The

DIVINER'S
TALE

Novels by Bradford Morrow

COME SUNDAY

THE ALMANAC BRANCH

TRINITY FIELDS

GIOVANNI'S GIFT

ARIEL'S CROSSING

THE DIVINER'S TALE

The
DIVINER'S
TALE

BRADFORD
MORROW

AN OTTO PENZLER BOOK

HOUGHTON MIFFLIN HARCOURT

BOSTON   NEW YORK

2011

www.hmhbooks.com

Library of Congress Cataloging-in-Publication Data
Morrow, Bradford, date.
The diviner's tale : a novel / Bradford Morrow.
p.   cm.
ISBN 978-0-547-38263-0
1. Dowsing—Fiction.   2. Supernatural—Fiction.
3. Serial murderers—Fiction.   4. Psychological fiction.   I. Title.
PS3563.O8754D58 2010
813'.54—dc22   2009047462

Book design by Brian Moore

Printed in the United States of America

DOC 10 9 8 7 6 5 4 3 2 1

For Cara

If a man could pass through Paradise in a Dream, & have a Flower presented to him as a pledge that his Soul had really been there, & found that Flower in his hand when he awoke — Aye! And what then?

—SAMUEL TAYLOR COLERIDGE

Everyday life is only an illusion behind which lies the reality of dreams.

—WERNER HERZOG

Part I

DIVINING
CASSANDRA

1

M Y FATHER, WHOM I trust as surely as yesterday happened and tomorrow might not, was the first to call me a witch. He meant it in a loving way, but he meant it. In later years, he'd sometimes say it with a defiant touch of pride. —My daughter, the witch.

I brought this on myself by warning my brother, Christopher, with all the raw certainty of a seven-year-old who believed she could see things hidden from others, not to go to the movies one August evening with his best friend, Ben. He laughed, like any older brother twice his sister's age would, and said I could take a metaphysical flying leap. I can still picture him, lanky, loose-jointed, tall as a tree to my eyes, wearing his favorite faded baseball jersey untucked over a pair of worn jeans and scuffed brown boots. —Hey, Nutcracker, see you in the afterlife. Turning, he clomped down the porch stairs two steps at a time to the waiting car. I remember lying in long orchard grass in the field beyond our house, listening to the restless crickets scraping their bony legs together, and waiting for the meteors to tell me when the worst had come to pass.

At first the sky was calm. Just an infinity of cold stars and a few winking planets out in the void, carving their paths through the darkness. Maybe I got it wrong, I hoped. But then so many shooting stars

started chasing across the night I couldn't begin to know which of them had carried my beloved laughing brother away. The crickets stopped their chorus as the whole field sank into silence. I sat up and gasped. How I wished what I saw above me was a great black slate instead of a brilliant light show. Defeated by my vindication, I walked back to the house and sneaked in the side door.

—That you, Cass? my mother called out. My mother, who could hear a mouse yawn the next county over.

—No, I whispered, not wanting to be me anymore.

Christopher never came back. Neither did Ben or Ben's father, Rich Gilchrist, who was the town supervisor. The funeral was attended by half a thousand people. That happens when you are a well-liked local politician and chief of the volunteer fire department. Not to mention a decorated war veteran. Many men in dress uniforms attended from all over Corinth County in rural upstate New York and across the Delaware into Pennsylvania. Phalanxes of fire trucks bright as polished mirrors lined the road beside the churchyard cemetery. People wept in the wake of all the eulogies, and afterward the bells tolled. It was the second big funeral in as many years—Emily Schaefer, Chris's classmate, was killed the year before in what some believed was not the accidental death the authorities declared it—and our town still hadn't recovered. Whereas before we followed one hearse to the cemetery, this year three coffins were carried out together after a joint service, one draped with an American flag and two smaller unadorned ones behind. To this day I can hear the bagpipes playing their dirge.

Family friends and Christopher's inseparable band of buddies—Bibb, Jimmy, Lare, Charley Granger, my favorite, even the brooding Roy Skoler, who slipped out back to smoke—came over to our rambling farmhouse afterward, and everyone ate from a smorgasbord and drank mulled cider and spoke in low shocked voices. As for myself, I hid upstairs. I felt guilty, bereft. Also angry. If he hadn't so simply ignored me, things might have turned out different. I barricaded my door that night and spent hours memorizing my brother's narrow freckled face, his edgy voice, his gawky mannerisms, his lame jokes, the Christo-

pherness of him, so I could hold him as long as possible in the decaying cradle of memory.

Instead of sleeping in my bed that night, I lay fitful on the floor, twisting around in my funeral clothes, hugging my doll Millicent, who was my first confidante and imaginary little sister. Why, I thought, should a grieving sibling sleep comfortably when her brother was stuck inside a dark box all alone? I felt hopeless, deeply discouraged. I didn't want my brother to be dead. I didn't want to be a witch. I had no interest in knowing ever again what might happen in this world before it did. My foresight was one thing. But to shift the flow of my brother's will so it might not collide with his fate was as impossible as reaching out to grab one of those falling stars, hold it in my palm, and blow it out. Still would be beyond me, had he survived when a woman fell asleep at the wheel and crossed lanes, flying head-on into the Gilchrists' car under a new moon. Which is to say no moon at all.

My mother, for all her Christian religion, sank into a numb depression and stayed there for a long time. When I called her *Mom* she only sometimes answered; more often she just looked blankly right through me. Since she paid more attention to me when I addressed her by her first name, Rosalie, it became a habit that stuck. She took a year off from her job as a science teacher and spent days doing volunteer work for the church. None of her good deeds, from serving meals at a homeless shelter to clerking in the United Methodist thrift shop, buoyed her spirits. Though I didn't want to believe it, some days I sensed she blamed Christopher's death on me. This she would have denied, if asked—I didn't—but it was there in a random gesture, a quiet phrase, a clouded glance. I do know she prayed for me. She told me as much. But I'm glad she prayed in silence.

Looking back, I see that I was trying my best to breathe.

If it hadn't been for Christopher's death, I probably would not have been raised by my father like I was. In Rosalie's grieving absence, my dad and I reinvented our kinship. He was far too wise to bury his own sorrow by attempting to transform me into some factitious son, tomboy though I admittedly and perhaps inevitably was. High-spirited and

gregarious, a magnet to a constant stream of friends, my brother had been nothing like his introverted sister, Cassandra, who more often than not kept her own company. Nep did his level best not to Christopherize me. Nor did I feel compelled to try to make my father into an older brother figure.

Instead, we began hanging out together, a fond parent and his punk kid. He drove me to school and picked me up. Together we made three-bean chili and shepherd's pie for dinners on the nights when Rosalie arrived home late. We listened avidly to his old jazz records, shunning the seventies pop music that filled the airwaves. Weekends I sat on a tall stool next to him in his repair shop, really just a converted barn near the house, filled with widgets, wires, gadgets and tools, boxes of tubes both glass and rubber, a thousand broken household things he, poor man's Prospero, hoarded for spare parts and used to fix whatever people brought to him that wasn't working. Radios, tractors, toasters, clocks, locks. He even mended a clarinet for some boy in a local marching band. Nep could, I marveled, take almost anything that had fallen into disrepair and make it new again. Young as I was, I recall thinking, He's the last of a breed, Cass. Don't take this for granted.

I was crushed by my brother's predicted death, stunned by my mother's disappearance from our lives, and inspired, warmed, and moved by my father, who, however much I'd loved him before, was a revelation to me. The man was possessed, in his quirky way, of genius. I thought so then and still do now, even in the wake of all these intervening years.

What needs to be said here is this. If I hadn't been fathered so much by him, I might not have become, like him, a diviner. For however skilled he was at transforming the ruined into the running, and however steadfast a husband and father, Nep—shortened from the whimsical if preposterous Gabriel Neptune Brooks—was born with a gift that went far toward making those other masteries possible. There had been many diviners in the paternal branch of the family. All had been men. Over the next decade, I became the first female in a lineage that extended unbroken back to the early nineteenth century, as far as our

family tree has been traced. This has been my blessing, my bane, and, aside from my own children, my legacy for better or worse.

It was as a diviner I made the discovery on the Henderson land.

Before Henderson's, I never had a fear of being alone. Walking in the forest or crossing some unfamiliar field in the predawn morning or darkening night never bothered me. As my father's daughter, I knew the flora and fauna here as well as I knew the names of my sons. I never worried about getting lost because I never got physically lost. Not in the field, not while divining. Besides, worrying never got anybody found.

Not that I wasn't used to coming upon things that were unexpected. Calm quiet and then the quick stab of discovery, those are, for me, the two poles of divination. Mine is by definition a loner's trade, a kind of work that involves spending a lot of time both in your head and on your feet, conversing with the invisible and sometimes the inexplicable. How often had I been dowsing a field in search of well water, or a mineral deposit, or something lost somebody wanted found, and thought, Nobody's walked here for decades. Possibly centuries. So what is this half-buried clawfoot bathtub doing out here in the middle of nowhere? Where is the plow that went with this lonely wheel?

You get pretty far out into the wild sometimes when you've hired on with a person who wants to settle fresh terrain. After the twin towers went down, I found myself exploring bonier, harsher, uninhabited land for people from the city looking to relocate, to Thoreau for themselves a haven upstate. But even before that, with so many people building their way into the wilderness, developing the backlands, I had been asked by locals to suss out the prospects of one tract or another. Analyze what the aquifer was about, the prospects of creating more Waldens in the mountains. And so it wasn't unusual to find myself way off the beaten track.

It was the third week of May. Rained overnight. The reeking skunk plants were well up and the delicate jack-in-the-pulpits wagged their cowled heads in the scrub shade. Overhead, mammoth clouds fringed in silver and charcoal flew hard and fast toward the Atlantic

coast a hundred or so miles due east. Noisy warblers flitted in the high branches. Redstarts and yellowthroats. Thrushes conversed, invisible in the near distances. The surveyors had finished up a week before I came out. Their Day-Glo orange flags dangled brazenly from branches — property lines for projected building sites.

Here was a four-hundred-plus-acre parcel that needed consideration. Maybe a hunter had hammered two boards together on this place once, or some early settler chinked up a winter cabin that had long since fallen down. Now it was a habitat for coyote families, black bears, whitetail deer, even the occasional shy fisher cat. Heavy swaths of sugar maple and tall ash gave way to sheltered fields ringed by wild blueberry and serviceberry. A beautiful land, neither worked nor spoiled by man, going back almost forever. A deciduous Eden.

Though I had never traversed this valley before, it wasn't entirely unknown to me. Christopher and I used to have a cave hideout in the rugged cliffs high above, along its eastern edge, and indeed my parents' house was but a few miles' hike beyond that rocky ridge. My developer client was looking to dig a pond large enough to call a lake, around which he planned to build an enclave of upscale homes. I almost felt — no, I did feel blameworthy doing my own survey of his lands so the tall rig could be brought in to drill. And before that Jimmy Brenner with his dozers and Earl Klat with his chainsaw singing and his skidder to make a pretty mess.

I had cut a dowsing rod and was walking, daydreaming a little. Whenever I sensed a sweet spot, even if the stick wasn't reacting, I stopped and looked around. A dowser who knows what she's doing can half the time anticipate where the land will give up its water beneath. A big patch of wild leeks reveals nearly as much as a witching stick does about a proximate trove of water near the surface. I drifted along through a thicket of shadblow and wood rhodies all waist- and shoulder-high. It smelled like strong spring, that sex and excrement odor of the world reawakening. There was a narrow curtain of lime-green and red buds at the end of this scrub corridor where the woods picked up and the land began to rise a touch. A redwing blackbird

cried out over my left shoulder not far away. Again, a telltale sign there would be at least a shallow vein of water here, as redwings prefer to nest in cattail wetlands.

I was feeling okay. My twins were in school. They wanted to go to camp this year, where they could play baseball and swim and be free of me, and I was going to let them. For all three of us this was a big deal. Because they were going to the same place, I knew Jonah and Morgan would be fine. Would have family right there to look out for them. Meant an empty house for me, but part of Mama Cass—one of my least favorite nicknames, and I had more than a few, from Andy to Assandra, given most people avoided the mouthful *Cassandra* when addressing me—looked forward to the prospect.

Not that I had a single iota of a plan for what to do with my fancy free, beyond the couple of add-on summer school courses the district administration had agreed to, at my request.

I needed the extra work to pay for the boys' summer away, which wasn't in my budget. Remedial reading for some younger students and a continuing education course in my favorite subject, Greek myth. I could do worse than wander behind Odysseus for a few months with my aging pupils, or discuss with them the twelve tasks of Hercules, the story of Pandora's box. I even proposed to screen that old camp classic, *Jason and the Argonauts*, with its stop-motion animated sword-wielding skeletons, ravenous Cyclops, and serpent-haired monster Medusa.

Then, without warning or any clear reason my mood should change, a black sensation just poured in, over, and through me. It felt as if a spontaneous, malevolent thunderhead had come flying fast over the ridge to instantly eclipse my world. I was, essentially and all of a sudden, deeply depressed. In retrospect, I wonder if I didn't weep. Must have blinked through my tears because I did move forward out of the flat scrub and into the edge of the forest there.

A girl. Maybe in her middle teens. She wore a white sleeveless blouse, bedazzled with large dark violet flowers, fanciful orchids or gardenias, which was knotted just above her navel. A denim skirt came down not quite to her knees. Barefoot. Her feet pointed outward in a

kind of loose relevé, like some ballet dancer frozen in the classic first position. Her wavy hair was brushed neatly, elegantly, over her shoulders, as if she were going to a party. She was hanged with a rope about her neck, not swaying in any breeze, but as dead still as a plumb stone. Her face bore an unaccountably serene, unforgiving half-smile. Her pale, quite colorless eyes stared straight ahead. She seemed somehow familiar, but that couldn't be right.

For one last moment of hope I thought, No, this was a doll. A horrific and perfectly wrought wax figurine. Lifelike to a fault. Its martyrdom here was ceremonial. Some sort of devil worship or maybe a terrible practical joke. Prankster drugged-up teens from a nearby town with nothing better to do than hold a sick ritual, a hazing in the middle of nowhere. Then I looked once more at the ashen face. This was no mannequin, no lifelike dummy. She was none other than a girl who was alive probably last week, maybe yesterday, and wasn't alive now.

I couldn't help myself. I wasn't thinking. I should have left her alone. Shouldn't have touched anything. It was a crime scene, after all. Instead, I went and embraced her. She was light as a dried cornstalk. A shed skin. Wasn't cold or warm. I held her in my arms and told her I was sorry, that I wished with all my heart I could have helped her.

Only after a moment of standing there whispering these words did it dawn on me that I myself might be in danger. Averting my eyes from the girl, I backed away from the woods toward the clearing a little. Numb, I studied the shadows shuffling across the ground. The outcroppings of glacial schist that jutted up here and there. The thin pools of standing water left from last night's rain.

Last night's rain. Her clothing was neat and dry, which meant her hanging happened sometime this morning. I was seized by the sickening prospect that someone was nearby taking me in, deciding how to deal with this unexpected, unwelcome intrusion. Like him, or them, I needed to think what to do. Slowly, in a quivering whisper, I began to spell the word *patience* backward. One of Nep's many quaint and sane methods for clearing the mind before beginning to dowse. But this was not a usual divining, and I didn't make it through all the letters be-

fore realizing that the immediate world had gone quiet. It would have been comforting to hear some birdcall. No air moved through the trees to rustle their budded limbs and first leaves. Gone were the tree frogs' peepings I had heard. The dark tide of feeling that had engulfed me before now switched into another register. I became alert and focused and oddly unfeeling.

A hasty breeze arose. The highest branches of the trees creaked like rusty harrow tines. I turned in place and looked back the way I had come. A narrow path to the south of the scrub flat, which I hadn't noticed before, led through the thick growth toward a copse of cherries and ironwood beyond. Deer trail, I guessed, nothing to do with this girl. I turned to face her again. What unspeakable terror she must have experienced. Yet it didn't look like she had struggled. She appeared shocked and forlorn, yet so eerily serene. Which was more or less how I felt, though not serene but rather momentarily emptied, blank. Seemed as if I should apologize to her once more, this time for having to leave her here alone. Her feet were only a stool's height from the ground carpeted with last year's dead leaves and long creeping lovely ribbons of staghorn clubmoss. Curious how the ground around her appeared completely undisturbed. As if she'd been put here by some creature with wings.

Without thinking, I asked aloud, "Is anyone there?" My voice sounded smaller than I had ever heard it before. Hollow, reedy, and helpless.

Faint as a half-forgotten memory, I heard a family of chickadees call to one another. Like distant silver bells chiming an hour, their song insisted it was time to leave. My feet began to carry me away from the clearing. I had the distinct sensation of being watched, if not by living eyes, then by her calm and accusing ones. Despite my desire not to, I kept turning, looking behind. I must have run part of the way. No one followed me, so far as I could see.

My truck was still parked on the grass just off the washboard country road. Crazy that the sight of an obsolete Dodge pickup that needed new brakes and rotors and had way over a hundred thousand rough

miles on it and no resale value could give me such a feeling of solace. I clambered in and started the engine. Couldn't have gotten a connection even if I owned a cell phone, which I didn't. The original Statlmeyer farm, which ran to thousands of acres when it was first settled, was the very definition of rural. They wouldn't be building any satellite towers around here for a country mile of years, despite how many developers rolled up their sleeves. My pickup jostled and jerked its way down the hill toward the paved road at the foot of the mountain.

I was hyperventilating, nauseated. Had to get to a land line. The old logging trail was not meant to be driven as fast as I did. A ride that had taken half an hour that morning took me no time at all to get back home. Strange how fear works. The farther from any personal danger I got, the less safe I felt.

"Could I get your name, please?" the woman on the other end asked again.

"Is there any way you can reach him wherever he is?"

"I told you Sheriff Hubert is out. Is this an emergency?"

"Yes, it's—"

"Hold on a moment."

Squeezing my eyes shut so tight they hurt, I began *e* and *c* and *n* and *e* and—

"Sergeant Bledsoe speaking," a man said. "You have an emergency to report?"

"Yes, yes. I need to report a girl, there's a dead girl, I—"

Bledsoe asked me questions one on top of the other. Did I know the girl? Could I give him the exact location? When was it that I made the discovery? Would I be willing to take them out there now? Was I all right, did I need medical attention, how soon could they send a patrol car by to pick me up, what was the name of the property owner again? I gulped out answers and he put me on hold for a long minute and came back on the phone to say they had contacted Sheriff Hubert and he'd already left where he was and would meet us at Statlmeyer's—no, Henderson's—within the hour.

I hung up and went to the bathroom. Washed my face with cold water and looked into the mirror. The visage I saw there was so contorted and distraught it seemed like that of a sister I never had who'd led a very hard life filled with chaos, setbacks, and secrets more terrible than my own. I had never before seen myself in such a harsh light. It was as if I had done the hanging.

Bledsoe drove me back out. He grilled me with questions I answered as best I could from within my daze. At least I had the wit to call my mother and ask her if she wouldn't mind dropping over so the boys didn't come home from school to an empty house. I thought it better not to explain what had happened. Other than the fact of that image of the hanged girl, I barely knew what happened myself.

"You're friends with Niles Hubert, I gather. He said to take good care of you."

I nodded. Not that Bledsoe saw me. He was driving fast with his lights flashing, no siren.

"How did you meet Henderson?"

"He was referred to me by Karl Statlmeyer."

"And when was that?"

"Two weeks ago, three."

"And what did he say?"

"He called me up and told me he'd heard good things about me and wanted to hire me to walk his land, dowse it, and give him some proposals about siting a pond and some possible building lots."

"And you do what?"

"I'm a diviner."

"And what does that mean?" His voice was low and flat, as dismissive as a slow flick of the wrist.

I was trying hard not to dislike Dennis Bledsoe with his shaved head and thick black eyebrows, one of which remained raised as if in a state of constant skepticism. Trying hard not to feel crushed by the way he seemed not to believe one word I said, and what he did believe, seemed to scoff at. He was just doing his job, I reminded myself, making necessary inquiries and all. But I had been to a few psychiatrists

over the years, attempting to cope with the trauma of my brother's accident, and more than one of them sounded like him. A little unbelieving, and not a little patronizing.

"Did you notice what time it was when you found the body?"

"I don't wear a watch, but it must have been ten-thirty, or a little after that. I left home after my boys went to school, got there and spent a minute cutting myself a witching rod, and started walking." I recalled the angles at which the cloud-softened sun shadowed her face. "Between ten-thirty and -forty."

"You can tell the time that closely without a watch?"

I didn't respond.

"So you only met Henderson that once. What's his first name again?"

"George Henderson. We didn't meet. He called me up out of the blue, offered me the job, and I took it. I can give you his number. I'm sure he's not going to be happy about this."

"No, I guess not."

Niles was there with another man when we arrived. He opened his arms and held me close for so long that if Bledsoe suspected Niles and I had a history it was confirmed. He released me, stepped back still clasping one hand, said, "Of all people for this to happen to."

"Nothing really happened. That is, to me."

Niles finger-combed his hair, an old nervous tic of his. Prematurely streaked white against brown, no doubt because of his stressful work. He gave me one of his cherished frowns — the kind of frown that between friends is really a smile. It was a mute conciliatory scolding, as if to say, Something happened to you all right, who do you think you're kidding?

This was already midafternoon. The many clouds had flown out to sea, it appeared, and the sky was a cool, pristine blue. We walked down the wet declivity, away from the road. A family of finches peeped and bounded in short acrobatic bursts through the air as we left behind the upper field and entered a fairly dense forest of second-growth maples and hemlock. We had to step over and around fallen branches strewn

like uninterpretable *I Ching* yarrow sticks tossed at random by snowy winters.

I was trying to keep my mind smooth. Back when Bledsoe first picked me up, I had decided I couldn't afford to see her again. I would escort them as close as possible, get them through that scrub flat to the edge of the stand of trees where she was suspended, and send them ahead by themselves. A lone veery called somewhere above us, sounding for all the world like a diminutive alien transmitting its code name back to the mother ship, *eerie, eerie.* Spring peepers were carrying on in a lowland off to our left. I could hear Niles breathing more heavily than a man his age ought to.

"How much farther you think it is?" he asked.

"Not much."

We hiked down through a kind of amphitheater of bluestone boulders shaped like huge loaves, which opened up into the northern end of the long scrub plain. I told Niles we were almost there now and in his kindness he anticipated me. Said, "I'm going to leave you with Shaver once we're close. No need for you to see this again. Sergeant Bledsoe and I can take it from here."

As we made our way through the thicket of mountain laurel, it occurred to me that here, of course, was Henderson's pond. A respectable lake, in fact, if he wanted to go to the trouble of paying for dozers to displace the earth beneath our feet. I glanced around. The flat was hemmed by impressive hills. Wondered if it mightn't even have been a shallow basin long ago that silted in like many do over time. Such irony. Had I thought of this earlier, I might not have bothered to wander farther. And if I hadn't, well, then what? I realized I had been somehow drawn away from my purpose here. This morning, without knowing it, I left off divining water and instead had begun to divine the girl.

I saw we were near and told Niles this was the place. She was just up ahead. Not even a hundred feet. Right at the curtain of woods. He told John Shaver, a thin, relaxed, kindly young man whose long white face reminded me of a pony I used to ride when I was a kid, to stay here with me. They'd be back in a little while.

Shaver and I didn't have to wait long. The two men returned in no time. By the look in their eyes I could tell something was awry.

"Nothing there, Casper," Niles quietly said.

How jarring his pet name sounded then, no matter that it went all the way back to our childhood together.

"That can't be right."

"You'd better come and show us where she is. We don't find anything."

Hurriedly we made our way in single file through the tall foliage. I was slipping into a panic because I didn't want to see the hanged girl again. But I knew I couldn't leave her out here unclaimed for another minute. She needed to be taken down from her gibbet, wrapped in the rolled tarp Bledsoe had carried in for the purpose, and taken home to her mother and father and family. I was soon enough running and had left the others behind when I emerged from the undergrowth to stand breathless and gasping at the edge of the woods just where I'd stood hours earlier.

There was no barefoot girl in a floral print blouse and denim skirt hanged with a rope by the neck. Everything looked exactly as it had that morning except for her not being there staring at me with those quizzical eyes.

I wheeled around and shook my head as Niles came up behind me with a face full of questioning. I turned toward the wooded cove again. Nothing. I walked swiftly to the very spot where I had held her in my arms, light as gossamer, but nothing remained of her. This wasn't possible. Niles was saying something about how we must not be in the right place, and I desperately wanted to agree with him and even began to say so. But when I glanced down, I saw my divining rod lying there among the leaves just where I had dropped it when I first saw her earlier, gazing ahead, so impossibly familiar.

2

ONE OF THE EARLIEST known female diviners in recorded history was something of a wild woman. Her name was Martine de Berthereau, the Baroness de Beausoleil. She was on my mind that afternoon, flickering in and out of it like the light through the budding trees as we climbed back out of the valley and I was driven home. Deep into the evening I couldn't shake the thought of her and what it sometimes meant to be a diviner.

Headstrong and wily, Martine was as tireless as a migrating hummingbird, fluent in several languages, a gifted mineralogist, an aristocrat who had no fear of dirt under her fingernails. A formidable character, she also had a weakness for alchemy, astrology, and dramatic flair. There have been other female diviners down the years, even famous ones. Lady Judith Milbanke, the mother of Lord Byron's wife, was well known for her gifts as a water witch. But to my mind none matched Martine de Berthereau. Her story has always fascinated and terrified me.

She made what some dowsers consider her most significant discovery the very year before Galileo claimed the Earth revolved around the sun, an idea that landed him in front of an outraged Inquisition. Theirs were heady times, the roaring twenties of the seventeenth cen-

tury. Shakespeare's generation had only recently passed, and Francis
Bacon was a rising star. Fresh, untamed ideas and their creators, like
exotics freed from a zoo, were suddenly running free, many of them
threatening to storm the papal walls. And the Baroness de Beausoleil
was seen by some as one of those very escapees. A unicorn, maybe. Or
a female griffin.

She had been traveling through France when her son fell ill. While
he slept off his fever behind the louvered windows of their room in
the Fleur de Lys, an inn not far from the central square of Château-
Thierry, she set out on foot to explore the village and surrounding
landscape. Her actions would not have seemed out of the ordinary,
except that rather than taking her parasol to protect herself from the
sun, she carried something the locals had never seen before. Wherever she went, Martine took a trunk carefully packed with all manner
of dowsing rods, known as virgulas, made of hazel and forged met-
als, an astrolabe, and other curious divination instruments. Followed
by a few smiling children and scowling adults, she walked the narrow
cobblestone lanes behind her virgula, speaking to no one. As a crowd
grew, she retraced her steps and circled back to where she'd begun.
There in the courtyard, as onlooking villagers murmured, the diviner
announced that right beneath their feet ran an underground stream of
mineral water, fortified by green vitriol and pure gold, with fantastic
healing properties.

A local doctor, Claude Galien, bore witness to what happened next.
Some questioned her; some denounced her. But rather than run to the
relative safety of the Fleur de Lys, the baroness demanded that the villagers form a committee of their most respected elders. The mayor,
the apothecary, the judge. Let them dig at just the spot she had chosen and discover for themselves whether what she claimed was false
or true. The hole was dug and waters rich in minerals were found, as
promised. Galien was so impressed he was moved to write a treatise
about the incident, which was published in Paris, in 1630: *La découverte
des eaux minérales de Château-Thierry et de leurs propriétés*. Though he suspected the baroness might have noticed the green discoloration on the

courtyard stones and deduced that seepage water leaching up to the surface would necessarily be high in ferrous sulfate—my mother the science teacher might say she used accurate data to reach verifiable conclusions by falsified means—he admired her strength of conviction.

For myself, I always believed Galien's eyewitness account of this miracle should have been the first step toward Martine de Berthereau's beatification, toward Rome's sanctifying her as St. Martine, patron saint of dowsers. How nice it would have been for me to point to her in my defense whenever Rosalie found fault in my divining. Instead, as the baroness and her husband dowsed many more mines on behalf of the royal house, and presented their findings to the court of Louis XIII and in particular to the infamous Cardinal Richelieu, her life began to spiral downward.

She had traveled the world—Scotland to Silesia to Bolivia, not to mention every corner of France—in search of ore deposits, silver, gold, iron, and other treasures hidden inside the Earth's bowels, and had discovered some hundred and fifty mines. More often than not her work went unpaid and discoveries unprospected. But when the good cardinal read in her reports that the deposits—many of which would later prove to be rich and viable—had been located using a forked wand, she was in for a fall. Accused by him of witchcraft, Martine de Berthereau, the baroness of "beautiful sunlight" as her name would have it, was remanded to the lightless state prison of Vincennes. There, with her daughter to whom she'd taught the art of divining, she would die in abject misery, separated from her son and husband, himself condemned to live out the rest of his days behind the iron bars of the Bastille. Not a pretty ending for what was otherwise such a strangely modern life. A woman of science. A world traveler, an adventuress. A working mom. An independent thinker willing to tread way outside the beaten path. Martine was what I always intended to name my daughter, had I ever given birth to a girl. I liked her nervy spirit, and before I knew much of anything about the dark days of the Inquisition, I hated Cardinal Richelieu for his cruel narrow-mindedness. If that was how religious men behaved, I didn't want anything to do with them.

Divining was always a bone of contention in our household. My mother and Nep, who was ten years her senior—forty to her thirty the year I was born—agreed to disagree early on in their romance about the scientific merits, or lack thereof, of the gentle art of divining. I always found it ironic that she who espoused verifiable facts was devoutly religious, while he who inhabited a world embraced by both postmodernist spiritualists and God-fearing old-timers wouldn't be caught dead darkening the doors of a house of worship. He could talk about the role diviners played in the Bible until he was blue in the face, but my mother would not be budged off her firm opinion that dowsing was a pagan practice at best.

—But what about Moses getting water out of a rock on Mt. Horeb? Nep might ask.

—That was a holy miracle, not dowsing, she would counter.

—How would the Israelites have lasted all those years in the desert unless Miriam was a diviner?

—Miriam's well was a gift of Jehovah and had nothing whatsoever to do with traipsing around in the sand with a magical wand.

—What about *Thy rod and thy staff shall comfort me*? If that rod isn't a diviner's rod, what in the world is it?

—It's a rod to smite atheists like you. Your father probably knew the old adage *Spare the rod and spoil the child*. More's the pity he didn't know one rod from another.

Naturally, they endorsed opposing ideas about what I should do when I grew up, and I failed neither of them. Few if any make a living at divining. So I followed my mother's footsteps as a teacher, substituting in social studies and geography, though I could lead an even better class in Greek and Roman classics if needed. And, as well, I took what our friends considered the unusual step of assuming the diviner's mantle in the grand tradition of the family patriarchs. Usually I felt fortunate to be born into a century when diviners were allowed to practice their art. You might be derided but never damned, laughed at but not locked up. But given where it had taken me today, fortunate was the last thing I felt.

Yet my father, whom I revered even more than the great Martine, had never betrayed any concerns about his own divining, or bringing his children into the guild. Divining was just part of his life and never bore with it the threat that always seemed to shadow me. The first time I tagged along with him on a dowsing job I couldn't have been more than eight, a redheaded beanpole of a kid. A summer morning, the year after my brother was gone, Nep knocked on my bedroom door.

—You got anything going on today, Cassiopeia? he asked.

—Nothing much.

—Now you do. Get dressed, and put on your shoes for once. Wear clothes for a walk through brambles. We're going to look for water that's clever at hiding.

As we drove in the orange sunrise, I knew I was entering a world I'd figured would never be mine even to visit, let alone explore with my father. Not a little terrified, I was given a forked stick fresh-cut by Nep, who took some pains telling me just why he picked the tree he hewed it from—in this instance, a single-seed fruit tree—and precisely how to whittle the Y-shaped rod. He also showed me other tools of the trade.

—This is an L-rod, he said, reaching into a worn leather duffel and handing me a pair of television antennas bent at ninety-degree angles. —Some people call them elbow rods. You hold them out in front of you like so, having me grip them chest-high in my fists, their glinting tips pointed forward parallel to the ground.

—What do they do? I asked, trying to keep them from wobbling in my unsure hands.

—I let them show me which way the water runs when I'm bird-dogging a stream. You can make them out of whatever's lying around. Coat hangers, any kind of metal. My dad had a set forged out of solid brass, real nice.

—Why don't we use those, then? I asked, only to be told that wouldn't be such a good idea since my grandfather had been buried with them.

Next, Nep showed me what was called a bobber, a flexible wand

weighted on the end that responded by living up to its name, bobbing up and down, or wagging side to side. —It's best for asking the stream yes or no questions like, You drinkable? Ready to be tapped? Water is smart, Cass. Doesn't like the words *maybe* or *why*. *Why* is a word for philosophers and water is wiser than philosophers. Got that?

—Yes, I said, trying my best to stay with him.

—Never insult water or anything else you're dowsing for by questioning it, Are you sure? Once you get good at it, the right answer's the first answer every time.

He told me that diviner's tools are all extensions of yourself and nothing less. He finished by saying everything you divine is a reflection of yourself, and this, the only lecture he ever gave me, came to an end as he put all the paraphernalia except for the fresh rod back in the truck.

Then he set out with me, marching across some pale hay fields and through a thicket, listening for vapors' voices that rose from the earth to be heard and interpreted by us only. Whenever I saw his dowsing rod quiver, jerk harshly downward, drawn by subterranean forces, I did my best to mimic his every gesture. I watched his unmoving hands. Studied his face as it pulled into pucker-lipped focus. I heard him moan a bit, give what later I came to think of as an almost erotic sigh. I walked in his wake while he circled the site he'd figured was most promising. After handing me his rod, he pulled a pendulum out of his back pocket, a heavy hex nut soldered neatly to a length of jewelry chain. I noted his head move left and right as he gathered confidence that this was it, the mother lode.

—Dig here, he told the neighbor who had hired him to dowse, after several deep percussion drillings by the professionals had turned up nothing but pulverized crusher run and sulfuric air. —Hundred and forty-two foot, he said, emphatic as natural law.

I waited, quiet and full of admiration, not quite knowing what I was witness to here.

—That's all the deeper we got to dig? the man asked.

—Strong vein, too.

—But we drilled the better part of a thousand foot in other spots.

—Makes you feel short, don't it.

This was the dairy farmer down the road, from whom we would get free fresh milk and guano-dappled eggs and home-cranked lamb sausage in perpetuity, thanks to Nep the local water witch—I'd later wonder why they weren't called water warlocks—having discovered the plentiful underground stream in his otherwise dry upper pasture. He's dead and buried now, is good Mr. Russell. He was the one who gave me that little white pony who was a hobbler but as smart as a quirt.

3

STARRY NIGHT, THE DIPPERS high above. And the moon rising, bleaching the evening air so the grass looked like it had been
dusted with bone meal. Moon reminded me of a peach pit. It was
chilly out. Cold enough for me to see my breath, like a bit of March
in May.

Rosalie had already given the children supper when Niles dropped
me off. After a couple of hours of a gentle if numbingly repetitive deposition, he concluded by assuring me he would personally go back
to the scene, or *site* rather, since it did not appear to be the *scene* of
anything, in a legal sense. Said he would drive up after dawn, on his
own time, before work. Look around again. My conjecture that the
hanged girl had been there when I saw her—held her in my arms, in
fact—and was removed during the time I left to return with others,
might have carried weight but for the very real and problematic detail
that the woods appeared untouched.

Not one overturned leaf was to be seen. Not a disturbed twig. The
bark this time of year was tender, as pliant as kindergartner's clay,
after all the wet spring weather. But we couldn't pick out a single
branch that showed the least sign of damage from a rope supporting
the weight of a girl's body. The sharpest-eyed forensic expert would, it

seemed, have come away with nothing, not that they had the least intention of sending one out. My work in the archaic, quixotic field of
divination—a realm populated, in the eyes of many, by dreamers and
schemers, hoaxers and head jobs—didn't help my credibility in the
first place. I sensed, too, that had Niles not been my friend, the matter
would have been categorically dismissed.

We'd sat together in a conference room at a long table. Its mahogany lamination was curling at the edges, and I found myself nervously
picking at the corner of the table while I answered questions. In my life
I had never been in such a stuffy, closed room. The overhead fluorescents buzzed like hovering wasps. The two men went over the events
of the morning must have been half a dozen times, and half a dozen
times I told them the same story. Then Niles, not Bledsoe, surprised
me with an unexpected query.

"Can I ask you something of a delicate question?"

Startled by the shift in the rhythm and timbre of his speech, which
was much more tardy and lower than his usual voice, I glanced up and
nodded.

"Are you on any medications? Taking drugs for anything?"

"No."

"Nothing at all?" Bledsoe pressed, that dark eyebrow of his raised.
"We're not talking illegal drugs, just for instance an antidepressant or
maybe a sedative at night to sleep?"

"I sleep fine without. The answer is no. I'm not on any kind of drugs,
prescribed or otherwise."

"You have been in the past, though, isn't that correct?" the sergeant
continued.

I repeated, "I'm not on any medications now."

"Nothing to drink?"

"You can't drink while you're divining."

"Has anything like this ever happened to you before?"

"If it had, you'd have been the first to know," answering Bledsoe's
question while only addressing Niles.

"Casper, just another couple things I need to ask. Bear with me."

With these words, Niles offered me a smile of sympathetic complicity. Under any other circumstances that smile, which deepened the crow's-feet at the edges of his beryl-green eyes, would have been gratifying and made me believe the world was spinning properly on its axis rather than out of control. But at that moment, for that instant, I feared his smile. If it were a chalk drawing on a blackboard I'd wipe it away.

"Ask whatever you like, but the girl was there. I touched her with my own hands."

My defensiveness couldn't have been more crystal clear. I was feeling attacked, and now all of us knew it. Bledsoe started to say something more, but Niles raised a hand, palm down, in the sergeant's direction, and the room remained still.

"When you're divining—" Niles continued, in a mild but serious voice.

"Yes," staring at the wafer of artificial hardwood in my hand.

"—do you get into some kind of state of mind, say, that's not what you would think of as being your normal state of mind?"

"It'd be hard to differentiate. I don't really think about it since I'm too busy doing it."

"Is it like a euphoria, or *dysphoria* I think the word is?"

"I suppose it's safe to say I'm more sensitive to things around me."

"You're in a kind of heightened state of sensitivity?"

"I try to be. Extra-sensitive, extra-perceptive."

"You feel like you're communing with some alternate world, something like that?"

"I don't think of it in those terms. You know I'm not into mystical hocus-pocus."

"Is it like sleepwalking?"

"My father put it like this once. Dowsing is like drowsing, except you're asleep and intensely awake at the same time."

"What's the process?"

I sighed, placed my hands on my knees. "There is no process, if I understand you right. It's a science that can only be explained in metaphors. You remember when I visited Greece that time?"

Niles nodded.

"Watching the fishermen repair their nets was one of my favorite pastimes there. I loved the idea that you could take something straight and limp, twine and twist it on itself, and turn it into a completely different object. A big loose basket strong enough to hold whole schools of slippery wild fish. Pure wizardry. That's what I try to do. Just, my thread is so fine you can't see it. I'm weaving a net to angle for whatever I'm looking to find. It's my job."

Bledsoe allowed himself a quiet laugh. I refused to offer him a frustrated glance.

"Don't be offended," said Niles. "I'm trying to do my job, too."

"I'm not offended by you. But it's obvious your associate doesn't believe a word of what I've said."

"You're getting tired."

"I am, but that doesn't change what I saw."

Bledsoe stood, stating in a tone that showed he felt more sorry for me than perturbed, "All right, I got to get back to work."

That was half an hour before we finished at the station. Well, I thought, nodding as respectfully as I could manage at Bledsoe when he left, who could blame the man? He hadn't overly troubled himself with masking his disdain for the whole misadventure, but why should he? Anyone who heard what I was attempting to explain would think I was mad, no doubt. I felt way out of my element, both frightened and foolish.

"Cass, do you remember that time you called me in the middle of the night and said you'd had a dream that I was in a house fire? You were very shaken up. You seemed almost, what, shocked that I was even able to answer the phone, that I wasn't covered in burns."

"I was glad I was wrong," looking down at my lap and back up.

"Now don't misunderstand me, I'm not impugning you. What I'm trying to say here is you're a person of deep-felt intuitions who doesn't always get it right. I think you already know I don't doubt your prowess as a diviner. Some doubt, others don't. I'm one who doesn't."

"Thanks, Niles."

"No need to thank me because I choose to believe in proven instincts. I remember all too well about your brother. I remember an-

other time when you told me not to go camping in the Adirondacks and I wound up getting shot, nearly killed, by some idiot hunting deer out of season. There are plenty of instances when you seemed able to see better than anybody what was waiting around the corner in people's lives. I can't explain it, but I don't need to. You know me. I'm a boringly practical, down-to-earth man—"

I started to disagree, but he waved me off.

"—who tries to be as objective as humanly possible. Your mother was the teacher who told us about Occam's razor, remember? Simplest solution's usually the right one? A lot of people out here try to bullshit me. Hell, almost everybody I deal with does. You're not one of them."

"What are you getting at, Niles?"

"What I'm wondering is this. Do you think it's impossible you sometimes suffer from hallucinations? Don't answer yet. Let me finish. Let's say sometimes you hallucinate things that are there. Underground streams, for one. That quartz deposit at Mossin's. The time little Jamie Schultz ran away and you helped find him. Doesn't seem inconceivable to me that you might see things that aren't there sometimes. Things that should be, even could be, but aren't in any provable way."

"Are you saying *is* and *isn't* are the same thing?" I tried to smile.

As a way of protecting me from having to explain to my mother why I arrived home in a police cruiser, he drove his civilian car. Niles was like that, a gracious man. He asked after Morgan and Jonah on our way back to Mendes Road, where I lived. I told him the twins were fine but weren't happy they hadn't seen their godfather in a while.

"I've been remiss."

Jonah continued to excel in his studies at school, I told him, especially math. His was the kind of mind that noticed, when we were talking one day about Noah and the ark, that the name Noah was hidden inside the name Jonah, just as Jonah was once hidden inside the belly of the whale.

"Bible stories? Isn't that a little out of character for you?"

"I'm not some rabid atheist, just we don't go to church, is all."

"Well, Jonah's always been ahead of the curve when it comes to smarts."

"Just the other morning he heard me use the phrase *born and bred,* and he asked me, 'Aren't you bred before you're born?'"

Morgan, it looked more and more, would turn out to be the family athlete. "Coach Mosley thinks he has state-champion-level play in him. With just a little more discipline."

"Has he outgrown that glove I gave him last year?"

"You can almost see through the leather on the palm part of it."

"I'll look into getting him another one when I get a chance."

The tedious subject of James Boyd—had the boys asked about him again as I feared they soon surely would?—he bypassed altogether.

The interior of his car was, unlike the spare and spartan Niles Hubert himself, a clutter of broken toys, empty plastic bottles, paperback books, a purple plastic squirt gun, a cardigan sweater, a small blue rubber boot. The phrase ought to be *You are what you discard.* I asked him how were Melanie and their daughter?

"All's well," he said. "Adrienne's interest in photography's grown into a full-blown obsession. She doesn't go anywhere without her camera. She has shots of me shaving, eating, taking out the garbage, you name it. She even takes abstract artistic photos of the garbage."

We were used to this. These were the fond exchanges we made on normal days when we saw one another, so it made sense to conclude this abnormal one with our more habitual *How's it going?* reassurances. I knew Melanie Hubert was upset to this day about my having had the audacity to ask, despite the fact her husband and I were engaged once upon a time and never went through with it, whether he could see his way clear to being godfather to my twins. How could I fault her? Yet I will always be grateful to Niles for answering my request with an uncomplicated, brisk yes. Fatherless, at least the twins would have him around for birthdays, a couple of hours on Thanksgiving afternoon or New Year's Eve. To give them their modest, clumsily wrapped, but deeply appreciated presents on Christmas. Knowing full well this might cause strife with Melanie, he honored his role with grace.

But Niles couldn't help me further that night. Neither could my mother. After I thanked her and saw her off and put the boys to bed, I would have given anything to be able to call my father. See if he had an hour for a glass of Châteauneuf-du-Pape, his favorite.

Nep was the only person I knew who might have been able to bring deeper insights to the table, share at least a strong sense of the physicality of the experience I'd had at Henderson's that morning. He didn't need to shoulder my burden, though, and had his own problems to contend with. Instead, I put on an old vinyl of Duke Ellington, one I'd borrowed from Nep, cracked the casement window a few inches so I could hear "Mood Indigo" on the porch without waking the boys, and poured the wine for myself. Wrapped in my barn jacket, I sat back in one of the squeaky hickory chairs and did everything in my power to keep the image of the girl from overtaking my mind, or worse, my imagination.

4

THAT DAY BEGAN the fifth great turning in my life. A jolting addition to what I had considered my elemental four. Just as there were four directions and four winds, and just as Plato identified four virtues and Hippocrates four humours, my private little cosmology used to have its own four-cornered form.

My first turning had been Christopher. The unwelcome prophecy of his premature death and the opening up into other planes of risk it marked. Second was my genesis as a true diviner, which didn't happen until I was almost twenty. Third was the birth of my boys.

The fourth occurred just last year, when my father made his confessions to me. And here came this fifth flexure to upset my tentative balance once more and shatter the covenant I had made with myself to hew to the normal, the everyday, and leave visions to visionaries. The hanged girl, now present, now vanished like some grim will-o'-the-wisp.

It was the fourth turning that made it impossible for me to have that glass of wine with Nep and tell him what was up, get his measure. Last year, the summer before this one into which we were now moving, he entrusted me with a pair of secrets. Secrets that, for all my reputation as someone gifted with mind-reach, I might sometimes have dared to dread, but never finally guessed.

We had just finished an Independence Day dinner of barbecued chicken and baby back ribs, with all the fixings my mother could think of to feed the company of far-flung friends and neighbors and some of her Methodist churchgoing contingent. Rhubarb and strawberry cobbler was being served on the back porch when I noticed Nep give me a wink to join him beside a bed of blossoming magenta campions, his favorite flowers as they do well whether it rains or not. — Like you should strive to do, Cass, he once advised me, long ago. He asked if I wouldn't mind walking him to the pond. This was his settled way of indicating he had something important to say. I looked around to see what Jonah and Morgan were up to, glimpsed them playing some rowdy variation of kickball with a bunch of other kids, so smiled yes at him.

Sunny late afternoon. One of those overwhelmingly clear days when the ceiling of the Earth looks like it's painted with lapis lazuli. I took his wide gritty hand and down we went, as we had so often when I was growing up. Strolling the shore lined with vesper iris as purple as plums, with butter-and-eggs and wild basil, he told me he had a secret he needed to let me in on. But first he had to tell me something important. I didn't like the sound of any of this, despite the neutrality that shaded his voice.

— Is this going to be good news or bad news?

— Just news, is all. There's nothing to be done for it.

He shared with me in simple, flat words his doctor's diagnosis of probable early-stage Alzheimer's. The symptoms were classic and, I realized looking back, clear as the cloud-free sky that stretched above. How is it we sometimes neglect the nuances of what's happening right in front of us? He'd been missing appointments for no good reason, he who used to keep his personal calendar in his head and never wrote down a telephone number in his life. When I told him he ought to jot things in the handsome leather notebook I gave him for the purpose, he did, reluctantly, but then forgot to look at what he had written. He lost his way to dowsing locations a few times, this man who knew every square inch of the county where he was born. His speech wasn't

impaired, but sometimes he paused to search out the right word. Or would use curious clusters like *my food-rake* when he meant *my fork,* or *basement oven* for *furnace.* He had always loved wordplay, so these curiosities seemed more like unfunny jokes than indications of underlying illness. Slowness of mind was not in evidence that July day, however. Down by the pond any hint of dementia seemed light-years away.

— No, he said, answering my next question. — The doctor wouldn't speculate about time frames. Sometimes these things go on a very gradual track. Other times, not so slow.

— And in your case?

— They have no way of knowing, one of those deals just time will tell.

I hugged him tightly, told him how sorry I was and that I'd do everything possible to help Rosalie and to be there for him. He didn't respond other than to rest his chin on my shoulder. We stayed like that, out of view of the party back up at the house, for a minute or so. Then he took my arms with both large hands, gently pushed me away a little to look me hard in the eyes. Astonishing, I thought, to see that he already appeared older than when we first wandered down. How the idea of something makes its image manifest itself. Those blue eyes of his seemed more cumulus-gray. I had the same wide-set eyes, the exact color, Nep once said, of the Earth's oceans when photographed from space. At that moment they must have appeared sadder than at any other time in my life. How I wished, just then, my divining rod was a caduceus.

— Look at it like this. It's a sort of independence day for me. Everything I did in my life that I don't want to remember? Stuff that's bothered me over the years? Things people have done I'd just as soon forget? There's a humane side to the disease. A great erasure of all that went wrong.

— What went right, too, though, immediately regretting I'd said it.

— Well, there's that.

— It may just be pathetic wishful thinking, but maybe the good stays with a person.

Nep didn't give me much berth for such sentimentalism.

—The good is probably erased along with the bad. Tell you what, daughter. When I've arrived there, if I have any way of getting back to you on it, I will.

Made me smile a little. That was my father all over. I thanked him for telling me and, knowing it wasn't in his nature to dwell on things, asked about this secret of his.

He squinted at the horizon, then down at the placid face of the water before us. And told me that like his father, my grandfather Schuyler Brooks, and his grandfather before him, my great-grandpa Burgess Brooks, and his great-grandfather whose name was Jeremiah Brooks, and the patriarch of the family tree, Henry Hurlcomb Brooks—diviners all, and highly respected by anyone who prized water and minerals and every kind of thing that was lost and needed to be found in this county—he was a fraud.

I stood there waiting for the punch line, the interjection that would make clear what he'd said. He looked me back and forth in both eyes, unsmiling and unflinching. For want of some better response, I asked, but not as a question, —A fraud.

—You heard me.

Another pause. I watched a dragonfly come to us, hover for a moment, zip away.

—I don't understand, I said.

—A person who knows anything knows when he's experienced success by traveling down avenues of luck as opposed to roads of actual achievement. Mine's been a walk of pure chance.

—I thought you always said you create your own luck.

—Sometimes yes. More often no. Good luck is, well, it's something attained as a result of chance. The wind blowing in the right direction. Placing your foot on a path that will lead you to something. Just like bad luck comes to good people. South wind luck.

I frowned, waited for him to move beyond this posturing and get to whatever deeper point he was going to make. —I can't believe you're serious.

—Believe me, I'm telling you what I think.

—But how do you explain all those years of getting it right?

—A fraud, he said, and went on to explain to me that his father had made the deathbed confession, hoping his own son wasn't a fake as he felt he had been, despite his own work divining the parched and droughty world.

What about all the others with their respectable and dramatic names?

—I doubt but they were all frauds and fakes, to a man.

Had mere chance rather than mastery, I wondered, passed down the line from father to son, father to son, through generations of luck-blessed shams?

—You, though. You're the real deal, Cass, he said. —Sometimes women have powers men just don't. Either way, keep it to yourself. Our family has a good reputation, despite the naysayers, and many's the person trusted in us all these years.

—Many's the person who hasn't.

I was awestruck to think those outspoken critics of our family might have been right all along.

—But they aren't the ones that matter.

—I don't believe you, by the way. You have the gift.

He looked at his shoes and then up at me with a quizzical smile, as if we were in a dream, just as a crow shot noisily out from behind a stand of cattails across the ruffled pond.

—Wanted to set the record straight, he finished before starting to ramble back toward the house with me.

I don't know why I chose not to more fully engage him, address him with deeper sincerity, tell a truth of my own. But I didn't. Instead, I rewarded his honesty with some further hesitant glossing about how it wasn't possible for him to have been so successful and at the same time a fraud. Regarding myself, I was too terrified to offer him any insights. He said nothing more on the subject that summer and into the fall as he embarked on his journey into the shadowy waters of Alzheimer's.

By the new year, his condition having deteriorated more steadily

and swiftly than I could have imagined—which made me wonder if
he hadn't known for a bit longer than he'd admitted—my father was,
on off days, beyond discussing what I should have pursued that afternoon. He was still very functionally Nep. Active, just slower. He
labored away in his shop but didn't finish repairs as quickly, and he
turned down jobs having to do with electronics since for some reason
that field of interactive circuits befuddled and therefore annoyed him.
His work in divination was all but finished, and the torch now passed
to me. I felt, because of his malady, I shouldn't trouble him with my
own shortcomings and difficulties.

One of my problems was I still had my own business and reputation
to maintain. The mammon in me? Not really. But being the only female diviner in the region, reputation was everything. With the excep-
tion of Madame Beausoleil and those occasional others, diviners were
until recent times traditionally men, going back to the sixteenth century when Agricola wrote of miners using the *virgula furcata* to search
for gold. I didn't dare admit, even to my mentor, that I believed I myself was a mere charlatan blessed with odd good luck. I had mouths to
feed and a house that forever needed paint. It was too late for me to
consider any other vocation than the ones to which I had devoted my
life. Neither divining nor my part-time teaching would alone satisfy
the monthly mortgage, modest though it was, never mind my sons' ap-
petites, which weren't. So I cobbled together a living as best I could.
No going back, fake or not.

The thing was, for whatever little techniques I had developed to en-
hance my chances of, as it were, swimming along with the Brookses
—my own confession will come in due course—nothing I had ever
done could explain my forevisions, as we called them in our family.
Forevisions, of which there had been many more than the one about
my brother, though forevision had utterly failed me in divining Nep's
condition. I had been a self-doubter behind my witching stick, but
technique couldn't explain how sometimes I just knew what logic
would lead me to believe I shouldn't know. The two worlds of diviner
and seer felt different to me, but like the prongs of a dowsing rod itself,

there was some unifying connection between them. I had walked out
on both limbs but couldn't swear I understood either. Was the hanged
girl some forevision I couldn't yet translate into meaning? The very
idea left me suddenly exhausted and wired at the same time. I didn't
want the monster back ruining my life. The monster: shorthand from
my youth for a state of mind I couldn't avoid, understand, or bear.

Words such as *patience,* forward or backward, and *virgula*—words
Nep had known so well—now eluded him every once in a while, as
if they were butterflies and his net had holes in it, flaws in its webbing
he didn't know how to fix. I wondered if he remembered the word
halcyon. Not that many people would know it in the first place, unless
they'd been forced to. It was in my thoughts tonight for good reason,
jogged there unwittingly by one of Niles's questions. A word I hadn't
considered for the longest time, Halcion carried a real resonance for
me in my mid-teens. Widely prescribed in the eighties, the drug was
later proven, for all its benefits of inducing sleep in troubled insomniac
souls such as mine, to drive some to the edge of the edge, and yet others right over. I don't remember ever having apocalyptic feelings when
I was, as I privately named it, *halcyoned.* Yet I do recall more than once
having an impossible conversation with Christopher when everyone
else in the house was still slumbering.

What's it like there in the land of the dead, Chris?

Like nothing, like floating in warm flowers.

Can you see me?

There's nothing to see except your worries and hopes.

What do they look like?

Knives hovering over you.

The hopes, too?

The hopes especially.

These dreams were as vivid to me then as the smell of my red wine
and the distant, majestic hooting of a great horned owl counterpoint-
ing the Duke felt to me now, sitting on the night-chilled porch. They
had been so real to me, in fact, that I occasionally lapsed by mentioning them during casual conversation with my parents, who were natu-

rally alarmed. Their concerns over my mental health became an inces-
sant subject for a time. Switching doctors was their approach when
things didn't seem to be improving. After Nep refused even to consider allowing some priest-friend of Mother's to perform an exorcism,
they turned to Dr. McGruder, the next in a string of psychiatrists in
the city I wound up visiting once a week. He proposed I continue the
sedative for a time at a higher dosage, and they sanctioned it, innocent
of its contraindications. Nep harbored doubts but didn't have enough
magic within his powers to propose a different course of action. I recall thinking that *halcyon* was such a beautiful sound for a word, even
though its first syllable bears the worst of all possible images while the
other carries so much promise. *Hell. See yon.* On the one hand, *see hell
yonder?* On the other, *see beyond hell.* It was a drug I used for about a
year to retreat for a few hours from my waking life.

I never threw out any leftovers from the pharmacopoeia that was
prescribed to me over the years, and, of all things, having dug through
my pillboxes looking for some light sedative before sitting outside
with my thoughts, I discovered a few powder-blue Halcions from the
bad old days. I weighed them in my palm and marveled at the lengths
to which Nep and my poor mother had gone, back when I was not so
much older than the girl I saw that morning at Henderson's, to help
me step away from the unhappy world of forevisions. This Halcion was
just one of the many means they were forced to explore in the quest of
driving my monster away. They loved me dearly, I knew, but I couldn't
have been the easiest daughter to raise. I dropped the pills into the toi-
let, along with all the rest of the old cache, and flushed. If I was fated
to go through a dark phase again, I was going to do it on my own, no
doctors, no drugs, no fake halcyons.

I was tired, couldn't feel the cold anymore. Couldn't see the girl
anymore. And I couldn't hear their questions. The moon and stars gave
off a generous nocturnal calm. I sank into myself, blessedly thought-
less, and, after a while, driven inside by my cold feet and fingers, I shut
the window and lifted the needle off the clicking, spiraling groove of
the vinyl disc which was all played out. Before I went upstairs to face

my pillow, I stood in the dark with a hand on the newel post. Stood there quite some time listening, all but asleep on my feet. Everything was silent, tranquil. No voices from the past, nor any mirages. The boys hushed and untroubled in their rooms down the hall from mine. Not a mouse moving in the wall. A dense, serene stillness. I climbed the stairs, fumbled off my clothes, crawled into bed. I doubt I dreamed, although I, like Nep now in his different manner, wouldn't remember one way or the other next morning.

5

HENDERSON HAD PAID a hefty freight for the four hundred unlevel acres of wooded and snaking ridges whose jagged cliffs looked like teeth biting down on the valley bowl below, but he sure didn't know much of anything about what he purchased. Niles was able to ascertain that with one call to the phone number I gave him at the station. His only concern was whether he himself was in any kind of legal trouble and, more to the point, if his development had to be curtailed.

—Not if you haven't done anything wrong, Niles said.

—Of course not.

—Well, then there's nothing for you to worry about.

He was given the story in abstract terms, Niles offering him the sketchiest possible version as a way of protecting me from criticism, while at the same time seeing if Henderson knew anything that might shed light on my encounter. Long shot, but he thought it was worth a try. He told Henderson that while doing the work he had contracted me to do, I discovered something unusual on the property. No, there was no need to discuss specifics as it appeared that the matter was nothing more than one of mistaken identity. Still, if he had a moment to answer just a couple questions? Whatever was needed, he was only too happy to cooperate. Niles asked Henderson, had he been out to

the acreage recently? He hadn't. Had he granted permission for anyone besides the surveyors and Ms. Brooks to be on his land? He had
not. Never authorized anyone else to go out there to hike, hunt, maybe
camp? No.

Henderson evidently interrupted to ask about my character. Was I
on the up and up? Should he have checked around a little more carefully before sending me, sight unseen, out onto his property? Sheriff
Hubert assured him that my integrity wasn't in question. And asked
if Henderson happened to have the best number to reach the prior
owner, Statlmeyer. That was the same Statlmeyer sold him the four
hundred acres, right? Henderson — and this gave Niles a mute laugh,
he admitted to me — corrected him. Four hundred and sixteen acres.
I mean, at some point, who's counting? Yes, Karl Statlmeyer, Henderson said, after giving Niles the message I needn't bother doing any
more work on his behalf and should send him a bill for the hours I had
put in. Niles said he would pass the word.

He reached Statlmeyer long distance from home that night and que-
ried him about ways to access the land on foot other than from the
logging road we'd been using. Turned out Statlmeyer wasn't any more
helpful than Henderson. The acreage had once been part of his family's enormous landstead. He used to let some distant cousin's kid hunt
the land in exchange for throwing poachers off and replacing the No
Trespassing signs around its boundaries. But that was years ago and he
and the boy had fallen out of touch. When Statlmeyer himself finally
walked around the place, he told the sheriff, that was enough. The dirt
and trees were worth more money than they should ever have been,
out in the middle of nowhere. He had been only too happy to dump it
on Henderson. Was there anything more? Niles thanked him and said
that would probably do it.

My phone rang early the next morning. I asked him what if anything
he had learned overnight, and he told me about these conversations
with Henderson and Statlmeyer.

"Finally got nowhere," Niles said. "Because there was probably nowhere to go."

He had stayed up late after that, studying a survey map of the area,

and in fact there did turn out to be another possible path down to the spot where I saw what I saw. Much tougher trail, if a trail at all. Maybe another approach would render another result. Or, rather, any result. Would it be asking too much of my mother to take the boys again?

"If you don't feel overly upset," he continued, "I think it'd be useful if you walked back in with me."

"You believe me about the girl."

"I'm not saying that. What I'm saying is you might see something I don't."

"I'll call Rosalie right now."

"You'll be waking her?"

"She was up at five, guaranteed. Always is."

The boys were sleepyheaded and grumpy until they found out they were going to spend their Saturday morning with Nep. The affection was mutual. He never failed to brighten and revert at least a little to his old self when the twins came around. For kids their age—turned eleven this eleventh of April, a couple of precocious Aries—they were quite sensitive to his disease. It both fascinated them in a boyishly morbid way—Jonah and Morgan could sit cross-legged side by side and watch a spider methodically anesthetize a web-caught moth until it was ready to devour its prey—while, at the same time, they drew from deep reservoirs in their spirits some profound sense of human mortality. They also held their grandmother in high esteem, despite their sense she was a bit too religious for her own good, and willingly embraced doing any little thing that might help her help him.

"Hurry up," I urged.

One of my worst mothering—or misguided "fathering"—mistakes was when I had allowed them, far too early on, to try a sip of my morning coffee. Now there was no going back. Like little demonic connoisseurs, they objected to the cups of Sanka I made to move things along.

"What's the big rush?" Morgan asked, pushing his long brown hair out of his face. His hair, which he grew out the previous year after many evenings of family debate, was one of the few physical traits that

differentiated him from his otherwise identical brother. That and the small acorn-shaped scar on his cheek, a badge of honor received during his one ill-starred season trying and failing to play hockey. Otherwise, both were tall, trim, strong, narrow-shouldered boys, with long hands and knobby fingers, and sharp-boned faces whose kind but keen hazel eyes were arrestingly wide-set — even more so than mine. When one of them looked at you, you knew you were being looked at.

"I've got to be somewhere."

"Somewhere where?"

"Out at the Henderson place."

"I thought that's where you were yesterday."

"Well, I got to go back there this morning."

"Something's not cricket. What's the deal, dude?"

The moment offered me, for the thousandth time, a strong insight into what Nep must have faced when I was their age, although fortunately neither of them had shown the least interest in divining. I had privately concluded last July that I might best be the end of the line in that regard. The future would have no further need for people bent on dialoguing with the earth. In another generation or two, highly advanced versions of our by-then-medieval subterranean magnetometer technologies, our seismic refraction transmitters and VLF receivers, our shrewd machineries of prying and spying, would become so ubiquitous that a diviner might have as much a place in the world as an ostrich-plumed quill pen. Divining was a fading art few cared about anymore. Who could expect them to? Lost arts are by definition just that. Lost as Marcus Terentius Varro's play, *Virgula Divina,* which either satirized or celebrated divining, but because its manuscript disappeared centuries ago we will never know. What responsible mother would push her children to take up an ancient art fated to become another curiosity chucked onto the huge trash heap of outmoded human ideas?

"The deal, dude," I called back from my own bedroom where I was slipping on my sweatshirt and jeans, "is I'll tell you later. And don't call me *dude.* Word?"

"Way not word," said Jonah.

"Yeah, why not?" Morgan asked, crunching pretzels from a bag his grandmother must have given him.

"A dude's a man, that's why not."

"You're wrong, Cassandra. Everybody who's anybody's a dude."

"And while you're at it, don't call me *Cassandra*, either," I said, taking the pretzel bag from Morgan and handing him a peach, which he bit into without a pause.

"You call your mom *Rosalie,* am I right or am I right?" his mouth full.

"Keeping it real," Jonah approved, laughing.

"Just because I do it doesn't mean you have to. What's the matter with *Mom?*"

"What *is* the matter with Mom?" Morgan asked Jonah.

"Got me, dude. Something in the water."

They were dressed, fed, and in their grandmother's car by a little after six. Rosalie gave me a far more afflicted look of questioning what I was about than she might have meant to. I think she was accusing me of a transgression over which she needn't have worried. She never liked the idea of my overnight infatuation with James Boyd, but neither did she like it that I remained a single mother with no clear prospects or much evidence that I was looking. I dated from time to time, out of the human need to hold and be held, to be able to tell myself that I was yet among the living. Still, though I respected Niles too much to pursue him, he and I made my pious mother nervous.

"Thanks for this," I said, kissing her on the cheek before she drove away. "You know I wouldn't ask unless it was important."

"When will you be back?"

"Shouldn't be later than lunchtime, but I don't know for sure."

Niles pulled up not long after they left. This time he was in the cruiser. I couldn't decide whether or not it was peculiar that we didn't say much more than hello to each other while we traveled down Mendes Road, past houses, trailers, horse and cow pastures, out toward the rural county route that would take us back to Henderson's. He seemed

preoccupied, so I left him to his thoughts. Besides, I was feeling apprehensive and didn't mind the silence. He was wearing civilian clothes today. Plaid jacket over a blue jean shirt, worn chinos, even more worn hiking boots. Our drive was quiet but for the news station on the radio. Suicide bombing, roadside car bombing. Brutal rape, a murder. Our never-ending catastrophes followed by the weather forecast, traffic, sports. Then the same cycle all over again. By the third repetition that today would be partly cloudy, sixty degrees, with a chance of afternoon showers, I asked Niles if I could switch it off.

"No problem," he said.

We drove past the widened logging road I had taken the previous day that led into the old Statlmeyer farmlands. Continuing up the two-lane for another half-mile, Niles slowed to a crawl.

"Somewhere 'long about in here," he said, and without looking handed me the folded map that'd been nesting in the rubble of paraphernalia — walkie-talkie, notepads, a holstered pistol, sunglasses, handcuffs, the works — between his seat and mine. It occurred to me, and so I said it, "Your cars are such junkyards, Niles."

I side-glanced a sort of acknowledging smile, then spread the map on my legs to study it. Given my own devotion to maps, I was surprised at myself for not having done the same thing he did. But with all that land at my disposal, I hadn't thought I would need to go in with any preliminary homework under my belt. Counted on experience to carry me through. There was the line of dashes on the topo he must have been referring to. Another logging trail, it seemed, although it didn't look like these woods had been timbered since way back when leather tanneries proliferated in the region and razed the hillsides to harvest hemlock bark used in the process of turning cowhides into shoe soles. It was, in fact, a pretty out-of-date map. I mentioned this and he said, rightly, that's what made it valuable.

We drove too far, not having seen the least hint of an access. He pulled a U-turn and crept back along the rough shoulder of the paved road on the wrong side of the median. Not that it mattered on an empty stretch like this. I studied the tangle of roadside foliage, much

of it not yet fully leafed, though there was a patch of large leggy aged forsythias all abloom, like a wall of gaudy fire that we passed by, quite lovely even in their decrepitude. We kept going but there was no sign of any former entranceway.

"Maybe the mapmaker made a mistake," Niles suggested.

"Cartographers are mortal, too," I said, and as I did it simply dawned on me. "The forsythias. Turn around."

"What?"

"Let's go back. Those forsythias. They're not native. Telling by their size they must have been planted a pretty long time ago. That's where our other trail's going to be."

He turned around again, drove us back to the bright yellow partition of flowering bushes, and parked. I felt I had now earned my berth. We paced up and down the hedgerow. No gap anywhere. Just a long cheery monolith of odorless blossoms. Only after we'd hiked around the top end where the forsythias petered out and made our way along the far side of the flower wall did we find some hint of what we were looking for. All sorts of trees. Some were native; others were cultivars clearly planted. Tulip poplars, black walnuts, a few stands of white paper birch, dogwood, jack apple, black haw.

"People lived here once," I said.

"Seems like."

We saw it at the same time. About a hundred feet into the woods, a vague but distinct trail. Another hundred feet along the curving path —a human path, much too meandering for deer—was a Styrofoam cup lying on its side, half-hidden by young fiddlehead ferns.

"Could have been Townsend's people," Niles said.

"Surveyors don't get to where they have Townsend's reputation by dumping on the land they're supposed to be measuring and marking. Besides, we haven't crossed the property line yet. No ribbons."

"Still, doesn't necessarily say a thing. You know what, though. I'm having second thoughts about you hiking down in here with me."

"No way. You asked me to come along and I'm coming."

"I made a mistake," he said, then surprised me by pulling a small

digital camera out of the shoulder-slung rucksack he'd carried with him, which I assumed had only a bottle of water in it, or an orange, and took a few pictures of the cup. He produced a clear plastic bag and what looked like forceps, knelt, plucked it up by the lip, and looked at it closely before stowing it and marking the position with bright yellow plastic tape, pulled from a spool that was also in the sack, which he tied around a branch above the spot. Methodically, he spent the next minutes circling the area doubled over, looking, he told me, for a cigarette butt. "Tobacco and java are like hell's version of peaches and cream. Anybody who'd be sloppy enough to leave a cup here wouldn't have the horse sense to field-strip their butt. I'm seeing nothing, though." When he stood back upright, he looked me in the eye and asked what struck me as a strange yet obvious question.

"Do you sense anything or anyone?"

I breathed in deep, cleared my thoughts away as best I could, but I felt no presence here. I told him I didn't and said I wasn't used to divining people, as such.

"I still think you should let me take it from here. I'll walk you up to the car."

"No, Niles. I appreciate your concern. But you know I need to be here, too."

He shook his head, said nothing further, turned his back on me, and continued along the trail.

The birds were riotous this morning. Warblers carrying on like some piccolo orchestra gone joyously mad. So noisy it was almost annoying. As I walked, looking right and left and above me, and sometimes behind, a fitful chill ran through me. Then a wave of curious fatigue as we made our way inevitably toward the central overgrown floodplain that lay at the bottom of the slope. Even though Niles was, while walking ahead, disturbing the fallen leaves and undergrowth, breaking dead limbs and branches where he stepped on them, it seemed clear that this had been a thoroughfare of sorts. Lightly used, yes. But used. So I was thinking, Who would bother but somebody who relished solitude, or who preferred that others not see their deeds, or both? But then, it

could as easily be a poacher trail. Many were the evenings at my parents' farmhouse, which was much more remote than mine and indeed closer to Henderson's, when we heard gunfire during months not set aside for such activities.

I didn't mean to drift but drifted despite myself into watching Niles Hubert ahead of me in the scape. He and I had known one another since grade school. I climbed with him in trees, we broke arms together, played marbles, sword-fought with ash sticks, jumped side by side on his parents' tottery rusted rickety trampoline. He was my first kiss, an awkward and premature blunder that cost us the better part of the summer—we were all of twelve; summer was eternity—before we recovered from our rampant shyness to speak again, hang out, carry on. After that we reconnected as real friends. The purest kind you can count on. He became more worldly-wise than I did, for whatever reason, as we edged along, hand in hand, from our early through midteens. He wanted more from me than I was able to give him. But we were inseparable. How we loved to sit in a quiet remote place, backs against a maple tree, and kiss—having made it a kind of research project of our own, in light of that first debacle—kiss so long that our lips swelled, making us look like we'd eaten a bucket of warm Bing cherries. Nobody thought we would be with anyone else but each other.

Then, almost imperceptibly, my problems started up again. The monster took to whispering in my ear. Its voice sounded like fine-grained sandpaper rasping against stone. It seldom appeared in the form of a beast or being but came to me more like a mystifying cloud in my mind, a cloud of deep rich rose not unlike the color your hand acquires when you cup your palm to a flashlight in the dark. If the hanged girl was another instance of the monster, it had rarely revealed itself to me in such cruel and forthright form. The monster had always been simple and swift as a thought, the merest suggestion or outward trace of a thought. When I was in a period of—what to call it?—remission, I could easily keep these phantom thoughts to myself. But that wasn't always the case.

I remember once there was a teacher named Thomas Lowry whose

wife was friendly with my mother; they did church business together. She spent a lot of time at our house doing committee work for church programs and brought her little girl along to play with me, even though I was too old for her. A conscripted babysitter, I recall thinking how much I'd rather have been out with Niles than stuck at home with this round-faced, freckled girl half a dozen years my junior. Still, an inherent loneliness in her drew me to Jenny, and so I did my best to entertain her. One day, having run out of other ideas about what to do with my charge, I invited her to swim in the pond.

—No, she said, afraid the fish would bite her.

—But there's only trout in there, Jenny, I assured her. —Brown trout and rainbows with their sides all covered with pretty spots.

—They'll hurt me, she insisted.

—They won't hurt you, honey. They don't even have teeth, not really.

She wouldn't hear any of it and yet I, for reasons that shall remain forever unclear to me, understood what really was going to hurt her. Because the monster was at work in me that time, I saw in a halo of understanding that I needed to let her know her mother wasn't well, she might be quite sick in fact. —You should take extra-good care of your mother, you know that?

—But I already do, Jenny softly replied, no doubt wondering what was the matter with me.

—That's good, it's important for you to keep doing that.

The psychological anatomy of this behavior, the neurobiology that ranged behind it in my frontal lobe or wherever it came from in my brain, to this day I do not fully understand. I hadn't meant to be cruel or unthinking, but of course she went to her mother crying. And, of course, Rosalie stormed down to where I was sitting on the short dock cooling my feet in the slimy duckweed and scolded me for being so mean.

The girl's mother, it would soon be revealed, was ill. Not because of me. The poor woman had her stomach cancer for some long time and even knew about it. She and Mr. Lowry had decided to keep it a secret.

A terminal tumor. What point was there in darkening everyone else's spirits around them? They figured they would keep up a brave façade for as long as they could. In retrospect, I admired them entirely and, even after all the therapy, could not help but detest myself. It was one thing to know. Another to say.

I shared what had happened with Niles, who thought I was acting weird again, like during the time after my brother died. He distanced himself after that, I believed, although he has sworn it wasn't so. We saw less and less of one another as I saw more of city doctors. In my immaturity, I wrote it off that we somehow staled on each other. Probably was my fault because, for reasons I couldn't then comprehend, reasons I didn't have any will or way to talk about, I wasn't ready to do some of the things he, with his hormones raging at the hot high tide of adolescence, openly desired. I feared he grew tired of waiting.

I also wondered if he wasn't a little afraid of me. Niles, not generally the fearful kind, was nervous that his beloved girl was possessed, touched in the head. He might have thought it uncanny and even useful when I told him he ought to study for a pop quiz coming up in our history class—it did, but he wrote it off to my mother knowing ahead of time from a colleague and letting me in on the knowledge. He considered me clever perhaps for telling him his truck clutch was about to go—it did, but I might simply have noticed a different sound when the gears shifted, nothing more. But when I told him that I could have sworn I saw dead Emily Schaefer walking along in the moon-cast tree shadows down by the stone rampart one night when I couldn't sleep, saw her turn and look up at me in my window, and that she was disappointed in me, that did throw Niles off. It would have anyone. And as he withdrew, my mother filled the vacuum left in his wake. When I mentioned Emily to her, she had even less patience with me than Niles. She preferred, quite wisely, that I weather this aberrant season out of the public eye and even took a term off teaching so she could homeschool me while I improved.

Improve I did. I sometimes suspected her of pulling invisible strings behind my back, such that her handiwork may have lain behind Niles's

absence. This I now doubt, but I'll never quite know for sure. At any rate, I do recollect being in bed one frosty autumn night a few months into my exile, staring up at that same pale meniscus of a moon that had cast shadows on poor Emily, and deciding I'd had enough of forevisions. Even if I believed some special knowledge had lodged itself in my heart or head, that's where it was going to stay. And, if it were possible, I would gird heart and head against such fantasies which, even when accurate, brought little peace or succor to anyone. Myself included. That night I made my first covenant to do my very best to become, for lack of another word, normal. To unpleat, smooth, and ease the patterns of thought in my mind.

Even now I didn't experience a regretful wistfulness following Niles into Henderson's land. I never indulged in any bitterness toward him for moving on with his young life. What else should he have done? Occasionally, I allowed myself to remember the ways in which Niles and I made love — yes, we did have a brief, predestined season together in our twenties, after I matured some and before he became enamored of Melanie — and cherished the images of those times. He even asked me to marry him, in part, I always thought, because that was what everybody naturally expected, including us. Our engagement, however blissful, was short-lived, and that was that. I still felt so strongly connected with the man that regret was not a word in my emotional vocabulary. What I felt was comfortably safe as we headed toward what I believed, equally strongly, would be an abyss of some kind. A dead end that was quite alive.

It was like this. Years ago, in my early teens, I bought for fifty cents a huge fat folio of a book at the annual local library sale. I wanted to find a Greek or Latin dictionary, but all they had on the table was Mathews's *Chinese-English Dictionary.* I told myself, with all the sense of pride that accompanies such an outlandish purchase, that for half a buck I was going to be the only person in this whole damn county who could speak Chinese. When I got home, I cleared my little oak bedroom desk and sat the tome down before me. I opened it up to a chance page, *Lu.* Page four thousand something. The first entry, in bold type, showed what I

later learned was an ideogram. And beside it, the English translation: "A bad road; the road is bad." Not too promising. The next word translated to "A sacrifice by the way, before a funeral." Nervous, I read another entry. "Dangerous ways; dead end," and closed the volume. What came as a grand disappointment and revelation was that I would never learn Chinese, but I would always navigate difficult paths. This was my nature, I believed, and serendipity had brought me certain proof. I never opened the book again. But I still own it.

"Niles?"

He had gotten pretty far ahead of me, or rather, I had fallen behind. I could just make out his red and purple jacket through the crowded mesh of tree limbs. In another week or two, he would have been invisible behind a thick scrim of leathery green leaves.

"Niles, slow down."

He walked a little farther and then I saw him stop, not necessarily because of me. It wasn't as if he turned and shouted back my name or acknowledged my calling out to him. I hurried down the path, through zigzags of toppled trees, huge trunks fallen so long ago that moss and wild mushrooms had taken up residence on their woody carcasses. He was standing over a knit cap, his jaws flexing as they habitually did whenever he was upset. Bright pink, with a black tassel. It wasn't clean, but neither was it so dirty that there was much chance it had languished here lost all winter. He photographed and bagged it, marked the location again with tape. I was speechless. Without exchanging words, we both searched the forest floor but found nothing else.

Niles said, "Your description didn't include a pink cap."

"That's because she wasn't wearing one."

He was weighing what to do. "Any sense of how far we are from that grove where you allegedly saw her?"

"Allegedly?"

He didn't respond.

"I'm guessing we're not that close," I answered into the quiet. "Another three, four hundred yards."

"I know I asked you yesterday, but are you absolutely sure you took us back to the same exact spot where you'd been earlier?"

"No question. Besides, you saw my divining rod was there."

"That doesn't prove much. You could have dropped it anywhere along the way."

"Niles, I didn't lead you to the wrong place. She was there before. I swear it on the twins' souls."

That took him aback. Did me, too. In a life of dealing with doubters, this was, I realized, the most I had ever longed to be believed. I began to understand why it was that he decided to bring me along. It wasn't because he needed my help. To the contrary. He had intended to try to help me with a serious display of earnest regard on his part — the calls, the map, the off-duty time reexamining a place that wasn't in any official way of interest to him. No crime seen, no crime scene. He wasn't humoring me. Niles wouldn't bother. More that he wanted to help me regain balance and come around to accepting the fact I'd suffered some kind of phantasm or waking nightmare as I had when I was young. But the pink cap plainly scuttled his purpose some.

We walked on. The birdsong thinned out. Just some complaining crows floating by overhead. The trail disappeared, then reappeared now and again, and we managed to stay on it, more or less, all the way down. I had no reason to believe it would lead us to the hanging ground, but when it did I remembered this copse of ironwoods and black cherry trees with razor clarity. Niles did also. We hiked, him first, along the same narrow path I had surmised was a deer run and quickly came upon the clearing where, on its farther verge, stood the beetle-branched tree. It looked for all the world like a photographic negative of a lightning mass, St. Elmo's Fire done up in black.

She was as absent this morning as yesterday afternoon. The walnuts and maples glistened in wan filtered sunlight. Niles and Bledsoe had combed through this scrub before, but he went searching again now while I stayed behind, in a blind of bushes. How was it that the birds were so voiceless in this spot? Birds always were to my mind the very freest of all creatures. Why they avoided singing in a landscape so natu-

rally suited to them was beyond me. As if their silence were condemnatory.

I stood just where I had the day before. While I could mentally paint the hanged girl right where she had been, there was no willing her back into being. For the briefest moment I felt remorse, and not a little shame for having dragged Niles down here in the first place.

I had to admit to myself it must have been a cognitive slippage, a gross delusion. To have held her in my arms, though? I was mired in confusion. Wanted to leave here now, go home to my boys and forget any of this happened. I was wasting everybody's time. Niles, my mother, Nep, the twins, even Bledsoe and Ponyface, had all been put out for no good reason.

Then Niles materialized from the scrub. His face was as pale as an anemone. In his gloved left hand he was holding a long light brown snake. It dangled there, dead. Quietly he said, "Let's get you out of here." His revolver was drawn, I saw. He held it in his right hand pointed earthward. The snake was a rope.

6

THE REST OF THAT confessional Fourth of July sailed by in a haze. My father and I strolled back up the hill together, quietly from the quiet space of the pond, toward the laughter and chatter around the house. There wasn't more to say. He knew the import of what he told me, and I was still weighing what he'd shared. No doubt he understood his daughter was shaken. Wouldn't take the very least diviner — and all of us are diviners, one way or another — to predict that. Before we were within earshot of the nearest partygoers, some of whom had gathered on a flat knoll at the periphery of the lawn to set up the annual amateur fireworks display, he said, almost whispered, — All will be well, Cassandra. Trust my word.

Trusting him was what I had always done. Like second nature to me. Like nature itself, not second, not first. Just nature. My faith in him wasn't simply going to evaporate like fine rain on a hot stone.

We were approaching the group. Morgan saw us and called out, — Hey, where you two been? Hurry up already.

Jonah added, — Yea now, time to get the sky lit up.

— Coming, Nep shouted back, bright and smiling as if life's path were only merciful and infinitely smooth, without a single pit to fall in.

I thought, Let's slow everything down. It's only early twilight.

—Can't shoot the fireworks off without the general on the ramparts, one of Nep's pals pitched in.

How beloved he was, my father who had always done things his own way. And how these many people on the back porch, and over along the side of the house playing croquet, and the ones setting up the fireworks, and those inside the house helping put the leftovers into the fridge—how they were going to miss him when he went away. I know morbidity and sentimentality are brothers, like the Greek gods of sleep and death. But it was hard not to say to him, and I didn't bother to suppress myself, —I love you, Dad.

He stopped us—we were arm in arm—and replied, in a flat voice unexpectedly filled with an edge of warning, —I think you have the gift. It's a real gift. You mean something when you see something. Let's never talk about this again.

We were swallowed up into the crowd as dusk gave way to nightfall. I tried to keep a game face, smiling among dowsing agnostics who doubted my gift and others who'd hired me and now had overflow ponds and sweet-water wells in unlikely places. For his part, Nep seemed wholly engrossed once more in playing host, while showering bursts of billowing bright pink and silvery blue coneflowers exploded in the night sky above and everyone oohed and aahed. He was cutting up with his old friends Joe Karp and Billy Mecham and big Sam Briscoll whose diet, so far as I could tell, consisted strictly of chaw and brew. Jonah and Morgan were there, too, having glommed on to these firebirds, not wanting to miss one moment of the big light show. Not far from their group I noticed some of Christopher's old gang, Bibb and Lare. Was it possible that Roy Skoler was there, too, talking with them? He hadn't been invited, as far as I knew, and later, when I went over to say hello to the gang, he had disappeared.

By now the fireflies had started their own orgiastic light show all around us. A nice man a few years younger than I named Will Hutton, whom I had gone out with a couple of times, stood next to me during the fireworks as we exchanged pleasantries. I noticed my mother saw us together and nodded to me, smiled, at which I genially frowned

back. Will had, one blizzarding February afternoon the year before, taken me and the twins to Rollerworld, where we endured an hour of skating ovals to loud hip-hop and heavy metal. His was, I knew, a generous gesture, and I appreciated it. But Jonah and Morgan, then nine going on ten, insisted it was a *total sissyass* outing, and though I chided them for their ingratitude I couldn't in all honesty disagree with them. When he called again, I seemed to be forever busy.

After Will moved on, Niles stepped over to tell me he and the family had to head home a little early. His girl, Adrienne, suffered from terrible asthma, which was acting up, and they'd forgotten to bring her inhaler.

—I want prints of some of her photos of the party, I said, trying to smile, though it was only Niles I wanted to talk to now about what had been shared at the pond, and that would have to wait for another time, a neutral moment.

—You all right? he asked.

—Never better.

—You seem distracted.

—Thanks for coming. Hope Adrienne feels better.

When the fireworks concluded, those who didn't leave retreated to the house to talk and drink some more. Having confirmed for myself that Morgan and Jonah were still preoccupied whooping it up with their grandfather and his best buddies, I took advantage of this exodus to retreat to my favorite place here, a bluestone bench beneath a tall white pine on the far side of my mother's vegetable garden. I sat down, my head in a mild vertigo.

It was all too strange. It had always been all too strange, my competence as a dowser. Believing my ancestors had been touched by some divination god, I had talked myself into hoping that some of their blood genius was my rightful inheritance. Yet Nep's news, if true, shared on a day meant for the celebration of independence, was, appropriately enough, also relieving. I might not be alone. Might be freed from the years of guilt I'd felt, always believing my father was an honest master, while I was merely his impostor apprentice.

When I turned nineteen and officially added my name to the illus-

trious roster of divining Brookses, that's when I went professional with
my well-meaning subterfuge. The day before I was to go dowse for the
first of many clients Nep would pass along to me, nepotist that he was,
I drove down to the historical society library, then to the county assessor's office. There, under the guise of fulfilling my teacher's responsibilities, I studied vintage geodetic and recent soil survey maps of the
tract I was to walk the next morning. I was sure that left on my own,
without benefit of some inside knowledge, the only movement my diviner's rod would make was from my hands shaking out of embarrass-
ment and the fear of failure. And I hit pay dirt right out of the gate, to
roll a mildly mixed metaphor and an awful truth into one.

There it was—on paper quite well preserved since nobody had
bothered to look at this document for over a century—tucked in the
northwest quadrant of the property in question. A marshy pond, small
one. Not even big enough for the mapmaker to have bothered scribing
its name, assuming it ever had one.

The map was dated 1883. If the gentleman who drew it, one Ameri-
cus Granby, hadn't been many decades dead, I'd have loved to give him
a big hug. As happens when a spring is weak, during the intervening
century the pond had filled with runoff sediment, the residual swamp
dried up, and cattails had given way to jewelweed, joe-pye, and a riot
of huckleberry bushes. But I knew just where an underground source
like as not lay, untapped and ready to be rediscovered. What was more,
the soil survey told me that the aquifer was bedrock and, as such,
twice as likely to hold water in its fractures as, say, glacial till. I was
all set.

Nep came along. Said he wanted to be aboard for his maiden's
maiden voyage. See his Cassiopeia shine like a star. No one was more
impressed than he when I strode across the flattish fields shag-rugged
with thigh-high grasses, my witching wand that I had cut from a black
cherry tree held before me, until I came to the location of the long-
defunct, forgotten pond and put on quite a show.

—Right here, I said, matter-of-factly, exhibiting all the confidence
in the world. I had already learned by watching my father how to tense

the tip of the divining rod to jerk down, palms up with thumbs holding either end of the fork in the traditional manner. Easier than playing Ouija, though the violence of the yank earthward toward the vein of water did surprise me. Nearly took the bark off the branch. My left wrist and up into my forearm even hurt. That was strange, I recall thinking, before recovering my actor's aplomb and reiterating this was the mark. My client brought out his backhoe the same afternoon and dug a test hole ten feet, at precisely the depth I had prescribed. Within days it was half full of water. Not a gusher, but good enough for Cleve Miller's needs. Many years later, Morgan and Jonah would go swimming with his grandkids in the nice third-acre pond that was excavated there the same summer. It even bears a name now. Cassandra Pond.

That is a true story.

I became as addicted to nineteenth-century geodetic maps as an October squirrel is to acorns. Clandestinely made copies of everything at the county assessor's office, cloaking myself in the flimsy robes of the dedicated teacher. I collected soil surveys as well, with their analyses of loams and drainage. Of channery and meltwater streams. Of tuff and varve. I became a dedicated scholar of the area's geology, its river systems and tributaries, its complex aquifer. I studied sites on paper for days before actually setting my diviner's feet on dry land to perform my mime's routine. The time spent in the field doing the witching was the least of my efforts. I became, by my lights, little more than a benevolent trickster.

Business grew. From every couple of weeks to once a week to twice to half a dozen times. It even interfered with my teaching obligations. More and more when the principal called me the night before to say I was needed to teach state capitals to Mrs. Peabody's eighth-grade class the next day, or Mr. Vieiro's social studies group, I would have to decline because of a prior commitment to work elsewhere. Guilty as I felt about my methods, I was getting my jobs done. My clients were almost all of them impressed by the results and eager to recommend me to others.

The times I pronounced a spot viable and it came up dry were

nearly always because the original surveyors had made mistakes, mistook outwash till for glacial, say, and thus my failure occurred because there was simply no water to be ferreted out. These were cause for double humiliation. I might have felt better about failing if I felt better about succeeding.

The most important, and disconcerting, early event in my divining —my second turning—came one day when Nep wasn't feeling well and, without benefit of any of my usual preparation, I had to fill in for him at the local trout hatchery. Seemed their gallons-per-minute output had dwindled down to nothing and they would lose thousands of fish if I wasn't able to find what the drillers with all their engineering know-how, their clamshell bucket rigs and big sharp rotary drills, had not. My plan, my ruse, such as it was, involved doing some scouting, then stalling until Nep felt well enough to undertake this himself or I had time to pore over some face-saving maps of the site's geologic and hydrologic history.

This hatchery was set in a valley flanked by long, hunchbacked hills and in whose wide basin ran a glistening stream littered with glacial stones. In a normal year, the valley would be greener than envy. Hadn't been a normal year, though. Some seasons of low precipitation in spring and summer, and light snowfall during winters, had left our region in rough shape. Our water tables were way down. Grass looked like Shredded Wheat. Leaves drooped on their sagging branches. My garden tomatoes were the size of walnuts and just about as tough and dry. A reservoir one county over was well below capacity—you could see the top of the old church steeple peeking above the water in the middle of the dam where the ill-named town of Neversink had been submerged when they built it, like some provincial upstate Atlantis. Work was plentiful for both me and Nep. People who used to look down their noses at diviners were driven by dry wells to give us a chance.

The hatchery valley was all tans and browns. Looked like an old sepia-toned photograph of itself instead of the real thing. Skinny, gulping trout in their long pools were crowded in thin, slow water. Made me

sick to think of them poaching in their earth-bermed tanks. I saw I had to make this work, somehow. Given the direness of the conditions, it would be unethical to stall. So, my heart pounding in my throat, I began the search. Would that my Y-rod were some magic wishbone which if broken over my knee might bring me luck.

I knew I was wasting Partridge's, my, everybody's time, but I couldn't think what to do except fare forward. The hatchery man, who'd forever scoffed at us Brookses, had already exhausted conventional means of trying to locate sources, and his budget was getting tapped out. My services were nowhere near as expensive as the excavators', who would have been content to dig his place until it looked like an open-pit mine. If I hadn't known this before, the talus from failed test drillings that I literally stumbled on in the nearer fields would have tipped me off to the frustrations earlier contractors had met with.

So I started thinking counterintuitively. Where was the most unlikely place to strike water here? Where would wily water, water with shrewd savvy and maybe a sense of humor, lay itself up? I climbed due east toward a prominent rise in the valley, far above what would be considered the water level of a given terrain. My rod held before me, more security blanket than dowser's tool, I began crisscrossing, back and forth, weaving the land as is the custom, up this knotty little rise.

Partridge, whose huge brown coveralls and lobsterman mutton-chop sideburns were a sight to behold, lagged behind. He insisted on watching my progress, even though I told him I worked best when left to my own devices. A relief that he'd dropped back, since I didn't want the man to witness my growing desperation.

Then it happened. Just like that. My forked stick without warning bent down hard and leaped cleanly out of my hands. I managed to stifle what would have been a most unprofessional scream and woke right up from my petit malaise. The moment was surely comparable to the shock newborns experience when grabbing that essential, painful first breath of air. It is not too much to describe it as a birth. A part of me was born, right there. An essential part I don't to this day fully understand and may never.

I picked up the rod and got to work, having many times seen this phenomenon manifest itself for Nep. Believing he had always been the genuine article, having as yet no reason to question him, I was just following learned behaviors. I marked the spot with the heel of my hiking boot and climbed east away from the location twenty or so paces. Here I began diagramming a circle around it, as if I were tethered to the divot by an invisible string. Nothing, nothing, and now again the witching stick yanked down and I swear I had not a thing to do with it. Again I heel-kicked the spot. I continued circumnavigating the central mark until I discovered—or my stick, or some force of nature did— another live vein, and another. By this time, Ben Partridge had caught up with me, sweating enough to half fill one of his evaporated trout cisterns without my help.

—What's going on? he asked, wiping his considerable brow with a red handkerchief.

—You have two rich veins running northeast to southwest there and over there that merge right here, pointing to my original strike. —Give me a minute and I'll tell you how far down.

I had never tried this before, at least not without knowledge of what maps had proposed my result was to be, but put into use a technique Nep said went back to my great-great-grandfather. Standing at the center of the circle, I held my switch before me and began to count. Five feet, ten feet, twenty, thirty, at which point the tip of my stick began moving. When I hit thirty-three, it dove downward. At thirty-four, the tip of the rod eased back up again. Was I somehow making this happen?

—Good news, I said, containing my astonishment. —You don't have to go deep, either. Thirty-three feet along here, I suspect forty or thereabouts at most down there.

He sat both fists on his big square hips. A cedar waxwing, looking for all the world like the beautiful feathered dinosaur that it, in fact, was, perched atop a white pine as if to observe this moment of curious grace. —That's all?

—By the way, I added, pulling out my pendulum to dowse the

strength of the flow, —you've got a regular river down there. Even fifty gallons a minute wouldn't surprise me.

A weak breeze rustled the skeletal and naked raspberry bushes and small bleak pines that made their homes up here as Partridge and I gazed back down the hill and across the long field toward his house and siloed barn and collection of outbuildings that surrounded the hatchery. This was going to cost him a bundle in aqueducting, if he decided to believe me.

—You're sure about this? he asked.

That breeze, as if on diabolical cue, calmed.

—Let's see what the water says.

7

WE CLIMBED BACK out of the valley for a second time in as many days, the birds curiously trilling again. Niles called headquarters with information and instructions while I leaned against the trunk of his car, wishing I'd never heard of George Henderson or his land. It wasn't long before several more cars pulled up along the road at intervals. Some police. Some plainclothes. Detectives, I assumed, but I know little or nothing about that world. Niles spoke with them. I couldn't hear what he was saying but don't recollect at any time in the past seeing him more grave or focused. Half a dozen men and a uniformed woman fanned out along the stretch of asphalt and vanished into the woods. Niles afterward went with them, having left me once more with pony-faced Shaver. I could hear the dispatcher's voice and the distorted voices of others coming from Niles's radio unit in the car. The moment was dense. I might describe it as clotted. As we all have sometimes done when dreaming, I wondered if I wasn't awake inside a nightmare. Even occurred to me to pinch myself, try to shake it off. But there was no waking up.

Now another car came at a clip from the opposite direction. Two more men got out and spoke with Shaver before themselves heading down through the trees. Their radio unit was left on, too, and between

it and the crackling choppy voices on Niles's, the former tranquillity along this isolated reach of road was shattered.

"How're you doing today?" Shaver asked, a look of concern on his pale face.

"All right," I told him, offering a smile meant to let him know he needn't worry about me. What else could I say? Yet it dawned on me that my life, for the foreseeable future, was categorically changed. No, what I had witnessed meant things were very much not all right. Nothing was going to be the same whether they found my hanged girl or not. I was invested in her in ways I couldn't yet appreciate. Much as I tried not to acknowledge it, she had already begun to haunt me.

"You have any idea how long the sheriff wants me here?"

"Just long enough for them to make a preliminary sweep. He didn't want to keep you a minute more than necessary."

"Necessary for what?"

Shaver flashed me a look, as I was missing the obvious. "To identify the body as the same one you saw. If they find it."

"Don't you think that if they find a dead girl it's bound to be my same girl?"

"Maybe, probably. Not how it works, though."

"Isn't there a morgue where I could do it?"

"That's what will happen if they don't make a pretty immediate find."

Fact was, no one was available to drive me back home. Niles hadn't anticipated any of this and he was improvising. My getting home was understandably the least of his concerns. I took a slow, long breath. What a lovely agate sky hovered above, punctuated by fluffy silver-gray clouds that hinted of spring rain rather than snow. The earth awakening after its long icebound sleep. It was flat-out insane, I thought, that such natural beauty should preside over a world bent on fostering such viciousness.

"Is it all right if I sit in the sheriff's car?"

"Sure. Smoke?" he said, offering me a cigarette.

He was trying to be kind—"No thanks," I said—but I had to be by myself.

In the car I heard the dispatcher in conversation with someone who was on the way with a dog. Said it would take them an hour to get her boots on the ground, was how he put it. For a while I just ranged in and out of listening to the communications. Found myself marveling at how these people could actually understand what was being said, the distortion so thick and the beginnings and ends of words seemingly snipped off and bleeding into thin air. A dialect, like all dialects, with eccentricities and rules all its own. I'd traveled overseas only once—to visit Greece and Rome, see the places I had read about in Homer and Virgil (who was considered a wizard in medieval times because his name was wrongly linked with the virgula)—and this was like that: hearing foreign tongues and sensing you can almost comprehend what they're saying. Just not quite. I heard my name come crackling over the radio, too, which gave me a jolt. Didn't catch the context.

What caused me to feel her near me again, I don't know. I could no longer hear the dispatchers' voices, or anything else. The girl was look-ing at me, I knew it, sitting in the back seat of the car. I dreaded turn-ing around. Couldn't bear to see her again, whether she was somehow truly there or a figment of fantasy. I remained motionless, unbreath-ing, caught in a kind of suspended animation. Once again I hoped I might have fallen asleep and was dreaming. Then a soft musical laugh-ter, far away, began to emanate behind me. The gentle laughter, or per-haps weeping—they can sometimes sound uncannily alike—of a girl, insinuating itself as if through a small tear in the fabric of a wall of si-lence. No, it was more than one voice, I now realized, and not laughter or crying at all, but several voices talking at once, a melody of ques-tioning. I couldn't help myself and glanced in the rearview mirror. Three girls, their faces floating in the narrow glass.

No closing my eyes this time, no spelling *patience* backward. I turned, whispering a shrill "What?" but no girls were there. Relief shot through me followed by a fresh terror that I had now passed into a realm for which there were no logical words. Tried to revive my

breathing, wiped my cold and beaded forehead with my jacket sleeve. About this one, I knew at once, I would not tell a soul.

Niles had left the cap and Styrofoam cup on the seat there, objectively real things, without a doubt, and curiously comforting for the fact. The length of rope lay beside them, too, preserved like the others in its own plastic bag. Looked as if they were archaeologist's treasures destined for a museum. As I turned and slumped in the seat, defeated, I was left once more with a mounting panic that all this activity was in vain. By the end of the day I would look more the fool for having been the impetus for all these earnest people to leave behind whatever they had been doing this morning to come up to a lonely expanse of forest and tramp around, only to find what Niles and Bledsoe had already found, and what I myself seemed to keep finding—nothing. Niles would catch some pretty merciless flak from his colleagues, I imagined. Behind his back if not to his face. And as for myself, I would become a fully confirmed pariah.

Now another vehicle, a dark blue SUV, materialized over the long rise up ahead. A hyper-alert female German shepherd with a gleaming coat of brown and black fur arrived with her handler. Shaver opened the back door of Niles's car and grabbed the bags that safeguarded the rope and cap, handing them to the man who restrained the tracker dog on a long leather leash. He opened the plastic pouches, not touching their contents, and offered each to her wet nose. After she scented the things, the pair disappeared into the curtain of green like the others. Minutes piled upon minutes with nothing to fill them.

Impatient and drained, I decided to walk up the road to stretch my legs, distance myself from this latest misperception. Shaver said he preferred I didn't venture out of sight. Made me feel like Morgan and Jonah must sometimes have felt when I issued them similar edicts. But whereas the twins would have bristled and openly revolted, their mother just shook her head, unspeaking, and began to walk, hands slung deep into her pockets and eyes fastened to the shoulder of the road, studying its pebbles and bits of debris as some geomancer might. But unlike a geomancer who could read such stones, I didn't under-

stand what had brought me here, headed toward what I was increasingly convinced would be the confirmation of just another dead end.

The sun was high now. Well past midday. I strolled up far past the end of the forsythia hedge. The road was straight and I was within sight of Shaver, so my withdrawal from the immediate scene didn't go against his request. Today I should have been doing a thousand things at home — laundry, reading, helping Jonah and Morgan with their weekend homework — instead of biding time here waiting for something awful to happen.

As I walked I tried to block out where I was and why. My mind was rarely as adrift as it was this morning, but I weighed its anchor, imagining what the twins were up to, and found myself in my parents' living room. My father was there and the boys were there with him playing cards, poker I expect since that was what he and I used to play. Count Basie grooving on the turntable. Rosalie asked me if I'd had anything to eat all day, and I told her no, just some water this man Shaver had given me, but that was about it.

That's not eating, that's drinking. Here, let me get you something.

I followed her into the white kitchen and, answering another of her questions — she somehow knew the story I'd refrained from telling her this morning — said Niles hadn't really taken me back to the site with any expectation of discovery. That he did it more as a way for me to find closure.

She asked me what Niles was possibly thinking. How was I to find closure by not locating what I was sure I had seen?

Her point was well taken, but I reminded her that she more than once got down on all fours to shine a flashlight under the front porch to confirm when Chris and I were young the fact no ogre lived there.

Not quite the same.

Exactly the same.

You were little kids.

Niles isn't treating me like a child, if that's what you're getting at.

I switched back to my father and the boys. They were watching a baseball game on television. Yankees, their favorite poison. Nep used

to know every Bronx Bombers player stat going back to the twenties and listened to games on the radio in his workshop all season long. More and more pieces of that great puzzle were getting lost now, except for times when vivid pockets of memorized information came back with a vengeance. Both boys, especially Jonah, who carried a sea of numbers within him, had gotten it into their heads to pick up where their grandfather was being forced to leave off. A great deal of baseball talk, career numbers even for obscure players, filled our house, especially when Nep was around. Jonah was showing off his prodigious math skills, adding, subtracting, multiplying, dividing, even squaring players' uniform numbers with the same elegant ease with which Joe DiMaggio ran bases after swatting one into the distant bleachers. What does DiMaggio's jersey number plus the Babe's plus Yogi's times Mantle minus Stengel less Guidry divided by Jeter equal?

A-Rod, said Jonah, with unearthly calm.

What's Lou Gehrig times the square root of Whitey Ford?

Easy. That's Whitey himself.

Then I was back in the kitchen with my mother, who asked me, straightforward and disarming, Are you and Niles still, is there still something going on between you two?

While I had anticipated her question, saw it on her wary face, it nonetheless came as a disappointment even in this imagined conversation.

How could you say such a thing?

There's still something there between you.

There will always be. Sentimental as it sounds, first love makes its own special stamp on people's hearts. But he has his family and life. And I have mine.

She handed me a plate with a ham and Swiss sandwich on it sliced in half, some chips, and a garlic pickle. I was so hungry I felt faint. As we made to go back into the other room to join Nep and the twins, my mother offered the simple, sane kind of apology only lifetime intimates can make — Cass, I'm sorry, I just worry about you so — and I was seized abruptly from my fantasy and drawn cascading hard back

into this other, waking life and the hand on my shoulder was not Shaver's but rather that of Niles, who was saying my name.

"What?" I asked, looking past him down the road and seeing I had managed to walk quite a distance from the cars. "What's happened?" It was clear from his eyes that they'd come up with more than nothing this time. "You found her, didn't you."

"No, listen, Cassandra."

"Well, what? What's that look mean?"

"We found a small encampment partway up the far slope. In an old hunter's cabin, looks like. Some canned food, water, a blanket. I thought no one lived on this land."

"Was anybody there?"

"Not a soul. We figure it must be a squatter or some illegal hunter but couldn't find a blind in the trees anywhere. I'm not sure what we got."

"So now what happens?"

"Couple investigators are taking pictures, making an inventory, see if they can't start putting together an idea of what's going on."

"I guess you'll have more questions for Statlmeyer and Henderson."

"For you, too, maybe."

We had started walking back down the long gradual hill toward the cars. I felt my chest compress.

"Is it all right that we talk like this if I'm going to be questioned again? Tampering with a witness or along those lines?"

"Look, Cass. I hate to tell you, but you're not considered a witness to anything, as such," he said, then went on in a softer voice, "There aren't real grounds to bring charges of making a false report, but it is a crime, you know."

That took me by surprise. I tried not to let it show, but Niles knew me too well.

"Nothing'll happen, don't worry. Your divining, or whatever it was, did lead us here to this other find."

"Bledsoe thinks I'm a hysteric."

Niles kept walking. "Doesn't matter."

"Who knows, maybe I am."

He made no response. As we continued along the shoulder of the road, I had such an urge to take his hand. This was a feeling I hadn't experienced with Niles Hubert in well over a decade. And even as the stirring faded — as well it might — I could hear my mother's voice up-braiding me for having had the thought. But mine was less a sexual urgency than a need to reconnect with the tangible world. To hold a known hand. How ungodly and unusual could such a small desire be?

We were not quite within hearing of Shaver and the man he was now talking to, either someone who had entered the scene while I was away or one of the men who'd gone into the woods and returned, when Niles took my arm at the elbow and said, gently, "I think, Cass, you need to be very careful of yourself. I think you may need some help. I'd like to try, if you'll let me. There's a very good woman I know who might be able to talk to you. And if she feels she can't, she knows some excellent people who probably could. Will you let me do that for you?"

"But what about this camp?"

"What about it."

"You wouldn't have found it without me."

Niles thought about that and said, "Occam's razor. You bring enough interested people to bear on any land or locale and they'll probably discover something there. Plus, here's another one you'll recognize. Curiosity breeds convergence."

Occam's razor we'd learned from my mother. The second phrase? Nep. Niles didn't forget things.

I needed badly to go home now. I started to ask him if it would be permissible for me to leave, when we heard a commotion below us on the road and saw one, then three, then all the men who had earlier headed down into the forested valley. They had emerged in a group from the woods and were standing together on the road, talking loudly, excitedly.

Niles and I began to hasten toward them when we both caught sight of the uniformed woman. A girl was walking beside her, clutching her

arm. The girl seemed afraid and dazed and exhausted, clothed in a dark dress that was wrinkled and filthy, as was her long pale brown hair. Though I was running now, I closed my eyes and opened them.

None of it was a mirage. Just before Niles and I reached the others who were crowded around the girl, it began to sprinkle. Soon enough a misty rain blew down across the hills. The forsythias along the roadside, their many branches festooned with gaudy, cheerful flowers, sparkled with the fresh droplets and nodded up and down and side to side in the freshening gusts, as if offering a host of conflicting opinions.

Part II

IN SEARCH
OF SANCTUARY

8

My mother's family was originally from Maine. Mount Desert Island and environs with its stony coasts and steel-blue harbors and sea-scraggled pines. When Henry Metcalf, her father's brother, died, she inherited a handsome old quaintly decrepit lighthouse and its keeper's cottage on a small isle, really just a big bump of largely forgotten land in the ocean. On a clear day, if you squinted and looked carefully, you could see Covey Island from Otter Point on Mount Desert, midway between Baker—whose lighthouse still worked—and the eastern tip of Little Cranberry Island, farther out in the Atlantic than either. This inheritance came a couple of years after Christopher died. Rosalie, Nep, and I made the all-day drive to see to Mr. Metcalf's funeral arrangements, put in order whatever needed to be, and hear the will read. At Covey, a whole new world was opened to me, one in which water was anything but hidden.

We instituted a family habit of going up every August when the heat and humidity crept from the coast into the mountains at home and made daily life difficult and sleep impossible. Too, Rosalie thought the change of scene would be good for me, help me to shake the fore-visioning spells that had plagued me from time to time. Nep and I learned, after our own landlubber fashion, how to sail the white dory

that had been bequeathed us, and my mother and I harvested mussels in low-tide beds that flourished along the virginal shores.

We had but two neighbors on the island. One, Angela Milgate, was a thoroughly reclusive widow, a professional hermit of sorts. The other was a perennial absentee, even in high summer months. Often as not, it felt as if we owned the whole place, which until midway through the last century the Metcalfs still did. A small, unprepossessing family cemetery lay near the center of the just-about-thirty-acre island, its antique headstones surrounded by a weathered wrought-iron fence and a grove of pines. Here the lifelong islander Henry Metcalf rested in peace beside his son, his wife, his brother William and sister-in-law Winifred — my maternal grandparents — and other Metcalfs from earlier years. What with wild blueberry bushes and scented balsams, arrowwood and sweet gale, with broad Atlantic vistas in every direction across the ever-changing water, and also the lighthouse — deactivated around the turn of the twentieth century, its stairway passable but crumbling, its round tower so beautiful on its rock foundation — the island was nothing shy of magical. A true refuge.

It was here I fled with Morgan and Jonah after school let out for the summer. I was well aware they didn't want to go all the way up to Covey, especially in early June when the black flies were out in stinging legions. Besides, camp was to start in a matter of ten days and this side excursion was a nuisance, not to mention that Morgan's baseball season was in full swing. But they weren't fools, my boys. They saw how frazzled their mother had become after the incidents at Henderson's. Saw me come home devastated the afternoon that girl was found. She was alive but dehydrated, with a story to tell but little or no will to tell it. Nor did she have any apparent grasp of the questions asked by the policewoman who had taken temporary custodianship of her after she'd finally appeared from behind an outcropping of monolithic stones that resembled, as Niles said, a tumbledown Stonehenge, where she had been hiding from the searchers and the police dog. She stared ahead at nothing visible, like a spooked, cornered wildcat. Ignored the water Shaver offered her. A candy bar that one of the men

rummaged out of a pocket she also disregarded, utterly indifferent. If she had been standing there in some alternative dimension from which she couldn't see any of us, her response could hardly have been less engaged. We were like ghosts to her. Not merely ghosts, but ghosts she couldn't—or wouldn't—perceive. I had felt disconcerted before, but watching this girl only left me feeling lost. Bereft, even, and as alone as she surely imagined herself, no matter what her real circumstances would prove to be.

Suppressing a mother's impulse to go comfort her myself, put my arms around the poor thing, I stood aside, at the perimeter of the concerned crowd who had rescued her. I didn't have the wherewithal to begin seriously to connect my vision of the hanged girl with this half-feral soul, but couldn't help myself. She looked to be in her mid-teens. A little older than the other girl. Strong cheekbones, full if pale and cracked lips. She was wearing a dark violet dress with a beige Bakelite or maybe alabaster pin above her left breast in the shape of a rose. Unlike the hanged girl, she was the opposite of pristine. Her dress was torn, and her pretty pin was muddied. Her cocoa-brown eyes were bloodshot. Her dirty hair was garnished with leaves and twigs like some wood nymph, a modern-day disheveled dryad.

The immediate conclusion everyone reached, as became clear from the talk going around among the men, was that they had a runaway on their hands. Were they right, I thought, whatever she escaped must have been well worth running from. This was tough terrain under the best of circumstances. But to have lived out here for as long as it took to turn her into the dirty rag that she was now meant she had slept through some cold nights, and wet and chill days. She continued to peer before her with an intensity so staunch and focused that I found myself glancing in the same direction she was. I assumed if anyone could see what so engrossed her, it would be me. But she wasn't looking outward. She was gazing at something within. And what she observed there gripped her attention more than anything we offered her. Unlike the hanged girl, she wore a pair of simple black shoes. They were mucky and one of the laces was missing, but at least she wasn't barefoot.

Niles glanced back at me. I knew what his eyes meant to ask, a question he couldn't pose aloud without risking ridicule. What was happening here? he wanted to know. I wished I could help him, but with my own eyes tried to let him know it was beyond me. At least just then. With that girl. I felt every bit as lost as she seemed to be. Maybe more so, since she at least in theory understood what had caused her to be here.

They wrapped a gray wool blanket around the girl and helped her into the back seat of Niles's car. The policewoman climbed in beside her. I sat in the front. The rest of the officers and investigators returned to the field to glean what they could. Ours was a quiet ride back toward town. Only the woman spoke. She asked the girl her name, speaking to her in tones and words that seemed more appropriate to someone much younger than this, handling her trauma with kid gloves.

Where were her mom and dad? Were they at home? Could she tell us where she lived?

Nothing.

Okay. Was there anyone else in the woods they should look for who needed help? Did she have a brother or sister who would like to know she's safe? Wouldn't she change her mind and have some water or this candy now? Was she feeling warmer? Nobody was going to hurt her.

The girl stared ahead as if in a vacuum.

Cómo te llamas? the officer even tried, just in case. *De dónde vienes?*

There was nothing for it, but I admired the woman's tender persistence. Before we reached the station—the ride seemed to take forever—an ambulance intercepted us on the road and some paramedics took over. I caught a lift in the ambulance to the hospital and from there Niles had arranged for someone to drop me off home. He said he'd call once the girl was examined, and the child welfare people and a counselor arrived to begin the process of getting her entered into protective custody. He wished he could take me to Mendes Road himself but he had to get back to Henderson's and afterward to the station.

"You going to be all right?" he asked.

"I don't understand any of this."

"The girl's safe. She's in good hands now. You should be happy, Cass, not stressed."

"But I don't get it."

"Something good happened here, that's all you need to get. Imagine if you hadn't seen whatever you saw yesterday, imagine if we didn't go looking this morning. She couldn't have lasted much longer by herself. And she seemed bound and determined not to come out of there on her own. As far as I'm concerned, you saved her life."

I shook my head.

"Take care of yourself, go easy. *Patience* forwards and backwards, don't forget."

Once home, I took a long hot shower. Made myself a cup of tea and sat with it as it grew cold. My evening didn't promise much more peace than the day had given me. Rosalie was driving the twins over within the hour. They were all but manic, she warned me. As it happened, my fantasy about them playing poker and watching baseball with Nep was wishful thinking. My father had suffered through one of his badly disoriented days, it turned out, and wasn't up to playing anything. He might have sat with Jonah and Morgan and watched, or at least looked at, a ball game, but none had been broadcast.

What was I doing all day? the boys wanted to know the moment they walked in the door. What about yesterday? What was going on? they asked over and over, and these were not needy children. They demanded to be told what and who we were up against. For them, it was never just one or the other of us in our small family left to face the harsh world alone. We three were always a unit. An us, a *We*.

More than once they had been in fights at school over some classmate's accusing them of having a mother who was crazy as a loon. Screws loose, bats in her belfry, the madwoman of Mendes, all that clever, contemptible nonsense some kids — too often practicing to become clever, contemptible adults — are so good at ladling out. One time Morgan was suspended for a week after blackening the eye of a boy who had called him a bastard, son of a witch. Without a doubt,

some sniping parents condoned at least the spirit of their children's accusations. If I had been teaching Darwin rather than such—to them—harmless subjects as geography and ancient mythology, more than a few would have been after the school board, arguing at the top of their Creationist lungs to have me removed from the premises. A number of Rosalie's fellow congregants at church felt the same way, but since I went to church mostly just for weddings, funerals, and the occasional baptism, they could hardly throw me out.

Secretly proud of Morgan for fighting back, I canceled all work scheduled for that week and homeschooled him, as my mother had me, once upon a time. I like to think he learned more during our days working together than he'd ever have learned in class. Either way, unless Niles managed to keep this recent incident quiet, rumors were about to fly rampant, thanks to these same gossips, of my discovering a dead girl who not only was not the same girl they found alive and lost in the woods, but who wasn't found at all. I could already imagine some of the things they might say.

I made the whole story up to get attention for myself.

The girl was my secret daughter whom out of shame I had forced to live in the forest since infancy and in a fit of rage I personally hanged her.

No, she wasn't my daughter, she was someone I kidnapped, then hexed so she couldn't incriminate me, struck her deaf and dumb, and abandoned her that night in the woods so I could support my earlier absurd claim that—and so forth.

Variations, some milder, some wilder, of these stories would find their way along the grapevines out there in the community, especially among children Jonah and Morgan's age. I was determined to remove us from the vicinity the very day after final classes and not return until the twins started camp. Between now and then, I could only hope that the supposedly runaway girl's situation was resolved.

Our truck barely made the drive north. We overheated twice on the way up and had to stop along the interstate to give the engine a chance to cool down. The boys informed me that this was its swan song, its farewell performance.

"*Adiós*," Jonah said.

"Goodbye, cruel world," echoed Morgan.

They were laughing so hard about the steam coming from under the raised hood, while other cars on the highway cruised past, that my frustration about it soon gave over to laughter as well.

"All right," I said. "When we get there—"

"If we get there," said Morgan.

"—we can look into selling it—"

"For about fifty cents."

"More like we give them the fifty cents."

"—and get something new."

"New *used,* you mean."

"We can afford what we can afford," I said, trying to stay with the mood. "Tell you what, though. I'm going to let you two pick the car."

"Now you're talking—"

"—turkey."

We laughed some more as the engine whined, coughed, complained, then finally turned over again.

"I set the budget, turkeys. But you pick the wheels, dig?"

Both groaned. They hated it when I tried to talk hip.

"We'll see what there is to see and our people will get back to you on it," Jonah finished.

What contrarian minds we come equipped with. At that moment, when my two bastions of strength were picking up the slack, trying to help me move past problems, giving me good advice with humor and their personal brand of quirky respect, I found myself shadowed by a feeling of having let them down. I couldn't help but think that if they had a father, another provider in their life, they would be riding right then in a real car. Not this absurd smog-belching artifact. Though they might put brave faces on it and insist otherwise, they deserved a father. Someone accomplished in the world who would love them as much as I—well, almost as much—and show them how to fix things that were broken and make things that weren't there before. Nep had served as a surrogate. Fathered them like they were the sons he never had. Or rather, as he had fathered Christopher during his short life. And he'd

always been brilliant in his understudy role. But now he was sometimes there, sometimes not, and I felt his absence to the marrow of my
bones, as both daughter and mother.

"You all right?" Jonah asked, after some miles in silence.

"You bet," I assured him, and briefly grasped his hand.

Once we grocery-shopped, then rolled past the stores selling cu-
polas with their weathervanes turning in contradictory directions and
fields of lupines by the ragtag tourist zoo, we stopped for crab rolls at
a pound in Ellsworth, where we also bought ourselves live lobsters
plucked from a holding tank. Crossing the causeway from the mainland onto Mount Desert, I could smell the salt air and my heart quick-
ened. Toward the end of the long day, we finally parked our poor limp
truck in the municipal lot in Northeast Harbor and boarded the Bunker & Ellis launch that would carry us out to the island.

For all their initial reluctance about coming north, the twins were
happy to be on the mailboat that doubled as the ferry here, and so
was I. Familiar coastal islands glided by, pine-haired rocks with their
pink pobblestone beaches in the bundling water. Out in deeper water, lobster buoys looked like gaudy painted Easter eggs. Henderson's
woods, with its perplexing vision and voices, could not have been farther away, and that realization set my spirits flying. I gave Morgan a
spontaneous hug from behind. Instead of wriggling away he hugged
me in return, wrapping his wiry strong arms around my lower back
while still facing forward toward the ocean. In another year he would
be almost as tall as his mother. Jonah leaned against the rail beside us
at the front of the mailboat, pointing as harbor porpoises lunged and
stitched the ocean swells some hundred yards to starboard. His cheeks
were lit up from the sea winds.

This was a moment people long for in a lifetime. The Greeks didn't
have a word for it, they who had words for everything. Not a single
word in English could compass such equanimity. I believe the Bud-
dhists refer to it as *a peace which passeth all understanding*. It was like
that.

The cottage was more of a wreck than I had expected. It had been a

harsh winter up here. The front porch floor was peeling and in places looked like a great potpourri of dark red flower petals, and a few shingles were missing from the roof. Several fresh cigarette butts littered the grass beside the porch. That was odd. Had some lobstermen come ashore and rested on our steps, or a dayfaring family out for a sail looked in through our windows?

Inside the house, on the first floor, the sheeted furniture and rolled rugs and all the rest of the chattels seemed fine. There was still plenty of propane in the tank, and the electricity was working. However, we discovered that one of the seaward windows was broken, and inside the upstairs bedroom where I always stayed we found the feathery bloodied remains of a black-back gull that had flown, or been blown, right through it. The room was, remarkably, undamaged by rain. I had never seen such a thing before but figured there must have been quite a storm sometime in the past days that disoriented the bird and slammed it, with a heavy whip of wind, into the glass. We three got the window boarded up temporarily, scoured the stained floor, and buried the huge sea bird, and within a few hours, just before sunset, had the place more or less up and running. I was determined not to treat this unusual mishap as an omen, wasn't going to let it intrude on my renewed sense of calm.

Weary though we were, Jonah carried the big lobster kettle down to the goldening shore, past corridors of beach roses, *Rosa rugosa* with their devoted drunken bees, and filled it with saltwater while Morgan got a driftwood fire started in the pit. Tradition was that the first night was always a dinner of lobsters — *bugs* the boys called them, adopting local slang — and we weren't here to break with tradition. I set the table and lit candles and a hurricane lamp, leaving the overhead lights off that first night as a way of clearing the world away, literally blacking it out. We had our supper and stayed up late talking. When I finally sent them to their shared room, finished the dishes, put out the fire with cooking water from the pot, and extinguished the candles, I was deliriously tired, deliciously so. Waves crashed on the shore under the spray of endless stars. I felt as if I could sleep for a week.

The Metcalfs had been no lovers of modernity, and while the family had allowed electricity to be cabled to Covey back in the twenties when the other outer islands were serviced from Mount Desert, a telephone was never installed. No one was going to call. I went upstairs, carrying my lamp ahead of me, and, ignoring the newly boarded window, climbed into bed feeling safe from the world for the first time in weeks. I who never said prayers even said one of thanks, a Nep-like agnostic prayer.

Dear Lord, if you're out there somewhere listening, I want you to know how grateful I am for your giving us protection during our journey, and please I ask you please let these days we have here be peace-filled and undisturbed. Thank you for watching over my sons. Amen.

9

Hard sunlight so filled my room the next morning that I came awake in a literal flash. I was shocked not to find the bloody, thrashing seagull on my bed, where it had been just a moment before. In my nightmare, a figure hovering outside my window had cradled the gull in its arms like some demonic madonna, before burning each of the bird's eyes with the tip of a cigarette and throwing the helpless creature at me through the glass. I breathed in and out, tasting the sweet briny ocean air, trying to slow my pounding heart. Hearing no one astir, I figured the twins were sleeping in after yesterday's long drive, which was just as well. Sheltered though I was in truth, I questioned whether Covey was far enough away from Henderson's to be the sanctuary I'd sought. Rather than force myself out of bed and trek downstairs to prepare breakfast, I pulled the pillow over my head with the idea of stealing a few moments in order to think.

I didn't want to admit it, but my monster was back, aroused from its sleep, ranging around my perimeters. That much I had to acknowledge. A nightmare was just a nightmare, but I could no longer deny that the hanged girl bore all the hallmarks of one of my forevisions, though as forevisions went it was the most inscrutable, baffling one I had ever experienced. Unlike in times past, when I could see some di-

rect correspondence between what I foresaw and people or events in my everyday life, this time I could make no such connection. The question was, What was I going to do about it? Or, more to the point, Was there anything I could do?

What finally decided me on leaving Little Eddy for Covey Island was, among other things, that the police investigation, largely based on forensics and the work of the expert Niles had me meet, preliminarily concluded that I had in fact suffered a hallucination. Some mess-up in a visual neural pathway. Plausibly Charles Bonnet syndrome, but my age and perfect eyesight didn't fit the profile. Peduncular hallucinosis was suggested, but I presented with none of the typical accompanying symptoms. Optic neuritis, schizophrenia? Not likely. In the end, they settled on a probable transient stress disorder, a delusional episode. If nature abhors a vacuum, authorities deplore the inexplicable.

The therapist was well-meaning to a fault, a woman who cited James Thurber as a possible fellow sufferer, saying the cartoonist who wrote "The Secret Life of Walter Mitty" saw an old lady with a parasol walk right through the side of a truck once. A large rabbit spoke with him about world affairs from time to time. On another occasion, he witnessed a bridge rise lazily into the air, like a long balloon. She was, in essence, assuring me that even those afflicted with mild madness have a creative, viable place in our culture.

"Imaginative people such as yourself are sometimes carried away by the very thoughts that make them special in the first place," she had proposed. "But it's important not just to understand the difference, but feel it in your heart. Feel the difference between reality and the fantastic make-believe that you experience as real."

I remember lowering my eyes as she finished uncoiling this string of thought that reduced me, I felt, by its implication to a kind of infantilism.

"To be balanced, you must know how to distinguish between dreaming subjective experience, such as your waking nightmare, and objective living experience. Does that make sense to you?"

"It does and thanks," I answered, knowing this was the only response that might spring me from her soft leather chair.

Point was, I hadn't been dreaming, but none of them had the least tangible reason to believe me, nor was there any hard neuroscience or accepted psychological model known to them that might connect my "vision" of the dead girl to the discovery of the lost girl. So, what I saw never "objectively" happened. The rope we found that day came back from the lab with no identifiable evidence suggesting any possible narrative that would indicate a recent hanging. The fibers were too weathered and weak to readily support the weight of even a child. As for the Styrofoam cup, it did turn out to have been dropped by one of Townsend's survey team, a cup from Crowley's General Store in the small downtown of Little Eddy, hazelnut with sugar. The pink knit cap was the girl's. She apparently lost it while running, trying to avoid being seen by Niles and me when we descended into the forest. And though the search and investigation were supposed to have been an in-house affair, with details kept under strict wraps, word got out, I assume courtesy of Bledsoe. Much of the story was picked up, with errors and exaggerations abounding, by some regional papers and beyond. Not as if I had a clipping service, but my phone started ringing, and most of the people on the other end with questions for me weren't locals. A few unfriendly letters, most of them unsigned, populated my mailbox. A call from Rosalie's pastor offering to speak with me. Turned heads at the grocery store. Even the boys had gone a little quiet on me, not knowing what to say.

Only after I got the call from Matt Newburg, the school principal, telling me a number of concerned parents wanted to remove their children from my summer school class, was it clear I might want to consider getting away for a while. When he added that my continuing education course on Homer and Virgil was canceled due to low — that is, *no* — enrollment, all nine people having pulled out, the die was cast. For obvious reasons, I myself postponed the dowsing appointments on my schedule. I was in no state to ramble around alone in some remote field or woods. Never before had the uninhabited earth seemed threatening. And the telephone might as well have been an exposed live wire.

Even my phone call with Rosalie was charged. When I told her my

plan and asked her blessing to use the cottage as an escape, she said
fine, but made her own request. She and Nep wanted to join us the
following week, after we had opened the house and got settled a bit.
Nep's health being what it was, she thought it wise to move our annual
August vacation forward this year. Given all that had been going on,
time together seemed imperative.

"Wonderful," I agreed, before getting off the phone. But I knew
what it meant. Knew she was traveling here to talk. To hike with me
the craggy hard-going shore of the island, picking our way along while
she detailed everything that was wrong with my life that I already knew
was wrong with my life. No doubt she intended to warn me—to protect me from myself, as she would have put it—that when the monster
was near, I needed to be especially mindful not to speak about matters best left buried in the past. My mother had mapped all the chinks
in my tinfoil-thin armor. The thought crossed my mind, as we said
our goodbyes, that I ought to tell her I didn't want to discuss Christopher or any of his, and by turn our, long-dead secrets while we were
at Covey—a place he had never known—but decided against saying
anything. Perhaps once Rosalie arrived and breathed in the purifying
ocean air, her worries would disappear much as I hoped mine would.

For his part, Niles assured me I shouldn't worry about the garbage
that was written in the papers or what people were saying, insisting I
shouldn't be ashamed or distressed. He met me nearly every day after
the encounter, during his lunch break or whenever he could get away.
Out of public view, we walked together along the outskirts of the local firemen's park, or around the far side of a nearby lake. During the
drives through the green, anonymous hills to meet him I sometimes
felt like a discreet lover hooking up with her married boyfriend. My
nerves were so jangled and thoughts so given to shadowy feelings of
guilt that I might as well have been up to something adulterous like
that. Instead, I tried to heed his advice to stay proud, calm, strong, not
to worry. But I knew his voice too well, and the look on his face proposed he himself was worried. When I asked what Melanie thought,
he pulled a frown and said, "Doesn't matter," which was easily inter-

pretable. She no doubt warned Niles he risked hurting his reputation by continuing to associate with his crazy childhood friend.

Niles, though, didn't treat me as crazy. He treated me with respect, cutting through the nonsense in the news reports and telling me the truth about the found girl's story. Her name turned out to be Laura Bryant. No feral child, no dryad, the girl had been missing for some two weeks. She disappeared at a train terminal on an early May morning. Laura and her mother had gone to a riverfront station to meet her father, who was returning from a business trip. His train was running behind schedule because of track work down the line. Wind coming off the river was stiff, and though any ice floes had long since melted away, it was chilly. She told her mother she wanted to go to the car and get the coat and cap she'd left behind. The parking lot was plainly visible, right on the other side of the tracks, and her mother said no problem, just hurry back since he's arriving any minute now. So Laura, shivering a bit, paced down the platform and up the stairs to the enclosed overpass, a glass and girder affair, and while a southbound train rumbled into the station, temporarily blinding her mother's view and distracting her, the girl vanished, as many children do, into the awaiting void.

The whole scenario was so simple. The southbound pulled out soon enough. Laura's mother glanced toward where she had parked but she didn't see her daughter. Dawdling, most likely, or maybe she was in the overpass that straddled the tracks, looking out its windows. Well, she would get a talking-to, Mrs. Bryant was thinking. Laura's father's train arrived, greetings were exchanged, a welcome-back kiss. Then he asked, Where is Laura? The woman explained what had happened and together they walked to the car. The coat and cap that Laura had gone to fetch, because it really was quite cold with that wind coming off the water, were missing, and so was she. They began looking around for her. Began asking people in the lot if anyone had seen a girl with brownish-blond hair, fifteen years old, wearing a new dark blue dress, the color of a violet. They canvassed shop owners to ask if a girl had come in, maybe used the restroom. Rang doorbells of houses by

the station. No one had seen her. No one could help. Their day descended into chaos.

Niles continued to tell me about Laura's recovery as he learned more about her. Said he wanted to keep me current and keep current with me. Whenever he called me *Casper,* however, I couldn't help but think of myself in cartoonish terms. *Casper the Friendly Ghost.*

Within several days of being found, Laura overcame her diffident muteness and asked what was going on? Who are you people? Where am I? She made tentative eye contact with those who were looking after her, though it appeared she had been traumatized into a kind of inconsolable shyness. She did finally express interest in food, and when a plate was set before her, she ate heartily. She seemed to answer questions to the best of her ability, but Niles couldn't tell whether she was groping for information she couldn't express, or holding back what she didn't want to reveal.

When he visited her in the facility, she recognized and acknowledged him. Asked if Renee, the female officer, was coming again. Still, during those first long days it was as if she was in reversion, had backtracked a few years and was thinking with the mind of a younger, terrified self. Or else she was some sort of bravura actress, coy as a chameleon.

"Damned confounding," he said.

Apropos of nothing, she announced after breakfast one morning that her name was Laura. Said she knew that was only part of her name but claimed not to remember more. She apologized about this, since the people trying to comfort her wanted so badly to know.

"At least she knew she was Laura," I told Niles, who was relating all this to me. "Names are doors to ideas."

Laura went on to say she lived by a river that was very wide and there was an old church by this river she remembered quite distinctly — Niles said he racked his brain trying to recall anything up or down the Delaware that matched this. The river changed color all the time, from brown to blue to white, and across the river was a mountain. Before she was here, she said, she lived in a house. She was sorry she couldn't

describe it further. No, she couldn't make a drawing for them because she would be inventing and what good would that be? They wanted her to draw it anyway? She made several, all different. She pushed aside the paper and colored pencils. Didn't want to draw anymore. The pictures were a waste of time. Besides, she wasn't some baby and she'd had enough of this childishness.

No, she answered another question put to her. No, she didn't know anybody in the forest. She hated the forest. She hated the filthy hunter's cabin. The roof leaked and it was cold at night and her fire kept going out whenever she fell asleep. She hated the guy in the long car who came and went but mostly left her alone there, locking her in the shanty with a bar through a latch. No, she didn't know who he was. No, he didn't tell her why he took her there and warned her to stay, or else. He had said horrible things to her while he touched himself, threatened to kill her if she didn't behave. Said he could make bad girls disappear right out of this world. No, she didn't know anything else now. That was all she knew. And the next day claimed not to have meant a single word of any of it.

At the same time Laura was recovering physically, while offering her confusing, contradictory, and questionable stories, I gathered from Niles that discovering her identity wasn't finally that difficult. A matter of circulating the girl's image and a basic description of her for other departments to check against their missing-persons databases.

It all transpired within the week. A match, a positive ID. The river turned out to be the Hudson, not the Delaware. The mountain across from it was Bear. She lived in the village of Cold Spring, where the train station was but a block from the river. The church proved to be the Chapel of Our Lady Restoration, perched on the water's edge, a Greek Revival temple with Doric columns that might as well have been facing the Aegean as the Hudson. A place where people used to pray for the safe return of mariners.

Reuniting Laura with her family was most important both to Niles and to the child welfare services people, but when Renee told Laura her parents were very excited that she was safe and were driving here

to be with her, the girl's response was a crosscurrent of enthusiasm and alarm. Under the circumstances, not an unexpected reaction. A background check on the parents turned up clean—no records, no warrants, no traffic tickets even, just an upstanding family of comfortable means—and so Laura would be released into their custody and that would more or less be that, although child services would recommend individual as well as family counseling.

The attention turned for a time to investigating her purported abduction. In light of her failure to provide any further workable description of this man and his car, other than that the latter was long, there was little to work with beyond the possible pretensions of a scared girl. No fingerprints other than hers were traced on any of the small cache of supplies at her makeshift camp, and the only footprints they found, largely erased by the rain, were the size of a girl's Laura's age. No one had come forward to claim having witnessed her being abducted, or accompanied by anyone on the road. The investigation edged forward into a vacuum. Nothing supported her claim of having been the victim of kidnap, while everything pointed to her being a frightened runaway.

I hadn't seen Laura since the day she was found; it wouldn't have been useful to her or healthy for me—and now that her situation seemed settled, I told Niles I was taking the boys and escaping to Maine for a while.

"No reason not to. You know that by leaving you're giving some people more reason to talk. 'What's she skipping town for?' Not that they should stop you."

"Don't worry, they won't," I said.

"If I need to reach you—"

"Don't forget you got to push pretty hard on the numbers to dial me up there, since the island has no phone service, land, cell, or otherwise. The mailboat still swings by whenever there's something to deliver, so you can get me a message that way, over sea waves instead of airwaves."

Which was what brought me back to the present in my sun-drenched room. Those sea waves were shoving against the nearby shore, washing

away what was left of the nightmare. They had fascinated me from the first time I came here, how unpredictable were their rhythms. Never set a metronome by waves, it occurred to me, unless you want to play the music of the spheres. I could hear the scuttle and scraping of stones as the water withdrew, and the deep thrumming of some fishing vessels out there in the distance. Could also hear the boys downstairs now, banging around. Smelled the bacon they were frying, savory against the brined air. I rose, dressed, sat by the window looking out at the ocean for a few more quiet minutes before I heard Jonah calling me down to breakfast. As I descended the steps I felt a surge of pity for Laura Bryant. Pity, and a kind of solidarity. After all, neither of us had convinced anyone of anything, had we?

10

FOREVISIONS. IT HAD BEEN a good long stretch since they had visited themselves upon me. In the wake of intuiting that my brother was in grave danger, I experienced what could be described as an unholy string of these forevisionings. My mother certainly thought of them that way — unholy.

None were as monumental or significant as the one about Christopher. But I seemed, for whatever reason, to be able to know what was going to happen around me. I could and did predict the number of kittens Hodge Gilchrist's pregnant tabby would bear. Hodge was poor Ben Gilchrist's younger brother, and we were thrown together by our grieving parents after the accident that took both our older brothers, the idea being that our playing together would be healthy. I foretold the genders of all five kittens — two males, three females. And their colorings — three more tabbies, one marmalade, one chestnut. Hodge wrote down what I predicted, sealed it in an envelope, and gave it to his mother for safekeeping. At the time, the woman commented on how cute our game was. But when the litter matched what I had imagined, Mrs. Gilchrist, who must have heard the rumors about how I had foreseen my brother's death, and therefore possibly her husband's and son's, maybe even hex-murdered them both, didn't like me hanging around with Hodge quite as much as before.

There were other things, small things that in themselves mattered not one whit, but that I'm sure drove my poor mother to distraction and provoked prayers this odd phase would soon pass. I knew who was calling when the phone rang. That's Griselda, Griselda from the school board, on the line. There's Margaret Driscoll, probably wants to know if we have plans to drive to the city so she can catch a ride with us. I'll get it, it's going to be Niles anyhow. I knew what time it was, within five minutes either way, day or night, whenever anyone asked. Sensed the bluebirds weren't going to nest in the box atop the wooden corner post of the kitchen garden this season, though they had every year for as far back as we could remember. And when they didn't, I silently predicted my mother would say, as she did, — So the birds took this year off.

Equally easy to predict was Nep's proclaiming, — That's my daughter, the witch.

Life went along like that.

Yet much of what I could see, or foresee, had to do with death. These forevisionings — Nep's coinage, too big a word for me at the time, but it stuck — made me the most uneasy. I felt relief only when circumstances proved me wrong, and I felt none whatsoever, not even in some appeased private dark corner of my ego, when I wasn't. One could make an educated guess as to the size of a cat litter. Even predict genders and colors. But when I went over to the Gilchrists' house to visit the newborns after school, I didn't dare say that the chestnut kitten, who was rushing about and playing with every bit as much vivacity as the others, and who had such a healthy coat and winning personality, wouldn't live very long. I didn't say it and didn't want to think it. Her name was Lucy. I spent as much time as I was allowed, doting on her, giving her treats. Looking back, I wonder if Hodge's mother didn't insist he stay away from me after my little Lucy — Cassie's favorite kitty — was found lifeless one morning. It didn't seem fair that I could be seen as somehow responsible. In retrospect, though, it makes a kind of awful sense.

During this time I became increasingly isolated. Hodge wasn't my best friend — Niles was that, though I'm sure he sometimes wondered what he was doing hanging around with this wobbling, spinning top

of a girl—but Hodge and I had been close. And it hurt to lose both Hodge and Lucy in one fell swoop. My brother was gone as well, and with him went his gang of friends I loved to follow around, even Roy Skoler with his dog as friendly as Roy himself was not, and especially thoughtful Charley Granger, whom I always had a terrible crush on but never told a soul.

—You're like gum on a shoe, Christopher taunted me, inaugurating the nickname *Gummy* which I was not unhappy to shed when the day came. I passed through a hard, friendless time after I stopped telling people my forevisions and before Nep took me under his divining wing. His loving aegis.

Never an indoor girl, I spent much of this period outside wandering about, especially once the snow began to melt. Edging the east border of my parents' place was a rugged stretch of up-and-down land that was good for nothing except solitary tramping—a gnarly mess of steep slopes littered with stones and bottomed by soggy springheads chock-full of waterlogged dead trees, woodpecker trees. Just my kind of land, and I put in many hours ranging that world, which abutted what was then Statlmeyer's wilds. It was a pastime I never stopped enjoying, which later fed into my wanderings as a diviner. When we started coming to Covey I wandered even on this small island, starting with a wind-beaten footpath above the shore, then clambering down to tidal pools closer to the island's edge. I'd take that same walk with Rosalie when she and Nep arrived. This morning, though, I ferried with Jonah and Morgan over to Mount Desert. We picked up the old Dodge—still mud-splattered from my frantic drive out of Henderson's—and, good to my word, drove across the causeway to the mainland to visit used-car dealerships.

"Now here's pure class," Jonah said in mock awestruck tones, standing next to a squarish enormous box of metal wider than it was tall, at once silly and sinister. Black as a coal chip, with coffinlike lines, its chrome glinting like cutlery.

"The total wheels," Morgan agreed, running his hand along its grille, which made my heart sink. "A hummin' Hummer."

I said, "I don't like it."

"But Cass, this here's the ultimate road jockey."

"Hold on. You guys don't think this is ugly?"

"Work of art. Terminator's got ten of these suckers in his garage."

"Look, it's a fake war toy, a tank without a turret. All show and crow."

We test-drove it for a few blocks. First time ever I wished my sons had licenses. Let them drive this big dumb metal box that felt claustrophobic and clumsy as I steered it along. Even at that, their happiness made me happy, but fortunately the price exceeded any budget I might muster, so I wouldn't have to break my promise.

"Well, what do you think?" asked the salesman, an earnest fellow with sad eyes.

Morgan said, "Nah. Not for us."

"Too military in its feel," said Jonah, with far too straight a face.

Been had again. We looked at other offerings elsewhere. A silver contrivance all humped up in the back, some throwback to the forties. A mini-something too small for the three of us to fit inside. And everything beyond my means, no matter which dealership we visited. At the end of the day the boys announced they could live with the pickup. We never knew anything other than, so why switch now?

"Just get it tuned up once in a while," Morgan suggested.

"Like, uh, every other century?"

Without directly responding, I surprised them by pulling into the first service station I saw along the main road headed back through Ellsworth. Tune-up, brake check, transmission check, new tires, whatever was essential—the works. Some dowsers out there would have taken a pendulum to the truck engine to divine what was needed. Some witchers would even have dowsed the integrity of the mechanic. For myself, I'd had just about my fill of divining for the time being. I read the man's eyes and liked his handshake, asked him a few questions and he gave me straight answers. He even razzed Morgan about his Yankees cap, Boston being the only team that mattered in these northern reaches. I trusted him, and that was divining enough for me. "By the way," I added, before we were given a lift to the ferry. "Would you mind washing this filthy thing?"

Back on Covey, I experienced a sensation of the simplest joy. That of being a good plain adequate parent. What could be better? My feet were sturdy on the earth as I took a late-afternoon walk around the island, having left the boys at the cottage. A grounded solidity settled over me. All was well, and would be well—I could almost hear Nep saying the very words.

In places where the path was overgrown with low-lying inkberry, bearberry, and other weather-distressed scrub, I was forced to climb down toward the beach, slower going because of the rocks. The tidal pools that had been a grand obsession of mine when I was younger never quite lost interest for me after I grew up. I had my favorites, memorized from years of making this stroll, and I took time to glance into them, see if anybody was home. Though the tide was out, most of my holes were empty except for dwarf darting fish. Partway along, however, I came on a spidery iridescent crab left behind when the water withdrew. Trapped as it was, back-and-forthing in the shallow basin, it might have been cause for considerable fun in the old days. I would have looked around for just the right stick with a small fork on the end, like a pygmy witching rod, tried to scoop up the poor fellow and place him back in the surf. If I happened to be playing with a pail, I would have become a one-girl bucket brigade, filling the pool as high as I could so it wouldn't dry up before the next tide rolled in. Had I a sandwich, I'd tear off pieces, throw them into the water, and watch him tentatively pinch at them, his eyes on their stalks undulant. As it was, today, I took pity on him, wading into the basin, where I gingerly picked him up and set him back in the Atlantic.

On the way back, as I collected some pretty volutes and a whelk, the eerie sensation of being watched came over me. Feeling the fool, I glanced around but of course saw nothing. The delusion did not last, fortunately. Why is it we sometimes like to frighten ourselves for no reason? I put the shells in my pocket to add to the collection on the mantel.

In bed that night, as I drifted away into a dreamless sleep, I realized that for the first time since Henderson's, my world was showing signs

of recovering balance. Or, that is, rediscovering balance. Just there, just then, for a blessed moment my corner of the universe seemed as stable as the granite the lighthouse had stood on for over a hundred years and which the ocean had pummeled and thrashed for eons. Sometime during the night, I woke, or believed I woke, and briefly listened to the waves below and wind above as stars waltzed across the window, and thought I heard the voices of those three girls singing, a trick the ocean and its breezes liked to play on me when I was a girl myself.

Strange but nothing frightening. Instead, the oddly soothing music of nature imitating man, miming its own creatures. Wasn't it possible that a breeze had happened to flute its way through the partly opened windows of Niles's car back at Henderson's, to sing like this? What I would have given to convince myself of it. Even so, the hanged girl and the lost girl and the strange laughing voices were fading from my waking, and even sleeping, life. Niles was diminished, too. The Bledsoes of the world were deep at the bottom of the sea. Even my parents were reduced to the far corner of the canvas. It was just me and my twins.

Morgan and Jonah made their own breakfasts next morning, peanut butter sandwiches and coffee, from what I could tell, and headed off to the shore even before I came downstairs. Couldn't blame them for finding something better to do with themselves, after I'd mentioned at dinner that I had to hike up to the cemetery to do the spring cleaning before Rosalie and Nep arrived. Another of the annual Covey routines. Make sure winter hadn't toppled any of the thin marble headstones or the wrought-iron fencing, clear out any fallen branches from nearby trees, tend to our ancestors' resting place.

When I saw the reluctance on their faces — Morgan in particular had little patience with, or fondness for, this part of the Covey cycle — I told them they ought to go off and do their own thing in the morning, that I could get it done myself. Neither disagreed, though Jonah did allow himself a small jab about not seeing any more ghosts.

If only to sidestep the issue, I told him I didn't believe in ghosts.

"Good idea," he said, as a father might to a guileless child.

Following suit with another peanut butter sandwich for myself and filling the thermos with the coffee they had left for me, I grabbed a leaf rake and a pair of gloves from the sea-grayed wooden garden shed and strode up past the lighthouse toward the center of the island. Before entering the pine woods that topped Covey, as they did Islesford, Cranberry, Baker, all the islands around here, I turned to look back at the steel-blue convexity of ocean and its few lobster boats out for the morning haul. It didn't seem at all fair that Henry Metcalf, who sought only to preserve this beauty for others, should be finally denied by death the chance to see once more what I myself could witness by merely opening my eyes. Ghosts ought to exist, I thought, if only to revisit such ineffable simplicities as this.

A path led up between boulders, then leveled out through a forested plateau to the cemetery. Winging overhead, a young osprey. Underfoot, bluebead lilies like tiny bursting stars in first bloom that would grow pretty berries in a month capable of making you very sick if you ate one. Bluebeard flowers, Nep called them. The dense, ever-present perfume of balsam fir and white pine pitch. In the distance, hidden by rock and foliage, the purring engine of a boat. Not so unaware as to have forgotten I was alone in the womb of the woods for the first time since seeing what I saw, I reminded myself that this was Covey Island, not Henderson's valley. I had been coming up here for years, for decades actually. This was where my mother's people lay at rest—and therefore my own gentle ancestors—as unhaunted a place as I could imagine.

Winter hadn't been quite as rough on the cemetery as on the cottage, which was far more exposed to the ravages of icy wind and snow blown fast across the winter ocean. While warm sunlight pooled into the flat clearing ringed by conifers, I had a sip of coffee before getting down to work. Thanks to heaving frosts, some of the headstones were leaning at various angles, but none had fallen over. I pried open the creaking gate as wide as its rusted hinges would allow and began raking the corners of the fenced enclosure where leaves, twigs, ends of branches had collected.

This was the kind of work I loved. Nothing open to tortured second thoughts, nothing psychologically chancy, nothing ambiguous or risky, just pure and simple labor whose results you could see transpiring before your very eyes. I must have worked for an hour or more, lost in the act of clearing debris from this sacred mortal space, piling it on a huge flat stone at one end of the clearing where we could burn it later.

Sitting down to take a break and eat the sandwich I had brought with me, I wondered how Nep was faring this morning back home while Rosalie began packing for their trip north. As I ate I fantasized what it would be like to live on Covey full-time, try my hand at the same sort of subsistence farming and fishing the Metcalfs had managed over that last century. The obvious impossibilities of such a life soon flooded the fantasy and capsized it like a matchstick rowboat swamped by a freak wave. There was nothing here for Morgan and Jonah, nor any paying work for me who, at any rate, couldn't farm or fish my way through even the mildest Maine year. Still, as passing fancies went, it was a nice one. I stood, tossed the sandwich crust into the woods where a chipmunk or rabbit might like to finish it, and returned to my raking. Another half an hour would do it, I figured. This would please my mother, I knew, as she sometimes liked to come up to this peaceful and secluded spot to pray. I could see the appeal. Perhaps raking and praying weren't such dissimilar acts.

Soon a human rustling, a muted cough, caught my attention and I glanced across the cemetery clearing. Some pine boughs scythed the air, though there was no breeze to push them. Didn't mean anything necessarily — I had seen this curious phenomenon many times in the woods, as if supposedly inanimate trees got it into their heartwood heads to conduct an unseen orchestra. Another noise followed, though, a pebble plucking its way across the earth behind me like a skipped stone but on dewy grass instead of flat water. I begged myself not to look back at where I had heard the sound, but couldn't suppress my curiosity and so I did, a not quite involuntary reflex.

No one and nothing stirred. My first thought was, Please, no more

madness, but then I realized that of course the boys must be having fun at my expense.

"Morgan," I rebuked, and then a little louder, "Jonah, that isn't funny."

I leaned on my rake and listened for a moment. Was that a snort I heard?

"Boys, stop it already."

Neither I nor whoever it was just inside the shroud of leaves and needles moved or made any sound. I placed a deliberate hand on my hip to show them I was not amused.

"Instead of playing tricks, you two ought to get over here and help me."

More silence, followed by a thickish branch snapping deeper in the woods. Then came a sharp grunt lower in timbre than I had ever heard either of their preadolescent voices make, though I knew it had to be them. Nobody else on the island ever came up here.

"Guys?" into the ether.

The pitiless games boys will play. They would hear about this later, I decided, and continued with my work, pausing now and again to look up and listen. Naturally, it passed through my mind that this might have been another manifestation of the monster. But—how to explain this?—it just wasn't. My heart didn't beat with the same flutter, my breath didn't scallop and shallow itself. No divination was at play here.

I did wonder what animal might have made the noises, if they hadn't been Morgan and Jonah's work. There used to be a small population of deer on this island. Rosalie said that Henry Metcalf never tired of telling the story of how a black bear suddenly appeared on Covey many years ago and vigorously hunted this small family of whitetails—only a few generations of them—down to nothing, wiped them out. He surmised, puffing his habitual meerschaum pipe, that it must have swum across the cold Atlantic water from another of the islands. Then, once all the deer were gone, the bear disappeared, too. Probably swam back to where he'd started from, Henry would finish, with his broad, toothy islander grin.

And now they were all gone to dust. The enterprising bear. The hunted deer. Henry himself there beneath my rake tines. The earth would gather us up, circle its arms around all of us finally, and there would be rest one day for both hunter and all the hunted. But for the moment, even here at the heart of the island where its dead were cradled, such rest was not for me as yet. I was being spoken to, it seemed, by someone gone to dust and another who had not. As I gathered my things to return to the keeper's cottage, I had to acknowledge, if only quietly to myself, that my haven might not be immune to the wanderings of the dead or the living. All the way back down through the pines I kept looking over my shoulder.

11

THERE WILL NEVER be a right moment to make my confession about James Boyd, so now might as well be the wrong one.

I met him a dozen years ago on one of the most sweltering days in a fiendishly hot summer. Early July, and Corinth County was powder. When you walked you raised puffs of dust with every footfall. Where usually healthy streams ran, now trickling ribbons of slow tired water edged downhill, stalling, often disappearing altogether before reaching the next tributary. With this drought came more work than I could ever handle. Divining for years by then, I had never been so overwhelmed. I barely slept that whole prior month of June. Found myself pulling all-nighters, sometimes sneaking in an hour of sleep after poring over maps, then putting in long days ranging the baked earth with my switch, more than once wondering why I bothered to keep up appearances. Not an easy season in my life.

Since finding Partridge's water, I'd developed a knottier perspective about my craft than I had before that strange moment at his hatchery. After all, I had discovered water on his stubborn knoll without knowing item one about the locale. Behind my assurances that I appreciated Partridge's conversion — not to mention his apologies for having

ever doubted us Brookses in times past—lurked a profound confusion about what had actually occurred. What was more, it happened after that, again, then again. So, not having any better idea, I proceeded with my fourfold method of research and theater, of reading the landscape and truly divining, and met with my share of successful dowsings. I did the homework when I could, still not confident about relying on what seemed like quirks. But in the field, on site, when none of the background data was paying off, I'd begun to allow myself the gamble of moving beyond the knowable.

I had a better than modest reputation. Didn't hurt that Partridge, normally a dour and reserved man, sang my praises. —That woman diviner saved my hatchery, he claimed. His deliveries of stock took him all over nearby counties and across the Delaware to the south and the Hudson east, so my esteem among those who bothered to listen spread far and wide. James Boyd's father, Robert, heard about me down this quaint grapevine.

As fate had it, I went to the Boyd place every bit as unprepared as I had Partridge's. He's dying, was what I thought when I heard the despair in Robert Boyd's voice, and it tripped me into agreeing to come over before I'd had time to do my homework on the tract. I scolded myself for having had the audacity to go there without having studied first. Wasn't this, after all, what I told my students never to do? And yet I was my own worst student, working here on a wing and a prayer. Not even a prayer.

Given all this, I could have done without James Boyd's first words, as I shook his hand. —Don't think for a minute I believe in any of this. I'm only here because I was asked to be here. No offense.

He was standing in the deep shade of a dead-leaf-laden pergola by the porch and, having come from the already blinding sunlight, I could barely see him or anything else.

—No offense taken, I said, squinting. —Where's your father?

—He couldn't make it up today. So it's just me.

—Sorry to hear that, I said. —He sounded very concerned. Making small talk.

—This place means the world to him. Me, I don't get it. I don't like the country. Too much nature, Boyd said as he let go of my hand. I'd almost forgotten he was still shaking it. —If that's what he wants, though, far be it from me to stand in his way.

The house did look unlived-in. Pollen and dust hid any shine the yellow clapboard might once have boasted. What seemed to have been a flourishing perennial bed was growing rampant, weedy. A length of picket fence around what had been their vegetable garden had fallen over. But one could see what a bucolic oasis this had been in its heyday.

My eyes had adjusted and now I could finally see his face. Prepared as I was to not like him for all his urban aggressiveness, I was thrown off by what I felt when I looked at him closely. He was the handsomest man I had ever met. Had an ideal, classic face with an aquiline nose, a clear brow that belied the tenor of his unattractive words. He was unshaven, with carved lines in his chiseled cheeks. Unruly dark brown hair. Dusty hazel eyes with irises finely rimmed as if by a fountain pen.

He was silent for what I took to be a disconcerted moment. Then, in a neutral voice, said, —You're not what I expected.

—You thought I'd be a warty witch from a Wicca coven, maybe? I said, raising my eyebrows. Hiding my stream of thoughts while fishing his.

—Touché, he replied, and offered a conciliatory smile.

We walked around the outside of an old springhouse where he thought the sick well was located. I was not surprised to learn, as he talked while showing me the rest of the land, moving from shade to shade, that the illness I'd intuited—the cancer I had heard in his father's ardent voice on the phone—had kept Robert Boyd from traveling or tending to the land he clearly had loved.

—What about your mother?

—She died a few years ago. It's only the two of us.

—I'm sorry, I said, wondering if he had his own wife and family. There was about him an air of detachment, isolation. —Now then. Your well's giving brown water or no water, or what?

—Just turn on the faucet and up comes a gruelly, stinky sludge. That and air.

—If you wait for this drought to pass your well will come back on its own, you know.

He shrugged. —My father doesn't want to wait.

Pointing to a peach tree that stood at the margin of the yard overrun by drought-crisped grape leaves and fleece flowers, I asked, —You mind if I cut a small branch off that?

—Take the whole tree, for all I care.

His voice was lightly gravelly, as if he were sifting through pea stone for his words. I knew from the first moment I shouldn't have been interested in him, let alone mesmerized, but I was. Still, how much I would have preferred it if he had at least made an effort to be genial.

—Look, maybe you'd rather I left.

—No, no.

—It's just that you, we don't know each other very well, and you seem very resistant to the idea of divining—

—We don't know each other at all, actually.

I approached the once-stately, now-shaggy tree which, if it housed a daemon inside its boughs and trunk as the Romans believed, would very much want to help me discover water somewhere near its sagging leaves. After searching for just the right forked branch, I cut my switch and, doing my best to ignore my host, who after a while disappeared inside the house without a further word, began walking the land in a simple herringbone pattern.

Midmorning gave way to late morning. Late morning gave way to early afternoon. More than once I felt the rod kick a smidgen, give me a hint, but each time it went idle again. It was always something of a conundrum to know, really know, when the divining rod was acting of its own accord, as opposed to reacting to its handler's fancy, antsiness, or distress. James appeared with a bottle of water, but I waved him off, thanking him but wholly centered in my concentration. In retrospect, there's little doubt the tide that day had turned, insofar as I had to be patient with him in the morning, but it was he who was forced to show patience with me later. And, with all the years I have had to winnow

through my memories of that day, it astonishes me that I cannot identify just what happened or when it happened that James Boyd and I,
two people who didn't know each other, had nothing in common, and
were even mildly hostile toward one another, slipped into another register altogether.

James Boyd was not, for all his masculine attractiveness, my type.
If I could be said to have a type. My ideal man was more solidly of the
earth. He could peel a hard-boiled egg with one hand and knew the
names of birds. Could do his own cabinetmaking and properly plant
potatoes. But James Boyd was a through-and-through city person who
preferred avenues to roads, restaurants to kitchens, art museums to
county fairs. In his book, potatoes were for ordering *au gratin,* not
planting in the ground. A warbler was someone on the stage of the
Met, and a loft, his loft, had nothing to do with hay.

Yet something was happening. I could feel him watch my progress
from the window across the long field. When I glanced in that direction I saw his face dart away from the glass. I wondered whether if he
weren't there staring at me I would be more focused. But soon enough,
having walked through a thin copse of raspberry bushes, looking for a
tonal variation in the plants and grasses, then back some paces to the
north of my tracks, I realized I was misplacing any possible blame. This
whole misadventure was my own doing.

What I would feel next, I assured myself, would be akin to what the
Greeks meant by the word *eureka.* In my quasi delirium, I talked myself
into believing I would discover water at any moment now.

I was mistaken. I couldn't even formulate an idea of where to walk
next. I'd have given my eyetooth for a fracture trace analysis of the sub-
strate just then, but failing that I began to think there really was no water here. Now that the day was coming toward its close, I faced plod-
ding to the house to tell James Boyd—who had driven from downstate
expressly to supervise on his father's behalf this water witch, this impostor as he viewed it—that I couldn't locate what they wanted. I
dropped my stick on the ground and meandered dizzily toward the
sullen red sun, my back running with sweat, my arms and legs clammy

with the heavy whiteness that had settled over the scape. Even the crickets had gone mum.

—You don't look so good, he said, after I knocked on the screen door.

—I'm sorry, I whispered. Coming out of the thick hot air into the relative cool inside the house only made me feel more ill. Two James Boyds, each interposed on the other, were helping me down a musty hallway.

Most of the furniture in the house was sheeted, though he had undraped the living room leather sofa, which felt sticky against my skin. Before collapsing on it, I had caught a glimpse of myself in the pitted pier glass next to the fireplace and saw I looked as pale as one-percent milk. How foolish of me to have refused the water he had brought for me earlier in the afternoon.

—This sort of thing never happens to me, I slurred in the spinning room.

—Look, it's a furnace out there. Maybe you've got sunstroke.

I must have passed out, because the next thing I knew he had brought me a glass of water, helped me hold it, much as one might a sick child, and was smoothing my damp hair from my forehead and kissing it gently. Instead of pushing him away, I just lay there and felt him touching me, and let him.

What we did together was so natural and simple. He was unlike any lover I'd ever known. Gone was all his belligerent arrogance from earlier in the day. I was kissing the real James, I told myself. Not that other incarnation. Tender, yes, but also thoughtful, daring. I was swept away into a new dizziness under the touch of his fingers and tongue. We spent the night together in his parents' room, as his own was still outfitted with only a twin bed. On the dresser was a framed photograph of James's mother. Sitting in a gingham dress under a parasol, smiling as if her happiness and the world would never end. Before we switched off the lights, I held the picture in my hands.

—I think I would have liked your mother, I whispered.

Though we opened all the windows, the heat did not give way much

during the night. The full moon seemed like another sun. To this day, I believe we believed we did love each other for those few hours.

We woke long after dawn, having scarcely dozed, and made love again with even more conviction in the hazy sunup light than when we'd been hidden from each other's eyes in the dark. Having barely eaten the day before, I was ravenous, and despite my lack of sleep felt much better. He did his best in the kitchen. Stale toast and blackened bacon. Bachelor cooking, but I relished it.

—I want to give your land another try, I told him. —Today I've got promises to keep at other places. But I can come back in a couple of days, if that's all right with you.

—More than. You've made a convert of me.

—No, no. You ought to stay a nonbeliever until you have reason to change your mind. Let me find your father his water and then you can convert.

—I think, speaking of him, we should keep what's happened to ourselves.

He had to get back to the city and took my phone number, after making tentative arrangements to come back up to meet me for my second attempt. I recall driving home, bedazzled, a little afraid of myself and him and where this might lead.

The weather let up some by the next time I saw him. A heavy downpour struck during the night and the long grasses were dripping wet. I had allowed myself to hope he would call to confirm our meeting. Or at least say hello, acknowledge somehow the bond we had formed, however tentative and new it was. I contemplated phoning James's father to ask for his number but thought the better of it, trusting James would show up as promised.

Arriving early, I did what I might have tried in the first place. Returned to where the original well had been dug and, using a crowbar that I fetched from the truck, I pried away its capstone. A sulfurous iron smell rose forth. I thought I could hear faint movements in the liquid far below. Snakes, or frogs. Never a good sign in a well, because when they die they're not going anywhere. I peered down into the

rank darkness, admiring the mason's handiwork of laid-up stones rim-
ming the circular cavity, then dropped a pebble and heard a dull mushy
thud when it hit bottom. It occurred to me to use a pendulum—one of
Nep's heirlooms, a pyrite hexagon—to see if a vein of unfouled water
lay beneath the bedrock of the old-timers' well. Or, if yet another ran
nearby that might be asked if it was willing to be moved—there are
times and techniques for doing such a thing. What did I have to lose?

The pendulum hovered over the well and made no motion. When
I moved it a few yards to the northeast of the mouth, it began gradually to gyrate. This was what I had been looking for. I tried again with
a hazel virgula that also belonged to Nep, and, yes, it nosedived at
the same spot. I stacked a little cairn of stones right there and sighed,
looking at it. What should have been the simplest thing I'd made madly
difficult for myself. At least I would have good news for James when
he got here.

James. Telling by the sun it was nearly noon. Although we hadn't set
an exact time, I supposed he would have arrived by now. Maybe traffic
in the city had hung him up.

Before long, misgivings began to set in. Had he gotten back to his
loft downtown and decided he'd made a ridiculous mistake? Yet he
seemed sincere in word and gesture that night and, too, in the telltale
morning, when the ecstasies of evenings often look so barren under
the klieg lights of dawn. Our encounter had brimmed with promise,
so I had felt. Despite its suddenness, there was nuance and comfort to
our touch. Now I had to question all that.

The depressing dread of being stood up began to take over. More
from nervousness than hunger I ate one of the sandwiches I had made
for us, a little picnic packed in a wicker basket. Drank some warm
lemonade and marveled at how strange it was to be sitting here waiting to rendezvous with a man my first instincts had been to dislike and
distrust, but who I now believed was capable of breaking my heart.
Your common sense, Cass, I warned myself, has flown the coop. Then,
like that, his coupe appeared in the drive, leaving behind it a halo of
dust, and I had to make some swift attitude adjustments.

When he climbed out of the car, his first words were, —None of this is my fault, please, I'm sorry for being so late. After an embrace and kiss, he added that a work-related matter had held him up, nothing to do for it.

—What makes you think I came here just to see you? I teased, trying to lighten up.

—Well, what else is there around here *to* see?

—Water, for one. Are you hungry?

Yes, he was starving, he said, smiling. Chicken salad with fennel on peasant bread? Perfect, better than Four Seasons. He asked if I was feeling myself again. Said I looked worlds better than before. For all his polite nonchalance and easy elucidations, my paranoia about James Boyd didn't feel entirely misplaced. After he finished eating and we'd filled as many awkward silences as we could with small talk, I showed him the cairn and gave him the good news about my discovery.

—You're sure about this? he asked, echoing nearly every client I'd ever dowsed for.

—Sure as sure can be. The primary source will be in a sidestep pocket, probably not much farther down than the original well was dug. Your family and maybe even people who were here before have been living off a leak from the main fount. Not the strongest source I've ever seen, but more than enough for your needs. Or, I mean, your father's.

—That's something, he said, comprehensively unbelieving. His eyes were on me again, as they had been before.

—Everything okay? I asked.

—Definitely.

—Are you all right about what happened with us? I asked, regretting my words the instant they left my mouth.

—Of course I am.

—Good, because—

—Let's go inside? as if to prove his point.

We did go upstairs and take off our clothes and make love again, and it couldn't have been more manifest to me that the heat of our re-

cent night had, like the heat wave itself, begun to abate. By the time we dressed and he—a mere hour after having shown up—said he had to run back to town without offering any of the expected platitudes as he left, I knew, while I collected my dowsing instruments and disheartening picnic basket by myself, that what had seemed so propitious was instead a one-off bust. Indeed, speaking with Robert Boyd on the phone later that evening, to tell him I had been successful in discovering his water for him, he said, in passing, how delighted James and his wife and little girl were going to be when they heard the news.

—James and his family adore the place, he explained, his weak voice raspy yet full of hope. —This will give them a chance to get it back to where my wife and I had it once upon a time.

I hadn't the heart to inform him his son harbored no other intention than of dumping the Boyd farmhouse to the first person with a line of credit and a cheap lawyer the moment he died. But toward Boyd the elder I had nothing more in me than to wish him the best with everything. I even said, —God bless and good luck to you, because I sensed that would be meaningful to him. Seven weeks later my pregnancy would be confirmed.

12

MORGAN AND JONAH WERE waiting for me, sitting impatiently in the violet shade of the cottage porch roof when I returned from the little graveyard. Both sprang to their feet when they saw me put the rake away in the stone shed, and came running through the tall speargrass, calling out more or less at the same time, "Hey Cass, you just missed him."

"Missed who?" I asked, half-hoping Niles had gotten it in his head to come to Covey for some reason, Niles who wouldn't flinch at noises made by my prankster sons or a harmless woodland creature that I, who infringed on its domain, had startled into retreat.

"I don't know," said Morgan.

So it had been the boys after all. "You mean the same 'him' I missed in the cemetery a while ago?" I frowned. "Who do you guys think you're kidding."

"You mean you saw him, too?"

"Actually there were two of him and they looked amazingly just like you."

Finally, I thought, turned tables on them for once. But instead of bursting into laughter and conceding that they'd been busted, they stared at me in plain confusion.

"I don't get it," said Jonah.

"Come on, give it up. You were trying to spook me at the cemetery."

"Totally no way," Morgan insisted.

"So who was this man looking for me?"

"We never saw him before."

"Jonah?" I asked, licking my thumb and rubbing some dirt off his cheek, at which he lightly winced.

"That's right, we don't know him. But he knows who you are. He said—"

Morgan interrupted. "He knew our names, too."

"Well, what did he want?"

They looked at each other and back at me, their faces unwontedly blank. My hands were trembling, so I placed them on my hips in the hope the twins wouldn't notice. "Did he at least tell you his name?"

Names are doors to ideas, it occurred to me once more. What idea was eluding me here?

"He didn't say."

"Why didn't you ask?" I demanded, exasperated.

"We just didn't," Morgan answered, now defensive, palming his long hair out of his face where the wind had ruffled it into his eyes.

Must have been someone from Cranberry or Mount Desert, I thought, turning toward the house, or a newspaper journalist from back home who had nothing better to do than follow us up here in search of some continuation of the Henderson story. But no, a journalist would have waited, and besides, my story was already yesterday's news. Anybody who would have taken the trouble to boat over from one of the other islands wouldn't have departed without leaving a name and telling the boys what brought him all the way here.

"Where'd he go?"

Both eagerly pointed down the dock path.

"You two head inside. I'm going to have a look, see if I can't catch up—"

"Look, he did say one thing," Jonah broke in.

"What was that?"

"He said he'd hate to have to come back but would if you forced him to. What did he mean by that, Mother?"

Hearing him call me *Mother* took me aback. Made him sound so vulnerable. I had no idea what to tell him. All I knew was that I was both angry and terrified, and that it was best not to let my boys see it. "I don't know what he's talking about. Did he mean it in a friendly way or threatening?"

"He wasn't friendly or unfriendly," said Jonah.

"He seemed pretty serious, though."

"I need you boys to stay inside while I go find out what this is all about."

"But—"

"Please," I said, more firmly. "Get inside right now. And lock the door."

"Come on—"

"Lock it."

As I ran down the path, stumbling, sliding on loose stones, I couldn't help but think the obvious. James Boyd, after all these reticent years, had read or heard about his sometime lover's recent travails and gotten it in mind to pay her, so to speak, a visit. Judge for himself whether she should be allowed to continue raising these reported sons he never met nor once bothered to contact. Made me furious to imagine him reentering my life. Furious and frightened. Would Jonah and Morgan ever trust a word I said again, if he let them in on what I always assumed was a tacit covenant between myself and their extinct father? I could only hope they would understand and forgive. By the time I reached the dock, out of breath, I had reconsidered this assumption. James Boyd had no interest in me or them, I realized. Even if he had, there was no way he would put himself to the trouble of traveling all the way to Covey Island to make his cryptic point, whatever that point could possibly mean after so much time. If not him, though, who?

I peered along the curved rocky shorelines in both directions, looking back from the far end of the dock, and saw no one. Without pausing to think twice, I sprinted up the hill along a narrow path that led

directly over the island to the houses on the far side. This trail, since it offered no lovely views—and because we never visited those on the other end, nor they us—was rarely, indeed almost never, used. Nor did it show any signs of having been taken by anyone recently. When I emerged from the green thicket to make my way down through a glass-slick slope of talus, I saw no smoke coming from Mrs. Milgate's coal-stove chimney, and the adjacent house looked dormant as well. A postcard picture of tranquil island life.

It had been a couple of seasons since I last encountered Angela Milgate. Small though the island was, she really did keep her own counsel. Because of this, I felt every bit the intruder myself here as I sheepishly climbed her wooden steps and quietly knocked on her door. She didn't answer, though I could swear I smelled baked beans, or burned syrup maybe, wafting from the open windows. Her pair of duck boots were neatly placed side by side next to the doormat, and their leather uppers, I saw, were still wet from a recent walk down to the water.

"Mrs. Milgate?" I called out as loudly as I dared. "You home? It's Cassandra Brooks here."

Either she wasn't in the mood or else was napping, and so I decided to try my luck at the other house. Since the tide was out, I walked a beeline across the kelp-strewn muddy flats past where a cormorant perched like some elegant angel of death atop a beached skiff whose hull was the worse for wear. Not a boat one would want to take to sea. When I knocked on the front door, it swung open slightly. Sensing the place was long abandoned, I stuck my head inside and shouted, "Anybody home?"

Uninhabited houses, derelict houses, always have some kind of unwritten symphony going on in them, and this one was no different. Tiny crumbs of sound, dim little cracks and creaks made by nothing other than the walls talking to one another. I once heard a recording of what was purported to be the sound of solar winds and was reminded of it then as I took a few steps inside. The furniture was old, springs corkscrewed up through the upholstery. The musty air itself seemed tired. Whoever owned the place showed as much indifference

toward it as James Boyd did toward his poor father's farmhouse. Careful where I stepped, I toured a few of the downstairs rooms. It was when I discovered more fresh cigarette butts in the kitchen sink that I realized I had no business trespassing here. And besides, I had begun to worry about leaving the boys alone for so long.

Stepping out of the woods once more onto the ramparts above our dock, I cast my eye across the open waters and saw an unfamiliar outboard boat with its white crest of wake water receding into the horizon line where the ocean met the mainland. Small as a sesame seed shrinking into a poppy seed. There was no guarantee that the man who had spoken to Morgan and Jonah was aboard—I realized I hadn't even asked them for a description of him—but I hoped he was. Still, I made a cursory search along the coast to both the east and west of the landing, my thoughts racing in useless circles, and came up with nothing.

As I climbed the hillside back to the cottage, I had to admit that while the noises at the cemetery probably were either those of an animal or my imagination, the man who spoke with my sons needed to be treated with a different order of respect and wariness. My parents' arrival was still a couple of days off, and that evening I decided to raise the flag that let the mailboat captain, Mr. McEachern, know I wanted him to stop at Covey while making his island rounds. I needed to get to a telephone.

We ate a quiet dinner and went to bed as rain started falling, having secured the downstairs windows and doors—a rare measure. The next day low clouds moved hastily between the ocean and overcast sky like random thoughts under a proven theory. Jonah, Morgan, and I stood on the dock after lunch, waiting for the mailboat to arrive. Choppy seas used to unnerve me a little but island people, as I'd become in my way, don't take the waves as much more than, well, waves. Hurricane waves, tropical storm waves—those mattered. You didn't have to be a hydromancer to know today was only a nice chop. Our clothes were snapping in the brisk breeze. The air and water shared the yellowish-green hue of a healing bruise.

"Do we have to go?" Jonah asked. The boys were scanning southwest, where Mr. McEachern would be arriving from Mount Desert.

"Yeah," said Morgan. "Relax. It's not like he did anything."

Much as I knew they loved riding in the Bunker & Ellis and poking around the old general store on Islesford, I also was aware that they, still on their way to becoming island people, were nervous about sailing in rough seas—never failed to make them sick as dogs—but were far too proud to admit it. I was torn. Didn't want to leave them here by themselves, yet didn't want to force them to make a seasick passage. My strong intuition was that the man had left, having gotten his message across. Rosalie was going to be able to clear this up for me, once I got her on the line, I was certain. And if not her, then Niles might know what it was about.

"Besides, we have our own stuff to do right here."

"Such as?"

"Just stuff," he answered, rolling his eyes. I decided I needn't drag them along, that they would be fine. Needed to remind myself they were making a sacrifice to be up here with me in the first place, and it behooved me to give them as much time to themselves as they liked.

Their descriptions of the man were vaguer than I might have hoped, not to mention contradictory. Morgan insisted he had brown eyes; Jonah was sure they'd been blue. They did agree he had black hair, was wearing a Windbreaker, and had a tall forehead. He was on the pale side, Jonah noticed, and wasn't too tall. Certainly didn't sound like anyone I knew.

My approaching ferry lay on the horizon, a mere indistinction almost as small as the mystery boat had been the day prior. Before long we could see its prow knifing the water between some bobbing eiders and guillemots, carving it into greenish-white wakes. Drawing close, the mailboat soon enough docked, the surge of wash heaving it up and down as the captain tossed his bowline, then stern, which Morgan caught, then handed off to him as he jumped onto the plank dock to tie up.

Mr. McEachern—a ruddy-faced, bull-shouldered, soft-spoken man with a tidy gray beard—asked how everything was. I told him I needed to ride with him to Little Cranberry and then be dropped off back here when he was done with his rounds.

"Might not be before sundown, if that works for you. I got some extra drops today."

"That works," said Morgan brightly.

"Take your time," Jonah added.

"You two make sure there's a place to come back to, you hear me?" I said, hoping my trip to Islesford would prove a big waste of time. My nerves had been tight and tense as piano strings these past weeks and I wondered if I hadn't overreacted. When one is spooked, every little thing seems charged with meaning.

The mailboat reversed its engine, crabbed away from the dock even as I was speaking those words. I watched the boys wave to me, and I waved back as the boat set out over the wide wild water. I did ask Mr. McEachern if he happened to have ferried anybody over to Covey the day before, and he said no. He also answered no to my question as to whether, to his knowledge, anyone had been inquiring after me or my family in Northeast Harbor. Mr. McEachern constituted a kind of central sounding post in these islands, saw and knew everybody, heard or overheard everyone's news, their doings, their scuttlebutt. No gossip himself—indeed, a through-and-through gentleman—he wasn't given to disclosing all he knew. But he was a noticer, too, a conscientious soul, and would have told me if he had heard anything that might be cause for concern.

The post office and general store on Islesford, as Little Cranberry Island was also called, reminded me of my youth, when we used to come here for basic supplies. Nep made a practice of treating me to red licorice sticks or jawbreakers from big Ball jars on the counter. Its smell, a warm combination of pipe tobacco, gingerbread, and drowsing dusty dogs, remained the same over the decades. So did its look. A conjunction of stuff, which in any other locale would seem eccentric, here made perfect sense—deep-sea fishing tackle and homemade fudge behind the glass counter, life jackets and greeting cards, buoys and bottled milk. The telephone was behind the cash register. Not private, but since no one was here aside from the proprietor, who was half-deaf, it didn't matter.

Rosalie and Nep's line was busy, so I called Niles. Was surprised to find him in.

"How's your disappearance going?" he asked.

"Not quite as invisibly as I'd hoped. We had a visitor to Covey yesterday. Showed up unannounced, left more or less the same way. I have no idea who he was, and it's not like he was willing to say."

"Go on."

"There's not much to go on about," I said, and told him the small balance of what I knew. "I'm trying to reach Rosalie. Sounds like it could be something to do with money being owed maybe."

Niles didn't necessarily agree, saying he didn't know what it sounded like.

"I'm almost afraid to ask, but what's happening with Laura Bryant?"

"Nothing more, really. She's back home. Turns out she had a history of running away, so it fits a pattern."

"I feel bad for her."

"So do I, but it's out of our hands now. She's getting help, I hear."

"Good," I said, and wondered if Niles was reminded of my having been a sometime runaway when I was younger than Laura Bryant. I felt self-conscious about the parallels and knew it was wisest to leave the matter unspoken.

"Her mother tells me Laura would like to thank you in person, talk with you a little."

"I'm not so sure, Niles."

"Well, I can give you the number if you change your mind," he said. "By the way, I heard that Henderson is going ahead with his development plans."

"It's a shame to think of those beautiful woods being all carved up."

"Weren't you one of his first hired henchmen?"

"Henchwoman," I said, but couldn't argue the point.

"If your man comes around again, get his name why don't you."

"Will do, Niles. Thanks," and we hung up.

Finding the line at my parents' still busy, I decided to take a ramble along the lanes of the village. I had time to kill and always liked this

seaside place, with its piles of old wooden lobster traps baking in the open air, its children playing on porches or riding their bikes up and down the dirt roads, its high-steepled white church that seemed so legitimate and necessary here, where men went out on the water every day to make their living. From the near distance, gratingly loud yet not visible, came the distinctive noise of kids racing around on four-wheelers. Like swarming locusts they buzzed, reminding me of the days when my brother and his raucous gang were obsessed with riding them through the Corinth countryside. Not a pleasant memory to interrupt the serenity of my otherwise calming stroll. When I returned to the general store and phoned again, I finally got through.

"You ought to know that's impossible," she stated in response to my question whether she might be enough in arrears on some bill causing the township to send out a collector. "I've never missed a deadline paying my taxes or a bill in my life. Your father used to tease me about it, don't you remember? Called me the *Pollyanna of Payables*. He had to be there for some other reason, but listen, Cassie—"

"Yes?"

"Seems to me the obvious answer is that the twins are being a little inventive. Maybe somebody dropped by from the other side of the island and chatted with them in passing, and they just got it wrong what the fellow said."

"Well, that wouldn't be any more like them than you forgetting to square away some debt. Besides, I checked over there and no one was around," mentioning the smells of Mrs. Milgate's baking and her refusal to answer the door, though leaving out the cigarette stubs because I knew Rosalie would shrug them off as the meaningless ciphers they likely were.

"Cassandra. You're there to take things easy and that's what you should get back to doing. Your father and I are looking forward to spending time with you."

"We are, too. Do me a favor, though, and don't bother Nep about this. I don't want to worry him more than I already have."

She agreed, and that was that. I didn't relish leaving the matter un-

resolved but saw no reason to press it further. Besides, I had spoken to the only two people who might shed some light on it, and they were less concerned than I might have imagined. Best leave it as a dead end, I thought, walking back toward the piers, knowing that it was going to gnaw at me anyway, just as he intended, whoever he was.

I waited for what seemed like forever on the town dock, looking out past the fleet of anchored lobster boats and floating clusters of brown rockweed. Overhead, gulls scolded my impatience as I paced the weathered planks. Finally the sturdy ferry returned in heavy slant-light pouring through the thin fog that had accumulated. It hugged the stony shoreline, making waves as it did, and drew alongside. Rather than waiting for Mr. McEachern to tie her up, I jumped on as the mailboat hammocked in backwash waves.

The windows of the house burned a warm amber as we approached the island. The lighthouse, glowing white like some robed sage in the dusk, looked contemplative and wise. Secure there on its promontory. Yet Covey seemed so solitary to me this evening, almost desolate against the Atlantic expanse. Its dock fragile, mere pilings surmounted by a course of stalwart boards jutting out into the sea. Unthinkable that one would feel confident walking on such a frail thing, but in a moment I would, trusting it the same way I trusted the boys had spent a trouble-free afternoon with the island to themselves.

It was growing dark swiftly, the air a dense inky blue. The packet's running lights were on, green and red. Only a couple of other passengers were aboard, an old woman and a little boy, headed back to the mainland after visiting relatives. I apologized to them for having to make this unchartered detour on my behalf, while wrapping my sweater around me against the moist chill. Was this how things were going to go from now on, taking unchartered detours? I wondered, as the boat rode high swells, then made a graceful and deliberate circle past the clanging bell buoy.

Thanking Mr. McEachern, I informed him my parents were coming to join us and asked, would it be possible to run them out from North-east Harbor?

"I'll take care of it," he said, in his broad Down Easter accent. *All tek kay-ah ovett*.

As I began my climb up the well-worn path, I looked over my shoulder and saw the mailboat's running lights grow smaller and fainter, heard the grinding rumble of the engine fade. Twilight assumed preeminence by the time I reached the keeper's cottage. Light pouring from its windows welcomed me back. The first stars were out, brave throbbing pinholes poking through the soft haze, declaring themselves from the coldness of space to be more than tiny sparks, but suns, sons of suns, huge in their own neighborhoods.

Jonah and Morgan had gotten it in their heads to replicate our first night. Candles on the table. The fire pit roaring. They had brought out all the leftovers from the nights and days before. Quite the beggar's banquet. Canned chili, oyster crackers. And, though we didn't have lobsters, they managed to collect enough mussels to cook in seawater and kelp to make a meal.

"Everything all right here?" I asked, as Jonah ceremoniously handed me a cup of fresh coffee.

"Morgan burned the house down."

"Didn't mean to. Just one of those things."

"But we built it again before you got home."

"That's a relief," I said.

"So what's your story?" Jonah asked. "You find out who that guy was?"

I studied his face when he said this, looking for any telltale gesture that might suggest yesterday's visitor was an embellishment or whimsy, but he was all earnestness.

"No idea," and began helping them set the table.

"Cassandra—"

It was never a good sign when one of them addressed me by my full first name. No matter how many times I'd asked them to desist, they proceeded after their fashion as if I hadn't uttered a word. "Yes," I said, scowling a bit.

"We had a board meeting when you were on Little Cranberry and—"

"We've decided we're not going to some wipeass summer camp."

"Right, forget that bullshit."

"Guys, please let me pretend I'm a good mother who isn't raising children that use words like *bullshit* and *wipeass*. Humor me that I haven't raised a couple of barbarians."

"Point is, we're staying with you," said Jonah. "You need us around."

"I appreciate what you're saying. Just, let's sort this out tomorrow."

"Nothing to sort," Morgan said with finality.

His brother added, "Now come on. Dinner's going to get cold."

Mussels never tasted sweeter. Fiddleheads never more buttery. The coffee, though muddy, might as well have been some gourmet espresso. My boys had prepared a feast to remember. And made a decision which, for all their foul-mouthed assurances otherwise, was a real sacrifice as well as an act of devotion.

13

WHAT A CEASELESSLY spinning spider is memory. The unseen pack of four-wheelers on Islesford continued to buzz in
my head after dinner that night, drilling through to an aural memory
of Christopher and his tight-knit gang of friends in the bad old, good
old days. Half a dozen boys in all different shapes and sizes, most of
them a little older than my brother, which was fine by him since — not
unlike my own boys now, my boys who constitute their own small
gang — he never really thought of himself as a kid.

— Childhood's for weaklings, Cass, he once told me. — You got
that?

— Got it, I said, thinking if that's what Christopher believed, it must
have been right.

— And weaklings are for the birds.

I nodded, pretending to understand.

Ben Gilchrist was the number-one man in their gang. While he
wasn't the oldest, he was the tallest, which brought him a measure of
respect. Built to rip-roar his way through life, he often egged the others on to greater, madder glories. I have wondered over the years if he
lived so fast and hard because he knew deep down his life wasn't fated
to run the full stretch, guessed he was destined to be a sprinter rather

than a marathoner. That his father was the town supervisor gave him a false sense of privilege of which he took full advantage. Whenever he or Chris or any of their gang landed themselves in trouble, chances were good that Rich Gilchrist would get them off with little more than a slap on the wrist.

There was Jimmy Moore, whose sallow, round face was sprayed with a constellation of freckles, and whose tiny eyes were dull as a sow's. Jimmy was possessed of a mean streak and took pleasure in throwing rocks at sparrows and other small creatures, though I never once saw him hit any of his targets. Then there was Bibb Spangler, who always reeked of his father's aftershave. He seemed forever in a daze, which made me wonder if the heavy odor of cologne might have affected his mind. Bibb was always ready to do anything. If the gang decided it was a good idea to hike up to the cliffs overlooking the quarry and dive headfirst onto the shale below, he would do it without thinking twice. Less that he was stupid than staunchly committed. There was also Lare Brest, whose name was a constant source of nasty gibes that I, tagging along with the gang, didn't comprehend, although I laughed long and hard with the rest of them, sure that whatever they were saying must have been funny.

A boy named Roy Skoler came around sometimes. He was the oldest, the only one who smoked publicly and could get away with buying cigarettes and beer for the others if he wasn't asked to produce identification. Nobody knew where he lived, and he never seemed to have to answer to any parents, a freedom the other boys openly envied. He owned a rifle and was always followed by a big friendly hunting dog. Chris and Ben went shooting squirrels with him and that dog once or twice, as I recall. His thin upper lip was shaded with the hint of a mustache, and I remember he always wore polished shoes, Sunday shoes, even in the woods. There wasn't much Roy Skoler and I ever had to say to one another—an unspoken lack of ease defined our relationship, such as it was. He more or less ignored me and I, by turn, tried not to get in his way. One thing about Roy I remembered with absolute clarity. He never smiled. Not only that, but when you smiled at

him, he looked away. Almost as if it was too painful for him to witness. The guys in the gang took this as a further sign of Roy's superiority and coolness, but it made me uncomfortable. I reassured myself that his demeanor—not only didn't he smile, but he rarely frowned, his face a mask of remoteness—meant I ought to feel sorry for him, since he must have been unhappy. But for the most part I tried not to think of Roy at all.

Last was Charley Granger, who always treated me the kindest and spoke up on my behalf whenever the others didn't want me coming along on some adventure. With his hair a rich chestnut color always tousled and spilling over his forehead, with his broad shoulders one higher than the other, with his warm hazel eyes forever attentive, Charley was plainer than most good-looking boys, but his spirit gave him what I would later think of as an almost Apollonian attractiveness. It was always Charley who intervened when the gang, sharing a bottle of whiskey Roy had managed to procure, got it in their collective head to make me the brunt of some stupid whim.

—Hey, Chris, how long you think your sister can stand on one leg holding the bottle for us? Bibb might say.

—On top of her head, Lare would add.

—While she's saying the Lord's Prayer, Ben might chime in.

—Not sure. I could imagine Christopher shrugging, wary but unwilling to stop the flow of banter.

—Maybe we better find out.

—Once you find out, then what? Charley would inevitably ask.

—Then nothing, is what.

—What's the point in knowing nothing?

—Ah, Charley, shut up.

And so the moment would pass.

I hate to admit it even now, but Charley brothered me much more than Christopher when the gang was gathered, and protected me as best he could against the others.

Our rural truck culture required a vehicle with which to nurture its youth. Decades ago, a horse would have been a boy's dream, but

now the four-wheeler served that purpose. I dreaded the day when the twins awoke to its irresistible necessity in their lives. It was loud. It went fast. It was dangerous. It burned fossil fuels at a furious rate. It could be souped up, driven illegally. It got broken, which meant you could fix it and have a legitimate excuse for getting grease all over yourself. Black smeary badge of honor. What more could you want?

During those last months of Christopher's life, racing his four-wheeler with the gang became a consuming mania. His four-stroke, single-cylinder red turbo was intended as Nep's birthday and Christmas gift rolled into one, though my brother would never make it to Christmas. Rosalie was, predictably, dead set against it.

—He's going to kill himself on that thing, she said.

But Nep, who personally built it from parts stripped off junked machines, understood the magnitude of the moment in a Corinth County boy's life, the transition toward manhood that it marked. And he prevailed.

The gang did their racing as far away from their parents as possible. They liked their sport rough and tumble. The more eroded and difficult the terrain, the better. Helmets, goggles, gloves were spurned. Any of the boys who left home wearing safety gear in order to convince their folks they were being responsible dumped this extraneous stuff in a heap, like the worthless debris they considered it, once they got to their makeshift speedway. I came along, piggybacking on my brother's ride, but was left literally in the dust once we got where we were going. Charley was the only one in the bunch who didn't own an ATV, so when they got together to race, he and I were sidelined. We'd watch and chat a little, except when one of the other boys loaned him his dirt muncher for a turn.

—Get it together, Gumshoe, Chris had said, one afternoon.

—I'm going as fast as I can.

Our mother had left me in his care. The story was, we were headed over to Ben's to meet with the guys and check out Bibb's new wheels. And the story was true, if incomplete. We did swing by Ben's. And Bibb did in fact have a refurbished ATV that was chopped down to the

barest essentials — no mudguards, no lights, no rack, nothing beyond its frame and mufflerless engine. But once everybody had converged, the lot of us went tearing off down a steep hill behind the Gilchrists' house, fording a treacherous quick-running creek, and up a wooded hillside until we reached the summit, a mile from anywhere. Here was a rugged track that snaked up and down pitted ravines, gullies, across flat stretches, on land nobody seemed to own. We — well, the gang — had the run of the place, no matter whether it was private or state. Could create mayhem and make as much noise as they wanted without one single soul knowing the better.

A steamy afternoon, humid and with green thunderclouds building in the northern sky. The ball of sun had lowered into a snarl of maples along the west apron of this makeshift arena, causing the world to glow solemn purple. They had run a few races. Bibb pulled an airborne wheelie over past the hairpin turn, he claimed, though I never saw it, and Bibb was ever one for hatching stories, especially when they made him look heroic. The clearing went from smelling redolent with mushrooms and the heavy dank perfume of rotting and living leaves to the acid tang of scorching oil and unfiltered exhaust. I kind of liked both scents equally, truth to tell. Charley and I sat on a long beech log, not talking much, in part because of all the whining, reedy racket of the engines.

—Wish you knew how to ride one of these? he asked, cupping his hand to my ear.

—I already do know.

—That's not what Chris says.

—Chris says wrong.

—So you been taking it out in the middle of the night for a spin?

—Did last night.

—Did you now.

—Sure did. Laid down some rubber, too.

—Well, Cass, you've always got a surprise up your sleeve.

—Don't tell Chris.

—Oh, he said with the affectionate, knowing smile of an older child

who can see through a younger child's white lie. —My lips are sealed like the seal of Solomon.

In retrospect, and even at the time, exchanges such as this were a sign of Charley's decency. He was well aware I didn't know a clutch from a kick starter but wasn't about to betray me to the others.

Jimmy Moore had won two or three races, and before the light dimmed much more, the time had come for the gang to play their most insane game. *Turding* it was called for reasons that were utterly obscure to me at the time, though I sensed it wasn't a word to repeat at the dinner table back home.

What turding resembled most was jousting. Another instance of engine and wheels displacing the horse in country life. Four-wheeler supplanting four-hoofer. Lare Brest had seen a reenactment of a medieval tournament when his family vacationed at some theme park in Florida, and he came home full of stories about knights and lances and throwing down the gauntlet. Nobody agreed with him that the guys should wear costumes like those of the stuntmen-actors he witnessed, but it wasn't long before the gang became knights manqué in heavy metal T-shirts and camouflage cargo pants, armed with stiff branches fallen off trees, and began testing their wills against one another on an uneven straightaway in this wood-ringed clearing.

The rules were few. It was forbidden to aim the tip of a lance at the head of the opponent. A chest shot was fair, as was a hit to the shoulder. For the most part they simply played chicken, swerving at the last moment to avoid a head-on collision, or bashing the front of the other's machines with their lances rather than the riders themselves. Their injuries were generally cuts and bruises to the hand that grasped the branch, which often snapped and splintered on impact and went flying into the air. Whoever was left holding his weapon intact and had made the run without falling off, won. Whoever lost his lance, broke it, fell off his ride, bailed in any way, was deemed *turded*. If there was no contact and neither rider swerved away, it was a scratch and immediately replayed.

Jimmy was on a tear that evening. Both Christopher and Ben lost

on their first charge, my brother escaping injury and, more important, humiliation by simply being left with the stub of his lance at the end of the run. He'd made a pretty valiant effort at jamming the thing into the front suspension of Jimmy's four-wheeler but aimed too low and caught his lance in the dirt. Ben, for his part, lost control of his wheels and nearly crashed headfirst into a thick ash tree, tangling himself instead in its lower leaves and toppling his ATV. Bibb was no match for Jimmy. He dropped his ramrod long before he and Moore were within striking distance, and Jimmy caught his shoulder with a clean blow, knocking him hard to the ground. Fortunately, he hadn't been moving too fast and rolled a few times like a thrown doll. When he climbed to his feet, I thought he was crying at first. Instead he was laughing — a bit hysterically, but laughing, which meant he saved face. Lare had already taken off for home, and Roy Skoler, who was hanging out with us that night, lit another cigarette and begged off quietly, saying he had no interest in getting killed, so it came down to Charley to end Jimmy's streak. The defeated kids lined up their vehicles, like soldiers on metal stallions awaiting review, and revved their engines while they waited for the two to get positioned at the far ends of the track.

Roy took Charley's place beside me on a rock outcropping well behind the line of drivers, where Charley and I had moved to a safer distance from the action after Bibb lost control and went flying. He had a flask and offered me a sip.

—I don't want any, I said.

—Just a little to toast your boyfriend Charley good luck.

—He's not my boyfriend.

—Sure he is. Everybody knows. Now come on and give him a toast for luck.

—Let me smell it, I said, and recoiled at its harsh burned-sugar stink.

—You're not supposed to sniff it, you're supposed to swig it, Gummy.

—Don't call me that.

—Okay, he said. —I won't, but only if you take a sip. One won't hurt you.

My first taste of alcohol. My tongue and throat were scalded. I felt as if I were breathing bitter fire out my nostrils.

—Ain't that yummy, Gummy?

Coughing as hard as I was, I couldn't speak.

—Take it easy. You all right?

I continued to gag as he clapped me lightly on the back.

—What you need's another tug. That's what the pros do.

—I don't want—

—No, here. That's a girl.

I could hear the engines racing wildly, crazed, as he held the flask to my lips with his right hand and, with the open palm of his left hand pressing against the back of my head, eased more down my throat.

—There now. Much better.

He must have worked swiftly because I cannot remember him setting down the flask, cannot remember any sequence of acts between that second drink and his moving one of his hands between my clamped thighs, kneading me with rough clumsiness. With his other hand he gripped mine and forced it on his hard pulsing lap. I bit his tongue when it pushed itself past my teeth into my mouth, and I remember hitting him as hard as I could on the side of his head with my fisted free hand, at which he slapped me right back with far more strength than I possessed.

We sat stunned, silenced, each of us in our different way. Though I wanted to, I refused to allow myself to cry. It was Roy who spoke first.

—That's not very friendly.

—You're not my friend.

—I thought you'd like that. You like watching it enough.

—Do not.

—You got a pretty good eyeful last week.

—I never saw anything, I lied, heart racing.

—Keep it that way, he said, and forced another hideous kiss on me, his thin tongue in my mouth once more. I didn't dare struggle again but blanked my mind of all thoughts and waited for it to be over.

This can't have gone on for too long, but it might as well have been a

vile eternity and only ended—violence interrupting violence—when we were abruptly torn away by shouts, though not at us. A pandemonium of yelling kids at the center of which were terrible shrieks like those of a rabbit being carried off by a fox to its final destruction.

—Say a word about anything to anybody and you die, he told me, holding my head back with a tight fistful of my hair. —Believe that.

I knew the screeches had to be coming from one of the gang, but I'd never imagined that a boy could produce such a high-pitched sound. I was finally crying as Roy and I ran in the ringing and shaded air to where the others were gathered, all gesturing wildly. There, under the headlights of Jimmy's four-wheeler, I saw Charley Granger writhing on the ground, clutching at his face, blood seeping between his fingers. Ben and my brother got him on the back of Ben's four-wheeler. With Christopher and me leading the way, the whole gang went racing down the mountain as the last light was giving over to nightfall.

Charley did lose that eye, and Roy Skoler disappeared for a while from everyone's sight. He needn't have warned me not to tell a soul about what happened, because it was the last thing on earth I would ever have done.

The gang essentially disbanded after that, which was fine since, as Christopher told me a few days later, home from visiting Charley in the hospital, it was time for all of us to grow up already, anyway. My parents didn't permit me to go see him. They felt the poor young man ought to be allowed his privacy and didn't need visitors who weren't his closest friends. Since no one could possibly understand what a close friend I considered Charley, I sat down and wrote him a long letter telling him how awful I felt about what had happened, that I was thinking of him every day and night and wished him a speedy recovery. I signed the letter *Your devoted friend* and never sent it.

Part III

REVENANT IN THE LIGHTHOUSE

14

HERE WAS ONE OF those mornings sailors loathed but I loved.

Dense stringy fog wrapped itself around Covey Island, looking like exquisite silver scarves slipped by the breeze off the necks of mermaids, as Rosalie once said. *Sea smoke,* some island people called it. She and Nep were arriving today. Given there was no sun to tell us dawn had broken, it was lucky I'd set the alarm clock. The boys and I had agreed to get up early to clean and straighten. All three of us wanted the cottage to look picture-perfect for their grandparents. I can't have been the only one to whom it occurred that this might be our last family gathering on the island.

"Good," said Morgan. "They won't be able to get here before the fuzz burns off."

"I wouldn't count Mr. McEachern out no matter what the weather," I said.

"But we're totally socked in."

"Let's get to it anyhow, what d'you say."

They dragged broom, mop, rags upstairs and I started in the kitchen. Rosalie had always been a more meticulous housekeeper than I. A kitchen I considered passable would to her be just this side of grimy. I

wanted her to be happy. The soot-dusted coal stove was first, there
in its antique black splendor, bathed in light from windows that radi-
ated a translucent gray, and against whose panes a gently blown mist
whispered. I pulled off the grates and began by emptying cinders and
ash into a bucket. Again I thought, like up at the cemetery, I loved this
kind of work. So gratifying to see immediate results. With students,
you never knew. You work hard to teach them, then years go by before
they might become heads of state, or wards of the state. And with divining you never were sure if you accomplished anything until the hole
was dug. Things had certainly turned out well with my boys, mopping
away upstairs now, though I remembered being so dismayed when the
results of my liaison with James Boyd became as visible as the bucket
of ash I carried to the fire pit.

Since I was thin and tending toward tall, my pregnancy began to
show — at least naked in front of my unwashed mirror — by autumn
the year of my encounter. *Show,* I thought at the time. What a word.
As if it were a performance, an exhibition of a work in progress with a
collaborator nowhere to be found. I took to staying at home, keeping
out of the public eye. My parents saw less of me than ever and I didn't
return friends' calls.

I was living at the time in a converted barn. Rent was cheap. Pas-
toral views were framed by every wheezy, breezy window. An ancient
hornets' nest that put me in mind of a huge molten brain hung in the
cherry tree outside my bedroom casement. The owners of the property allowed me to ride their aged horse that lived with a few goats
on the floor below mine, in trade for my feeding them. My well-worn
books I arranged on cinder-block shelves made with planks of rough
hemlock, slivery wood that had been left in a corner downstairs when
the board-and-batten building was raised.

Mostly, reading was how I passed my hours. Reading and worrying.
My three cats braved the times with me — Homer, so named because
he was partially blind and loved to sing; Herman, in honor of Melville,
whom I considered a late-born Roman epic poet; and Sybil, because
the others followed her around as if she knew where the action was

going to be. They had chickadees to stalk, mice to chase, and a big late-season vegetable garden to play in. How often, those days, I found myself wishing I were one of my cats. I used them sometimes as excuses for canceling further divining work that summer and early fall. I must have sounded daft or lazy. I can't make it there today, my Herman is lost. My Homer is sick. Sybil's about to have babies. I felt as free as a nail in the wall.

Where I lived was only a short drive from my parents', which made my absence the more pointed. For all my autonomy, my childhood bedroom was still there, and I missed it. Missed Nep, missed Rosalie. Niles, of all people, would be the best friend outside my family I could possibly trust to have any insights as to what I should do. But Niles had married in June and we tacitly agreed to observe some decorum and distance.

Instead of calling anyone I knew, one morning I telephoned an abortion clinic in New York. Made arrangements, set a date. The relief I felt when I hung up was staggering. What had I been thinking all August? That I was actually going to bear this poor doomed love child? An accidental embryo the result of a betrayal? It would be criminal to bring this baby into the world, I believed, terrified I might unfairly hate it from the moment I laid eyes on its face and recognized its father's exquisite, treacherous features.

Having now emerged from the stupor of not knowing what to do, I telephoned Rosalie and invited myself over for dinner. My mother and father had always been straight with me, and clearly the honor must be returned. I wasn't so foolish as to think either of them was going to like what they were about to hear. But I didn't have enough Boyd-like indifference in my heart to hide my disgraceful mistake from them any longer. I would need moral, or, as I imagined Rosalie would reckon, immoral, support to get through the abortion. The time had arrived for me to come clean.

Nep greeted me at the door with a hug. —Been a while, stranger.

—Is that her? my mother called from the kitchen where we joined her.

They had decanted a special bottle of wine and their moods were buoyant, which made me feel all the more petrified.

—Here's to homecomings, Nep said, raising his glass. We drank and my father and I sat down at the kitchen table while Rosalie continued with dinner preparations at the nearby counter. She asked over her shoulder about the cats. What a shame this one was sick and the other lost. So glad he found his way back home. Nep inquired about my dowsing. Would I be able to help him more before the snow flew?

—And by the way, Rosalie added. —How many kittens did Sybil wind up having?

—Actually, Sybil didn't have any kittens, I said, lowering my eyes.

—That's sad, my mother said, setting her knife on the cutting board. —Stillborns?

—No, Mom.

—Maybe she just got fat. False alarm, Nep joked.

—Well, Syb is a little fat. But she was never pregnant.

—Pseudocyesis is what that's called, Rosalie said, ever the science teacher. —So it was a false alarm?

—No, I knew she wasn't pregnant.

—What in the world would possess you to say she was, then? That's not like you.

—Don't worry about it, Ros, said Nep. —I'm sure Cassie here can explain.

I glanced up at my father, then at my mother's worried face, before finally confessing, —Homer and Herman are fine. They've been fine all along. I feel horrible and ashamed to admit this, but I haven't been at all truthful with you.

Rosalie came and sat down with us at the table. —What's wrong, Cassandra?

A hesitant silence intruded before I said, quietly, resignedly, —I'm pregnant.

The look on Nep's face was one of such supreme dismay I can picture it in my mind with precision even now. I didn't dare glimpse at

my mother to confirm her anger and humiliation. Now came a longer silence than before.

Rosalie finally spoke. —Please tell me it's not Niles's.

—It's not, I said, wishing like anything it was.

—Well, whose is it? Her staccato voice was filled more with fear than hostility.

—You don't know him.

—Whose is it? It's hers is whose it is, said Nep.

Pressing forward, my mother continued, —What's his name?

I told them everything. Nep might have paused at the surname Boyd, I couldn't quite tell. We always kept each other informed about the various places we dowsed, and he had an elephant's memory before the Alzheimer's. He had already gotten up from his chair and had his arm around my shoulder, and Rosalie was holding my hands across the table, flexing her fingers hard and unconsciously.

—So now what? she said. —Does he know?

—No.

—Shouldn't we contact him? Nep asked.

—No, never. What's next is I'm going to have an abortion. By next month this will all have been a bad dream.

—Over my dead body, Rosalie cried out, standing.

Nep said, in a tight strained measured way I never heard from him before or after, as he sat again, —Let's all be quiet and be quiet right now. Let's not get ahead of ourselves, or behind, either. We're a family and we've had problems in the past and we'll have problems in the future and this is one more problem we will work out together. He folded his fingers together on the table before him and stared at his hands, as one might a chess piece before making a crucial endgame move. —I do have one question.

—Yes?

—Have you given consideration to keeping it? I think your mother already expressed her opinion about the matter. And you know she and I don't always agree on things of this nature, her church and mine being different—

—What church? Rosalie said. —Where's an address for it? I'd like to attend one of their services sometime.

—but, and not that this is anyone's decision but your own, I believe the three of us would be able to manage it if you went ahead. Who knows, maybe when the father finds out, he'll do the honorable thing and—

—I never want to have anything to do with him again.

—Devil's advocate's never my favorite role, my mother said. —But don't you have the ethical responsibility, if not a moral one, to inform this person he's gotten you pregnant? Aren't there maybe legal consequences involved in not telling him?

Her points were well taken. But ethics, morals, laws simply weren't of overriding importance to me at that juncture. I think if James Boyd had left it alone after the one night of intimacy I might have felt less adamant about despising him. But driving up two days later and knowingly putting me through the paces a second time, aware he intended to turn right around, having told me nothing whatsoever of the truth, made me bitter. I could only imagine what a multitude of emotional games he was playing with others in his universe. Wasn't my business. But neither was my life, including my pregnancy, any of his.

—I don't care, is how I responded to her question. —He abandoned any rights to anything having to do with me. Besides, I do know him enough to know that this is the last thing on earth he'd want to trouble himself about. He's not that kind.

Rosalie came and offered an embrace. She did so with such a painful smile I was petrified. —There are other solutions to the problem, she said, her voice cracking.

When Nep rose again and put his arms around both of us, we reached the end of the dialogue. We managed to eat. Back at the barn, I had left plenty of food and water for the cats, figuring there was a chance I wouldn't be home until tomorrow. I spent the night in my old bedroom.

Even in the safety of this childhood haunt, surrounded by old familiars like my worn doll Millicent and my frayed Pooh and my

favorite books like *The Runaway Bunny,* whose pages I leafed through hopelessly, and all the other comforting childhood memorabilia, I was wildly restless. As were Rosalie and Nep. I heard them through the wall, getting in bed, getting back up. The house would fall quiet for a time, then more muffled discussion would ensue. Talk, whisper, moan, talk.

Somewhere in the midst of it all I experienced a profound recollection. Here was precisely the consternation and gut pain I felt that night, so long ago, when we learned Christopher had been in his fatal accident. Death and the promise of life. It was hard to imagine they could inspire such identical responses in me. Although I can't begin to reconstruct the sequence of thoughts that led me to this conclusion, it was sometime after I connected my dead brother with my as-yet-living fetus that I decided to have the child.

If my parents were willing to suffer the temporary indignities of gossips who were going to have a field day with me, the unwed, unattached mother, then so could I. Let the backstabbers have at my back. Wasn't like I hadn't been their mark before. What was more important, I had the chance to turn a wrong into a right. To take the ugliness out of what had happened by besting it, maybe even transforming it, with something the absolute opposite of ugly. These thoughts may have trodden across the line from realms of cold maturity into those of rather fanciful idealism, but in retrospect, they led me to make the right choice.

My drafty, quasi-converted barn might have been habitable for a single woman but it wasn't the best environment for a mother and her newborn, so I moved back home that fall. Reluctant initially to accept my parents' offer to stay with them for a while, I did have to admit that I craved the company, if not the comfort, that being with them afforded me. At night, I settled down in my childhood bed facing the dormer windows with my mewling gang of cats and stared sleepless at a moon-and-starlit view memorized into a personal mythology over more than seven thousand nights.

The months dropped away as I swelled and sphered. The scandal-

mongering came to pass and then faded. I spent more time reading about the rearing of children than anything by Euripides. Told Niles over lunch at a local diner what was happening, Niles whose wife was also pregnant, I thought ironically, even though there was no irony involved. He, as ever, avowed a heartfelt loyalty, a lifetime bond that neither this nor anything else would sunder, and offered to support me in any ways he reasonably could. I made an excursion to the city to buy all sorts of baby things. Sewed infant clothes with Rosalie. Built a crib with Nep. And then built a second, identical one after learning from the obstetrician that I was expecting twins. For all my stack of self-help textbooks and admonitory advice from my mother, I could never have anticipated how much physical labor — far beyond the labor pains of delivery — was part of rearing babies. I was a total neophyte, and no forevisioning or divining would wipe that basic deficit away. Like every new mother, I improvised my way through their infancy.

Not one day or night went by without my worrying that James Boyd would suddenly appear to disrupt my life all over again. But he never turned up, never called. By becoming such a thorough absence, he allowed me to stretch him, as it were, like a canvas on a frame. With provident care, I molded a new father for these boys, and amazingly, Rosalie and Nep didn't contradict me, even though they must have known I chose to fill in some blanks with pure invention.

What my boys grew up with was that their father was a handsome and hard-working man whose job forced him to be on the road more often than he'd have liked. When he finally had to make a choice about whether to settle down or stay on the road, he chose the road. We lost touch. The last I heard, he was successful. A rising star in his own life, but a shooting star in mine. No, I don't have a photograph of him. He always said, A photograph is yesterday, a person is now. And now is better, just ask yesterday. I never met his parents. His mother was deceased, though I spoke on the phone with his father. A dignified voice, a kindly man I thought, also dead now. And that was that. My boys and I had each other and we were a trinity to contend with.

One last thing. As hard as it might be for Morgan and Jonah to do

me this favor, I wanted them to promise never to bring up the subject of their father again. They knew the whole story now, so further questions would only lead us in unhappy circles. For the most part they abided by my wish.

This was the best I could manage. Of course, over the years we'd had to contend with the rumors kids at school had picked up from their magpie parents that challenged the credibility of my story. One day I would have to tell them the truth, I knew. How many times I found myself wishing that Niles hadn't fallen in love with Melanie Lyons, now Melanie Hubert, as I believed he was the one man who would have been capable of raising my sons with me. Under the circumstances, he did what he could. And the boys, initially growing up in the same house as I did, before I saved enough money to make a down payment on my modest place on Mendes Road, turned out better than in my most optimistic fantasies. They were finer, more intricate companions than I might ever have imagined.

The butcher-block counter was scrubbed. The zinc sink scoured. The window glass washed. The shelves of canned foods tidied, tins of Nep's favorite Norwegian sardines in mustard stacked high. The kitchen table was polished. The pine floor mopped. I joined Jonah and Morgan upstairs to finish preparations in the bedrooms and bath, then came back down where together we spruced up the greatroom with its worn but lovely kilim rugs and antique furniture left from Henry Metcalf's days. Wound the old brass ship's clock on the mantel. Arranged a nosegay of wildflowers from the yard. Rosalie's dominion was ready.

Outside, the fog had thinned. Sun soon broke through as an offshore zephyr picked up. Since we didn't know exactly when they were going to arrive, we decided to take a late lunch down to the dock and wait while those mermaids' scarves blew away to Newfoundland and a rich aquamarine sky was unveiled in their wake.

We packed two baskets with more food than we'd ever need. Bread, cheese, olives, some salmon cakes left over from an earlier dinner, almonds, oranges, even a can of Nep's favorite sardines. Jonah took his

dragon kite, Morgan his fishing rod. I told them I'd be down shortly to join them. Just wanted to change my clothes. Off they went with the baskets and other gear. I watched out the greatroom window as they filed down the narrow path around the edge of the island and out of sight. Beyond them stretched a sea so blue it seemed unreal somehow, as if I were inventing it.

Upstairs, I changed into a white poplin sundress Rosalie had bought for me last year. Put on the charm bracelet Nep gave me when we first visited Covey, a piece of jewelry that was a necklace way back then and now served, twice wound around, as jangly wrist jewelry. Brushed out my hair, which was wavier up here by the ocean than back in Corinth County. The face I regarded in the mirror was not as rested or settled as I might have hoped. I tried smiling, but the effect seemed strained. Yet I knew it was important that I recover as much of that blessed serenity I'd experienced on arriving at Covey as I possibly could. I gave it another try and saw, just on the other side of the veil of distress, a truly smiling Cassandra.

That's more like it, I thought.

Time had come for me to join the twins on the dock. I arranged a straw sun hat on my head, as now it was bright outdoors, put on sunglasses, and headed down the path. The breeze blew in wavelike crests so all the low foliage on either side of the path—oysterleaf and cinquefoil and innumerable others—was lashing and switching. I took in a deep breath of the pristine, polished air. Because of the earlier chowder fog, few sails were to be seen, even though the afternoon had developed into a perfect one for sailing. Lobster boats were chugging around, making up for lost time. I rounded the corner of the bluff and caught sight of Jonah's kite aloft toward the southwest, and Mount Desert beyond. Then I remembered I'd forgotten my camera. Even though yesterday was indeed never going to be today and the images I wanted to capture would never be more than mere memory jogs, I still had it in mind to document the occasion. In all my focus on looking nice, I had left it on the bench by the front door. Wouldn't take but a moment to retrieve. When I turned to run back up to the cottage,

I saw a young girl, pale as an albino, standing slightly above me beneath the towering lone white pine that grew beside the path, a wind-blasted skeleton of a tree with stiff straight green-fringed arms pointing in all directions. She was staring at me as if I were an unusual sighting. As if I were what birdwatchers call an *accidental*. Half-smiling, half-frowning. Though I didn't recognize her, I assumed she must have strayed over from the other side of the island, but that didn't quite add up, given I had found no one there. She was wearing a blindingly bright pink shirt tucked into orange clamdiggers, an outfit whose neonlike colors made her stand out against the backdrop of short sage scrub and pale stone. Blue-black hair cropped ragged across her forehead, cut in such a way that she appeared to have wisps of sideburns. A boyish little girl with gray eyes and narrow lips pink as the inside of a conch shell. Barefoot. She might have been impish but for the slightly impatient jut of her jaw.

"Hello there," I said, taking off my sunglasses.

She said nothing in return but continued to eye me with undisguised curiosity, as if I were the stranger, the trespasser, the oddity. It almost seemed like she was, how to describe this, *colorized*. As if she were in a restored film whose tinting was oversaturated and just a tad out of focus. She made the surrounding landscape appear subdued.

"And who are you?"

Still no response, except that she tipped her head, birdlike herself now, to one side. Maybe she was shy, or had been told not to speak to strangers. Maybe she was a mute.

"Are you looking for somebody? You lost?" I asked in a gentle, motherly voice, but to no avail. She continued to gaze into my eyes with that quizzical look on her face.

A mood came over me that I didn't expect or like. Suddenly, I didn't want her to be there. Puzzled, I glanced away, out toward the Cranberries, long thin green-brown conjoined smears on the shimmering plate of ocean, then returned her stare.

Moving as slowly as if she were underwater, she held out her hand no higher than her waist, palm up, as her half-smile widened a touch.

Cradled there was what looked like a skipping stone, mottled gray and white with something akin to a face on its flat surface. Now, black as wet tarmac, a large dog appeared out of the underbrush to sit beside her. Panting like it had run a long distance and wanted to rest in the shade. He seemed a sweet enough mutt, wore a wide wet smile, as panting dogs do. I was inclined to reach out and pet him but didn't dare.

Were it not for my monster, this encounter wouldn't have been cause for alarm. Mild surprise, yes, since to my recollection no one had ever ventured from the north end of the island over to our side. Perhaps also some wonder about how oddly luminous she seemed against the landscape, though this could be a simple feint of light. But the sharp dread I felt made me worry I had become downright paranoiac. Whoever this girl was, I didn't have the strength of heart to find out. Didn't want to know. My parents' landing on Covey and the first images of our family's reunion would have to be left to individual and collective memories. No way was I going back to fetch my camera.

"Well, okay, goodbye," I said, in a falsely cheerful voice.

She continued to smile, sort of, and said not a word.

I turned around on the path, the wind picking up some, and my feet led me away from the cottage, the androgynous girl, the huffing black dog. I hoped she would remain silent, not say goodbye. Walked hurriedly, stumbling once, then again on a narrowing in the rocky trail, wanting to look back to see if she was still there and somehow assuming she wasn't. She made no utterance and her dog didn't bark. There were no sounds beyond my fast shallow breathing and those of wind and waves. Soon I saw Jonah's colorful dragon kite cutting quick arabesques in the stiff breezes above the beach, and as I rounded the precipice Morgan came into view at the end of the dock, casting into the surf. Beyond the twins, so far out toward Mount Desert that they couldn't see it yet, I was certain I glimpsed the white of the bow-ripped jade water and the small silhouette of the boat carrying my parents toward my sons and me.

Halfway down the rock path to the dock I did turn and look back.

As I might have expected and had certainly hoped, the pallid girl was gone. So was her smiling dog. I closed my eyes hard, rubbing them with my fingertips to clear my head, then opened them again. Nothing loomed before me but the path, the sage scrub, the pine with its long bows tousled by the wind. As I turned and continued down toward the landing to join the twins, it occurred to me that I hadn't even noticed whether the waif and her black mutt had cast shadows.

15

HOW OFTEN DO WE use other people as screens upon which to project our obsessions? Our discontents, dreams, desires, and fears? Well, I always thought, often enough that it's a wonder the whole waking world isn't simply viewed as an endless improvised film. One with as many screenwriters, producers, and directors as there are actors.

Imagine. The history of the world as an endless stream of simultaneous epics, with all the humans who ever lived acting as both stars in their own autobiographical pictures and extras in the movies of everybody they ever met. Most of us like to think of ourselves as working in the realist tradition, making our movies true to life. But there are times in each of our countless films when the celluloid jumps its sprocket or the digitalization cascades and crashes, and we are left with something unrecognizable, a story that bears no immediate resemblance to what had been the prior throughline. We want to send the scene back for redraft. Something's wrong with the plot, we cry out. The dialogue is flawed. There's a continuity gaffe. The acting isn't believable. We need another take. *Cut!* we want to shout into the mouthpiece of our tin megaphone. But, nothing doing. The shot is already in the can, ephemeral as memory itself because memory is its medium.

Not knowing whether the girl was real, to use that mysterious word, left me walking the rest of the way down to the shore in full recognition my movie threatened to veer even deeper into the fantastic. But for all my love of myth, I had no desire to traffic in fantasy. I wanted my personal film to be the simple, straightforward story of a young woman who has her problems but is blessed with two brilliant children, loving parents, and maybe somewhere in her future a man to complete the standard architecture of the cast. I wanted my movie to be interesting, but also ordinary. No Martine de Berthereau-like tale with all its drama and tragedy. A film whose true profundity lies in its deep ordinariness. But that didn't seem to be the way my life was arcing.

Jonah's dragon kite was still curling boldly in the breezes high above the stone beach and Morgan was still casting from the end of the dock. The boat was a good quarter-hour away, what with the strong headwinds prevailing. And so I decided to challenge the validity of this documentary of mine. That girl hadn't the right to frighten me away from my own house, I decided, and probably hadn't intended to do so. I went back for the camera, chiding myself.

It lay where I'd left it on the front porch bench. The house was undisturbed. I met no one along the way up or back down. Nor should I have expected otherwise, although I was determined to have another look, when Rosalie and I would take our traditional walk the next day, to see if anyone was staying with Mrs. Milgate. If so, in case she had forgotten, it would be prudent to tell her about the dangers of the lighthouse, which wasn't in good repair and was certainly no place for children to go exploring. Our few No Trespassing signs — they still read "Lands of Henry Metcalf" — were nailed to trees across the meridian ridge of the isle, not because we were worried about intruders but rather because we couldn't afford to spend the thousands it would cost to repair and insure the old tower. One downside of being on an island without phones was that if anyone needed immediate medical attention, it wasn't the easiest matter to arrange.

I looked behind me up at this imposing lighthouse of ours. So white

there in its tapering maleness. Imagining my mother seeing it from the boat as she gazed our way, I felt a mild twinge of daughterly anxiety. It had been some time since we lived under the same roof, and I could easily divine what her response might be if I shared all I had seen, all that had been happening to me. Nep's less active presence in my life only redoubled my sense of vulnerability.

Was I intimidated by Rosalie? Perhaps the religion she so comfortably wore was off-putting, dismaying somehow, and daunting in its certitudes, at least to one who saw the world as a place in which the lack of certitudes was the only thing to be sure about. Not that she was ever overly pushy about her Methodism. She wasn't some pious pedagogue with a cross in one hand and a strop in the other. My mother was far more subtle than that. And, never to forget, she had lived for more than three and a half decades with a man who was as secular as the gadgets he repaired and the earth he walked with his fragile diviner's twig. No, I wasn't afraid of her as such. Just aware of the warp and weave and tangle that was our relationship.

Nep looked years younger when he stepped down the seesawing plank, his cheeks wildly aglow from wind and sun. Mr. McEachern helped him off after Rosalie had come ashore, and the boys hoisted their bags from the boat.

Whether because of the fresh soft air or because his mind was calmed by arriving at the island, Nep looked to be having one of his good days. His eyes were quick and clear. In profile he appeared as distinguished as a sea hawk, sharp-featured and worldly. His illness weathered him, but less in a diminishing than in an ennobling way. An ivory cable-knit sweater was draped over his shoulders, tied loosely by the sleeves at his neck. His mane of white hair streamed back over his finely boned head. He was wearing a pair of faded blue dungarees, a beige linen shirt, and some old docksiders, sockless as a schoolboy. I snapped a photograph of him for my permanent album. This was one of those moments I knew I would need to remember.

"How was the trip? You must be exhausted," I said, as Jonah and Morgan accepted their grandmother's embraces and shook Nep's hand, all very manly and dignified.

"Flew by like a breeze," my father replied.

"A breeze for him, maybe," Rosalie said, "but that drive isn't getting any shorter."

She thanked Mr. McEachern, whom she had known since her childhood days up here, with a kiss on each cheek. He, in turn, thanked her for the chocolates she'd brought for his wife.

"Tell her I'm sorry they're a little melted from being on the road all day," she added. Nep reached for his wallet to pay for the ride out, but Mr. McEachern would hear none of it, boarded his boat, and powered off back toward the main island.

We sat on large smooth blue rocks that had served many a generation as natural seats down here near the water while Nep and Rosalie rested, found their land legs after the choppy transit, and had something to eat before venturing up to the cottage. To everyone's delight, Morgan made a grand display of his casting techniques and Jonah got his kite back into the sky. For that brief hour it was as if time had turned backward and I was allowed, against all rules, the chance for a peaceful scene in my Cassandra Productions film to be crafted precisely as I wished it. Contented children playing under the admiring eyes of their mother and grandparents; calm solicitude among the tribal elders; the weightlessness of easy banter among people who were used to one another. A respite.

Eventually, we made our way up the hill in fits and starts. The boys took the lead, lugging the bags. With stops to rest and admire the flowers and the shimmering islands in the distance, my parents and I followed behind. Furtive, hoping Rosalie didn't notice, I scanned either side of the path for the neon girl and her dog, her silent smiling black dog that looked, it dawned on me, just like the one that used to traipse around behind Christopher's gang. How they loved that beaming mutt, Roy Skoler's hunting dog. Though the world was crawling with black dogs, I knew there was no point in inquiring at Mrs. Milgate's whether any children were visiting her. My heart sank at the recognition.

Doing my best to set my worries aside, I threw myself into the reunion that night in the cottage, and for the next few days that followed.

We sailed the boat one afternoon to Otter Cliffs and Thunder Hole, where the sea spouted straight up into the sky. We sailed to our favorite unpeopled island and musseled the shallows of Lamb's Bay, whose sea wrack Nep called "wrack of lamb." We stargazed together from the flats above the cottage, the lighthouse blocking out the lower constellations that went wheeling into the black sea. We puttered, weeded the perennial garden, played board games.

It seemed like the sweet ordinariness I longed for had settled over me like fairy dust, except for a brief moment when I could have sworn I smelled cigarette smoke through my open window before turning off the bedside lamp to sleep. I sat stunned in the dark. There was nothing to do, was there. Having discovered the fresh butts at the cottage and in the dilapidated house, I should have asked Jonah and Morgan if the stranger had been smoking. Too late now, though. By asking, I would only provoke more questions from everyone, Nep included, and I didn't want to do that. Best to just let matters unfold as they would, bide my time until I could clearly see if there was fire behind that smoke.

16

NEXT DAY, MY MOTHER and I set out as we always did for our trek around Covey's shores. This usually took us several hours, less because of the hike's length than the sheer ruggedness of the shingle that edged land and sea, not to mention our habit of lingering over every little treasure we found. A clump of beach peas, a spider web woven in a rummage of rocks, some pineweed whose flowers were tiny as diamonds. The sky was calm and the face of the water was flat as a fallow field. A few clouds shaped like white mushrooms edged the eastern horizon; otherwise we walked beneath an inverted bowl of paling indigo. Nep and the boys stayed behind to do their thing. They had made noises about fixing one of the propane pilots on the stove and maybe doing some fishing.

We talked about Nep first. She floored me by saying, right off, that he had gone missing not long before they were to drive up here.

"Why didn't you tell me when I called?"

"Because he'd been found by then and I didn't think there was much point in worrying you."

"Where was he?"

"They picked him up walking along Mendes Road. Seemed like he was headed to your house, is what Niles said."

"But why would he — that's quite a ways."

"We have no idea and he doesn't seem to remember."

"Wouldn't he have a hard time knowing the way even?"

Rosalie's response surprised me. "Once a diviner, always a diviner, I guess. Not only that but I swear I saw mischief in his eyes. I think he was having a good time of it, if you want to know the truth."

My dear wayward father would one day finally wander right over the edge of the earth, I realized while hiking there along the beach littered with the rubble of sea scree. How horrified he would be if he knew I'd been reading some books on medical dowsing, on how to use pendulums and aurometers to identify detrimental energies and to eradicate negative thought-forms, in the hope of finding a cure. I knew better than even to bring it up. As a fellow diviner mentored by the man, I was to be abandoned by the one person I knew who truly fathomed the mysterious nature of the act. And as his only child — the only one he raised into adulthood — I knew the coming separation was going to leave a titanic emptiness in my life.

Rosalie told me that aside from his capricious, willful, unannounced march toward Mendes Road that day, he seemed to have entered a plateau phase. His aphasia, still relatively mild, was at times less depressing to him than a source of gentle laughter. When he referred to his shoe as a *hard sock,* or called a plate of scrambled eggs *yellow gravy,* he would catch himself and marvel at what a slippery slope his neuropathways had become. The doctors deemed this promising. He'd always been an apperceptive man and this served him in good stead. His sporadic lack of focus and tendency to misinterpret what someone had said was "often episodic rather than strictly progressive," Rosalie told me, and I couldn't help but notice her lingo had been affected by visits to the clinic.

"I know I've been pretty distracted these past weeks and haven't been as much of a help to you as usual," I confessed. "But I must say he seemed almost his old self at dinner last night. A slower Nep, for sure, but Nep."

"He has his good days and bad days. I'm hopeful he'll have only good days up here."

Hearing the concern behind her words, I looked over at Rosalie and for the first time noticed the ways she'd changed since Nep began his decline. Some people get stronger as their mate fades, as if the body knows by instinct it must compensate, keep the balance, lest it too begin to slide into the abyss of illness, while others grow weaker alongside them. My mother, for her part, looked robust, her hair recently dyed toward its original auburn to beat back the encroaching silver. She carried her compact, lithe body with a kind of stylish confidence unique, in my experience, to true believers and their counterparts, the self-assured atheists. No agnostic tentativeness infected her posture or stride. Her chinos and white blouse, her white running shoes and sensible straw hat, her handsome rose bandanna, all gave her the air of a mother and wife who was very comfortable being Rosalie Metcalf Brooks. But her jet-dark eyes were mildly sunken, the fragile skin beneath them white as vellum. Worry lines that had always given her forehead and cheeks distinction, making her look wise and serious beyond her years back when she was younger, now trenched themselves deeper into her flesh and extended their reach.

We walked a ways in silence, watching the gulls wheel and play. Far off, creeping along the line where the blue of air met the water's deeper green-blue, a huge tanker drifted northward, no larger than a millipede from my vantage. Casually, as if it were a part of my routine, I peered up past the rocky, eroded banks toward the woods' edge but saw neither a girl nor a smoking man.

After a minute Rosalie spoke again, breaking the thoughtful quiet.

"I've been meaning to give you this." She pulled from her back pocket a postcard and handed it to me, adding, "I kept it aside from the rest of the mail I brought up for you from Mendes because I wanted to wait until we had a chance to be alone."

The card, unsigned and without a return address, bore the image of a fresco in the basilica of St. Francis of Assisi. It depicted a group of women weeping over the dead and haloed saint while in the background a strange and incongruous figure in white, its back turned to the viewer, climbed a golden tree toward a heaven of green clouds. *Il pianto delle Clarisse,* read the printed title on the card, *The Poor Clare*

Sisters weep over the death of St. Francis. On the reverse, in simple childish block letters clearly meant to disguise the writer's identity, the penciled note read, *Leave me alone, little girl. I'm giving you fair warning.*

Just as the sender intended, I was horror-struck.

"What does it mean?" Rosalie asked.

"I don't know what it means," standing still in my tracks.

"Any idea who—"

"I don't know who."

"Have you been in an argument with anybody?"

"Not a soul," I said, knowing my minor unpleasantness with Bledsoe would never trigger anything this harsh.

"You think it has anything to do with that man who spoke to the boys the other day?"

"Mom, I honestly have no idea what this is about," I answered, hearing that unfamiliar appellation strike a formal note between us with the same startled impact she must have heard. I asked myself aloud, "How are you supposed to leave somebody alone if you don't know who they are?"

"Cass. I need to ask you something, mother to daughter."

I looked at her, wishing I could buy time to catch my breath. Not that by catching it I would have been able to divine where that pretty postcard or its blunt directive came from. "Sounds serious."

"I spoke with Niles about what really happened down on Henderson's land that day."

"You must have pressured him," I said, and slipped the postcard into my jacket pocket before stooping to pick up a spindly gray spike of driftwood that was perfect for a walking stick. The death of St. Francis, patron saint of birds, that was the scene depicted on the card. Quite a prescient choice of imagery, I thought.

"A little. But he knows how concerned I am, and there were so many different versions of the story I heard—"

"I could have told you myself, if you'd asked."

"Well, I didn't want to put you through it."

Under our feet the beach rocks clacked hollowly, scraping and chattering against each other. A petty argument among stones.

"Cassandra, do you have any idea who that girl was?"

"Laura Bryant? I would have thought Niles told you all about her."

"Not her, the girl you thought you saw before."

"No. I did think at the time she seemed familiar, but I don't know why."

"Was she a composite of sorts?"

"You mean like in a dream when we combine people we know into new ones?"

"Something like that."

"No, Ros. She was her own person. I swear I didn't make her up."

That gave her pause, but only for a moment. "Did she look at all like Emily?"

A jolt of recognition vaulted through me. The hanged girl, I now realized, did look like Emily Schaefer, my brother's classmate who died the year before he did. With my walking stick I knocked down a small stack of flat stones someone had piled meticulously, from largest to smallest, there in the middle of the path. Someone? Morgan or Jonah, must have been. I didn't want to think otherwise.

"I already told you. Maybe you should have asked Niles to read the transcript of my deposition, if you were so concerned about putting me through it again."

"Don't be angry with me, Cass. It's just that I'm worried sick."

"I know what you're really worried about," I said, spontaneous as a slap.

Rosalie made no reply. How could she have responded, anyway? We were the only two people who understood what unsaid words lay behind what we had just broached. We two and, I now began to fear, perhaps the man who wrote this obscene and absurd postcard, although his presence in my life made less sense to me than the hanged girl, the found girl, less sense than anything. Surely Roy Skoler could have nothing to do with this. I hadn't laid eyes on him for almost thirty years and had heard nothing about his doings.

"You're not right about that," she countered, unconvincingly. She removed her hat, gathered her hair back behind her ears, and replaced it. A familiar tic. "After hearing what happened and watching you these

past couple of weeks I wonder if you aren't headed into a really bad patch again."

"Who's to say I'm not already there?"

Covey was meant to have been our haven, but here was the confrontation we had been sidestepping for years. If we were ever to have a bond after Nep — our mediator, our family's glue — left us, we needed to brave these troubled waters. Ignoring the issue of Christopher seemed to be what both of us wanted, had always wanted, but I had to wonder if this recent confluence of events was going to make forestalling impossible. What would I have given to lie down on a tuft of beach grass here in the sun and take a nap that would last all summer.

"You really think that?"

"No, I don't know. Besides, I'm not a kid like I was then. I have more resources to work with."

"That's good to hear. Because unless you're keeping a whole world of secrets from me —"

I shook my head, though of course I had been.

"— you're not even close to being where you were those years after Christopher passed, up into your teens. I doubt you even have a clear recollection of what it was like when you ran away that time. You were gone three nights, four full days. We thought we might have lost our other baby, too."

"I was just hiding from the world."

"Near the same woods where they found Laura. Don't you remember how terrified your father and I were?"

"That was a long time ago. It's more a dream now than anything and I wouldn't mind leaving it that way."

"I wonder if you don't do a little too much wakeful dreaming for your own good."

That caught me off-guard. "We all do our best," I murmured.

"Look, Cass. I don't want anything except for you to know I'm concerned. And that you should feel free to talk to me about anything anytime. Come to me first. Open up if you need to. I'm here for you, you know."

"Thanks," I said, having no better idea how to respond to this. "I'll give what you're saying some thought."

"But I haven't really said yet what I'm saying."

"So what you're saying is—"

"Don't you think it would be a good idea for you to get some counseling while the boys are away at camp?"

"Niles made sure I saw his therapist person, and we pretty much got nowhere. Let me be frank with you. I have no intention of going to another psychiatrist, another therapist, another legalized drug merchant. There's nothing more they have to give me."

She remained quiet.

"I'm perfectly fine," I said, hoping that would end it. I knew Rosalie had come up here to be with me, and within the parameters of her own sense of motherdom she was doing the right thing—which reminded me of a saying of Nep's, *Do right because it is right,* a beautiful phrase Rosalie attributed to the Bible but really comes from Kant. I did appreciate what was unselfish in her words even as I disdained what else I knew she was subtly trying to negotiate with me.

We had stopped walking. Had made it nearly halfway around. The two houses on the other side of the island were pitched on the widest of the many sheltered coves that gave Covey its name. They were in view now, framed by tall droopy spruces. From where we stood there still seemed to be no signs of life in either. Shingled with traditional unpainted cedar and streaked dark brown from years of heavy weather, they had a crepuscular look, like two petrified dinosaurs. A humble jetty reached into the lapping water where some buoys bobbed, those of lobstermen willing to come out this far. I saw that the cormorant's skiff hadn't risen with the tide. Gulls squawked overhead, birds I always thought of as malicious, their yellow beaks stained with that red spot like blood. Seagulls were supposedly the souls of dead mariners, and today I believed it.

"You know that's not true," my mother said. "You're not fine."

"I'm clearheaded enough to know I don't need more tedious therapy sessions and designer antidepressants."

"It's good advice you're ignoring."

"Besides, I don't have time for such self-indulgence. It doesn't look like the boys are going to be away at camp after all. They said in no uncertain terms they didn't want to go."

"And you let them make that decision for themselves?"

"I'm not going to shoehorn them into going somewhere they don't want, in the name of making them have fun."

Rosalie walked along beside me for a time, dispirited. "I only wish you were more religious. Having faith, believing, would help you more than any human therapies."

Not wanting to tread into this subject, I did say, "I have faith. It's my own kind of faith. But I don't *not* believe. You ought to know that."

She said nothing.

Hoping to keep the peace, I finished, "Listen, I know you're worried for good reason. When we go back down I'll look into it. No promises, hear, except to give it serious thought and maybe have a conversation with somebody."

"Fair enough." She brightened a little. Of course she saw through my attempt to mollify her but knew when enough was enough.

We were about to pass by Mrs. Milgate's house, the smallest on the island.

"She's away, seems," said Rosalie, noting the closed curtains. "That's unusual for Angela. Bless her, I hope she's all right. She's the last person on the island who knew your uncle Henry from the old days."

I wanted to tell my mother about that burned-syrupy smell of baked beans but thought the better of it, not wanting to wander back into the quicksand of her concerns, saying instead, "Should we go knock?"

"You know how much she covets her privacy. I don't think dropping in unannounced would sit too well with her," answered Rosalie as we hiked toward the farther cottage, whose sunned linen curtains were also drawn. I wondered, Had they been drawn before? I couldn't remember. It occurred to me, the sometime outsider, what a dangerous choice it was to be a hermit. Your trade-off for privacy was to thwart the company of others who might help when you most needed it.

"Are you sure we shouldn't go back and check on Mrs. Milgate?"

"When Angela wants us to come by, she always gets in touch, lets us know through Mr. McEachern," which put an end to it.

Before our exchange about my suspect mental health, I was tempted to broach with Rosalie my curious encounter with the little girl and her grinning dog. Now I knew I had to keep that to myself as well, if for no other reason than not wanting to be accused of further delusion. I consoled myself with a new theory that the girl might have been part of a boating party that put to shore. Perhaps she had meandered away, went scouting while her parents slept off their lunch on the beach back by one of the hive of small inlets where they'd moored. Smoked a cigarette or two. Yes, that was it. This made such sense I couldn't believe I hadn't thought of it before. No phantom, she was just a girl given to taciturnity, shy, like I had been when I was her age.

When we rounded a cliffed corner that would take us along the western edge of Covey and back toward home, we saw a colorful flotilla of sailboats, some with orange sails, others red, turquoise, bright lime-green. Must have been a race. They were all going in the same direction, half a mile out. A lustrous mirage flying across the wide water. They were every bit as bright and blurry as the girl had been, I assured myself.

Rosalie said, "I have one more thing I want to talk about before we get back."

"That sounds serious, too," smiling in a vain attempt to lighten things a little.

"I'm afraid it is. Niles's wife came by to visit me the other day."

I didn't like the way this was headed any more than the previous business. I waited for Rosalie to continue.

"She's worried about you and Niles."

"Poor woman," I said, wondering for just a passing instant whether she would have been capable of writing the warning on the postcard. Unlike Niles and myself, but very much like my mother, Melanie was a regular churchgoer, a devout believer. The card did have religious imagery on it. But then I pictured Melanie Hubert, whose faults were

no more serious than being overly sweet, a little too convinced of her own goodness. Still, in her darkest hour, she wouldn't have been capable of sending such an ugly threat, would she? "You know Lucretius's saying *Fear begets gods*—"

"I know it because you've told me a hundred times. You also know I couldn't disagree with him more strongly."

"Melanie's a case of fear begetting devils. I'd set her straight if she wanted to ask."

"You'd already left for Maine when she came over."

"All the more reason for her to stay calm. Niles will always be one of my best friends, and neither she nor anybody else is going to change that. But Melanie has no need to be worrying about me and Niles."

We walked most of the rest of the way home in silence. No doubt I was deluding myself to think Rosalie was satisfied. But despite the conversation's downward turns, I hoped the air was cleared between us, at least on a few thorny subjects, so we could now continue our time together without outside distraction.

Early afternoon. The tide going out. Some sandpipers were mincing in the shallows ahead of us. We rambled past a dead horseshoe crab, which Rosalie taught me during one of our walks around Covey years ago is not a crab at all. More akin to a spider, she'd said. An arthropod, not a crustacean. And while the Lord's given them three hundred and fifty million years to learn better, they still swim upside down, clumsy as sots, truffling for sea worms and bottom grubs. For all their primeval armor and a sharp tail like a fencer's foil, horseshoes were about as threatening as a clump of seaweed. Nep hadn't been the only one to try to teach me about the teeming world. I needed to remember that.

Interrupting both our reveries, I said, "Thanks for talking with me, Rosalie. I know it's not easy, and I know you care. It means a lot."

"You're my daughter," she said, simply.

It went unsaid that the pact about Chris, that old concealment so many years silted under that I sometimes doubted its ultimate veracity, need not enter into the dialogue. Neither of us wanted to look at

it, think about it. Christopher needed, in his way, to stay dead in order for us to stay sane.

The keeper's cottage was in sight now. Smoke rose from the fire pit, wafting our way. Bracken air hovered above the beds of beached kelp left exposed to the sun, their blanket of protective sea pulled back by the fingers of the tide. Three figures, our men, were making their way down from the house to the fire they had built. One waved to us, then all of them did and we waved back.

17

THIS PACT ABOUT Christopher's past wasn't one I pondered often. A year might go by and only the quickest disquieting flicker of it flew through my head, like one of those shooting stars that drew their ephemeral lines down the black sky the night he died. It was as if my secret with Rosalie were shut inside a metal safebox, pad-locked, then left out in the rain so long that it had rusted solid. There was no reason to harp on it just now, whether or not Rosalie fretted that my monster might unhinge it, as it were, and crack the box open for all to see. Nothing and no one had opened it in times past. For all the doubts I had about some of my mother's convictions, I was loyal to her.

Toward Christopher, too, I still felt an abiding fidelity. He and I shared so many good times together, and I needed to tend to these most, like heirloom roses in the front bed of a memorial garden. It was Christopher who taught me to tie my shoes. Chris who helped me memorize my multiplication tables. Chris was the one who showed me where birds' nests were secreted away in trees and the right way to climb up high to see them. When I had chicken pox, Christopher read to me from my children's books for hours on end and cooled my fore-head with a wet washcloth, fearless about getting sick himself.

Nor had Rosalie misremembered my having been in the woods above Henderson's before. But she barely knew the half of it. Once, she and Nep left me in Christopher's care when they had to spend a whole day and late into the night in the city attending—hard to imagine—a funeral in the morning and a wedding in the afternoon. The reception was to run late, so they instructed Chris not to leave me unattended. There was plenty of food and soda in the refrigerator, and he already knew how to light the oven to heat up the casserole she had prepared for our dinner. He needed to make sure I had enough to eat and got to bed by ten.

—I'm not a baby, I protested.

—I'm not a babysitter, he agreed.

—Don't you two wander too far from home, she admonished him.

—And I don't want your friends in the house while we're out, understood?

We understood the second rule, but the minute they left, Christopher began stuffing his pack with food and told me to get my boots on because we were going to spend the day being Indians in the cliffs. A whole day with my brother to myself? I was thrilled. The cliffs were sacred terrain to him, which made it all the more special.

This was the year before four-wheelers became the sole means of transportation, so we hiked for a couple of hours off the beaten track so as not to be spotted by any of our parents' acquaintances, making our way along a hogback thick with pines until we were finally close to the cliffs. Everyone Chris ever brought here, including me that day, had to go through quite a ritual of induction. Adults were never to know about this secret hideout. To make sure they didn't, all visitors—there weren't but a few—were blindfolded and led by a rope tied around their waists up and down some rugged, trippy land. It wasn't a short hike, especially blindfolded. Once visitors were out of sight of any recognizable landmarks, they were unmasked in woods that looked just like other forested acreage in our area, except for the caved cliffs, purported by my brother to be old Indian dwellings. The idea was that only Christopher would know the hideout's precise location.

When he removed my blindfold, I yipped with excitement. He was right. This was a perfect place for some Indian families to reside. It perched on the westerly side of a steep and treacherous ravine, at the base of which snaked a creek where they must have hunted deer and rabbits and fished brook trout and had lots of fresh drinking water. One of the caves in particular had a blackened ceiling which, even in retrospect, made my brother's theory plausible. Certainly, someone had wintered here long ago.

—Now we're Indians, too, I said.

—Get some kindling, Pocahontas, he commanded in something meant to sound like the voice of a warrior, and soon we had a small fire going. We pierced hot dogs on the ends of branches he sharpened with his knife and ate our lunch in fine style.

—What's a funeral? I asked. —I mean, I know what it is. But have you ever been to one?

—A funeral's where they lock the dead guy in the last room he'd ever see alive if he wasn't dead. And all his friends hold hands in a circle around him and they say nice stuff about him and bawl a bunch. And then they put him in the cold ground and that's where he lives until God comes down from his cloud and gets him out.

—And then what?

—Then he's in heaven.

—What happens there?

—Don't you listen when we're in church?

I shrugged.

—Nobody knows what happens exactly, except you can't cry. No tears in heaven, Cass, because it's a place where nobody remembers how to cry.

—Oh, I said, wondering whether you would be able to remember how to laugh up there in heaven, if you didn't remember how to cry.

—Now, little sister. Are you ready for me to go capture some bad men from another tribe?

My heart sank a little. I knew what this meant, however clever Chris thought he was being. —Sure, I said, putting on a smile for him.

—Good. Keep this fire going, but don't let it get too big, hear?

Within half an hour he returned with Ben Gilchrist, Roy Skoler, Emily Schaefer, and another girl, all of them blindfolded and holding on to a rope that was tied around the waist of the person in front of them. It was quite a sight. Christopher never looked more triumphant.

—Look who I caught trespassing our tribal lands, Cass, he said, barely containing himself. I saw that Roy Skoler had already taken off his blindfold and was looking at me with those unflinching eyes of his. Roy had bottles of beer in his rucksack and a pack of cigarettes. Emily and the other girl brought marshmallows and graham crackers, which they immediately offered me, both of them taking it upon themselves to mother Christopher's kid sis. I never saw Ben or Christopher smoke before, but there they were, coughing and pounding their chests as they did.

—Peace pipes, Chris whispered to me. —Old Iroquois custom.

The party was more fun than I liked to admit, I who'd selfishly wanted my brother all to myself. The girls were full of questions about what I was studying in school, which movie stars I liked best, what sorts of things did I enjoy doing on weekends. They toasted s'mores and cooked more hot dogs. As the afternoon slid toward evening, the sky shifting toward an eggplant hue, they disappeared in twos and threes into the woods. Left on my own by a fire burning down to hissing coals, I wondered if they were ever coming back. I both did and didn't know what they were doing, but it didn't matter so long as Christopher said everything was all right and would take me home pretty soon.

Emily Schaefer was the only one of them who wasn't drinking, I noticed. At one juncture she and I were alone in front of the fire. She had come back from the woods all disheveled and with a dazed look on her pretty face and pine needles caught in her hair.

—Were you wrestling? I asked.

She hesitated. —That's right.

—Did you win?

She looked at me, I'll never forget, and gently, delicately brushed

my cheek with the back of her fingers. The spontaneous act of affection from one girl to another. —I don't think so, she said.

—Well, who won?

Emily shook her head. —I must look a mess. Would you mind picking the leaves and stuff off my back? I can't go home like this.

While she sat cross-legged and poked the coals with a stick, prompting them to flare again, I kneeled behind her, brushing the needles and dirt off and combing her hair with my fingers.

—I hear your father is a diviner, she said. —That he can find things that are hidden.

—That's right, I said, proudly.

—My father thinks he's cracked but doesn't cause any harm.

This made me wince, but even that young I'd begun to expect such comments. She was waiting for a response, so I said, —What do you think?

—Well, I think the world's a strange place, she answered.

—I guess so.

—Oh, it is, Cassandra. You'll see when you grow up. Meantime, thanks for making me look presentable. You're a good friend, she said, surprising and delighting me with this declaration. To this day I wonder whether we mightn't have become real friends, were she still alive.

Everyone loudly complained when Chris announced they had to submit to being blindfolded again in order to be led back out. I got to tie the blindfolds, so I didn't mind at all until my brother tied mine so tightly it made my head hurt, his breath stinking as he did, and led the protesting group back the way we had come. Roy Skoler was behind me in the single file and I remember him muttering drunken nonsense that might as well have been some foreign language. He touched my hair once or twice and jerked hard on the rope, trying to make me trip. Though he scared me, I never let on, doing my best to ignore him. Besides my brother, I decided in my blinking blindness that the only one of the group I truly liked was Emily. She had the face of a sad saint, I thought. And when she was nearby, she'd taken it upon herself to make sure I was glad to be there with them. Amazingly, my brother

tucked me in bed by ten that night and even read me to sleep after swearing his sister to absolute and irrevocable secrecy about the activities of the day.

—Princess and chief must observe total silence, or die.

He needn't have threatened me on pain of death, as I never tattled. I probably idolized him even more for his crazy daring.

For all that, were I forced to face facts, I would have to admit that my venerated Christopher had never given my mother, or me, quite as much cause for the pride we always felt toward him. Other stories I knew about Chris—other things he allowed me to witness because he probably considered me too naive to recognize them for what they were—never diminished the adoration I felt for my brother. Over the years there were nights when I lay in bed, face-down in my childhood pillow, crying enough to make heaven drown, wishing he were still around rather than in that "last room" he spoke of. He calculated his sister's love and correctly relied on my hero worship to secure my conspiratorial silence.

18

THANKS FOR BEING so good with the boys," I said, sitting beside Nep in high grass and ferns, our backs against the sun-warmed white bricks of the lighthouse the day after Rosalie and I talked our way around the island.

"Nothing easier."

"I know they can be a little exhausting at times, with all that back-and-forthing they love to do, finishing each other's ideas, piling it on."

"Like we used to when you were—" searching for the word, "short."

"Young, yes. I guess we did at that."

"Feels good to be with them. With you, too."

"Idem," I said, reviving a term from our old code language. Meant *same here* and dated back to when I was first trying to learn Latin.

Some of what we spoke about was in words. Some was communicated with our eyes. Some came through the fragile bony flesh of the hands we held, unabashed, an old man and a woman who felt every last one of her thirty-six years. Our conversation was similar in tone but different in content from what we discussed during that Fourth of July. This wasn't another turning. I wanted no sixth turning. Indeed, if I could reverse some of those five turnings, my life would be better.

Nep told me he'd heard about both my visioned and found girls.

"People say — provoking things," he explained, pausing again to capture the words needed to complete his thought. "Me in the room with them."

"And they don't realize you're listening?"

"Not so much."

"So you've become the dreaded fly on the wall."

"Flies don't hear as well as I do."

"I'll bet you've been hearing them say your daughter's crazy, gone off the deep end what with her hanged girl and all."

After a moment, he said, "Why do you care?"

"I only really care what you think."

His gaze held mine so long I finally averted my eyes, looking down at the glistening grass where a row of tenacious ants marched not far from my crossed feet. Nep tightened his grip on my hand.

A little chagrined by my next question even before I asked it, I still was desperate to know. "Has anything like what happened to me at Henderson's ever happened to you?"

"Not the same."

"So you have seen something similar, is what you mean?"

"Everyone has. Even dogs, cats, birds."

I wondered if he had quite understood me, but his lucidity this day, in this sea-strong air and sitting on this piece of familiar earth, was unquestionable. Feeling a little like I was imposing some makeshift Platonic dialogue on my poor father, who never would have willingly played the role of Socrates, I asked, "Why is it that people, unlike dogs and cats and birds, laugh at those who see something they don't?"

"Because people, unlike animals, have a great — capacity for contempt."

Here his articulation was in full swing. His words made me recognize that my mentor absolved me, in his way, of feeling guilty about how most people had taken, or mistaken, what I witnessed in Henderson's valley. This came as an enormous relief. If I could accept his absolution, it would be a giant step toward pulling myself back into my own life.

I looked down at the column of ants, admiring them as they streamed ceaselessly through their intricate jungle of blades and pebbles, what had to be a tedious tract for them to negotiate, but for me represented a single stride. The comparative nature of everything, I mused. One man's mile was another's inch, one's truth another's fallacy. Was Rosalie's insistence on there being a god, a holy spirit, a virgin mother, an only-begotten son who died for our sins before being resurrected—was it any more discountable than my own appalling vision, and the forevisions and divining I'd wanted people to believe?

I loved myths. Taught them to others. But I cherished my gods as ideas, symbols, and I knew it. So was I among the contemptuous rather than the faithful? Our planet was roiled by believers who despised other believers who didn't believe what they believed. It was so apocalyptically palpable one could feel the world quivering with the frustration of it all. Was I any better than the next scorner?

"Are you saying I shouldn't worry about what they think one way or the other?"

"Why should you?"

"But you always cared about reputation when you were divining."

"I made a mistake," he said. I waited for him to continue, but he just sat, looking curiously across the overgrown meadow toward one of the old stone outbuildings, another structure on Covey I warned the twins to stay away from. A nice mansion for clever mice. Must have been a supply shed at some point, or maybe a large root cellar. The shingled roof had partly caved in. Most of its windows were long since blown out, leaving it open to the weather, though one pane remained intact, if ajar, and in it was a reflection of the lighthouse.

"Yes?" I glanced in the direction of the shed.

He rose to his feet, quietly, letting go of my hand.

"Nep, what's the matter?"

"The not-friend in the cloud I'm seeing."

"The what?"

"Who are you?" he insisted, wading through the grasses, his finger-

tips brushing the waving green spear tips that resembled an unmowed field of delicate June hay.

"Who is—Nep, where are you going?"

There was nothing to do but follow him. Our Platonic dialogue had come to an abrupt end.

"All right," he not-quite-answered.

I stayed close behind, wondering if this was one of his fugues or, as Rosalie called them, his *walkaways*. His disease suddenly extracting him from the everyday world to send him on some phantom mission he believed needed to be accomplished. Get somewhere he didn't really have to go. Or worse, where there was no getting to.

When we reached the stone hut, he peered inside through one of the empty windows. I did, too, alongside him. A damp cool earthen scent gave from the darkness, the ripe still air of a cavern. A fearsome-looking black and white spider, an argiope, had spun herself a huge oval web protected from wind and weather and was perched, waiting at its flexing center for prey. He took a couple of steps away from the shed and peered at the glass pane with great intensity. I looked at it, too, but saw only clouds moving across its dirty face.

"What is it?" I asked. "What not-friend?"

"What do you want?" not addressing me but turning around and gazing toward the top of the lighthouse, shielding his eyes from the sun with a saluting hand. "There," and pointed at the iron railing that enclosed the gallery, the catwalk used in the old days as a lookout post. Something white and fluttery dangled, hard to see, as we were both looking directly into the sun. With great purpose, he strode back up the rise to the door at the base of the lighthouse, fumbled in his pocket, and pulled out his set of keys, one of which fit the padlock.

"Dad?" squinting upward into the glare, then back at him.

Without a word, he opened the metal door, entered the gloom of the tower, and began climbing the circular staircase. My duty now was to make sure he didn't get hurt. As we crept our way along, hugging the curved and shadowed walls of stone, I found myself hoping against hope that he had seen the same girl I did a few days before. The mute

girl with her black smiling dog. If together we saw a mutual specter it would change my life then and there. My gravity would return and I'd be able to believe in myself more than I had in months, years. After all, I hadn't told Nep anything about her.

He climbed steadily, not saying a word. I trailed close behind him. Some edges of the stone steps had crumbled, and fresh chips and fragments of granite lay loose on them. We both slipped and caught our balance and I again said, "Dad?" But there was no stopping the man. Another door, this one unlocked, opened onto the gallery. From echoing darkness into windy light we emerged. The island spread beneath us. Beyond the roof of the keeper's cottage was an unimpeded view of the ocean. The gnawing, sizzling waves striking the shore were audible. Sea birds flew below us along the coast, the tops of their feathery wings reflecting sunlight.

Nep caught his breath and made his way nimbly around the gallery, clutching the wobbly handrail until he reached the place where a rope was tied to one of the iron palings. Grabbing it, he began to pull hard, hand over hand, much as a fisherman might haul in his line to see what he had caught.

A crude figure, fabricated from old mattress ticking and stuffed sheets, emerged over the railing and flopped like the rag doll it was onto the gallery floor right at my feet. Eyes, nose, mouth, ears were painted in black as if by some child on the oblong and misshapen cloth head. Its arms were open-ended tubes of sackcloth crammed with rags. The face was without any clear expression, but straight lines that curled up at the ends on either side of the head were meant to suggest the hair of a woman. In her arms she clasped another doll, which I recognized at once, my own from childhood. Millicent, looking tatty and wind-bedraggled, had been stitched onto the breast of the grotesque figure which, I now saw, was hung around the neck with the rope. I wanted to scream but swallowed it back.

My father and I looked at each other. There really wasn't anything either of us could say. I tore Millicent free from the mannequin arms that clung to her and held her to my own chest, tears flooding my eyes.

If whoever he was, the person who arranged this, wanted me to leave him alone, he wasn't making it easy for me to oblige him.

We discovered in the watch room of the lighthouse, where the broken Fresnel lamp mirrors faced blindly outward toward the four horizons, another cigarette butt and a crumpled piece of waxed paper. He had gone about his business calmly enough that he had even taken time for a smoke and sandwich. How many times had this intruder trespassed Covey?

"Nothing about this to Rosalie and the boys," I rasped more harshly than I meant to.

"Nothing," he said, turning away from the mannequin on the gallery floor and heading back down the tower.

"It's very important that you understand me, Nep. Are you sure you do?" as we reemerged at the bottom of the stairs and padlocked the door again.

"I understand—nothing about this to them. Don't worry."

For a quick, weird blink of time I had to wonder if Nep hadn't done this himself. He possessed a key to the padlock. He'd been caught on his way to Mendes for some inexplicable reason and might have kidnapped Millicent on another foray in which he hadn't been found missing. Nep was the one who drew my attention to the effigy dangling from the railing far above in the first place. Perhaps this was all some practical joke—inept and upsetting, but benevolent in design—that he hoped might give me second thoughts about my original vision of the hanged girl. I could easily discount such poor judgment as impaired mental function over which he had no control. It would be nothing for me to forgive him, I knew. So I asked. "That wasn't your little prank, was it now?"

His confused look put this idea to rest.

After everyone else had gone to bed that night, I told Rosalie it seemed to me a good idea if we all caravanned back to New York together. She reluctantly agreed, saying maybe we could come back to the island in August, if the stars aligned themselves properly. My sense was that she capitulated to leaving so abruptly in the hope I intended to

seek the help she'd proposed. I wasn't sure one way or the other what to do. All I knew was that it was time to leave Covey, the sooner the better.

Rosalie did have one request. Said her heart was set on all of us going to the summit of Cadillac Mountain to see the sun rise. This involved getting Jonah and Morgan up at around three in the morning so we could catch a predawn ride with Mr. McEachern over to the island. The twins had been there once before, but that time, through a series of mishaps, stops to rest, to massage leg cramps, to look at a flight of peregrine falcons—false sighting—we missed daybreak by a good half an hour. Cadillac, named for the French explorer who once owned all of Mount Desert and then went on to found Detroit, was the highest point on the eastern seaboard. The place where one could be among the very first in America to glimpse dawn.

After packing our things, we went to bed early on our last night. I didn't catch one wink. The image of Millicent in the crudely fabricated arms of that effigy would not leave my mind, no matter how many times I told myself there was nothing to be done about it. At three we were up and dressed. After closing the cottage, we hiked by flashlight in the bracing ocean air down the path to the dock with our bags.

The sky was loaded with stars. Blizzarded by them. The breeze off the water was crisp and hard. We could hear Mr. McEachern's motor idling even before we could see his boat tied up, all lit like a toppled Christmas tree. When we got to Northeast Harbor, his wife, Loreen, met us at the pier with hot coffee and cocoa, and we crammed into the McEacherns' station wagon and drove the park loop to the mountain. Rosalie drank hot chocolate and the boys and I downed the scalding coffee, trying not to spill it on our laps as the car bounced along in the dark. We parked near the summit. The sky was already brightening. I took Nep's arm and we walked up the path through sleeping tables of pink granite, now and again shouting ahead to the boys, telling them to slow down.

None of us wanted to miss it, and none of us did. Jonah and Morgan were at the bald plateau top waiting impatiently with Loreen McEach-

ern and Ros when Nep, Mr. McEachern, and I finally made the peak. Knotty threads of clouds wound around the horizon like bunting above the Atlantic before us and Frenchman's Bay behind. Some were thin and long, trails of brilliant crystal afloat in the sky at our feet. Others bunched upon themselves, becoming incandescent in the new light.

Speechless, we were literally on top of the immediate world. Then, the first flash fed over the burning lip of the sea.

"Look!" Jonah shouted.

"Here it comes," cried Morgan. "See that, Nep?"

I glimpsed my father's face as light, gold and orange and pink, illuminated its every crag. A sunsetting man watching the sun rise. I wanted to linger in the moment, but it all went by so fast. Now it was dark, now dawn. Glancing at the others, I saw the twins seemed ablaze, as did my mother, who stood between them. The glow caught in Mr. McEachern's beard and Loreen's white hair.

Rosalie pointed. "Look, there's Covey."

The wind began to whip up a little as it often does at sunrise.

"It's wearing a cloud hat," said Nep.

And it was. A shroud of white had settled on our island.

"It's so beautiful," I said, trying not to wonder what other nightmares might be hidden beneath that innocent morning fog.

"*Divine* is the word for it," said Rosalie.

I looked down, then away from her. The pink undulant granite of Cadillac seemed like the brain of some ossified beast, the Earth's brain, dried out where it was exposed here, covered with lime-green and purplish lichen.

"It's just the world, is all. What more do you want?" said Nep.

Rosalie walked over to us and put her arms around her husband's waist and mine. We watched for a time in silence, none of us moving. The sun had become so blindingly golden, such a radiant perfection, that despite my agreement with Nep's thought, I couldn't fairly contradict Rosalie, either, or dismiss that loaded word of hers.

Words, I thought. The word *divine,* in particular. It seemed my life had been locked in a chess match with that one. Nothing about the

diviner Cassandra was divine, not when she had access to such private hells. Except for being part of nature. Nature's the only divinity.
This was what I told myself as the sun now fully crested the horizon.
I couldn't help but wonder, despite being moved by all this beauty, in
what mad corner he was hiding down there in that divine expanse.

19

EVEN BEFORE NEP and I discovered the hanged effigy holding Millicent, I knew I couldn't stay on Covey Island forever.
The cottage couldn't shelter me. The lighthouse that once guided ships
through darkness and peril could not protect me. The absence of a telephone failed to keep voices at bay. As isolated as our beloved island was,
my family could not shield me from anyone who wanted to slip ashore.
I could no more hide from this taunting and elusive stalker—not
to mention from myself—than my patron saint diviner Martine de
Berthereau could hide from her nemesis, Cardinal Richelieu.

Not that the house on Mendes Road, which had clearly been broken
into sometime after we left for Covey, would feel safer than the island.
Quite the opposite. Yet I knew it was imperative that I take a stand, as
unbowed and unbothered as I could manage. Also, it seemed essential
I make two visits of my own—one by arrangement, the other surrep-
titious. I needed to go meet Laura Bryant, glean some sense of what
caused her to run away, learn if there wasn't more to her story than
she offered Niles and the others, perhaps even discover why I divined
her in the first place, if that was, in fact, what happened. And casting
my wariness to the winds, I had to return to Henderson's valley, too,
trespassing this time around rather than dowsing the lonely place on

commission. What I hoped to find there was nothing. Absolutely nothing at all. But unless I went, I couldn't silence the forevisioner voice
inside that hinted otherwise.

Our family caravan arrived back home in upstate New York by late
afternoon. The newly tuned pickup ran like some strong old race-
horse, or solid dray horse anyway, that had never lost its feel for the
track. I thought, If only there were roadside repair shops where we
could drive ourselves in and request a personal tune-up, a spiritual
overhaul.

As we pulled off Mendes into the pebble driveway, I asked the twins,
"Why don't you two begin unpacking the truck while I go inside and
check on the house?"

"We'll go first," said Jonah.

"Right, that man might be in there."

"Or another girl hanging from the rafters in the kitchen."

They were half-mocking, half-serious.

"You can't," I said, adopting the cavalier tones in their voices, even
though I felt a queasy churning in the pit of my stomach. Not a feeling
I was accustomed to, or one with which I had much patience.

"Why not?" Morgan asked.

"Because I have the key and you don't."

Both laughed. "Since when do you need a key to get into our
house?"

"Got that right," Jonah agreed with his brother. "Everybody knows
this is the easiest place to break into in Little Eddy."

"I'm still going in and you're still staying out," I said. "And tomorrow we're getting new locks. Now start unpacking already."

Inside, the rooms were preternaturally still. Even the afternoon
songs of all the birds were stifled until I raised windows in the kitchen
and living room downstairs to get some fresh air through. Nothing
seemed tampered with, nothing even minutely disturbed. The creaking
stairs — a sound I had always been fond of before, its small music com-
fortingly familiar — frazzled me as I climbed to the second floor. Tread-
ing down the hall toward the bedrooms, indeed now making more

noise than I normally would, as if my pathetic racket would frighten anyone hidden in a dark corner, I noticed I was breathing through my mouth in shallow gasps, my tongue dry as stale bread. So ridiculous, I thought. It's not like any real harm, any injury, had come to anyone except in my cruel imagination. Calm down, for crying out loud.

Other than Millicent missing from her usual place—leaning back against the pillows of my bed, legs splayed and arms open, her red hair wildly flying on either side of her button-eyed head—everything appeared just as I had left it. I looked in the boys' rooms, the closets, bathrooms, my small study. Scrutinized every window on both floors. Even checked the attic. Once more it seemed as if a creature with wings had been at work, although this time there was no chance of my having hallucinated. After I told the boys they could bring the luggage in, I furtively put Millicent back on my bed where she belonged. I was relieved, if mildly confused, his intrusion hadn't gone beyond the simple theft of an artifact from my girlhood. That, and the industrious task of spiriting her all the way north to the lighthouse gallery. Whoever did this was not bereft of energy.

The first call I made after we settled in was not to Niles, but to Paul Mosley, the baseball coach. Exhausted though I was from our early morning and long drive, I urgently needed to make as swift a return to normalcy as possible, and the boys—regardless of their laudable, loving impulse to protect me—needed to get back on track. Mosley was something of a Darwinian, I knew. Whatever made the team fittest. The best able to outwit and survive the opposition. And he adored Morgan. Plans for my son to go to sports camp had changed, I told him. Was there any possibility he could still participate in the local summer league, even though he hadn't gone through registration and tryouts?

"Best shortstop in his age division? I think we can dream up a way to get him in."

Morgan was, at first, heroically reluctant. "I thought the idea was we were going to take care of you," he said, putting a stoic face on it while barely containing his excitement at the prospect of playing after all.

"Mr. Mosley's agreed to relax the rules—"

"No way. Moses broke a rule?"

Their nickname for the coach, because he taught them to live religiously by the laws of the game. Called them the *Team Commandments*. Thou shalt not steal anything except bases. Thou shalt covet thy neighbor's score. Thou shalt not bear false witness except when arguing with the umpire. A Christian Darwinian.

"Maybe bent them a little so you could join late."

"That rocks," said Morgan, pumping his fist in the air.

"Off the charts," Jonah agreed, after a small hesitation.

"You sure about this, Mom?"

"*Mom—?*" Jonah asked Morgan, rolling his eyes.

Morgan, not looking at his brother, corrected himself. "Like, you're good with this?"

"It's not as if you're going to be away twenty-four-seven. You can save me during your off hours."

"You'll come to games?" Morgan asked.

"As many as you'll let us," I said, smiling at Jonah, who seemed a little lost.

Not hard to understand why. For Morgan, Covey was going to have been little more than a brief detour on the road to a version of the summer he'd been promised all along, but Jonah had no team to join. Math had never taken sufficient hold in our local consciousness to have inspired much by way of summer clubs. He couldn't even get his own hapless mother to successfully solve a sudoku puzzle with him—a game at which he excelled—let alone convince a single soul among his peers to play. What I meant to propose to him as an alternative went against sworn promises I had made myself, but new circumstances pleaded new ideas. Whether Jonah would be responsive or not was another thing, and, I had to admit, hanging out with his mother wasn't quite the same as swimming in a camp lake with a bevy of boys his own age. I waited for a moment when he and I were alone to run my idea past him.

"Jonah," I called out into the backyard not long after Morgan had his news and left to shag balls—the endless vitality of youth—with a

couple of friends at a nearby field until the last of the sun died. "What are you doing?"

"Trying to fix this imbecile lawn mower," he grumbled. "Like have you noticed the grass?"

"Got a moment?"

When he came inside, I flashed back to the morning, long ago, when Nep asked me a similar question. "You have anything on the agenda tomorrow?"

"Let me check my book," turning through invisible pages on his open palm and pretending to scan them. "Guess not," he said, then closed his hand.

"Now you do, if you want."

I told him I had listened to the phone messages and was offered a job dowsing for, of all people, Partridge, at the hatchery. I suspected, but didn't say aloud, that this was sympathy work—Partridge was loyal—and if anybody else had inquired I would probably have declined. But witching his familiar grounds might reconnect me with myself. Besides, I needed the money. What I did say was that I wanted to know if Jonah would be willing to join me.

"In case you run into any more dead people?"

"Enough talk about that. You coming or not?"

He hesitated. "You going to show me how you do it?"

"If you're there you'll see for yourself, won't you?"

"I mean, are you going to let me try?" not missing a beat.

"We'll see what happens."

When we retired that night, I remained restless in spite of my road-weariness and the anxious homecoming. Much to the boys' bewilderment, I had secured the seldom-used side door downstairs with a chair jammed under the knob. Its lock, buried beneath coats of paint, was stuck, and I was sure it was this door that had offered our intruder his access to the house. Through my half-opened window and its curtains drawn tight, I could hear the shush of the occasional passing car on Mendes Road and the rustle of leaves in the trees. I wondered whether I was really going to let Jonah attempt to dowse. Wondered how to

explain to Niles about Millicent without setting off a series of top-pling dominoes that might lead to even more problems. Wondered what that vague creaking was downstairs, that mild twitch in the floor joists, knowing full well that these were the subtle percussives of an old house that had been settling for a hundred years and would still be making the same harmless sounds a hundred years hence.

I finally phoned Niles after breakfast the next morning and arranged to see him later in the day.

"The bench under the white pines, far end of the lake," he agreed.

My second call was to the local locksmith to outfit the doors and downstairs windows with new locks and latches, after which Jonah and I dropped Morgan off at the ball field and then drove out to Partridge's hatchery.

A warm azure sky. The air thinner than what we'd been breathing in Maine, drier. We listened to music on the radio, some candied country stuff on one of the few stations we could receive static-free in these rolling mountains. We were quiet. Whenever Morgan wasn't around to trade competitive verbal repartee with his brother, Jonah reverted to the same outsider's reticence his mother had displayed through most of her youth. I deeply, fiercely, and completely loved both my sons, but long before Jonah set foot on Partridge's land that day I had understood that he—for better or worse—was more like his mother than Morgan. Since I never really knew James Boyd, I had no concept of whether or not Morgan shared traits with his biological father. Early on, I had determined not to torture myself with inscrutable questions like this. Nor would I, by proxy, torture my twins. But this morning I did allow myself to accept what I had known for years. Though Jonah harbored much more potential than to become just another Brooks diviner, I knew there was no point in standing between him and this aspect of his heritage. He was destined to go to college—both boys were—I was convinced. I didn't want either of them to be stymied in this rural community forever if they desired a different kind of life. Wanted to see them spread their wings. Still, it was going to be interesting to walk in Nep's shoes this morning and witness Jonah in mine.

Partridge probably looked like an old man from the day he was born. One of those people who has an antique demeanor from crib to crypt. Even so, he had aged eons since last I saw him at an Independence Day party he came to a couple of years back. It wasn't so much his majestic bald pate or his muttonchop sideburns, whiter than a trout's gills. It was more about how he moved. Glacially slow, top-heavy on a pair of slim pins, he strode with a painful limp across the flat from his house to where we parked, hand extended and a kindly frown on his face. A frown that would have been merely a frown but for the smiling eyes and pronounced crow's-feet at their corners.

"Good of you to come," he said.

"Good of you to ask me. I'm profoundly grateful."

Partridge only harrumphed.

"I should have phoned ahead, but you said to drop by whenever I could. This is my son Jonah."

"We've met," shaking the man's slab of a hand.

"So," Partridge said, looking at me as he asked precisely what I hoped he wouldn't. "This's the next Brooks diviner?"

"Don't think so, no," I said at the same time Jonah said, "You never know," our two same-sounding last syllables landing right on top of each other.

Partridge was amused. "At least you disagree in harmony." He chuckled, maybe at his own cleverness, then just like that the grin faded and he looked ancient again.

I fully expected him to bring up the doings on Henderson's land, but instead he got right into talking about his job. Maybe he hadn't heard, or didn't care, either of which was fine by me. Turned out he was expanding and needed two more wells. His granddaughter had recently gotten married and planned to build a house farther up the road, as her husband was going to join the hatchery business. "They got it marked out with stakes where they want to site. Opposite that old apple orchard across the pavement. You want me to come with you?"

"I can find it," I said, grateful this turned out to be real, not contrived

charity work. Also that Jonah and I would be by ourselves. "We'll go see what there is to see and come back to let you know."

"Good luck there, Jonah," he said, gnarling one of his eyes into what was meant to be a conspiratorial wink.

We walked along the shoulder of the road.

"Don't I need a rabbit's foot or something to do this right?"

"Nep sometimes carries a little bottle of water in his back pocket, at least he says it's water. To encourage the spirits. He calls it priming the pump. I don't do anything like that myself, but everybody's got their own way of going about it."

I had a lightweight backpack with everything in it I would need. My knife, a thermos of coffee, peanut butter and marmalade sandwiches, a roll of bright blue flagging tape, a small sharp hatchet with its leather sheath snapped on tight. The blade end of the hatchet I used for cutting marker stakes and the hammer end for driving them into the ground.

"I like him," Jonah said as he took off his sweatshirt and tied it around his waist. "Seems copacetic."

Copacetic. Where does he get these words? "He is."

"How about you?"

"How about me what?"

"You copacetic?"

There was no dissembling possible when Jonah was around. The boy was already a diviner. Beneath my façade of maternal tranquillity, I was in fact sharply conflicted about holding a witching rod in my hands, given what had happened the last time I did, and equally apprehensive now about my impulsive decision to expose Jonah to my diviner's world. What had I been thinking? But there was no turning back now. Jonah would never forgive me, and I owed it to Partridge for believing in me. Moreover, the underlying idea was to regain my footing here, display courage, not knuckle under. Yes, I was going to try to be copacetic.

"See those apple trees?"

"Those ones that look like dead Ents?"

"Dead ants?"

"Ents. Fangorn Forest? Never mind, Cass."

"There are some live ones in there, too, and that's where we start looking for a rod."

"A-Rod? You think he's out here in Fangorn?"

"Very funny. A Y-rod is what we need."

"Only one?"

"A couple."

"Now we're talking."

We crossed the road and looked around in the ruined orchard. I found and cut myself a decent virgula and hunted with Jonah until we located another. Jonah insisted on doing the selection, cutting, and whittling himself. Then we made our way back toward the proposed building site.

"There's all kinds of divining," I said, and held my rod directly before me, its tip pointed just above the horizon, elbows at my sides. "A remote dowser might grip his rod like this to test a direction. Deviceless dowsers use the palm of their hand, no tools at all. Map dowsers who work with the police on missing-persons cases wouldn't even bother to be out here. They'd lay out a topo at the station and use a pendulum to find who they're looking for. Nep and I aren't into any of that. Our family's tradition has always been pure field divining. We prefer to walk."

"So, Cassandra, let's walk already."

My attempt at a little lecture had fallen flatter than a floodplain. There was a proper way to handle this, and I just learned it from my student. I rested the rod forks against my face-up palms, hooked my thumbs over the ends of each stick with a firm light grasp, cleared a sudden unwelcome memory of the hanged girl from my mind, and determinedly began mending the flats. Jonah studied my hands and the way I wended along. I could hear his steady progress as he stirred the grasses and wildflowers, and wanted to warn him to be careful of the stinging nettles, but thought it best not to hover over him.

The sun warmed my hair, which still smelled of ocean. I traversed the zone back and forth but wasn't cluing in to anything. How I hoped

no one would chance to drive past and witness us performing this rit-ual as old as the pyramids. There they go, crazy as crumbs, I could hear them wag their tongues. The Brooks woman and her sad little boy. You can see she's deluded him into believing all her twaddle.

Any wonder, I thought, why I'm divining nothing. Too many noisy discouragements yammering away inside for me to be able to listen outward.

When I began again, my head quieted, I realized I hadn't heard Jonah for a while, so I stopped dowsing and saw he was working a part of the field farther away from the site than would be comfortably within Partridge's budget. No matter. He was so lovely out there, a tiny figure sailing across a patch of earth, hay field with low mountains backgrounding the scene, straight out of some Brueghel painting in one of my art history volumes. Part of me wanted to run and hug him. Another part wanted to march over and take that problematic, useless stick out of his hands and break it in two. Instead, I stood stock-still as I saw him lurch to a halt. I was certain I heard him calling out, but the breeze was behind me and lofted his voice away in its wing.

"What's that?" I shouted.

Again I heard but a scrap of sound and began to imagine the worst — a cornered snake, a rabid red fox — as I set out, jogging at first, then running full bore, my pack thudding heavily against my spine. The grass was knee-high so I couldn't see what he was staring at, frozen like a sculpture there.

"What is it?" I called out, doing my best not to betray my fear.

"I don't know." His voice was squeezed back tight into his throat.

No snarling fox, no snake curled like a spring ready to strike. His rod tip pointed down at a forty-five-degree angle and quivered as if some thrashing leviathan out of an old fable were hooked at the end of his invisible line.

"My God, Jonah, don't scare me like that."

"What's going on?" he asked, ignoring my mild hysteria.

"If I could answer that question I'd be the wisest woman this side of the rainbow," I said, kneeling to catch my breath, shocked by the impli-cations of what I was seeing. By rote I hauled the pack off my back, un-

sheathed my hatchet, and cleaved my own rod in half to fashion a stake. Awestruck, Jonah tied the flagging tape to the end, leaving a couple of streamers that reminded me of the tails on his coastal kite. He pushed the stake into the soft loam to mark the spot. When he stood away, the plastic tails fluttered.

"Blue ribbon, dude," I said, masking my shock at what had just occurred. I asked if he was interested in me showing him how to circle, triangulate, verify the find.

"But you wrecked your rod."

"Yours seems to work fine. You all right?"

"Let's keep going."

As we did, many sentiments convened in my head. The first was shame, because I'd never wanted him to divine. Hadn't I sworn to myself over the years that I would stop this vexing legacy from being passed beyond me? Second was a contradictory pride that he had taken an interest in learning, had allowed me to pass him this unwieldy and all but obsolescent torch. And third was a sense of validation that, yes, this was real. I had witnessed only validity in Jonah's eyes when he looked into mine for explanation. Right here was living proof Nep was not a fraud and I, when not working with the safety net of research spread beneath where I tightroped, was not a fraud, either. How I wished Nep were here to witness Jonah Brooks become himself.

On the other hand, I was glad nobody had seen us and that ours had been a moment of private grace, both substantial in its end result but also duly ephemeral since it would never happen again. With Jonah's help I went ahead and finished siting Partridge's wells, knowing that I would not send him a bill after all. I never got paid for the Henderson job, because for myriad reasons, not the least of which was that I had failed him, I never invoiced the man. Broke as I was, I now thought it better to scrape by on savings or a small loan from the bank using my house as collateral than take any more money from this craft that had left me in such a confused, exasperated state. Jonah had proven himself a diviner and that was going to have to suffice. Just because he landed on his feet this time didn't mean he needed to leap off a ledge twice.

Part IV

WIDENING CIRCLE, TIGHTENING CIRCLE

20

As I drove to the park, having left Jonah and his lawn mower at my parents' place so he could work on it with Nep, my thoughts turned to Niles and Melanie. She had no reason to worry about me and her husband, yet I was embarrassedly excited to see him. It dawned on me, as I got out of the truck, there was a fair chance I had always been so distant with other men because I had invented a kind of false marriage for myself with Niles. My request that he be the twins' godfather. Was it a ruse? Had I married Niles in absentia, been an illusory wife? If only I could cut a witching rod and dowse myself for answers.

My problem had always been that I could forevision what others ought to do but was too often blinded when it came to my own life, trainspotting my own future. Don't go to the movies, I could warn Christopher. If you need water, I might advise Partridge and so many others, you'll find it here. There's a girl in dire trouble in these woods, I could report, and even though she hadn't been hanged, hadn't died, she was there nevertheless. No hardy magenta campion like my father wanted me to be, I felt uprooted and more lost than ever. And, as I walked across the macadam parking lot to the well-trodden path around the edge of the lake where Niles and I'd grown accustomed to

meeting, I had to admit I was frightened about what I imagined was coming.

Under the gathering clouds and light wind that threatened an afternoon shower, some indifferent swans paddled along the far shore, making soft chevrons in their wakes. A man in an aluminum rowboat was fishing for bass. When rocked by his casting, the sides of the boat caught sporadic sunlight and flashed, as if he were trying to signal me some message but I didn't know the code. The minute I sat on the lakeside bench, I realized I should have brought something for Niles. Blueberries, a seashell from Covey.

He didn't give me much time to worry about it. His car pulled into the lot soon enough, and I watched him stroll the path toward me, hands in his pockets. A family had started a fire in one of the square metal barbecue stands held aloft on a steel rod in the picnic area. I could smell its burning charcoal briquettes downwind and across the water. A girl's laughter floated over with it. Otherwise, the park was vacant this afternoon. Maybe the darkening clouds and breeze kept people away.

I stood and gave him a strong embrace. The relief I felt at being in his presence was overwhelming, as if the lake were filled with warm lavendered water and I had just slipped into it. "How have you been?" I asked as we sat together toward one end of the weathered wooden bench.

"Been all right," he began, then said, "Actually, I've been worried about you, if you want to know the truth. I'm glad to see you got some sun. You look more rested."

Rested was not how I felt, but I thanked Niles anyway. "I know you might have thought I was being a coward to cut out like that—"

"No, I didn't, I thought you were being perfectly sane. Nep do all right?"

"He goes in and out. But some days up there I swear you'd never know he had any problems. He's especially wonderful with the boys."

"I didn't like the sound of that man showing up out of nowhere and harassing them, though. You have any idea what that might have been about?"

Here I hesitated. The postcard was in my jacket pocket, ready to be turned over to Niles. The story about Millicent's theft and the hideous rag effigy—my poor hanged girl brought to life, as it were, on Covey—was fresh as an open wound in my mind. Resurfacing memories of Roy Skoler's past with me and unfounded suspicions about him now simmered, fairly or unfairly, within. Much as I wanted to divulge everything, I knew that if I broached all this with Niles, no matter how hard I begged him to keep it to himself, hoping to avoid another wave of public scrutiny and humiliation, he would inevitably urge me to file an official report. Breaking and entering, petty burglary, unlawful trespass, harassment, who knows what all. An investigation would be launched. None of which I felt I could handle just now.

"They didn't seem overly alarmed by him," I said.

"You were, though."

"Maybe I overreacted."

"Maybe you didn't."

I looked at Niles there beside me and registered his distress. I could swear his hair had grayed even since the last time I saw him and that the green of his eyes was clouded by uneasiness. He looked both exhausted and worried.

"Niles, what do you mean by that?"

His response was punctuated by merry shrieks of the little girl whose brother was now chasing her around the picnic area. "Did he ever show up again while you were there? This man, I mean."

"I never saw him," I hedged.

"Casper, you know my business. When things aren't right, especially when it comes to people closest to me, I get concerned. Don't get me wrong, I'm glad your family had a good vacation. But something's off."

"You've become a diviner now, Niles?"

As on that morning in Henderson's valley, I was compelled to take his hands. They looked like uncomfortable creatures, careworn and very much in need of being held. I stared at them until, to my surprise, one of them reached over and firmly, rather than tenderly, took one of mine.

"Cassandra," he said. "You need to tell me what happened on Covey. Did you know about Mrs. Milgate?"

"What about her?"

Niles explained he had received a call from an investigator on Mount Desert, no big deal, just running a routine background check on any possible witnesses before the death certificate was signed and the file on an accidental death was closed. The Brooks family were apparently the only other people in residence on what was presumed to be her last day. Mrs. Milgate's body was discovered the morning after we left by a boy she'd hired to bring out her supplies from the mainland every week. He found her dead at the foot of her stairs. Clearly, a slip and fall. Been dead for days, the investigator said. Maybe as long as a week. No evidence of foul play but he was just wondering if anyone had seen or spoken with her before her mishap.

"That's horrible," I managed to say, dumbstruck as I was. When standing on her porch, noticing her wet boots and smelling what I'd wrongly thought were burned syrupy beans, if I had only been more forward instead of shyly whispering her name, I might have discovered that she was in need of help. Or no, not help, she was clearly beyond my help by then. But at least the dignity of having her eyelids closed and her body sheeted against creatures that would disturb it. Too, if Rosalie and I had only knocked instead of trekking past, had been willing to bend her hermitage rules a little, we might have found Mrs. Milgate. I hated the idea of her lying there, utterly alone.

Could the man have been behind this? A calling card of sorts, letting me know his postcard was no idle threat? I dismissed the thought. It was one thing to play mind games, quite another to murder a woman just to underscore some point.

"Have you told my mother? She's going to be really upset. Angela Milgate goes all the way back to her childhood."

"I wanted to talk with you first. Did you see her when you were there?"

"Not at all. But that wasn't unusual. She always kept to herself. I never knew her that well." I had always thought of Mrs. Milgate as the

guardian angel of Covey, more a legendary hermit than a real person who was old, stubborn, and far too proud to be pushed around by those who might try to save her from herself. Everyone who knew her knew she wouldn't have considered a tumble down the stairs as good a death as passing away in her sleep, but any death was preferable to being taken away from her cottage on Covey by well-meaning relatives and stuck in some nursing home in Ellsworth to rot in an unfamiliar room. Still, it was profoundly disturbing that she most likely made her last misstep while we were on the island, her only neighbors, ourselves cocooned on its far shore.

"Maybe you'd prefer to tell Rosalie yourself," Niles said.

"If that's all right with you."

"It's not a matter of police business, so I think you should."

Was there any other news Niles had to spring on me? I wondered, thinking again of the postcard burning in my pocket. "I'm of two minds about showing you this," I said, pulling it out and studying the faces of the mourners gathered around St. Francis on his bier, trying and failing once more to construe what the fresco could possibly have to do with me, beyond my affinity with birds.

He studied the image after I handed it to him, then flipped it over. "Same man?"

"I don't see who else it would be, but Niles, listen. I'm showing this to you as my dearest and most necessary friend, not as the sheriff of anything. People are allowed to send nasty cards to each other and it's not against the law. I need you to let me sort this out for myself."

"I'll have to think about that."

"Look, even if you found out who it is, there's no way I'd press charges. He hasn't done anything and pressing charges might twist the knife in the wrong direction."

"Is there a right one?"

"Besides, if it becomes a public investigation, I'm fresh out of Coveys to run to."

"One thing I can promise you is that nothing will be public."

"If Bledsoe is involved—"

"He won't be," Niles said, turning the postcard over and over in his restless fingers, and scrutinizing it again as if it were a tarot card whose arcana he couldn't quite interpret. "By the way, who do you know in Massachusetts?"

A few sprinkles of rain began to needle the pewter lake.

"Nobody, why?"

"The postmark on this card's Springfield, is all."

Startled, I took the card back and held it up. I hadn't thought to look myself. Inchoate and wrong-headed as they were, my reasons not to tell Niles about Millicent now seemed stronger than before. I went to him with the hanged girl and look where that got me, I thought. There existed a very delicate balance between this other person and myself. Any disturbing of it, I suspected, threatened a far messier calamity than if I left matters quiet and simply proceeded on my roundabout own. Niles, for all his gifts, would necessarily take a far more direct approach than I proposed to try. Laura was now paramount in my mind. She and I were, through the vision of the hanged girl, bound together in some way and she was my best oblique avenue of approach. Although I told Niles I had no idea what a postmark from Springfield meant, I knew perfectly well that if one were to drive from anywhere in Corinth County up to Mount Desert Island, the route best taken would be through Springfield to Worcester to Lowell and on.

"What can you tell me about Laura, Niles?"

The rain was picking up a little, pinpricking my face. Like it was showering needles.

"I thought you knew she's back with her parents."

"I mean her case."

"There is no case," he said, looking at me with eyes that fathomed I was withholding some of what I knew. Fortunately, he chose not to pressure me right then. But it wasn't as if Niles didn't have his own ways of proceeding with or without me.

"Those cans of food and everything in her camp, she managed to buy all that herself?"

"She admits she stole the food."

"How did she get all the way from Cold Spring to Henderson's?"

"She's a clever kid, tough in her way, bright as can be. She reminds me of you a bit, when you were young," he said. "Turns out she even has, or had, an older brother, too. He went missing years ago, left home without a note and hasn't been heard from since. It's my understanding he would be all grown up now and that the Bryants still hold out hope he'll show up one day. There's never been any indication he met with foul play."

I sat there stunned by the parallel of Laura and me both losing our older brothers and running away. What was more, I was stricken by the black thought of what it must be like to lose a child, an obscene idea that caused in me a moment of unusual empathy toward Rosalie. The disappearance of Morgan or Jonah from my life was even more inconceivable to me than the thought of my own death. I had to wonder, Would I have done any better than she managed to do after Christopher died and I made my brief disappearance? I would not.

Niles said, "You can understand how the Bryants are so relieved to have Laura back, and why they're grateful to you, whether you think you saved her or not."

"But where was Laura going? Did she say?"

"She wasn't really headed in any specific direction. Just wound up where fate took her, is what she insisted in her deposition, stowawayed in the back of somebody's vehicle. We have no reason not to believe her. Point is, she's back home and doing fine."

For reasons I could neither explain nor articulate even to myself, I somehow doubted that. "So why did she leave in the first place?"

"That's for a family counselor to help the Bryants sort out."

"And that's that?" I said, incredulous.

Here he hesitated, glanced away across the lake, then continued, "Well, you're not wrong. Nothing's ever as simple as *that's that*. I've done some investigating on my own, following some midnight hunches, and I've found out that Henderson's seems to be some kind of epicenter, how else to put it, of vanishings spread out over too many years to make a real discernible pattern."

"How so?"

"If you took a pin and stuck it on a map of the area, then tied a string to the pin and transcribed a circle starting all the way over at Cold Spring, you'd find that there have been several missing persons who'd been living inside that circle. All girls about Laura's age, and all with siblings who ran away from home before they did. But it's an epicenter in the middle of nowhere anybody would ever bother to look because there's nothing there to look for, not logically at any rate."

A numb apprehension, a vague idea just beyond my grasp, poured through me in the wake of Niles's words. Was it possible that Henderson's valley, richly beautiful though it was, would prove to be some hell's playground presided over by its own diminutive devil? Niles continued talking while these thoughts spun through my mind. He spoke of having contacted several colleagues in the towns where these girls had vanished as well as the ViCAP people at the Federal Bureau who live to screen and meld and discover patterns like this. Once more there was nothing really substantial for any of them to work with, and thus his idea would remain just that, a feeling or impression, a nagging if intriguing coincidence. And the world was flooded, as he put it, by nagging if intriguing coincidences.

"I'd like to see Laura," I told Niles, with a fresh urgency. "Would you give me her number?"

"She's already asked to speak with you, thank you herself. I gave her your address and phone, so here's hers," and dug a piece of folded paper out of his pants pocket. "Just be careful, Cass. I know you too well."

After passing me the sheet of paper, a crumpled little origami, he stood up and held out his hand. The rain was light but steady. I'd wanted to tell him about Jonah's dowsing, wanted him to sit with me a while longer without talking about any of this. But it was time to leave. Niles held my hand tightly, this time more tenderly, all the way back along the lakeshore. The picnicking family had already departed, I saw, and the flames of their fire were reduced to a green-gray smoke that lifted against all odds into the sky.

21

Jonah came along, having announced with a mock scowl on his face that he didn't trust me on my own. Besides, he wanted to meet the famous Laura Bryant. Her mother had returned my call, invited us to lunch, and given me directions to their house in Cold Spring. Morgan was gone to a tournament in Binghamton, where he would be staying overnight with the team, so this was my window. Not that I knew if I would achieve anything during another encounter with Laura, other than maybe finding some way to begin burying her doppelgänger, the hanged girl, and move on with the business of living.

For her part, Laura needed to thank me in person, so her mother said. I accepted the invitation, keeping to myself my doubts about having been directly responsible for saving her from peril. I had been a woman hired to do something she didn't finally accomplish, who saw something that wasn't there to see, and who happened in the meantime to stumble upon the whereabouts of someone she wasn't looking for. Hardly the biography of a savior.

We detoured, before crossing the Hudson, to a sculpture park set on hundreds of rolling green acres, Storm King, where we walked for an hour among towering I-beam cat's cradles, mysterious half-buried black monoliths, and burnished weldings of figures that Jonah com-

pared to the Martians in *War of the Worlds*. He assured me that most of what we saw was "way copacetic. I wouldn't mind being one of these sculpture guys someday. Get paid to make nothing out of something."

"I wouldn't call works of art *nothing*."

"They don't do anything, do they?"

"They inspire us to look at the world with different eyes."

"Math does that, teachers like you do. Diviners, even. But this?"

"I'm not sure it happens quite the same way."

"Nep being sick makes us look at the world with different eyes."

"That's a little closer."

"So what you're saying is that art and being sick are pretty much the same deal," he said as we walked across the mowed field toward the lot and got back inside the truck. "You don't really want to go, do you."

"Of course I do. I just thought a little contact with culture might be good for you."

"I see," he finished, unconvinced.

We were expected around one and it was already just after noon. Fact was, Jonah had it right. He knew I was stalling, knew that some part of Cassandra Brooks just didn't want to meet Laura Bryant. Wanted instead to climb aboard a fantasy schooner with her twins and sail down the widening Hudson, never looking back, gliding beyond Bear Mountain and under the Tappan Zee, past the red cliffs of the Palisades, Manhattan, and our own personal Statue of Liberty, out to sea laughing, giddy with freedom.

Instead, we drove across the ugly red-brown girdered bridge to Beacon and along a narrow highway that paralleled the train tracks and the river that bordered them, the sumac not yet blooming and catalpa flowers just past peak, through a tunnel carved out of solid rock and into the village of Cold Spring. Jonah acted as navigator, reading instructions off a piece of paper. It was a picturesque little hamlet of old Victorians, of one-ways and cul-de-sacs, its main street teeming with antique shops. Pedestrians jammed the narrow sidewalks, and some old-timers in suspenders played jazz standards in a tiny gazebo down near the train station where Laura had disappeared not that long

ago. A green trolley trundled up the hill, its bell clanging — San Fran-
cisco-on-Hudson — while a noisy contingent of motorcyclists garbed
in black leather revved in its wake.

I managed to get all turned around, my son duly snorting at me,
but before long we were parked on a quiet residential street lined with
oaks, locusts, crimson kings. Here was a neighborhood that, despite a
bickersome blue jay perched on a hidden branch overhead, bespoke
the deep calm of lives being led in domestic serenity. Not the kind of
place, at least on its tranquil surface, one would want to trade for a
makeshift hovel.

Hesitating in the truck, I sat thinking, You know we could just leave,
right now, phone with regrets, offer an excuse that an illness in the
family — there was one, after all — prevented us from making it over. I
felt as unsettled as the vista beyond the windshield was settled. Jonah
was already out of the truck, though, and soon enough we walked up
the brick path to a stone house dating from the mid-nineteenth century, mansard-roofed with slate shingles, a corner turret covered in
ivy, elegant hedgerows, and old plantings. Julia Bryant answered the
door even before I rang the bell. I was relieved I hadn't bolted, since
she must have watched us pull up, park, and pause.

"Mrs. Brooks?"

"So good to meet you," I said, not bothering to correct her, just as
Jonah piped up, "There is no Mr. Brooks."

"And you are?"

"This is my son Jonah," I said, flashing him a quick smile of
warning.

The entrance hall opened into a high-ceilinged room centered by
a staircase. She led us into a library lined with shelves populated less
by books than by objects, elegant tchotchkes. Porcelain figurines of
pirouetting ballerinas. Scrimshaw, Native American pottery. Nesting babushka dolls, Balinese puppets. Guessing that the Bryants liked
traveling, since many of their objects seemed to be from abroad, I
commented on a little carved bull, and she confirmed my assumption,
saying they had bought it in Lisbon a few summers ago. Jonah browsed

the collection, grabbing down a Mexican skull mask and holding it up to his face.

"Jonah," I said, horrified by its gruesome effect. "Don't touch."

"That's all right," said Julia Bryant.

"Please don't drop anything."

He shrugged me off.

"You had no problem finding us?"

"No, your directions were good," I said, hoping Jonah would give me a pass. "We stopped off at Storm King on the way over. Very beautiful."

"You should see it in the fall when the colors are at their peak."

What in the world were we supposed to talk about?

"How is Laura getting along?"

I swear I detected the shade of a wince but it was so swiftly replaced by a reassuring smile that I had to doubt. I needed to remember this was a woman who knew about loss.

"Laura's fully back to her old self. She went through quite an experience. We can't thank you enough for having found her. We're so grateful."

"Well, you know, I didn't exactly find her."

"Sheriff Hubert explained a bit of what happened, and I can't say I completely understand the situation, but no matter what triggered the search it was because of you that they went out looking. They'd nearly given up on this side of the river."

"I'm glad she's home."

Jonah said, "Look at this, Cass." He was holding a ceramic figure of three maroon devils, naked and cadaverous, with outstretched arms, blue tongues dangling from wide-open mouths, and a spiky forest of horns on their heads brashly painted with red and blue blood vessels. The central devil held a toothy skull in his hands, as if offering it with the message, *This is your fate.*

"We got that in Oaxaca, same place as the mask. It's a Day of the Dead grotesque meant to ward away evil spirits. Jonah seems to like the skeletons."

"Best put it back."

"Don't you think it's cool?"

Julia Bryant and I exchanged a mother's knowing smile.

"It is cool," I said. "But put it back."

As he did, he asked, "So when do we meet this Laura?"

"Let me go upstairs and get her, and then are you hungry, Jonah?"

"Definitely."

After she left the room, I asked Jonah if he was all right.

"Sure," he said. "The question is, are you?"

Although I assured him I was, we both knew it wasn't completely true. I needed to hear Laura's story because I was convinced it would open a window into my own, give me insight into who the hanged girl was, or what she meant. But did I really want to see what lay beyond that window?

Laura and her mother came into the room together from the foyer, Julia Bryant's arm over her daughter's shoulder. "I believe you two have met before," Julia said, smiling first at Laura, who stared down at the oriental runner, then across to me.

"We have," I said, and walked toward her with my hand outstretched.

Laura took it and glanced away, not with the fixed unseeing gaze as when she emerged from the woods, but with a kind of avoidance. "Hello again."

"You look much better than the last time I saw you."

"I wasn't in such great shape."

"It must feel good to be back home."

At this she finally looked me in the eye with what I perceived as gratitude. "I'm glad you're here," she said.

With that, we were led to the dining room, where Julia Bryant served us a lunch she had clearly spent time preparing — vichyssoise, focaccia, salad Niçoise — and the four of us conversed for a while. Jonah was nonplussed to learn that a fancy word like *vichyssoise* meant nothing more than cold potato soup garnished with some raw chives. Watching Laura during the course of all our small talk was, I now and

then sensed, like watching a chimera. She'd lived some kind of experience I, too, had lived. And we both seemed to know it.

Little of what was said during lunch registered with me. My hope was that I could politely get a little time alone with Laura afterward. Were the roles reversed, I had to ask myself, would I leave my daughter alone with this woman whose ghoulish vision led rescuers to her by happenstance? But then Mrs. Bryant unexpectedly offered me my opportunity, asking Jonah if he would like to see the tree house in the backyard. "It's quite a production. Laura all but lived in it when she was younger," she said. "This way she and your mother can have a chance to visit more."

After they left for the backyard, I said, "So," not quite sure where to begin. Light streamed from the bank of French windows behind Laura, illuminating her hair to an almost ethereal glow. She was a pretty girl, I thought, in a haunted kind of way. "You know, without all the leaves in your hair, I didn't quite recognize you at first."

Laura leveled her gaze at me. A benign, serious, but otherwise unreadable expression.

"Can I ask you a question, Mrs. Brooks?"

"Call me Cassandra, or Cass. Everybody else does."

"Did he tell you where I was?"

"Did who tell me what?"

"Who told you I was there in that forest?"

"Laura, don't get me wrong, I'm glad you wound up being found, but it was Niles and the others who saved you."

She gave me a mildly disbelieving look.

"Who is this 'he' you're talking about?" I continued.

"Nobody."

"But I thought you said—"

"Forget I said it."

"Actually, didn't you say he threatened you, said he could make bad girls disappear right out of the world?"

"I didn't know what I was saying," looking down at her lap.

We were already nearing an impasse. She's fifteen years old, I

thought, defensive for good reason. Why should she trust me yet? Nothing to be gained by pushing her on this point. Just move on. "Now can I ask you a question?"

"I guess."

"Why did you run away?"

"I didn't exactly."

"That's what everybody thinks."

"It's their problem what they think."

"I'm here to listen," I said, wanting to reach out and stroke her cheek. "I'd like for you to feel you can be straight with me. You told the police you were kidnapped. Is that wrong, too?"

"I don't know."

"And what about your amnesia at the child welfare place, was that acting?"

"Are you sure you're not just here to get more information for the police?"

"The police are done with both of us. I'm here for myself, and for you, if you'll let me. I honestly don't understand what happened to me any more than you seem to understand what happened to you. Maybe if we work together a little—"

"I can try."

"So if you didn't run away and you weren't kidnapped, can you tell me what did happen? I won't let another soul in on it if you don't want me to. I don't really have anybody to tell, anyway."

"Aren't you some kind of prophet who shouldn't have to ask questions like that? That's what they told me."

"I'm no prophet, just ask my mother. She's a walking Bible and I'm not in it."

"If you say so." The slightest hint of a smile.

"You know what else I say," encouraged by her response. "Not that you did, but I hope you know running away is a dangerous business. It doesn't take a prophet to know that."

"The world's dangerous everywhere," she said. "You want to see my room?"

"All right," peering out the windows to where Jonah stood with Laura's mother beneath the voluminous oak whose trunk was studded with slat steps that led up to the tree house aloft in the leaves. Julia was talking and pointing at where it was built, supported by a pair of heavy branches that pronged out from the trunk. I followed Laura upstairs.

"This is my new tree house," she said.

Her room was so bare it seemed more a cell than a childhood sanctuary. Rock band posters—His Name Is Alive and the Cocteau Twins—were taped to the wall by her bed. A hooked rug, a ladder-back chair by the window, which looked out over a side yard and the neighbor's house beyond. On a small table sat an old typewriter, unusual for her computer generation, and a stack of poetry books—Emily Dickinson, Sylvia Plath, Bob Dylan's *Tarantula*, along with Emerson's essays. Pretty mature reading for someone her age. On the quilted bed, sitting against the pillows, was a teddy bear with black button eyes not unlike Millicent's. Its stitched mouth was meant to form a smile, but the wavering line gave off an air of unsettled caprice.

"I see you like to read."

"Some."

"Me, too. What are you reading now?"

"I haven't been able to read much lately."

"Don't have the time?"

"Just don't feel like it."

She sat on the edge of her bed and I took a seat on the chair.

"I ran away once," I said.

The words came out before I'd had a chance to measure what their impact might be, without considering where they could lead our tentative, faltering talk. She didn't respond in so many words, but the look on her face wasn't difficult to interpret. Go on, it proposed. "Were you unhappy, is why you ran away?"

"I was upset by things that happened, sure."

"What were you upset about?"

How neatly Laura had managed to turn the tables so that she was discovering who I was rather than the other way around. Still, this

seemed my only path to the girl, so it made sense to follow it further. "My brother died and I couldn't figure out how to deal with his being gone."

"How did he die?"

"Car accident."

"But you weren't driving," she said.

"No, of course not. I was very young."

"Sounds to me like you blamed it on yourself."

I hadn't said anything of the kind, but Laura easily intuited it, which made me wonder about her own brother's disappearance. "You're probably right. Even though it wasn't my fault, I felt guilty for not being able to stop it. Did anything like that happen to you?"

"And you still feel guilty about it, seems like."

"Sometimes. But it's more that I feel helpless when it comes to things like death, illness, the big issues that come at us in life. I don't need to feel powerful, but I hate feeling powerless. You know what I mean?"

Laura pondered this, examining her chewed fingernails, then looked out the window. "I know what you mean," she said, finally. "Life seems to have a nasty habit of making promises it can't keep. Of not listening to you when you need to be heard. I even told my mother I didn't want to go pick up my father at the station. I knew I wasn't supposed to be there. I just knew it."

"What do you mean, you knew it?"

"You're the diviner," she shot back, her hands closing into fists on her lap. "You understand."

"You seem pretty angry, I hope you don't mind me saying so. Is that something you're working with your counselor about?"

"Him? He doesn't know blow. I just do it because my parents are making me. We talk for forty-five minutes about zero, zilch, zip. *Ska pop, sa pum, sa po.* Then I leave and my mother drives me back home. It's all stupid, but we've both got to do it to make people think we're doing something. Besides, if I try anything else, he'll know."

"The therapist?"

"The man."

"The man who took you away at the station, is that what you're saying?"

"Something like that," she said, eyes welling with tears I could easily see she didn't want to shed.

"So if you weren't lying, why did you change your story?"

"You say you want to be my friend, for me to trust you. Don't make me answer that question. You know, Cassandra, he doesn't like you any better than he must like me now. He said I'd be fine if I stayed, but if I left I'd wish I wasn't ever born."

"He said my name, knew who I was?"

"He never said your name, but I'm sure he knows it now."

I glanced out the window and saw that Jonah had climbed up the wooden ladder and was now in the tree house. He had both hands on what looked like a rickety railing that reminded me of the lighthouse gallery railing and was leaning over the edge, talking with Julia Bryant in the yard below.

"Jonah seems to like the tree house," Laura said, trying to shift the subject. "You know, I didn't really build it myself."

"Your brother helped you?"

"No, that's just the way my mother likes to remember things. He built it himself and I was only allowed up there by invitation. It was our private, secret world for a while."

Like my blindfolded walks to Christopher's cave, I thought.

It was close in the room and I was about to ask Laura if she wouldn't mind opening the window, as a little fresh air would have been welcome. Also, I wanted to warn Jonah to be careful, when I saw another boy up there with him. A young man, rather. He was thin, hollow-cheeked, with dark hair cropped tight across his tall forehead, pale lips and skin, and the faintest hint of a youthful beard. Unmoving and paying no attention to Jonah who stood right next to him, he was staring at me. The expression on his face was a combination of apprehension and arrogance, a diabolic, threatening look. Jonah didn't seem to be aware he was there. I glanced at Laura, who was still talking though

now I couldn't make out what she was saying, and again peered out the window to where he stood, insouciant, his brow-shadowed eyes still fixed on mine.

"Who's that boy up in the tree with Jonah?" I asked, my voice dry as dust.

The young man moved farther back away from Jonah, was partially obscured by the rustling leaves.

"Cassandra? Mrs. Brooks?" Laura was asking.

"That boy there, see him?"

Laura looked out the window to where I was pointing. "What boy?"

"Right there, plain as day, hiding behind Jonah."

Laura said, "I don't think—" just as he turned his back on us and, in the trembling play of shade and light, dissipated and vanished.

I knew what had happened. This time there was no question about it.

"I'm sorry, Laura," I said, forcing a small, apologetic smile. "My mistake."

She shrugged. "That's all right."

How foolish I felt in my disconcertment. Here I had come to Cold Spring, self-cast as a concerned adult wanting to check on the health of a distant ward fate had laid in her path, and in the hope of trying to understand the mystery of the harassing stranger. But now look. More monster, more madness.

"I think it's time we go join up with your mother and Jonah. I'm sure she wouldn't mind having him taken off her hands."

"He didn't seem the annoying type to me," Laura countered, perhaps feeling a little sorry for me. My face must have been pale as the white sunlight outside. "I think you've done a good job bringing him up, if you want to know."

"Thanks for saying so, Laura," now regaining my composure. What I saw, after all, hadn't been there, of course. "I notice you have a book of Emerson's there on your table. You know his line *My cow milks me?*"

"I don't think so."

"Sometimes I think my boys raise me rather than the other way around."

"Well, they've done a good job, too."

Nice of her, but right then I felt shattered to the core. I wanted to finish, as best I could manage, whatever it was I came here to do and leave this place quickly, never to come back. Before we walked to her door, I said, in a small impulsive voice, a whisper between confidantes, "You going to be all right, Laura?"

"Sure, probably, why not?" she answered, as assuringly as she could manage.

Roles reversed again, she put her arm around my waist and vowed she was fine, not to worry. I couldn't think of anything more to say. I wanted to go home, huddle with myself, regroup, and decide how to approach what I sensed was a great crossroads in my life.

Mother and daughter walked me and Jonah under the pendant trees to the truck. I kept my eyes on the ground as much as possible so as not to see the uninvited guest again. When we reached the curb, I embraced Laura, who finally offered me the same half-smile, half-frown as the Covey girl, before walking beside her mother back up the path. I felt my face drain, felt what could only be characterized as supreme defeat.

Driving back across the Hudson, I came to the unavoidable conclusion that much of what was happening to me was a function of a rampant, chaotic imagination. Some kind of lucid dreaming, unbridled and festering. Very real, more real than real, were the counterparts to these imaginings. The man, the cigarettes, the card, the doll. Living at the nexus of real and unreal was becoming all but impossible. In the silent cab of the truck, while Jonah napped, I began to wonder if Niles's therapist hadn't been right. Maybe I had begun to manipulate my world without meaning to, altering it into something unrecognizable. Just what kind of fantasy film had I been directing for much of my life? Maybe I was way out of sync with the objective universe.

That night, after Jonah had tramped off to bed, our house on Mendes Road seemed perplexed. I was projecting, I realized. But I couldn't

remember the last time the three of us weren't together. Morgan had called in the early evening to say his team won their afternoon game, and that he had batted in three of the five runs in their shutout victory. It made me happy to hear the jubilance in his voice.

"Good going, dude," I said.

"How was your thing?" he asked.

"All right."

"That bad."

"I can't say we had as excellent a day as you."

"I wish you could be at the game tonight," Morgan said, trying hard not to be wistful or homesick. Just a star who missed his fans.

"We're there in spirit. They feeding you all right?"

We signed off after making arrangements about when I would pick him up at the bus station. A mob scene of moms and diffident young ballplayers who really would prefer it if their teammates weren't there to witness all the hugs and kisses. I promised to be discreet.

"Thanks, Cassandra," he said.

"Hit a homer for me, hear?"

On the porch, I watched a dogtooth-yellow moon rise through battalions of clouds. I needed to think clearly, but my mind was as gauzy as those clouds, and any bright ideas I had seemed as obscured as the moon behind them. Questions and more questions pressed in on me. How was it my long-standing covenant to leave visions to visionaries, to hew to the everyday, had been broken that afternoon at Henderson's? How long had I been interacting with things not wholly there, and what was my relationship to the threatening things that truly were? I knew I must be a real diviner, had proof over and over again that I was, but what did my sense of being either genuine or a fraud actually mean if my waking truths were so far removed from what others understood as true?

The Greeks invented the word *character*. But to them it meant quite the opposite of what it means to us now. For us, character is what makes us individual, unique. We have *characteristics*. We're fearful or courageous. We're loving or cold. Our defining character sets us apart

from every other man and woman. For the Greeks, however, character was about what traits each person shares with all people. Our com-
monality with others was the mark of character. Each person was part
of the whole, and all the more so depending on the quality of his or her
character. No surprise, I preferred the Greek view of things, wished I
could be like everybody else.

My last question now, indeed the only question that really mattered
to me, was this. Could I, as a diviner, one damned with the gift of forevisioning, function in the world well enough to avoid the same tyranny
of treatment Laura so wisely was sidestepping, the same useless treatment my mother and even Niles would have me undergo? Jonah and
Morgan were what counted most. I couldn't take care of them if I was
locked inside the prison of professional help, I knew, but neither did it
seem possible to be a diviner, a witch, and not bring trouble into their
lives. My twins were eleven, healthy and humorous. They were socially
adept, more or less. They had grandparents who loved them. No, I decided, all might be well with an undivining Cassandra. Or, that is, well
enough. Surely I could recast myself so as to negotiate everyday life
the same as anybody. After all, wasn't I finally just another person who
needed to get on with life?

Who knows, maybe now everything had come full circle. Ourobo-
rus the serpent caught its tail in its teeth, why not I? What happened
today may have been good, I decided, against all odds. Today marked
a step away from the abyss, not a fall into it. Yes. My life needed to be
taken fully in hand. And by none other than myself. A new Cassandra,
as new as I could redraft her from the raw materials I had to work
with, would face the morning. The sun would rise. I would see it. And
it would be the same damn sun as everybody else's.

22

I WAS UP EARLY, the liquid melodies of the first thrushes my alarm clock. A heavy mackerel sky stretched overhead, the sun obscured behind it as the moon had been the night before. But my resolve was not dimmed. If anything it had sharpened while I slept. Today was Morgan's homecoming, and even though he'd only been gone overnight, I wanted to make it special. Special in an ordinary, commonplace way. I mixed buttermilk pancakes and fried some sausage and eggs for Jonah when he came down. In a small copper pan I heated some of Cleve Miller's local maple syrup, which filled the kitchen with a childhood incense. I cut a big white bouquet of fresh peonies from the garden and arranged them as a centerpiece for the kitchen table. Filled the bird feeder, which soon was crowded with goldfinches.

From the moment I woke up, I had been singing in my head a nursery rhyme that Rosalie, who was a great aficionado of such ditties when I was growing up, used to recite to me. It went,

> The cuckoo comes in April,
> She sings her song in May;
> In the middle of June
> She changes her tune,
> And then she flies away.

Which made me wonder, as the rhyme surfaced from nowhere, the way old memories can do, whether the cuckoo represented my unhappy visions come and gone, or whether I myself was the cuckoo. Maybe neither, probably both, but it took me by surprise, this lullaby I hadn't heard for over three decades.

There was no getting around Jonah, no fooling him, so I didn't try. When he asked, halfway through breakfast, "What's with you this morning?" I knew there was nothing to be gained by hedging.

"I've made a couple of decisions."

"Sounds scary. You want some juice?" pushing back his chair and walking to the fridge as nonchalantly as he could manage.

"No, not scary. Tomato, if there's any left."

"So what decisions? There's only orange here."

"Orange is fine. Well, for one I'm going to lay off divining for a while. I don't have any jobs scheduled right now, anyway."

He brought our juice to the table and sat, saying, "If anyone calls, I can do it for you, if you want."

"Well, Jonah, that's really sweet of you to offer. But I think it's best to cool it for a while," reaching over to squeeze his hand which rested on the table. He didn't squeeze back. Not that he was angry with me, just lost in contemplation and disappointment.

"So what else?" he said.

"I'm going to talk to Mr. Newburg about getting my teaching job back."

"The great Newburg who gets a couple of whiny calls from some dickweed parents and what's he do? Stand up for you? No, folds like a broken chair."

"He did what he thought was best for his students," I said, marveling at Jonah's vehemence.

"Did what he thought was best for his own ass."

"Don't use that language. You're too smart for words like *dickweed* and *ass*."

"If I was smart, you'd listen to me."

"I do listen to you. You're my compass. But I need to make money to

pay for the mortgage, the eggs and orange juice, and the best way for me to do it is to get my job back."

"This is because of yesterday. You didn't like the Bryants."

"Actually, I did, Jonah. But this is because I realized I haven't been myself these past couple of months, ever since I was out at Henderson's—"

"And saw that girl."

"—and thought I saw something I didn't really see," I said, wishing I could tell Jonah about the other three instances that continued to plague me, so he might have a better chance of understanding my position. "I'm glad my mistake caused something positive to happen, but it would have happened anyway. Laura's an intelligent girl. She would have climbed back to the road and flagged somebody for help soon, anyway. My being there was total coincidence."

"And you believe that."

"Sure do. You should, too."

He rose from the table with extreme dignity and left the room without a further word. This was not going to be easy, I realized, and empathized with Jonah to my very core. But my course was set, and I had to husband, as they say, my resolve.

That same Saturday morning, before we left to collect Morgan, I telephoned Matt Newburg at school, expecting to leave a message that he might or might not choose to return. Instead, I found him in his office. I explained that during my time away I'd had a chance to think about our conversation and some of the concerns parents and prospective students had conveyed to him earlier. I told him I understood their worries. Appreciated as well his awkward position and his need to view things with the big picture in mind. I asked if it would be possible to meet to discuss my status.

He said, much to my surprise, "Why don't you come in Monday morning."

I thanked him, hung up, penciled the appointment on the kitchen wall calendar. A good first foray, I thought, wandering into the front room and looking out the window at our horse chestnut for some

vision of another ghostly boy or girl that would contradict my mood. But no, only a woodpecker working its way up the bark, pecking for bugs. On an impulse, I opened the phone book and looked to see if Roy Skoler was listed. He wasn't.

At the bus terminal, the glum look on Morgan's face as he threaded his way through the crowd spoke volumes. Jonah and I, models of reserve in light of all the handshaking and hugs, glanced at each other, guessing in the second game he must have made the last out with the bases loaded, or errored on some clutch throw that handed the other team victory. Unceremoniously, Morgan chucked his gear bag in the back of the truck, climbed in, and grumbled, "Let's get out of here."

"What's happening, man?" Jonah asked, as we pulled out.

"Nothing."

"You can't win them all," I said, as trite as a stale fortune cookie.

"What're you freaking talking about?" Morgan challenged.

"I mean, it's clear from your mood the team lost."

"We killed them. They couldn't've sucked worse."

"So what's the problem? No 'hello,' no 'good to see you'?"

"I'm not in the mood, Cassandra, so spare me."

"Easy, dude," said Jonah.

"You can shut up, pipsqueak."

Without a further word being spoken, I realized what was wrong. "You didn't get into a fight, did you?"

"I'm too smart for that. They'd have benched me the rest of the summer."

"Who was it?"

"Who cares? Screw them, anyway."

"We'll talk later," I said.

"Forget it."

The rest of the ride home was tense. And here I had wanted so badly to listen to my twins do their routine, jousting and joking, but neither of them had much patience with me at the moment. Still, this incident—which, predictably, turned out to be a couple of the boys taunting the team's star player about his mother, new kids trash-talking him in an effort to secure a place in the hierarchy and drag him down a

notch—further steeled my resolve. Morgan was right. It didn't matter who ridiculed me with another tired accusation. What mattered was we move forward. One of Rosalie's pet clichés was *Consider the source and rise above it*. As clichés went, a decent one.

After lunch, the boys recovered some of their fraternal rhythm. Morgan's spirits revived as if he had shaken off an umpire's bad call and had to go on with the game. Suppressing my urge to tell them to lock the doors while I was out, I drove over to see my parents. Here I told them—sitting on the back porch, looking at the meadow that cupped the pond as if in the palms of its hands, a vista as familiar to me as my own palms—about my decision to take a hiatus from divining, my request to be reinstated at school, my desire to simplify life and get more into the swim of things.

"Like racerats swim," I could swear Nep said under his breath as he swatted at an invisible fly. "Churchrats."

"What was that?" I asked.

"Churchrats."

"Be nice," Rosalie interjected.

He looked out toward the woods and pale horizon beyond.

"Ever since Henderson's," I continued, trying not to reveal my distress at the strength of Nep's disease this afternoon, "I've been flying backwards and upside down and I'm tired of it. Hummingbirds can do that but I'm no hummingbird. An albatross more like. I have to pull myself together for you and the boys, if not for myself."

Rosalie sat as silent as a Trappist nun, clearly caught between a dawning optimism that her daughter had been visited by some archangelic clarion voice of wisdom, after so many years of wandering in darkness, and an apprehensive concern that there was some catch lurking behind this sudden transformation. "I've even been thinking," I continued, "that if it isn't an imposition, I'd like for me and the boys to come to church with you tomorrow."

"Imposition?" she said, breaking her silence with a beaming smile. "It'd be wonderful. How long has it been since Morgan and Jonah saw the inside of a house of worship?"

Nep stared into the distance.

"I can't guarantee they'll go along with it—"

"You're their mother. Tell them and they will."

"That's not quite how it works. They've got heads harder than anvils and I can't force them. Besides, how many times did you tell me to go and I didn't?"

"Your father was the reason you got away with that."

"Either way, I'd like to go to church tomorrow. I want to see if there's something there for me."

Nep shook his head. An unpleasant cast settled over his face. He wasn't in pain, so far as I could tell, but neither was he comfortable. He appeared pinched, as if some errant facial muscle had seized up. I glanced at Rosalie. To her, it seemed, nothing was unusually amiss. When she walked me to the truck, I asked about him. He seemed to have taken a sharp downturn since returning from Covey.

"Bad days, better days," she told me. The dementia flowed under the influence of its own unseen tides.

Dementia. Such an ugly word, like *death*, *decay*, *despair*. But his mind was losing itself, his words sculpting themselves into curious shapes. While I'd avoided thinking of his illness as dementia, strictly speaking this was precisely what was chasing him away from himself. Driving along an empty road to Mendes, I tried to imagine our lives without him striding around competently, modestly, in it. What a weatherless world it was going to be.

My proposal after dinner that the boys accompany me to church was met with a resounding hush at first, followed by a storm of raucous, disbelieving laughter.

After asking, "You're kidding, right?" and seeing I was quite sincere, Morgan shifted into one of his mock characters, the Minister of Sinister. "My deareth brethren," he lisped with sham melodrama. "Blessed be heeth that passeth through the eyeth of the needleth."

"Amen," his brother intoned.

As ever, the routine descended into playful sacrilege.

"Oh, Joneth, my childeth."

"Yea now, Minister Sinister."

"Thou hath sinneth and now must payeth for thy sineths."

"Boys, come on," I said.

Morgan grabbed a broom that was leaning in the corner behind the kitchen door. With grinning solemnity he raised it like a crosier in both hands, saying, "Prepareth to meet thy maker, you sinful scum-meth."

"God save me." Jonah laughed and fled the room, perhaps a touch worried that Morgan, still moody, might take the joke too far. "Save me from the fire and brimstone —"

Running after him, Morgan shouted, "Minister Sinister's coming to punish you."

The screen door slammed. They horsed around outside, yelling and yapping. One of those moments when I was grateful our nearest neighbors were hundreds of yards farther down the road, unable to hear us.

And yet next morning, after all the hijinks, without another word exchanged about the matter, they donned their blazers and ties and accompanied me to the service. We sat toward the back of the nave on one of the long mahogany pews, beside Rosalie who was in shock over our actually being there. Flanking me, the twins shifted some and stifled yawns but were otherwise on good behavior. The pastor gave a sermon on the healing power of soul-cleansing. Like most such sermons, or so I guessed, his was generic enough to feel tailor-made for my personal predicament. That was the genius of good preaching. The imagery got a bit out of hand — I couldn't picture running my soul in the Laundromat of the Lord's love, or drying it on the clothesline of contrition — but many of his points made sense. Whose spirit couldn't use a good scrubbing once in a while?

After a haphazard but earnest rendering of "Arise, All Souls, Arise," much of the congregation departed, but my mother insisted we join her in the annex, where they served coffee, juice, and doughnuts. I knew this meant getting in over my head, and the boys urged me with strident whispers to skip the reception. But I was drawn along by the stream of talking worshipers and the unvarnished enthusiasm of my

mother who, it was plain to see, reveled in all this. The congregants were upbeat. That is, until a few of them noticed me and gave me some of the looks I'd anticipated. What-is-she-possibly-doing-here looks. Even Hodge Gilchrist, once a bosom buddy but now grown up and married to convention, and his wife, Jane, gave me a condescending nod.

Many of these people would have heard the rumors of my fantasized discovery of a hanged girl in the woods. More than a few may have preserved a low opinion of my morals based on my having given birth to a couple of illegitimate children. Others disapproved of or were amused by my heretical divining. Part of this was surely paranoia. But part of what I was seeing — the turned heads, the mild grimaces, the shallow smirks — was as old as the hills surrounding this village church.

As I began to search out more friendly familiar faces, ones that might offer an encouraging smile, I realized — despite my teaching and Morgan's games — just how much an outsider I had become. Amazing how if you seldom attended the volunteer fire company's annual pancake breakfasts, or never went to the big June tractor parade in Callicoon, and if you avoided the various roast beef dinners at St. Joseph's and religiously skipped church, you really could live in a community and know almost no one at all.

Niles was not there, but Melanie was. So was Adrienne, who gave me and the boys a double take as if wondering where was her camera when she needed it to document a paranormal sighting. The twins stood next to me, eating glazed doughnuts topped with sprinkles and taking in the scene with mild impatience as my mother brought Melanie and her daughter over to say hello.

"Good to see you," I said. "Boys, say hi to Mrs. Hubert."

They mumbled something and stared at me, mutely imploring, Can we leave yet?

"Cass decided to give church a chance this morning," my mother explained. "What did you boys think of the sermon?"

They shrugged and glanced at me again for direction.

"Cass, can I have coffee?"

"Me, too," said Jonah.

"One cup each. Not another drop."

"I want some, too," Adrienne now begged, but was quickly and quietly told no.

The pastor walked straight up, took my hand in both his weighty ones, and greeted me by name. When the boys returned holding their paper cups of black coffee, he directed his fatherly compliments at each, to which they responded with suspicious nods. It was clear even from our brief conversation that Rosalie must have telephoned him beforehand and given him advance notice her wayward daughter and godless grandchildren were going to be in attendance, and to make sure to be a welcoming shepherd. There was little point protesting to her about it. I knew her purpose was to help me, and if in times past I would have groused about such blatant interference, these weren't times past. Everyone standing in this church was looking for help, and I was no different. We were all deeply tattooed by the most basic perplexities, I reminded myself, and my mother had sought her solace here from the days even before Christopher's death, surely spending hours now each week praying for Nep's health and my sanity.

"You ought to join us more often," the pastor said. "It's my understanding some of your friends from childhood are parishioners. One of them even asked after you recently. Seems he just moved back to our area. I told him your mother said you were going up to the family place in Maine a little early this year. He seemed eager to catch up with you."

"Who would that be?" I said warily, feeling ever less safe in this uncomfortable room. What childhood friends did I have beyond Niles and Hodge, neither of whom had moved away from Corinth County?

"I don't feel so well," Jonah interrupted.

"Me neither," said Morgan. "Maybe that coffee was rotten."

Appalled by their bravura performances, but also feeling I myself had now reached a new dead end, I said, "We'd best be going."

Rosalie naturally wanted us to linger but must have registered urgency in my eyes, so walked us outside where we said our goodbyes

and fled. On the way home, the boys launched into a chorus of complaints.

"Please let it drop," I snapped, sorting through my memory for a childhood friend who would bother to ask about me. "It was a good idea for us to attend church."

"Well, I don't see what good there was in it."

"Trust me, it was good," I said, grateful neither of them pressed me for a reason why.

23

L EFT BY MYSELF that afternoon, Jonah having accompanied
Morgan on bicycles to a pickup game over at the school grounds,
I rummaged around in the garage and found some empty boxes. I knew
what I needed to do if I was going to stay this course. Moving with
the steady deliberation of an automaton, I went around the house and
gathered my divining rods, my pendulums, my accumulation of geo-
logical maps, anything tangible that had to do with dowsing. I retrieved
my favorite dogwood Y-rod from the shed out back where I had been
soaking it in a bucket of distilled water and clove oil to keep it lim-
ber. Then I carefully wrapped all my virgulae, bobbers, and L-rods in
remnants of sheets I kept in a rag bin in the pantry and layered them in
the boxes, like little shrouded corpses placed in a paupers' graveyard.
The pendulums I put into brown paper bags and noted down which
one was silver, which was fabricated from stainless steel, which from
brass, even one that was simply an acorn tied to a string. I unloaded the
hatchet and other necessaries from my backpack and placed them in
the cardboard boxes as well. Part of me wanted to linger over each of
these precious old companions, but I knew I couldn't bear it.

Once I had everything crated, I sealed the boxes with packing tape
and marked each in black ink on the lids with the Chinese symbol for

divining— ⊦ —an ideogram that looked for all the world like a headless, armless dancing stick figure. With some effort, I pulled down the attic ladder, a wobbly wooden skeleton I never allowed the boys to climb and shouldn't have used myself, and hauled the boxes up under the rafters next to other paraphernalia left behind by former owners of the house. It smelled somehow of death up there. I couldn't move fast enough to finish the task.

As I folded the ladder back into the ceiling, I felt an overpowering, nauseating mix of grief and joy. It was nothing short of the burial of an old friend, an honored if wily muse. It represented the abandonment of one form of searching I trusted but didn't understand for another I understood but didn't necessarily trust.

In light of my mother's long tenure in the district and my own decent record on the job, I was rehired for the fall term. "You've always been a good teacher," Matt Newburg said, being far kinder to me than I anticipated. Given I had suspended my other occupation, he promised to try to move me into as full-time a schedule as he could manage. For no particular reason, I had never really connected with the principal. But here he was being unexpectedly generous toward me, a normal guy being nice. Granted, he was not the appropriate man to be forward with, but wouldn't a regular, normal Cassandra Brooks think Matt Newburg—who wasn't married like James Boyd or Niles; who held a responsible job; who wasn't unhandsome, but a sincere, solid fellow with large blue eyes—was someone to have dinner with one night?

"I appreciate your generosity."

"Just because you're going through a rocky time doesn't mean we're going to abandon you," he said, shaking my hand before I left.

That night, after sharing the good news with the twins and my parents, I found myself thinking, Why don't I put in a little effort to be less of a recluse, an overgrown tomboy dressed in the same worn jeans and faded flannel shirts I had become accustomed to wearing when not teaching? Revise my uniform of a tatterdemalion? At minimum I might ferret out a couple of blouses that would look presentable with un-

frayed blue jeans. Wear some nice shoes instead of my dusty cowhide boots for a change. Present a portrait of a woman interested in being part of the world around her.

This phenomenon of the new Cassandra labored along in fits and starts through the balance of June. Dressed in what Rosalie deemed "a pretty outfit," I went to a midweek vesper service and even exposed myself to a small social afterward while the twins and Nep stayed home to watch a ball game on television. There was no further mention of this supposed childhood friend or any sign of him, and I chose not to ask more about it. For all my effort, I went to bed more often than not feeling like I had gone about my day as a woman in disguise, a woman I scarcely recognized. Not someone I necessarily disliked, but neither was this new Cass I had fabricated someone with whom I really wanted to spend much time. My experiment, undertaken to prove the hypothesis that a person who donned new garb and attitude might acquire a new direction in life, had already shown signs of failure.

For all their good intentions toward me, not to mention loyalty stretched thin, Morgan and Jonah weren't quite sure what to make of their mother. Morgan continued suffering the taunts of his peers, not just because his mother was different but now because she was "trying to act different from different." And Jonah existed in a limbo, even more friendless than I had been at his age. It was clear not just he but both of them preferred the earlier, divining Cassandra to this incarnation bent on assimilating, against all odds.

What I needed was a renewed sense of perspective. A strong dose of Nep. He, I had to admit as ever, was the one man I really did want to talk to, if he was lucid enough, and so arranged with Rosalie for me to drop by. I didn't tell her how alarmed I had been by my last encounter with him. Or how ashamed I felt for having broken the philosophical bond we shared as father and daughter. I remained as firm a nonbeliever—or more precisely, humble non-knower—as before, for all the brave face I had put on it for Rosalie's benefit. Indeed, I was conflicted enough after the church functions and the banishing of my rods and maps to the attic that I wondered more than ever what any

deity possibly intended for all of us, large and little, down here on Earth.

Morgan was at practice — he was absent from dawn past dusk these days and, after the incident coming back from Binghamton, hadn't seen fit to invite me to any games — so Jonah and I drove over together. A sultry scorcher of a white sky had settled over the long low mountains. The faint wind that washed through the open windows felt good.

We pulled into the drive leading around to the back of the house, and there was Nep on the porch in a white Adirondack rocker he had built for himself years ago. Jonah jumped out of the truck and raced up the stone path to greet his grandfather. I lingered, wanting them to have a few moments together, and soon Nep rose from his rocker and they came down the steps toward me.

"Come on, Cass," said Jonah, mischievous, even defiant. "We're walking down to the pond."

"How are you today, handsome?" I asked, giving my father a delicate embrace, as light as his new frailty suggested I hug him.

"The pond — beautiful."

"It sure is. That's a good idea to walk down there."

Nep looked pretty clearheaded, his hand steady on Jonah's shoulder, more to keep himself in balance, I sensed, than as a display of affection for the boy. His white hair, as long as Morgan's these days, shimmered in the dazzling sun. With his sandaled feet, his untucked blousy white shirt over a pair of baggy white cotton trousers, he looked like an old sage, a homely monk drifting through nature guarded by pink spirea and powdery plumes of astilbe.

"Come on," Jonah cried out again, full-throated, then turned to me with his inquisitive eager eyes and said quietly, firmly, "I want to show him, Cass."

I opened my mouth to insist otherwise, but then thought, No. Jonah had the right. My quest wasn't his. Divining was a way of connecting with his grandfather. No harm in that.

"What have you been up to today?" I asked my father.

"Today?"

"Yes, what have you been doing?"

"Nothing. Not today."

"Well, it's a perfect day to do nothing. Don't you think so, Jonah?"

"Perfect," he agreed. "And a perfect day to show Nep something secret."

Another walk to the pond to disclose another secret. Though Nep was reticent, I believe we all knew what Jonah meant. I looked again at my father, more closely this time, and saw that some quintessence had departed. His self, once solid, had become porous. I had the distinct feeling of having filtered through these perceptions before, and the ones that were about to follow. Like I needed to remember back to what was about to happen ahead. In the end, no language was equal to expressing this quantum moment. My father was leaving me soon.

A great blue heron was startled from its motionless stalking as we came down past a low wall of broken stones. Jonah ran ahead, clapping his hands and shouting at the huge carnivorous bird as it rose unhurried from the shallow water on patient, nonchalant wings that were almost as wide as Jonah was tall.

"I need to talk with you about something," I said to Nep.

He followed the majestic bird's flight as it lifted away above the canopy of green leaves, heading south toward some other pond. Jonah descended into the woods, I assumed to cut himself a divining rod.

"I don't know whether you remember about that girl Laura they found in the forest?"

I gave him time to respond, but he said nothing. Tightening my hold on his hand for an instant, I felt him squeeze back. He was listening.

"It's just that I went to visit her and I think something's really wrong. The man, or whoever it is, who hung that mannequin you found at the lighthouse? I'm beginning to suspect he has something to do with Laura, too."

"I see," he said.

"And I think he hasn't finished with either her or me."

"I know how that is."

"How so?"

He didn't respond, so I continued into a realm of speculation I hadn't articulated even to myself before this moment. "This is very hard for me to talk about, and I don't want to betray a confidence, but I wonder if Rosalie ever told you about Christopher's involvement with Emily Schaefer's death. I've been thinking about it, and the place where she died isn't all that far from where I saw the hanged girl. I'm convinced she was a forevision, Nep. But the more I think about it I seem to have been looking backward and forward at the same time. Are you with me here?"

"I am."

"There was another kid there with Chris when Emily died. His name was Roy. You probably don't remember him."

"No."

"I didn't mean to see what they were doing. I was just playing around in these cliffs where we used to go and heard people arguing. She was really furious, it seemed to me, but you know how a valley tends to exaggerate sounds. Anyway, I have a terrible feeling that whoever stole Millicent and hung that thing in the lighthouse is the man who kidnapped Laura, and maybe even knew Emily and Chris."

"Chris? There's Chris right there," Nep said, pointing.

My heart sank.

"You mean Jonah?" My son was at the far end of the pond, past cattails where this year's redwing blackbirds were nesting. He was striding deliberately around the bank with the rod he had cut in the meantime, having brought a pocketknife with him for the occasion.

It was impossible. Lots of little words strung together on preposterous, coalescing ideas like so many glass beads on a Moebius necklace.

"Christopher's a witcher now, look at that," Nep continued.

Jonah came running up, a serious smile on his face. "You see what I've got, Nep?"

"That a boy."

"You probably know every underground stream from here to China, but I found one, too. Tell him, Cass."

Two generations of Brooks men stared at me, looking for their mother and daughter to bring this news into focus, to articulate it, and thereby make it real. I felt the tears welling in my eyes, wiped them away, and smiled as best I could under the circumstances. Pull yourself together, I thought. Be here with them now.

"Jonah came with me to Partridge's, and against my better judgment I let him give a try at dowsing."

"Partridge."

"The man who runs the hatchery. Big guy with huge frothy sideburns," I said, wriggling my fingers at either side of my head as if I were scratching my own muttonchops. Nep seemed to be drawing a blank, so I pressed forward, "Doesn't matter. Here's the point. It looks like there's another diviner in the family. Not that the world needs us and not that Jonah's going to make it his life's practice, but he's got the gift, it seems."

"The gift," Nep echoed.

"You want to see, Grandpa?"

"Let's keep it short, Jonah," I said. "We don't want to tire him out."

He went about with his divining rod held before him, awkward but game and earnest. Nep and I watched. The distress I had been feeling, trouble I badly wanted to discuss with my father, was overwhelmed by my raw insights into his own wayward head. Here before me was a mind whose memories had released themselves from their moorings, free to float wherever momentary whimsies carried them.

"No, I want to see Christopher do his thing," Nep announced, as if reading my thoughts and proving my point. Jonah walked with his virgula outstretched before him, gripping the rod a little too tightly.

"I'm not sure you're going to find what you're looking for here, Jonah."

"Let him try," Nep said under his breath.

Jonah walked away from the pond and out toward a field brimming with orchard grass and bellflowers, purple and white, that a neighbor farmer would be haying in the next couple of weeks. He zigzagged up and down the land while Nep and I tagged along at a distance. A red-

start flickered across the tops of the long grass, its black and orange feathers creating the illusion of a thrown cinder from a flame.

"Jonah," Nep said. "Come here a minute."

The boy looked up in the way a deer will when interrupted in its browsing. He walked over to where we were standing, about a hundred feet distant.

"Let me see how, how you're holding it. Walk back and forth here," his articulation returning some along with his focus. Jonah obliged, and Nep, letting go of my hand, said, "That's not—here, like this."

I hadn't seen my father holding a diviner's rod in what seemed like ages, even though it had been perhaps only a couple of years since I last dowsed with him. Jonah passed him the forked branch. Nep took it in his hands, palms facing upward as he'd always preferred, and he walked, slowly, deliberately, while Jonah shadowed alongside, watching every last nuance of his posture and movements as if life depended on it. I stood there under a sky unmarred by the slightest cloud and marveled at this small perfect moment, all other worries and concerns having temporarily flown away like that heron. Here was my father teaching my son a craft as basic and mysterious as the very pools of water that lurked in the stony clay beneath our feet. What, I thought, could be more harmless and precious than this? A dying man and a child on the verge of manhood practicing an old art together. Jonah had taken the virgula from Nep now and was walking the field on his own again, his hands lightly grasping the forks of the rod, palms directed skyward. I watched Nep watch him.

Jonah didn't divine any treasure that day other than his grandfather's heart. As for myself, when I got back to Mendes Road, another postcard awaited me in the mailbox. No stamp, no postmark this time. Just a photograph of a lighthouse bearing the legend "Cranberry Islands, Maine." *Last warning to stay away from the girl,* the handwritten note read. *How easy to slip and fall.*

24

OUR ANNUAL INDEPENDENCE DAY festivities were fast approaching. Nep probably wasn't equal to it, was Rosalie's opinion, despite his staunch refusal to cancel. It was tradition, he told her in his way, and traditions are to be kept and cared for. This was less than a week before the big date. Our family hadn't missed throwing the Fourth of July party in any year going back as far as I could remember, including the year after Christopher died and even that uncomfortable summer when the twins were three months old, blinking infants in matching cribs. I didn't know what to tell her. If Nep wanted to proceed, I thought, let's go for it. His friends knew he wasn't well. If they hadn't seen him recently, here would be a chance for them to reconnect. On the other hand, maybe he wasn't the best judge of what he could and couldn't manage anymore. Thinking this way made me feel like a traitor to his lifelong free spirit, though. Like some well-meaning Judas.

It was Jonah who took me under his wing. "You worry too much," he said.

We had finally been invited to one of Morgan's games and I found myself wondering, even amid a new impatience with myself as aspiring paradigm of normalcy, what to wear. How would other moms dress,

should my hair be up or down? I also wondered, far more cogently, which of the kids had given Morgan such grief about me that he'd all but shunned his mother after our return from Covey, and how should I act toward them or their parents if they got it in their heads to identify themselves? How should I respond to anyone who might ask me about witching the hanged girl? I had been second-guessing myself about everything under the sun — this vaunted damn sun that was the same as everybody else's — and I was beginning to drive myself to distraction. Were those really fresh tire tracks in the drive when Jonah and I got home from my parents' or was I seeing things again? Was it conceivable that someone had breezed through the new locks and lain down on my bed? The pillows seemed crushed and the bedspread rumpled.

Unaware of the postcards and my concern about another intrusion, Jonah nevertheless saw right to the heart of the problem. "You should go back to being yourself."

"You think?"

"I know."

The party was moving forward if for no other reason than to honor Nep's admirable stubbornness. This year a lot of the preparation was going to fall to me, so I decided I might as well get a jump on it and was doing some baking. Jonah had joined me and was sitting at the kitchen table, sorting pennies, nickels, dimes, quarters in rolls, having decided it was high time to get rid of his childhood piggy bank in favor of adult bills. Without looking up from his piles of coins, he concluded, "I believe in you, okay? I know you can handle it."

I glanced over at him with a grateful smile.

"Thanks for the advice, man," I said.

"Any time, man."

That evening Morgan's team would lose despite his three base hits and some deft fielding. Jonah and I sat in the bleachers on the third-base side to get the best view of him on both defense and offense. The crowd was large and loud. Parents and grandparents had settled themselves in folding chairs along the chain-link fences and siblings filled the stands, tracking every pitch as if the fate of humankind depended

upon it, shouting advice to players and admonishments to the umpire. Some families had done tailgate partying, and the smell of burgers grilled on hibachis lingered in the air. A buggy summer evening.

Sometime late in the game, I noticed his familiar face. He was sitting in the first row of the bleachers opposite ours, and I wouldn't have seen him had I not walked to the truck for the insect repellent I kept in the glove compartment. On my way back, I recognized Charley Granger in profile and was surprised by how surprised I was.

He was by himself, it seemed. Maybe it was the yellowish sodium ball-field lights playing tricks, but I could have sworn there was a little silvering in his brown hair at the temples. He wore glasses. Charley, my Charley, middle-aged. This must have been the childhood friend the pastor had mentioned. Obsessing about Roy, I'd forgotten about the obvious.

Charley was dressed in a faded moss-green T-shirt and black jeans. His elbows planted on spread knees and his palms tapping together as he followed the play. Without thinking, I drifted in his direction. I found myself wondering if he would be wearing an eye patch—I couldn't see one from this angle. Wondered what his older voice would sound like, if he would even remember me. I knew we would have to exchange some reminiscences about Christopher, make the sort of small talk I had never excelled at. As I hesitated, having drawn close, the crowd made a raucous sudden roar, and I turned to look at what was happening on the field behind the ghostly diamond grid of the backstop fence. I saw Morgan dive, make his catch, pivot like some avant-garde dancer, and throw the runner out at first. Cheering with the rest, I walked forward and placed my hand on his shoulder.

"Charley?" I said.

"Yes?" looking at me with his serene eye, the ruined one sewn closed in such a way it seemed merely shut in a benign, perennial wink. "My God, Cassie?" He rose to his feet, broadly smiling, and we reached out to embrace each other, not a little awkwardly, finally settling for a four-handed shake, a tentative kiss cheek to cheek, and palms grasping each other's forearms. "Look at you."

"I can't believe it."

"What brings you out here?" he asked, the same question I had for him. I pointed toward Morgan, who was jogging back to the dugout with the other players, the visiting team having been retired. Charley had returned to Corinth because his mother was moving from Little Eddy after years of complaining about the harsh long winters and how lonely she'd become in the wake of her husband's death, Charley's father.

"I'm sorry, I didn't know."

"Thanks, Cassie. She asked me to help her pack, oversee the closing on the sale of the house, be with her while she wrapped things up. So here I am."

A brief silence settled over us while we looked at each other, calculating the years, I supposed, reconciling the person before us with separate memories of the one we'd known. I broke this by asking if she was at the game. No, he said, he was here because two boys who were children of a friend, an old acquaintance, were playing. Their father would drop by later to pick them all up and asked Charley to watch on his behalf. "Roy Skoler, you remember him?"

Speechless, I nodded.

"He was living downriver a ways, near his wife's family in Port Jervis. Seems he and his wife broke up and Roy's moved back to Little Eddy, rented a place down by the river until he can find something more permanent. He's got his boys for the summer."

"That's nice," I mumbled, as an icy panic raced through me. "That he's got his boys, I mean."

"Well, of all the kids in the old gang, Roy's the only one who hasn't really caught much of a break in life. Bibb, Jimmy, Lare, they all got themselves good jobs, families, they're doing fine. Roy called out of the blue and came up to visit me a few weeks ago, before he took custody of his kids for the summer, and it was a less than pleasant experience. I feel kind of sorry for him. But then, you know I've always been partial to outsiders."

"Me, for instance?"

"Both of us, for instance."

How deeply unsettling it was that Charley, the best of my past, unwittingly brought with him the worst of it. Roy Skoler in Little Eddy—it wrenched my stomach, indeed I felt nauseated. Forcing myself to smile and try my very best to get back into the rhythm of this reunion with Charley, I said, hoping to change the subject, "If you're not sitting with anybody meantime, would you like to join me and my other son?"

We walked to the opposite stand, where I introduced Jonah. Before Charley could ask about a father, a husband, I explained with an abbreviated version of the same story I had offered the twins long ago, my old cover story that had begun to harden into a reliable reality. Hoping Jonah couldn't hear everything I was saying, I went on to paint a somewhat brighter portrait of life than facts would bear. Like a film editor cutting in postproduction in order to make the make-believe more believable, I allowed Cassandra Productions to screen for him my work as a teacher while downplaying my other vocation as a diviner. My documentary was mostly truthful, just there were a couple of scenes left out. The recitation calmed me some, and as we settled on the bench together my pleasure at seeing Charley gradually overtook the shock of having evoked Roy Skoler's name. More circles were closing around me, but I didn't need to be trapped by them. At least not here with my old surrogate brother sitting next to me after so many years.

We watched the game, the three of us now cheering, now groaning, but at the same time I caught up a little on Charley's life since the old days. After the four-wheeler accident, the surgery and long recuperation, the physical therapy to learn how to negotiate his way in a depthless two-dimensional world, he went to college in Boston, then migrated north, finally settling in a small seaside town.

"What do you do?" I asked.

"My liberal arts degree seemed the perfect launching pad for a career in antiques. Antiques, old books, folk art paintings. I've also become a decent cabinetmaker and restorer in the meantime. My shop's

in Wiscasset, up in Maine. Most of my business is summer people, so this isn't the best time for me to be away, but there it is. What do you do besides raising these handsome guys?"

"Wiscasset, you mean on the Sheepscot?"

Nothing was more reliable than pure chance. I told him about Covey. How we used to prefer Route One, along the coast with its bustling little harbors and pretty villages, to the quicker interstate with its non-existent vistas, straight corridors lined by indifferent trees. We had driven through Wiscasset many times, I said, floored to have been so near Charley over the years and at the same time chilled by the real-ization that Roy Skoler had been visiting Maine just as I was being tor-mented on Covey Island.

"Well, that settles that. You're a slow coastal highway traveler again from now on," he said, smiling and putting his arm around my shoul-der as he might have done twenty-five years ago.

I looked at his face and realized I had been unconsciously averting my eyes. Charley understandably misinterpreted this as my wanting to avoid getting caught staring at the sightless flesh where — if my brother and the rest of the gang had chosen less treacherous ways of killing time — his other healthy eye would be looking right back at me.

"Pretty hideous, you're thinking," he said.

"No, that's wrong."

"I'm more than used to it by now, but it took a while."

"I don't think it looks awful, Charley. I was just thinking it's a shame how some things happen that are beyond our stopping them, is all," which was the truth, flat out.

In fact, Charley's manner as well as his face were both so youthful and mature that I realized that my childhood crush had never really abated. That said, I wasn't so foolish or impulsive as to think that the half-formed yearnings of a lonesome little girl had any purchase on the present. It was good sitting there with him, though, despite the fact I couldn't help but wonder — I refused to ask — which of the boys on the field were Skoler's sons. "You remember my father, Nep?"

"Never forget him. He was kind to me after the accident, gave me

a ham radio and taught me how to use it. I still have the thing, works perfect to this day."

"Nep called what he did at his workbench, bringing old things to new life, the *science of resurrection*. Seems what you do is kind of similar."

Charley gave me an unabashed hard thoughtful look, then glanced away as the umpire cried, "You're out," and that was it for the game. The crowd had dwindled to relatives and diehards who would hang around until the last soul departed, taking in the warm evening air, analyzing the game, or others who, like my old friend, were standing in for absentee parents. I wanted to talk more but didn't know what to say other than "When is Roy coming to pick up his kids?" knowing that I needed to avoid encountering him if at all possible.

He peered around the throng. "Not here yet."

"Want to walk down to the dugout for a minute? I'd love for you to meet Morgan."

Jonah had said nothing to this point but was as fascinated by Charley as his mother. When we made our way to the wooden shed that served as a dugout, he finally piped up, asking, "So you knew my mother when she was my age?"

"Younger than you."

"It's probably hard to imagine me as ever being younger than you, but I was."

"Oh, no," said Jonah. "You still are, in some ways." He then asked Charley, "What happened to your eye?"

"Jonah—" but Charley was already answering him, and neither paid attention to my objection.

"I lost it in my early teens."

"It went bad?"

"No, I was playing a bad game," he said, then looked at me, perhaps weighing whether or not to mention that I was there that evening. He must have decided not to, because he finished, simply, "Lowest moment of my life, but also maybe one of the best things that ever happened to me."

"No way. How come?"

"When you can't see the same way everybody else does, it's your responsibility to see things others can't. Simple idea, I always liked it. Hard one to live up to, though. You know who said that to me?"

Jonah shook his head.

"Your grandfather."

Morgan joined us, cap slung on backward — a personal tic that meant his team had lost, his version of a black armband for mourning — and before I launched into any platitudes about sportsmanship, he warned, "Just don't say it, Cass. We blew it. It's just a game. No big stink," then stared at Charley.

"Morgan," I said, placing my hand on Charley's forearm. "Let me introduce you to an old friend of mine who was buddies with your uncle Christopher."

He shifted his glove to his left hand, wiped his right on his dusty white pant leg, and shook Charley's outstretched hand.

"Good game you played."

"Thanks," Morgan said.

How was it, I wondered, Charley could get away with saying this and I couldn't? The weight of a male voice in a fellow male's ears.

"You know Tick and Arlen?"

"Sure, so?" Morgan answered, his eyes darting over at Jonah, then down at his shoes.

"Their father asked me to corral them for him."

"I'll go find them," Jonah intervened, deciphering something on Morgan's face, and that conspiratorial glance he had shot his brother's way.

At first I attributed Morgan's mood to the fact he didn't like losing and didn't want to stick around. But as I listened to my son and old friend talk baseball, a universal language for people who don't know each other, the truth dawned on me. These were the boys who had been tormenting Morgan since we arrived back from Covey. It was clearer than the bristling stars above. I hurriedly asked Charley if he'd like to get together and talk more.

"I'd love nothing better," he said. "You all right?"

"My number's in the book," I blurted and gave him a hasty good-bye kiss, startling both him and Morgan by my abrupt rudeness. Grabbing my son by the arm—he yanked himself free and ran ahead of me toward the truck—I called over my shoulder, "Wonderful to see you again, Charley," as Jonah climbed by himself up the brief rise from the field, where the floodlights were being extinguished one by one, having apparently not found the two kids he'd gone looking for. I waved frantically for him to go on ahead and join his brother, then turned around and walked straight into the one man I was hoping to avoid.

For an endlessly long moment I looked into the fixed and staring eyes of Roy Skoler, who with his sons beside him said not a word. His face had aged, the eyes sunk some into their hollow sockets, and even in this light it was clear he remained as pallid as ever. And yet his jet-black hair was still so dark that I even wondered passingly if he didn't dye it. Though the years clearly weighed on him, he was ever the same slightly statured man who exuded a tough, wiry confidence that made him seem larger than he was. He broke our brief frozen tableau with the faintest hint of a smile—this man whom I had never seen smile—before taking a drag from his cigarette and blowing smoke out of the side of his mouth. Pushing past them, I strode toward the truck, behind my boys who in the growing darkness had seen none of this, my heart racing and thoughts in a tangling blur, wondering how it was possible to have kept acts as shattering and central as those that rushed to mind, secreted for so long, unexamined and inarticulable.

My rod was now directed at its own diviner's heart.

Part V

THE FIFTH
TURNING

25

I REMEMBER MAKING friends with a small stone. A smooth black river stone that fit in the palm of my hand like a little animal, yolk-shaped and fast asleep. She had a face, for sometimes it was a she. Blurry white smears on one side of the stone suggested eyes and a quizzical mouth that at times smiled and other times frowned. Quartz lodged in granite, maybe. One of my shoes had gone missing, but that didn't matter much since I went without a lot of the time back then. I was cold and shivered that first night even though it was August. I had brought Millicent with me but hadn't taken a blanket. Millicent was cold, too. She didn't say as much—Millicent never spoke in all the years I had known her—but we always shared similar feelings.

Dew settled over the predawn outdoor world where I resided those days and nights, so my hair and clothes and doll companion were damp when morning came. I didn't worry since I knew the sun would dry me off if I lay down on the rock that served as a kind of porch floor to the shallow scallop of a cave, out of sight of anyone who might be searching for me. I was sure they were searching, but I wished they wouldn't bother, for a while at least. I needed to be by myself.

—They're looking, though, aren't they? I asked the stone, waking her.

The stone agreed my parents were searching for their runaway daughter.

—Others, too?

—Others, too.

During the day, I didn't move around much beyond this cave, little more than the intimation of an open mouth in the rock really, where my brother and I had fantasized Iroquois warriors long ago lived with their squaws and papooses. Nobody would have known they were here, we figured, and so they'd have been protected from anyone who wanted to find them. Just as I was now.

I asked the stone, —Is anybody nearabouts?

The stone said, —No.

—So I'm safe?

—No.

—Who do I have to be afraid of?

The stone said nothing. I held Millicent close.

This was the place Christopher and I came when Rosalie and Nep were away for their wedding and funeral day that once. The secret place where some of the other kids in the gang would join us. Though I was always brought here on the rope leash and with a bandanna tied over my eyes, these precautions didn't finally fool me. By listening to birdcalls and the telltale crunch of the earth, the particular rustle and feel of its grasses as we walked, by sensing how my brother maneuvered past this patch of thorny wild rose and that tangle of ironwood, as I pictured them, I visualized roughly where we were. Nobody told me the way. What was more, I'd tramped my whole young life through these forests and possessed a moving picture in my mind of its dips and rises, meadows and streams, where the poison ivy was and where the wild leeks proliferated. He wasn't going to fool me, and he didn't. Until the day Emily died, he never knew that his secret was also mine.

Looking back, I see it was the very first place I ever divined.

My brother was dead and his funeral was over. My mother was mute and hysterical, and though my father tried to comfort me, I wasn't yet

able to hear him over the mournful, dirging bagpipes that were caught in my head. I couldn't stay in the house another hour. So I left.

I was hungry that second day, sick with hunger. It didn't seem right for me to be hungry, especially since I allowed myself the indulgence of drinking a bellyful of water from the stream. The pebble I'd found in my hand down at the brook when I dipped for water asked me, did I know what I was doing? Was this really where I wanted to be?

No, this was not where I wanted to be, I silently told the pebble. But my brother's lost and I don't want to be found.

—When did you see him last? the stone persisted, speaking in a whisper.

—I told him he shouldn't go.

—He shouldn't have gone, then, should he.

The stone's voice was flat as its face, uninflected, and very sure of itself. It was as astute and reserved as royalty.

—We both know that, I said.

For a period of time the stone, trying to be a friend, went back to sleep, leaving me in peace. I didn't know which was worse. Talking to the stone or talking to myself. Because when I spoke with myself, I felt unforgiving, whereas when I spoke with the stone, she offered advice like, —Maybe you should go home, Cass. None of what happened was your fault. Nep and Mom are worried. Go on and get out of here.

—Maybe tomorrow, I said.

There were other things I could have done but didn't. I could have made a daisy chain for Millicent, as I'd always enjoyed making them in the past. A wide rock-ridden field loaded with wildflowers that bloomed without fear of the farmer's hayer was farther north of the cave and full of daisies. I didn't make a fire with the matches Chris kept inside a plastic bag out of the rain at the back of the cave. I didn't go looking for that lost shoe, though I wanted to, because I knew I might be seen. I didn't cry. This I wanted to do, too, but couldn't bear the thought of giving in to something as cowardly and weak as crying. My brother, if his ghost was watching me, and I admit I did believe it was, would have either cracked up laughing or been angered by such drippy

behavior. I could have been afraid in the pitch dark but was numb rather than fearful.

The stone said, —On the other hand, maybe it's better you stay here. You're in a lot of trouble, you know.

She whispered that advice to me during my second night, a breezy night in which the trees conversed with one another, their leaves talking nonsense with abandon. Her warning grabbed hold in my head and repeated itself like a mantra, again and again, and was doing so a little after the sun rose and the birds' dialogue took over where the night wind and woods' left off. I would never have guessed her words— *maybe it's better you stay here, you're in a lot of trouble*—would be the same I'd hear from the first human voice I encountered during the madness of my flight and hiding.

The words came from a boy's mouth. Roy's mouth. They may or may not have been the first he spoke when he found me asleep on the long flat rock, sunning myself dry.

—I knew you'd be here, he had said.

I was so shocked by his crashing into my sequestered world that I hoped he and the panting black dog next to him were just some bad dream.

—Don't worry, I didn't tell anybody.

My blinking into the sun over his shoulder didn't make him disappear.

—Look, I brought you some food, he said, now very clearly in focus and quite real. He opened up a rucksack and offered me a paper bag that was inside, backhanding away the dog that nosed toward it. —Bologna, peanut butter, some bread. There's chips in there, too, and a couple of apples. I'll bring better stuff tomorrow, just tell me what you need.

—I don't want anything.

—You need to eat some bread at least. Even convicts get bread and water.

—Maybe I'll have a piece of bread.

—What happened to your shoe?

—Lost it.

—I can break into your parents' house and bring you another pair.

—No, don't, I said.

He sat beside me on the rock and observed me with the same open curiosity a cat might show a cornered mouse.

—How'd you know where this place is? I asked.

—Chris showed me, he claimed, but I knew he wasn't telling me the truth. —So now only you and me are the ones that know. You're safe here.

I remembered what the stone said about me not being safe, but Roy wasn't unkind or threatening in any way. Instead, he was nice and thoughtful and didn't do what I expected the first person who found me would do. That is, order me to come home this instant. He didn't shame me by saying my mother and father were half out of their minds with worry. All he did was offer to help me survive a little better until I decided on my own what to do. This is what I told both Millicent and the stone, after Roy heeled the hound and left, saying he'd be back tomorrow, promising not to tell a soul he had found me. —You'll be wanting more supplies. I'll take care of everything.

When I asked the stone what she made of all this, she demurred. I thought she might have been a little jealous, but the stone didn't care for Roy.

—We'll see, she said.

For all my stubborn abstinence, my martyr's will to fast, to starve myself until I was as pure as the stone in my hand, I couldn't help but eat some of the food Roy had brought. I fingered peanut butter from the half-full jar and ate one of the apples. When I hiked down to the stream to drink some more water and wash my face, I sensed I was being watched. I hid myself behind a hemlock and trained my eyes, sharp as a fox's, back up the hill and across its cragged ridge. Sunlight danced everywhere, near and far, in puddles and flashes where the thick leaves parted to let it in, then closed and playfully parted again, projecting what looked like a million fat blinking stars against a green sky. Nothing moved but light and leaves. No one was there. The stone suggested

I was afraid because a person had broken in on my fragile, desperate peace. She was right, I was sure.

That third night was the worst, crowded by nightmares. No sooner would I fall asleep than wake again, feverish from dreamed scenarios with Nep laughing at me, then baring fangs like some hairless wolf, and my mother giving all my clothes away to some girls I never saw before, saying that if they didn't fit go ahead and burn them because I never was much of a daughter, and another in which a man with no face was trying to push the stone into my mouth. The sun rose on an exhausted runaway, my fourth and last day in the cave. Whether from exposure or malnutrition, my skin felt every bit as on fire as the phantasmagoric clothes the dream girls were meant to burn.

—You all right? I asked the stone. —I'm not.

The stone was as mute as Millicent this morning. Maybe she had said everything a stone was able to say. Who knows, I thought, maybe she had died during the night.

—I agree. You don't look too good, Roy said, instead.

—How long you been here? glancing up in shock at hearing his voice again.

—All your life, he answered. —You were sleeping. I didn't want to wake you up. Look, I brought you a blanket.

He knelt beside me and wrapped the blanket around my shoulders. While the first part of his answer hadn't made any sense, he'd spoken with such unwavering conviction that I didn't argue.

—That's better, isn't it? he said.

I was shivering too much to speak but nodded my head yes.

—I'll make a fire, warm you up.

—No, I said, looking at the stone for guidance. The stone blankly stared back.

—But you're shaking like a stick. Here, let me—

—No, leave me alone, I cried out.

—That's nice, he said. —Here's the thanks I get for helping you.

—I'm sorry.

—You just don't know what's good for you, he said, and took my hair into his hand, knotting it like he had that time when the gang was

last together. —I'm trying to warm you up, is all. Nothing wrong with that, is there?

—No, I said, trying and failing to move away from him.

—See, that's better already, he hissed, snaking his arm around my waist and pressing his face against the side of my head. I felt too sick and afraid to tell him, No, it wasn't better. I wanted to flee, but he had my hands caught behind my back and forced me down against the rock where I'd been lying and dreaming terrible sleeping dreams only a few minutes before this waking nightmare began. Time twisted and broke, and what transpired was in a single, interminable gesture rather than several angry, awkward, violent ones. He had my mouth clamped under the weight of his palm. My jeans were forced below my knees, one leg off my kicking shoeless foot, searing pain, and I blacked out and remembered nothing more until I woke up a second time that morning being carried by Roy, cradled in his arms as if he were my savior, with his smiling dog, innocently full of life, bounding ahead of us. When he brought me back to the house, a transient hero for finding and saving me, it was he who lifted me across the doorsill, like some valiant groom bringing home his semiconscious bride. The police asked questions, mostly regarding where he'd located me and why I ran away. Since he obfuscated and postured with confident brilliance and I wasn't willing or able to say much to them, they left, reasonably concluding that the poor girl clinging to her dirty little doll was traumatized by the violent death of her beloved brother and had bought some time to grieve by herself at everyone's expense. No matter, she was home now. The doctor, who did little more than take my temperature, advised bed rest and nourishment. His patient made no noises of complaint because whatever had happened was already beginning to cloak itself in a mist of unreality. The episode slid into a deviation far out of the stream that was my life. It became over time an irrelevancy, without real cause or, I thought hopefully, when I thought about it at all, any ultimate effect.

I went back to the cave once, hoping to find my sister stone. To see if she still had a voice to speak with and, if so, what she might say. But, like Chris and Roy Skoler and my mother for a time, she was gone.

26

THE TWINS AND I picked up Nep and headed out in his station wagon past Callicoon, crossing the span into Pennsylvania in search of fireworks, which were still legal there. My mother gave me some money to help with the purchase, which I could ill afford alone, but refused to come along with us on this, our shady annual expedition. We weren't allowed to transport fireworks back across the border into New York and weren't sanctioned to light them up at our Independence Day celebration. But a number of people in these rural reaches, where municipal fireworks displays were even more amateur than ours, went ahead with their own shows, and Niles both watched and looked the other way. A form of social protest, was how Nep saw it. One that the Founding Fathers would have applauded. The right to bear fireworks should be in the Constitution, he used to joke.

"You look wrong today," Nep said to me when we pulled out on the road.

"I didn't sleep that well last night."

"She's wearing lipstick in case she sees Charley again," said Morgan.

"What's Charley?"

"I'm not wearing lipstick. You remember Charley, Nep. He was one of Christopher's friends. You always liked him."

"Well, if it's not lipstick, what is it?" Morgan goaded.

"Lip gloss. There's a difference."

"Don't remember," said Nep.

"Lip glue more like. Think of all the dust that's going to get stuck there."

"Point for Morgan," said Jonah.

"Point for nobody." Today of all days, on this Nep adventure I always looked forward to, I should have been in a livelier, lighter mood. But seeing Roy Skoler changed all that. I felt as if my life had been a jigsaw puzzle spilled on the floor, and a part of me longed to put it together to see what the picture looked like, while another part had grown used to it being unsolved and preferred it that way.

"You're unhappy," said Nep.

"I'm fine."

"You're unhappy."

"Well, look, I'm already doing a lot better with my three men here headed out to spend good money on bad contraband. How's that?"

"That's the bomb" and "Rock on," the boys exclaimed at the same time.

Which made Nep laugh, which made me try to smile.

And damned if we didn't shoot the works. Roman candles and strobing fountains. Vampire rockets that came in their own gaudy coffins. Ones that promised to send up silver whistling tails. Ones that crackled into chrysanthemums and Man-o'-Wars. Bottle rockets of every variety our under-the-counter dealer, a fellow Nep had dowsed a well for, had in his inventory. Several boxes of the hardware were loaded into the back of the wagon and hidden under blankets. The return drives from Pennsylvania always elicited the same kind of crisp trepidation one might feel if walking across live coals on a dare. I had a sense this could be our last such run. The laws were getting stricter and it wasn't fair to ask Niles to compromise himself any longer. Besides, there was the matter of Nep.

Early on during our venture he was bright as a sparkler. Yes, he voiced his opinion in his personal language of cobbled words sometimes—he

told Morgan to get a haircut, saying he ought to cut off his hat—but when we crossed the river, he told the boys with perfect clarity about water boils and how dangerous they can be.

"A vacuum of air stirs under the water and can rise up and pull a boat right under, like that," snapping his fingers.

Yet once we had finished with the fireworks dealer, he seemed to slip into a passing coma. A transient death of sorts, asleep with his eyes and mouth open.

"Jonah, give him a nudge on the shoulder. Real gentle."

He did, and my father came awake. Said something incomprehensible. Then drifted off again. At one point when we were recognizably close to the house he had lived in his whole life, he asked why we were going back to Covey.

"Everything all right?" Morgan asked him.

"Right as ruin," he misspoke, craning to look at his grandson as if he didn't quite know who the boy was.

Once home, we hauled our cache into Nep's workshop, where his old cronies Joe Karp, Billy Mecham, and Sam Briscoll—the three wise men, as they were known, though their wisdom was suspect over the years—were waiting to help sort through the munitions. Seeing them recentered Nep, grounded him back into his life. Their routine was sacrosanct. They drank a few beers, parsed the weather forecast for the hallowed event, decided on what order the birds would fly. Jonah and Morgan had been allowed to join this exclusive club when they turned seven. Same age Christopher was let in. Same age I was. We children of both generations weren't really asked to offer our opinions. Our role was more like that of a Greek chorus. When one of the wise men had a good idea, we sang its praises. In some ways, the half an hour of live fireworks after the barbecue was incidental to these more intimate preludes.

As I entered the kitchen to help Rosalie set out a late lunch, she was sitting at the round oak clawfoot table, holding a wet tea bag over her cup, watching it swing from side to side like a dowser's pendulum. Her chin perched on a folded hand as she studied the bag swaying on its short string.

"Self-hypnosis?" I asked.

"I didn't hear you come in," flushed like quarry out of her reverie.

"What were you divining just now?"

She laid the tea bag on a saucer and drank. No steam rose off the cup, so I had to wonder how long she had been there. It never ceased to amaze me that a woman whose life was so closely driven by a belief in the holy divine always recoiled when she heard the word used as a human verb instead of an ecclesiastic noun.

"Charley Granger called looking for you. Haven't seen him in years."

"He left Corinth a long time ago."

"A good guy, wasn't he?"

"I always liked Charley," I agreed, hoping she wouldn't divine me and my girlhood crush in retrospect. I told her where he lived now, what brought him back to Little Eddy, and asked if it would be all right to invite him and his mother to the holiday gathering.

"Of course," she said, and after a pause, "How'd he look? His eye, I mean."

"Looked like it was shut, is all," I told her, wanting to change the subject. "Speaking of which, have you seen Nep sleeping with his eyes open?"

"I don't like to talk about it. Did you get all your bombs and fire-crackers?"

"Enough for four Fourth of Julys."

"He married?"

"Charley?" I asked, disingenuous, wishing for all the world I could open up with my mother about Roy Skoler and the forevisioner's intuitions I had begun to have about him, all the while knowing a lifetime of unspoken rage and humiliation over what he did made any thoughts I might have about his current activities wildly suspect. "We didn't talk about it one way or the other."

She picked up her spoon, stared blinking at it as one might a hand mirror whose face was tarnished, then startled me with words as plain and frank as I had ever heard from her. "I just don't know what I'm going to do with myself when your father goes," and looked up at me, her face as stoic as my long-lost river stone's, but her eyes damp.

As surely as she knew me, I knew my mother. She would not want me to break down in tears with her. Early on after Nep and I bonded in the wake of Christopher's death, Rosalie had conceived of the two of us as suffering from some sort of *folie à deux*—a mutually shared or stimulated psychotic disorder—whereas I had often thought she was afflicted by a *folie à dieu*. She always considered herself the sanest of our tribe, and as a matter of fact her position wasn't easily assailable, although she too had her faults and demons. Though Christ took over where Christopher left off, I know that my mother had passed many of those years much more lonely and bereft than Nep and I had been, and no prayer group or Bible circle had been able to rectify that. They wouldn't now, fully, either.

I sat beside her and said, "This illness can be slow, can go for years, and you know there are stretches when he does really well," then waited for Rosalie to say something, but she didn't. "I haven't been much help to you since all this other business happened, but I'm doing better now. You can see that, can't you? And I promise to look out for you and Nep as best I can."

"Thank you, Cassie. Have you talked with Niles about that man?"

"Yes, everything will be fine."

"What about the postcard?"

"Don't worry over it," I said. "Why don't we get lunch ready."

At that, my mother managed to compose herself, pull her public persona back into place. I tossed a salad as she dished cold gazpacho into big cups. By the time Nep and the others joined us, our spoken and unspoken words were gone like the spent sparks of a pyro fountain. I watched her during lunch and thought how admirably strong she was for keeping up appearances in the face of such mortal trouble. On the other hand, neither Rosalie nor anyone in her ken was equal to taking on my memories of Roy Skoler's assault, another piece in this abhorrent puzzle. Nep couldn't do it. Certainly not Jonah or Morgan. Not even Niles. Nor could I burden Charley with such an old nightmare, Charley who had remained at least distantly friendly with Roy. I was as isolated as my father must often have felt during those days

of deepening illness. I ate and spoke with the others, but knew I was simply left with what happened. No dowsing my way out of it, no fixing it in Nep's workshop.

Once Rosalie and I had divided up final cooking responsibilities—she would marinate the mixed grill, I would make various salads—I drove the boys back to Mendes to ready things for the next day. Both offered to help in the kitchen and I welcomed their company. In an exchange with Morgan that was as delicate as a water spider dancing across a puddle, he confirmed the Skoler boys had been the troublemakers on the ride down from Binghamton. They kept it up during practice, before and after games, even off the field whenever they could.

"Have you thought about talking with the coach about this? Maybe he'd want to have a word with their father."

"Ratting to the coach would be total death."

"It's no good for me to talk to him either, is it."

"Answered your own question," he said, and continued slicing celery, carrots, and cucumbers, dropping them into a bowl of ice water where they would spend the night in the fridge.

"They said their father told them you'd been a psycho from the day you were born."

"He didn't know me the day I was born. He doesn't know anything about me, as a matter of fact."

"Then why did you run so fast last night when you found out the Skolers were coming?"

"I didn't run. Besides, they were meeting up with Charley, not us."

"You cut out pretty quick."

"Plus you barely said goodbye to Charley," Jonah added.

"I'll call him and apologize. It's just we needed to leave. I knew we had a long day today and tomorrow being the Fourth—"

"Seemed weird to me," said Jonah.

"But we like you weird, Cassandra."

"You're kind of weird yourselves, you know," I said, attempting some of Rosalie's courage.

"Thank God for weirdness," said Morgan, looking heavenward.

"Not him again," groaned Jonah.

"That reminds me. I want you to show extra sensitivity toward your grandmother right now. Not that you haven't been, just she needs your support more than she may be letting on. We may need to go with her to church again. Can you do that?"

They agreed.

"And to finish what we were talking about, Morgan, if I thought any good would come of speaking with the Skoler boys' father, I'd do it. But I know it would make things worse. Besides, you're too smart not to see what's right and who's wrong here. From what I can tell, you're doing everything right."

Morgan kept moving the knife across the butcher-block, proud and embarrassed. His cheeks blossomed a charming warm crimson. Looked like beautiful birthmarks, lovely blotchy flowers.

Later that evening I did speak with Charley. He was kind, even prescient enough not to mention the abrupt rudeness of my departure after the game. My fears that Roy Skoler might have poisoned Charley against me appeared unfounded. Perhaps all this was a little too close for his comfort, too. He asked if I wanted to go out to dinner later in the week, continue our conversation, and I said sure, passing along an invitation to join us at the Independence Day celebration.

After locking the doors and downstairs windows, my new nightly ritual, I undressed. In bed I lay in a darkness softened by the nightlight I had lately taken to leaving on and sifted through memories of Charley, in particular how hard he had tried to comfort me after my brother's funeral. Curious to have forgotten until now that he was the only person I had allowed in my room while the otherwise interminable reception went on downstairs. He respected me enough not to interfere with my grief by coddling me with trite clichés about death and love and divine will. He didn't try to coax me off the floor. Unlike the false and twisted sympathy that Roy Skoler would show me a few days hence, Charley's was true caring. Had I been capable of accepting his support, I might not have needed to run away.

As these thoughts began dwindling toward sleep, a dream image of

Christopher, Ben, and Roy smoking cigarettes—their supposed calumets at the Indian caves—rose to mind. In the dream, I turned to Emily and asked, "What's that smell?" but now awake realized I had spoken the words aloud. The faintest trace of cigarette smoke hung in the room.

"Who are you?" I asked, the question stuck like a wishbone in my throat. I swung my legs around and put on my robe. In the feeble glow of the night-light I saw that I was alone. On hands and knees, hardly knowing what I was doing, I crawled to the open window and peered down into the front yard. There was a figure under the tree. Leaning against the trunk, looking up in the leaf-shuddering darkness. The tiny burning tip of the cigarette flared orange as the man—I knew it was a man, and I knew who it was—took a drag. "What do you want?" I called down to him and, hearing nothing by response, said, "Leave me alone," echoing the very words he had written on his first postcard. Without saying anything, he filliped his cigarette to the ground, turned, and left in no great hurry. Around a curve on Mendes Road and out of sight, an engine started up and he drove away.

Clouds congregated overnight, blotting out the stars. When I woke it was drizzling and the sun was curtained behind roving mists. I knew how disappointed Nep would be if we were forced to cancel the fireworks and hold the festivities indoors. Too bad there wasn't some way to reverse-divine the rain. Rosalie and I exchanged worried calls and drew up contingency plans, but by early afternoon the clouds had shredded away and blue sky returned in promising patches.

Would it be possible for Jonah and Morgan not to torment me about my floral dress? About my hair pulled back into a decent imitation of a French chignon, my modest but unwonted makeup, my silver bracelet plain as a calm sunlit sea that was my sole bequest from Henry Metcalf, and my leather pumps which my sons in all their lives had never seen? The dress and shoes looked new because I had bought them on an impulse after my first encounter with James Boyd, having driven to Middletown, speeding most of the way, just from the sheer thrill of being loved, only to learn there was no use for them. Over a decade later

these clothes, the makeup, and all the rest came out, as Morgan might have put it, of left field. My question was quickly answered.

Morgan came up behind his staring brother, recoiled, and said, "What did you do with our mother?"

"That man on Covey must have kidnapped her and left this stranger here," Jonah added.

"That's enough," I warned, retreating toward the back porch door.

"Actually," said Jonah, looking at Morgan, "she looks pretty decent."

"Not half bad for —"

"Stop while you're behind," I cut him off, thinking that, as with all these routines, I was forever getting the last word in way too late. No matter. I noticed they themselves dressed up a little — not a lot, a little — more than usual. Morgan eschewed his baseball jersey for a light blue shirt with buttons, untucked but ironed and clean. And Jonah excavated a pair of chinos from somewhere deep in his dresser. The only change I requested was that he switch his T-shirt, one I hadn't seen before, bought online behind my back, whose chest was boldly emblazoned *Dowsers Do It Divinely*. We packed the food in picnic baskets and drove over from Mendes a couple of hours before guests would begin arriving.

Nep, in stellar form, helped us carry things in. He gave us wide-smiling hellos and more or less high-fived both twins. Rosalie must have trimmed his flowing silken hair that morning and though she would never admit it — nor would I ask in a million years — maybe even helped him shave. He looked like the father I had always known. Upbeat, unworried. Wearing his usual earthy-colored clothes — shades of wheat and cream, the pale greens of winter grass — he was luminous as the day itself had become.

Had I not known just how far he had wandered away from himself over the past year, I might have been fooled into believing, for a miraculous instant, that here was the same Nep I walked with, conversed with, last Independence Day. The man who assured me he was a fraud, as a way, I now firmly believed, of encouraging me to trust myself in a universe that never gave up its favorite secrets easily. My father was

not a fraud. Had never been a fraud. He knew I knew it. I had come to understand it was simply a rite of passage, the traditional confession of fraudulence. The true practitioner avowing falsity as a way of allowing the possible false one a means of respectable escape.

Working together, we lit a fire in the homemade brick grill. We squeezed lemonade from the haphazard pyramid of yellow fruit on the counter. We filled buckets with ice and loaded them with colas, beer, bottles of champagne. Morgan hammered the horseshoe stakes and helped Jonah set up the worse-for-wear badminton set. Soon enough the three wise men arrived with wives and kids and grandchildren, then others, and before the party was supposed to begin it was well under way.

I washed strawberries in the sink, watching out the kitchen window while cars parked on the grass by Nep's barn. The Hubert family, I saw, had just pulled in. Turning off the cold water faucet, I walked to another window where I could spy a little better on everyone before they came bursting in on the quiet of the big kitchen. Niles approached the boys where they were finishing stringing up the cat's cradle of a net. He grabbed Jonah from behind, lifted him off his feet, and swung him back and forth like a clock's pendulum, both of them cracking up. Morgan slugged Niles on the arm, after which Niles set Jonah down and chased his twin around the badminton uprights until he finally caught him — Morgan was faster than Niles may have thought — gently tackling and pinning him on the grass, at which point Jonah jumped on his back, toppling the three together in a heap. Though Niles and I had spoken since our conversation by the lake, once after my visit to Cold Spring and again after Melanie revealed I had been to church — "Are you a convert now?" he baited me on the phone — this was the first time I had seen him since the park. I thought, I'll never not love Niles and he will never stop loving me or my family. The best way to protect that is to be his friend, no more, no less, and leave off pretending there was any other possibility. I hung my apron on a peg by the door and plunged into welcoming the partygoers.

Melanie, whom by chance I encountered first, asked if I needed

help in the kitchen. Adrienne had already gotten a game going of sending the shuttlecock high in the air with some of the many kids. Nep
and his confreres gathered along the grassy rampart, readying bottle rockets and other fireworks for launching—all very serious stuff.
When Charley arrived, I worked to quell my sudden nervousness as he
walked straight over with his mother and gave me a kiss on the cheek,
introducing me as "Cassandra, my oldest living friend."

"That can't be." I shook my head.

"It's true, I was thinking about it last night. I knew you and Christopher before I met anybody else in that crowd. And I can't think of a soul
who dates back before you two. That makes you my oldest friend."

Charley's mother asked to be introduced to Rosalie, or reintro-
duced, since the two knew each other from the days Charley, Chris,
and I were children. I caught Ros studying Charley's closed eye and
thought to nudge her. Yet my sense was that he had grown used to such
stares and didn't seem to mind. I liked him all the better for his patience.

"Where's the wonderful wizard of Corinth?" he asked.

"I hope you're interested in fireworks, because that's all he's going
to want to talk about," she said, sighing.

We left our mothers to their reminiscences and set off across the
yard toward the rampart. Several people stopped us along the way
with greetings and embraces, Niles among them. "Charley was friends
with Christopher," I told him.

"I'm surprised we never met," shaking his hand.

"We might well have, who knows? It was a lifetime ago."

"So you must have known Cassie then."

"I did my best to keep her out of trouble."

I asked Niles if he'd said hello to Nep yet. Told him we were headed
that way, would he like to come along? He declined, saying, "I do need
to talk to you about something, though, when you get a chance."

"Look," Charley interjected, placing a hand on my shoulder. "I'll
wander ahead and introduce myself."

I nodded. "Catch up with you in a minute, if that's all right," and
Charley continued up the hill toward Nep's group.

Once we were alone, Niles said, quietly, succinctly as a sharp knife, "Laura Bryant's disappeared again. I got a call from the Cold Spring police just before I left, and another from her mother."

"They're saying she ran away?"

"I hate to tell you this, but she left a suicide note."

I was speechless.

"Typed on her own typewriter. She wrote she was going to drown herself in the river and not to look for her body because they'd never find it, as I understood from the detective I spoke with."

"That's — I don't know what to say. She didn't seem the least suicidal when I met her," I stumbled, mind racing. "Depressed, maybe. Problematic, maybe. But definitely not self-destructive," although it horrified me to think my original hallucination of the hanged girl might turn out to have been a forevisioning of Laura after all.

"Let's hope not."

"Is there something I can do?"

"Not really. Half the time in situations like this everything is resolved happily within hours. She may just be taking a brooding walk along the Hudson and will be home for dinner late. Happens all the time. But obviously if she gets in touch with you, let me know right away. Find out where she is and persuade her to stay put, if you can."

I nodded yes. Others had joined the festivities meanwhile, and I told Niles I had to get back to helping Rosalie before long but first had a few things of my own to tell him and apologized for not doing so earlier. The travesty up at the lighthouse and the minor but meaningful thievery of Millicent. The latest postcard. The night visitor smoking under my window. Everything except Roy Skoler's history with me, all of which — despite compelling circumstantial evidence that, to me, was so damning — really added up to empty charges that could easily be dismissed as the hysterical accusations of a woman bent on revenge. The last thing I wanted to do was come rushing to Niles with another version of the hanged girl who wasn't there.

"Two questions," Niles said, unusually annoyed. "Why are you playing games with me and what else are you keeping from me?"

"Believe me, I'm not playing games. I find none of this even slightly

amusing. I'm doing my best to keep my head above water, look at it that way."

"Fair enough," he said, but I knew it didn't end there for him.

All my instincts led me to want to leave Niles and everybody else and somehow go find Laura. But tonight I needed to resist letting her —or the part of me that was bound to her—edge me out of my life.

Not that I wanted to have the conversation with Melanie about gingerbread recipes. Or the one I had with the pastor about teaching young people the importance of tithing. I tried a distracted joke about "teaching them tithing when they're teething," but it didn't go over very well. I did my level best not to give in to the desire to spend most of my time as near as possible to Charley. He helped me tend to the barbecue after having had a long talk, insofar as it was possible, with Nep. For dinner, we joined Niles and his family on a raft of blankets spread out on the grass beside a virtual hedgerow of black and scarlet hollyhocks below the porch. If anyone spoke behind my back or gave me and my colorful dress second looks, I didn't notice them. Sipping champagne as the fireflies began their mating dances and the daylilies closed their cups for the night, I realized I had managed to let my worries slip for a moment away into the vesper darkness.

Soon the evening star was joined by another planet and another. The connecting dots of constellations punctuated the purple sky, and the moon rose looking like a piece of glowing citron hard candy that had been sucked by some giant child. It was time for us to send up our own brief spray of man-made stars to join them. I saw that Jonah and Morgan flanked their grandfather and his adjutants on the fireworks front, and that Nep was breaking the rules by allowing the boys to light some of the fuses. Maybe I should have been worried. Maybe gone over to warn them it was a little too dangerous. But instead I found myself glancing around to see if Rosalie was anywhere nearby, hoping she wouldn't put the kibosh on their innocent mischief. Some old-time dowsers used body sensations to recognize the nearness of a spring. A knee would ache, for instance, or a knuckle, when they walked close by a live vein. The old-timer in me, divining for possible peril, didn't

pick up any such telltale signs as I watched my boys hanging on Nep's every instruction and witnessed the trio of them cheering and laughing as they craned skyward to see the bursting, the booming, the scintillating crowns of light that crowded out the blackness above, almost succeeded in pushing the darkness from every corner in our narrow universe. Not for a moment, however, did it escape me what had to come next.

27

THE BIRDS WERE CLAMOROUS this morning. In my pack, a bag of cashews, an apple, water. Without my usual divining gear, the pack felt feather-light. Laura was on my mind, and Charley also wove in and out of my thoughts as I hiked this terrain I hadn't set foot on since I was a girl. I couldn't recollect whether Charley had ever been escorted by Christopher to the caves. Somehow, I thought not. I found it impossible to imagine him submitting to being blindfolded. He was ever the one boy in the gang who insisted on clarity of vision. What a black irony was that.

If Jonah and Morgan, whom Charley had taken fishing, knew what I was up to here, they would either have tried to dissuade me or insisted on coming along. So would Niles, Charley, or anyone else. But I needed to make this hike alone and hoped the nagging suspicion I harbored was mistaken, a fantastic paranoia, a falsity stirred by the monster in my head. After all, if Roy Skoler was somehow behind Laura's disappearances—an intuition so gossamer and even prejudiced, given my bad history with him, I didn't dare mention it to anyone—there would be no rhyme or reason for him to bring her here again. Yet wasn't it true that Roy had already committed at least two grievous acts in these woods? One when he violated me. The other when he

shoved Emily Schaefer to her death. Yes, shoved hard as Christopher grappled with them both, one fatal hand pressing Emily's chest while his other pushed against Roy in a failed attempt to separate them, instead helping propel her over the cliff. The three struggled briefly in what could have been a young lovers' quarrel, could have been an argument about anything, before she lost her footing and fell screaming to the rocks below, her screams echoing until they were blanketed by sudden silence. It was all I could do not to scream, too, as I scrambled away from the boys who looked up, hearing the scrape of kicked pebbles, and saw me in the cliffs above them, watching. I was not supposed to be there that day, shouldn't have followed and spied on them. I wish I hadn't. Though I managed to hide, crouching breathless in a huge thick stand of mountain laurel, eventually I did creep home where Christopher, who got there first, cornered me in the backyard.

— You didn't see what you think, he said, looking at me with ice-cold eyes.

— What do you think I saw?

— She slipped, is all. Nobody's fault.

— You pushed, is what I saw.

— You're just a kid, you don't know what you saw.

I was old enough to see the blanched panic in my brother's face. And young enough to be swayed by his insistence.

Emily's death was, after an investigation, ruled accidental. My hapless conspiratorial silence was sealed when, before the police even questioned Christopher and Roy, my mother took me aside and told me, — There are some things best kept in the family that aren't for others to know.

From time to time over the years I wondered whether Christopher's death wasn't an instance of the universe trying to rebalance itself in the face of our impudent little secrets and accord, in a real way, divine justice on Emily Schaefer's behalf. Wasn't it possible that until Roy met with some form of justice himself, this same wobbling universe would remain imbalanced? Yet for so long he had avoided punishment for what he did, imbalance had begun to feel almost normal.

Given all this, why wouldn't Roy feel most comfortable in the place where he had gotten away with other transgressions? I even found myself wondering whether Roy Skoler wasn't Statlmeyer's distant relative who had been permitted to hunt here in exchange for throwing poachers off the land and giving him some filleted venison. If so, he would have developed a profoundly intimate knowledge of the terrain. Not to mention a deep proprietary bias toward these still-uninhabited woods.

Time had come for me to walk them once more. No more putting it off. Any second thoughts, any small hope of avoiding a return to the cave cliffs and the steep climb down into Henderson's valley below were fruitless. The path this man didn't want me to travel, scattered with lurid sights he placed there yet demanded I not see, had drawn itself right up to my door. He and I now shared this path of his, and the "little girl" he demanded leave him alone had no choice other than not to. I was not unaware that this might be exactly what he wanted, but if so, so be it.

Funny how not just the sense of time but of distances changes after childhood. In my memory, this hike to the caves was long, arduous, a glorious misery of a tramp through tough land carpeted with bracken ferns that tripped you, bracket fungi that colonized the sides of trees and scratched your arms, poison ivy that covered you in a rosy rash. Not that it was now a walk in the park, far from it, yet I came upon the caves—which were fraught with such wonderful and horrifying memories—so suddenly I thought I might be in the wrong place. But no. Here was our Iroquois cavern with its blackened ceiling. Here was the recess in the granite bulwark where Christopher built his fires. The mountain laurel where I hid from Roy and Christopher was still here, but so leggy now it wouldn't shelter a soul with its scraggly leaves and shriveled blossoms. And though I didn't want to linger on it, here was the stone flat where Roy Skoler had assaulted me.

Not knowing what to look for exactly, I searched the caves and scouted the immediate area. A catbird mewled in the distance. A yellow butterfly fluttered around me like an airborne flame. Wind threaded through the needled evergreens. Nothing was out of the ordinary. This

was a peaceful place which—if rocks and trees and butterflies were burdened with opinions—was content not to be bothered by people anymore. I began picking my way downward through a series of mammoth stone tables that a glacier of untold strength had toppled and scattered across the face of this declivity thousands of years ago. A descent I had never before made due to its almost impossible geography. Here it was that Emily had met her death. The leviathan rocks all looked the same to my adult eyes, so I was spared the horror of knowing which was the one where her life had left her.

Below, where the steeps graduated into valley flats, the flora changed radically. Cliff hemlocks gave way to hundred-year-old cherries, towering beech, and black walnut. The shadows deepened as I crossed the meandering creek and worked my way into the edges of Henderson's valley. Unlike when I was here in May, the leaves were now full and fat and the canopy was an undulant green roof over my head. Like some land-bound mariner, I used the sun for a compass as I worked my way back toward the flats where all of this began. Every now and again I stopped to listen, half-expecting the birds to desist their singing. They were in clarion voice, however, as if nothing in the world would force them to silence.

When I reached the periphery of the thick scrub flats, I was startled by a jarringly bright yellow intrusion some hundred yards ahead, looming large, obscured by the tangle of vegetation. Without thinking twice, I made my way through the snarl and mesh of brambles toward this unnatural presence. Not until I reached one of Earl Klat's enormous bulldozers, standing there in its vainglorious bulk like some mindless metal behemoth, did I realize what was going on. Henderson's excavations had indeed begun, and before me was the dreary, heartbreaking sight of once-pristine woods now shockingly effaced. Towering mature trees felled by saws or uprooted by dozers, their chainsawed stumps skidded into massive heaps. Bluestone unearthed and pulverized without recourse. Ferns and flowers and the habitats of countless creatures expunged. I never felt more ashamed in my life for having been party to such devastation.

I stumbled around the site—for it was a site now, not a forest any longer—and saw where roads had been roughed out. Disoriented by all the upheaval, I tried my best to find the tree where I had witnessed the hanged girl, but it appeared to have been dispatched, along with native stands of blueberry, serviceberry, and everything else in sight. In its place, Klat's crew had begun to shallow out where I presumed the accursed lake was to go. Much like some wartime child wandering in circles after the bombing of her home, I moved in a daze, my purpose in coming here in the first place undermined by all the construction.

Construction, I thought. Misnomer if there ever was one.

Fortunately, no one was working on the long holiday weekend, so nobody saw the profoundly discouraged trespasser who finally left, having realized there was nothing to find. As I started back, I did notice that Laura Bryant's shanty had been left unscathed. Peeking inside, I saw that the workers were using it as a kind of canteen, storage out of the weather for gas cans and coolers. It obviously saw a lot of use now. There was a well-trodden path to the door that even bore some fairly fresh footprints—not those of workers' boots but rather of dress shoes. Odd, but perhaps Klat had come up in the world.

Impossible to imagine Laura living in this forlorn hovel. The tenable terror her kidnapper instilled in the girl—assuming she had been kidnapped, and I believed she had—must have been overwhelming. Why else would she stay put while he decided what next to do with her?

My ascent up the mountain went more quickly. I badly needed to get home. Be back among things comforting and familiar. See my boys, be done with this fool's errand. Other than my personal remorse and shock over Henderson's development, I had sensed nothing amiss in the caves or down in the valley. Memories were one thing, forevisioning quite another. Indeed I had to wonder whether my renunciation of divining hadn't taken hold—an oddly dismaying thought.

It was only when I reached the caves that I realized I hadn't eaten all day. I hauled the knapsack off my shoulder, undid the leather drawstring, and sat down on a wide cool boulder to have a drink of the now-warm water and eat my apple. Finishing most of it, I tossed it

aside and lay back to close my eyes and rest briefly before walking back
to the truck. I might even have dozed off for a few minutes.

A murder of crows cried like a nursery full of squalling babies. I
started, opened my eyes, glanced over toward them, and saw instead
that she was with me again. Dressed as before in a floral-print white
blouse and denim skirt, a beaded choker around her thin neck and
some simple silver earrings I hadn't noticed before, but this time she
was as alive and breathing as I was. She hadn't aged a day. Standing in
the light and shade that dappled her, she stared at me with a mixture
of curiosity, shyness, and impatience. She held my apple in one hand.
With her other she was pointing past me at something or someone. I
swung around and studied the shivering pines and cleft upright karsts
of stone for a face buried in the shadows, a concealed figure, but saw
nothing. When I turned back, she had lowered her arms and dropped
the apple on the ground.

I knew this was Emily Schaefer but knew she couldn't really be there.
For just a moment, I pondered whether we weren't both ghosts.

What I felt now was less fear than a curious deepening hope for her,
for each of us. There was no reason to try to speak to her, I sensed, so
I didn't. But I did want to get a closer look at her face, as this time her
eyes were not a washed-out pale near-gray, but of a distinct chestnut
cast. They appeared to be damp. Maybe she had been crying, I thought,
though not necessarily from sadness.

When I slowly rose and began to edge closer, approaching her as
one might a fawn in the wilderness, the girl didn't move but intently
stared me in the eye. A flinch in the air behind me, the snap of a finger
perhaps, and I looked but no one was there, of course. I shouldn't have
expected otherwise. When I turned to Emily again she had somehow
managed to climb the tree she'd been standing beneath and was now
moving hastily, uncannily, impossibly from branch to branch, an acrobatic wraith in the maze of green. These gestures were accomplished
with unworldly expertise. I watched her fully in her element now, my
mouth agape, frozen in astonishment and admiration. She moved with
grace and overwhelming fluidity and freedom, a weightless spidery sil-

houette against the sky. I didn't attempt to chase her. What would the point have been?

I wondered, leaving the caves and Henderson's valley, hoping never to return, if there was such a thing as a ghost of conscience. Yes, I thought. And I had just encountered her for the fifth and, as I fore-visioned it, final time.

28

THE CLOCK DOWNSTAIRS chimed once not long before the other sound, a delicate scratching, began. Maybe this sound was followed by a creaking, the type of music made by a child on a swing far away, or the kind sea winds sometimes played in the lighthouse on otherwise quiet Covey evenings. But I couldn't be sure and didn't move.

Charley had left after midnight. Perhaps he forgot something and returned to fetch it, hoping I wasn't quite asleep yet. I had gone to bed soon after he said goodbye, kissing me good night on the porch where we'd been sitting, sipping wine for hours after finishing the fried trout and stuffed eggplant I made for him out of my Fannie Farmer cookbook. We had talked about everything under the sun — the moon, that is — long after I shooed Morgan and Jonah upstairs and tucked them into bed. Now I was still wide awake, having turned out the last of the lights. A deep darkness settled over the house, the moon having set and the stars erased by clouds. All I wanted was to sink into my pillow with a fresh recall of Charley's manner and voice, rehearse once more the stories we had rambled through, some from our childhood, others about how we got to where we were. But as strong and soothing as these thoughts were, they couldn't fully compete with the interweav-

ing images of Emily Schaefer at the caves, not to mention the devastation of the flats below.

The night had reached that riddlesome stretch when a single stroke might mean twelve-thirty as easily as one o'clock, or for that matter one-thirty. So the clock struck that once—it was one—and slow minutes elapsed, during which I realized it couldn't have been Charley since I hadn't heard his car return down Mendes Road. My dormer windows were on the street side. His headlights would have been visible in the leaves of the horse chestnut out front if he swung back into the driveway.

In the blackness I slipped downstairs and checked the doors and windows, which were still secure. Looked outside, saw nothing astir, so returned to bed. Maybe, I encouraged myself, it was one of the posse of stray cats that marauded by most every evening, knowing handouts could be had here. Or the scratching could have been made by any of our nocturnal visitors, our resident skunks, coons, possums with their tiny albino eyes pink as babies' tongues, who launched into life when the sun was gone. I listened for another half-hour, hearing nothing further, before succumbing to exhaustion but not real sleep. The balance of the night was spent in a limbo between uneasy rest and edgy restiveness.

Next morning the twins routed me from bed with coffee and loud music. Morgan had practice—the boys of summer were steadfast as Sisyphus—and Jonah had plans to go back to Nep's. A few leftover fireworks needed dispatching, plus he was going to learn how to solder and see how the acetylene torch fired. Turnabout was fair play. How many mornings had I dragged them from their beds with coffee and jazz on the stereo as impetus to get ready for school when it was blizzarding out? Besides, it meant I could come back and spend some time by myself. Place the call to Julia Bryant and see what was happening with Laura.

If there was sage advice I could have offered Morgan about the Skoler boys when I dropped him off at the ball field, I kept it to myself, knowing he was on top of his own game in more ways than one.

Wiser to be restrained and wish him a good practice, asking only what time he would be finished. In Morgan's absence, Jonah asked me what Charley and I colloquied about after he went to bed.

Colloquied, I marveled. Mispronounced, but another new word.

"Whatever came into our heads," I told him.

"What came into your heads?"

"You guys, his life in Wiscasset, my teaching."

"What about divining?"

"Didn't come up."

"What about the hanged girl?"

"Jonah, why in the world would I want to talk about that?"

"Because her friend is back."

"What do you mean?"

"You didn't hear those sounds last night?"

I waited for him to go on.

"Well, I did. Morgan was still sleeping, but I heard something and set up lookout by the window. It was really dark, but I'm pretty sure I saw that Laura girl run from the house to the shed."

"You were having a dream."

"No way. I checked this morning before you got up and somebody'd been in there."

"I did hear a scratching sound, but it was one of the strays."

"It was her," he said with inarguable finality and a mild frown.

Surely Niles hadn't told Jonah that Laura was missing—he was furtive enough when he confided in me—but I decided not to telephone him to find out. The questions that would arise weren't ones I necessarily wanted to answer. If he had told Jonah, was I asking because there was something Jonah had to report? If he hadn't told Jonah, why ask unless Jonah had something to report? The classic damned if you did, damned if you didn't conundrum.

"I guess we'll see. If she's here, she's come for a reason besides sleeping in the shed. Meantime, let's keep this to ourselves, why don't we."

"What about Morgan?"

"I'm not sure. He's got his hands full with those Skoler punks and

maybe it's best left alone until, I mean if, she shows herself. If you're wrong—"

"I'm not wrong. But I won't say anything."

During the drive to my parents' house, Jonah and I were each lost in our separate thoughts. We found Nep sitting alone on the porch. Though a little ashen from all the activity and abbreviated rest of the last couple of days, he was still riding high.

"Hello, daughter," he said.

"Hello, pater. I come bearing gifts. Or gift, that is."

"Let's see."

"I hereby present you with one Jonah Brooks."

"And what does a fellow do with a what's-his-name?"

"Shoot off the rest of the firecrackers and hang out in the workshop melting metal and stuff," Jonah said.

"That so."

"That's what you said."

"If I said it before, that before's still good."

He'd gotten pretty adept at covering and I respected the effort.

"If you're too tired, you know, Nep—"

"Never. Chris here's welcome to stay."

I shook my head at Jonah, unnecessarily, as the boy didn't bat an eye. A little guiltily, I told him I had to run and asked if he'd say hello to his grandmother for me. Fact was, I had no interest in recapping my evening with Charley for Rosalie yet and felt a real urgency to return to Mendes Road.

The first place I looked was in the shed, a board-and-batten affair with a cranky wooden door and rusted tin roof, where I found neither the hanged girl nor the runaway girl nor anyone else. True, the shed was such a jumble I wouldn't necessarily have known whether somebody had slept in it or not. I searched the outer edges of our couple of acres, walked down Mendes this side and the other, hiked the thicketed woods behind our place. I even scratched my fingernails on the screened door and one window, trying to replicate the sound I had heard. Familiar, but in the bright light of day I couldn't be sure. Pull-

ing open the heavy cellar door on the side of the house, I called down into the dimness where the warped steps led, "Laura, you there?" No response.

Jonah's imagination, I decided as I brewed black tea in the kitchen in a failing effort to stay awake, threatened to become as brazen as his mother's. Which would be a shame. If the fifth turning in my life was any paradigm of what imagination can bring down on someone, I didn't want that happening to my son. Another of Rosalie's childhood verses streamed through my mind as I lay my head down on the table, her favorite passage from Ecclesiastes, *To every thing there is a season, and a time to every purpose under heaven . . . a time to be born, and a time to die . . . a time to kill, and a time to heal . . . a time to keep silence, and a time to speak—*

"Mrs. Brooks?" gentler than any dream or specter.

I didn't want to open my eyes.

"Are you asleep?"

I raised my head.

"Guess not anymore, right? Sorry," she said, sounding altogether human and looking the worse for wear.

"What are you doing here, Laura?"

"I think you probably know."

That I did or should wasn't for me to address at that moment. I saw the fingers of her right hand were bloodied, not with fresh but dried dark blood with one fingernail badly torn, and her cheek was scraped. I reached out, saying, "My God, what happened?"

"It wasn't my fault," she said. While it didn't answer my question, her response did confirm my suspicion she was in trouble beyond having run away. I led her by the arm to the bathroom, where I washed her hand and cheek as delicately as I could and, after warning her, "This is going to sting," peroxided them. Laura winced but made no complaint when I daubed the disinfectant on her wounds. I then bandaged her hand, saying, "We should take you to the hospital."

"Please don't make me go to any hospital."

"Why not? You're hurt."

"He'll know to look there."

"Who will know, Laura? The same man as before?"

"Yes," she said, surprisingly direct given how oblique and even evasive she had been when I visited her in Cold Spring.

"Roy Skoler, you mean," I said.

"Is that his real name?"

"I don't know. What name does he go by?"

"Christopher."

I felt suddenly nauseated. "Does this Christopher know you're here?"

"I hope not."

"When was the last time you saw him?"

"Night before the Fourth," she said. "He came to my house, just like he said he would if I tried to get away. My mother'd gone downtown to do some shopping and I was alone in the kitchen when I heard a knock on the front door. I thought, That's weird. Nobody ever knocks. People just ring the bell. I didn't even need to look through the peephole. I just knew."

A razor-sharp mental image of the Bryants' foyer came into focus, and I could easily situate myself at the center of the terror she must have felt. Amazed once more at Laura's innate diviner's intuition, her ability to see through that door, I asked her what she did next.

"I didn't think, I just ran to my room, grabbed my pack."

"You mean you were already packed to leave?"

"Listen, Cassandra. I was packed from the day I got home. I could hear him downstairs in the foyer, shouting, 'Anybody here?' like he was a family friend sticking his head in to borrow a cup of sugar or something."

She was shaking, staring past me over my shoulder with the same disconnected look on her face that I remembered all too well from the first time I laid eyes on her after she emerged from Henderson's valley. Part of me wanted to stop her from continuing. I didn't want her to have to relive this encounter. But if I was going to help her I needed to know, so I waited.

"I heard the downstairs door close and hoped maybe he'd left. But

no. I'm pretty sure he was at the bottom of the stairs when he called my name. I couldn't believe what he said next. He used the same line as the first time, like I was really supposed to trust him again?" She let out an exasperated sigh.

"What line?"

"That I needed to be more patient and everything would be all right. That he was sorry about some of the things that happened, but if I came with him he'd take me to my brother, that my brother was friends with him and still wanted to see me."

"That's what lured you away the first time?"

As Laura lowered her head and shook it in despair if not self-disgust at having been duped, I realized she had been telling the truth all along, had neither run away nor been kidnapped as such, but rather been spirited away based on a duplicitous promise. Feeling like some cross-examiner, I asked her how she escaped with him blocking the staircase.

"That was the easy part. There's a servant's staircase, very narrow. Nobody much uses it, except when my brother and I were little we thought of it as our secret stairway down to the kitchen. The minute I heard him start upstairs, I sneaked down the back steps and out the kitchen door. Why I got it in my head to hide up in the tree house instead of running away, I don't know. I guess I still thought if he didn't find me, he'd leave. And besides, my mom was going to be home soon."

Reaching over, I rested my hand on her shoulder.

"Next thing I knew, he was in my bedroom. I figure he must have been inside the house before when no one was home. How else could he have known to go there just like that. Anyway, you know what he did? He sat down at my typewriter, put in a piece of paper, and started typing—"

"The suicide note."

"What suicide note?"

"Everybody thought you wrote a suicide note before you disappeared."

She recoiled. "That's what he was typing? So when I do wind up

in the river it'll be my fault?" She closed her eyes, opened them. "I can't believe it. He was even wearing those kind of gloves, the yellow stretchy ones."

"Surgical gloves?"

"That's the kind. And when he was done writing my suicide note, what did he do but look out the window right at me, like he knew I was there the whole time. This is what happened," holding her hurt hand up and pointing at her bruised, abraded cheek, "when I slipped and fell trying to get down from the tree house so fast. I still can't believe I got away. It was like he knew every other move I made before I made it."

"Every move except the ones that got you safely here," I said, staggered by her story. "You must be starving," I went on, at a complete loss. "Let's get you something to eat."

I walked with Laura back to the kitchen, where with trembling hands I made us both sandwiches. Laura silently paced around the room, picking up things off counters and shelves, looking at them with unusual care, as if they were *objets d'art* like those her parents collected. It was disturbing yet mesmerizing to watch her scrutiny of each and every little random bottle of vinegar or salt shaker or juice-stained glass left over from breakfast. As if she had been deposited into my everyday cosmos from some other world and was doing her best to get the lay of the land. She was the same girl I had once been, I realized, Laura like the young Cass dragged kicking out of childhood into the tempestuous universe of adults without willing or wanting it.

"Why were you so upset about his name?" she asked, breaking the silence.

"Christopher was my brother's name."

"I thought you said he was dead."

"He is. Here's your sandwich," I said, reluctant to explain because I feared my explanation would create more confusion, and my instincts told me Laura didn't need more confusion just now.

We sat down at the table. She was so famished, devouring her food like some starved little animal, that I gave her my sandwich, too.

"I think, Laura, that once you've finished eating we ought to call

Sheriff Hubert. You remember him, my friend Niles? It's not fair to let people go on thinking you might have committed suicide. Niles needs to hear about this. You can trust him."

"I liked him and probably he's somebody you can trust, but you can't call."

"Why not?"

Here Laura hesitated, stared out the kitchen window at a rose-breasted grosbeak on the feeder there with its bright red splotch on the chest like a fresh bloodstain, before saying, "It was hard enough for me to get here, find you. Please don't make me run away again. I don't want to wind up with the rest of them."

"The rest of them?"

"He said there were others, lots of them."

That silenced me.

"You just can't tell anybody I'm here and that's that. No one but you can know."

"Jonah thinks he saw you last night."

"Tell him he was wrong."

"Not that simple, Laura. You didn't spend much time with him, but Jonah's not that easily thrown off. If you need to stay here for a day while we sort things out, both Jonah and my other son, Morgan, are going to have to know."

"I can't talk about this right now. What kind of bird is that?" she asked, pointing at the window feeder, and launched into a description of the birdhouse she once made in her father's basement workshop and hung in the tree where she could watch the sparrows coming and going. I listened as she talked, though a part of me couldn't help being deeply troubled by the moral dilemma her appearance at Mendes Road posed. It made perfect sense to her to insist that I not take her to the hospital; that I not call Niles to inform him she was here with me, undrowned and alive; that no one, including Jonah and Morgan, was to know about her. But I couldn't reconcile her desires with what the larger world, that of Niles and her parents, not to mention Rosalie and Matt Newburg and probably even Charley, would dictate.

"Why did you come here?" I gently asked.

"Because I don't trust anybody else."

"Is that why you ran away those other times? Because you didn't trust people?"

"They called it running away, but all I was doing was trying to find my brother. I always came home after a day or two, no crime in that. Everybody else gave up on him a long time ago, so why should I trust them to find him?"

"Don't you trust your parents? Your mother seemed like a good person."

"She is, but she doesn't understand me. I tried to tell her and she didn't believe me. And my father's a disappearing act. He might as well live in his office in the city."

I couldn't help but be reminded of James Boyd. Made me feel still more protective of Laura. "Why trust me?"

"Because you divined me that first time and nobody believed you, but I knew it was true."

"Laura, I still don't know what happened that day."

"You don't have to," she said, attempting a smile that was at odds with those intense, dispirited eyes of hers. "What about you? You trust me, you believe me?"

"Yes," I said.

We talked more, as if the wall clock weren't chiming away hours. Turned out she had enough money to live on for a while if she could get away with it. She had stashed it in her bag along with a few poetry books, a journal, change of clothes, even eyeliner, blush, hair dye—a vagabond's tools for disguise—and other incidentals. That she was sitting in my kitchen, undisguised and unequivocal, made it clear she was compelled not so much to run from what threatened her as to seek resolution.

"Let's make a pact," I said. "At least for the rest of today and tonight. I'll promise not to turn you in if you promise to work with me to straighten everything out."

She agreed, which I took as a great stride forward. My thought

was, simply, to convince Laura that to trust me was to trust Niles, and thereby thread the way out of this labyrinth. What I said was that the time had come for me to go pick up Morgan and Jonah, but she should wait here and would stay tonight with us.

"You're not going to disappear on me now? We'll make things right," thinking what a foolish confidence I hoped to project with my smile, my arm over her shoulder as I showed her to my room and told her she could sleep there for a couple of hours if she liked. "We have books in every room if you haven't noticed. Take down any you like. It goes unsaid to lock the doors behind me and not answer if anybody knocks."

Driving away, I glanced over my shoulder at the house there on Mendes with only our voluminous chestnut standing sentry, trying to ignore the fear that churned my stomach, and was more than ever torn about the actions I was taking and not taking. Nothing prevented Laura from being seized by second thoughts and deciding to up and run. At the same time, little or nothing prevented Niles from descending on the house to find her inside and save her from herself. Or even Roy Skoler from breaking in, if he knew where she was.

As so often in the past, how I wished I could sound Nep out on what to do. I wasn't about to hand Laura over without knowing she would be truly protected this time, but every intuitive bone in my body said that was not possible. Calling Niles meant sending Laura back to her parents all over again. Or else meant her entering a maze of accusations, denials, counter-accusations, depositions, lawyers, witnesses expert and not, a trial, publicity. One more nightmare to fill some newspaper columns for a day or week, perhaps give local news networks some temporary grist. Though I hoped she would be safe for the night, we both knew she couldn't hide with me for long. Laura was caught between dire impossibilities and, by extension and default, so was I. It was as if we were walking a tightrope in tandem as the knots at both ends were coming undone.

Maybe nothing I was doing was right.

No slouch, Morgan was on to me within minutes of getting into the truck. "What's the problem?" he asked out of the blue.

"I have no problem."

"You'd be a terrible base stealer, Cass. Eyes, face, hands—too easy to read."

The sun dazzled as we drove toward my parents' and I fumbled my sunglasses off the dashboard, slid them on.

"You broke up with that guy, is that it?" he persisted.

"We're not even a couple, how could we break up?"

"Got fired again?"

"Morgan."

"I know. You were walking around behind the house and found another ghost."

That was so close to right, my decision to tell him made itself. No way should I even try to deceive the boys about Laura, especially if she was staying with us, so I told Morgan everything. Including an apology for having discussed with Jonah the possibility of keeping the secret from him. "We three don't have secrets. They have a way of festering. Grow like tumors until they eat away at the heart of a family."

True as this was, the statement bothered me, standing on the farmhouse porch with Nep and Rosalie. Who was I to talk about the dangers of secrecy? My mother was still savoring Independence Day, the compliments she'd received from this person and that, thanking all us Brookses for the lovely time. Nep was staring at me. Not with one of his comalike looks such as when we crossed the Delaware, but vigilant as a falcon tending its brood. I did my best not to return his steady gaze with one of trepidation. It is not impossible that, in memory, I may have misconstrued his expression. But I swear I didn't. He was looking at his daughter with his usual depth of affection and was also divining her. Then, reminding me of the first times I ventured out with him in the field, he made that small unconscious sighing moan that presaged a find. A mature music of knowing. As Jonah came stomping up the steps, calling out, "Look what I made," Nep slightly raised his hand in a kind of secular blessing and said to me, very plainly, "You're right. Do what you're right," and I thanked him with all the gratitude I could summon.

Jonah's show-and-tell was altogether unexpected.

"Look, Nep taught me how to solder. So I made these elbow rods out of a bunch of brass tubing." He held them in front of him and began walking the length of the porch.

"Most excellent, dude," Morgan approved.

"We don't do that anymore, Jonah," I said.

"Sure we do. Let me try that, how's it work?"

I realized this might be a strange moment for Morgan, seeing his brother for the first time in the role of apprentice diviner. If so, he betrayed no discomfiture and threw himself into his own apprenticeship then and there.

"You hold them like this," instructed Jonah, walking beside his brother, scrutinizing the tips of the L-rods, explaining the sketchy rudiments of how it worked. Nep watched me watch them before looking down to study his hands in his lap. This is my final clear image of him, as I noticed my mother's uneasiness, not to mention my own, and brought the lesson to an end. We needed, I said, to get home.

I breathed a sigh of relief at finding Laura asleep upstairs in my bed. Despite the July heat, she had pulled a blanket over herself but then partially kicked it away. She lay clothed in a pale green camisole and jeans with both hands tucked under the pillow as if to protect them from any further harm. Millicent was cradled in the crook of her arms. She's only a child, I thought. A tired, timeworn child. I saw that she had folded her shirt neatly and set it on a chair by the dresser. Her sneakers were set side by side, socks balled inside each opening. Her blue leather knapsack stashed under the chair. A spare, self-minimizing person, I thought, whose goal it seemed was to take up as little space in the world as possible, perhaps even make herself so compact she might vanish into one of its niches. Seeing her there inevitably reminded me, too, of myself in that shallow cave. Except no Roy Skoler was going to get to her again, to pretend to save her or otherwise, nor was she left to share secrets with a river stone. Quietly as I could, I backed away and left the room, closing the door in silence.

Understandably, the twins wondered why she had run away again.

Why was always a most dangerous question, I advised them, because often as not, the answer turned out to be something you didn't want to hear.

"She knows what she's doing," I said. "At least as much as anybody can. Our job is to take care of her until she has a chance to catch her breath, figure out what's best for her."

Though they were curious about our stowaway, Jonah and Morgan were also sharp enough to hear through my words and see it was I who needed to catch my breath, figure out what best to do. They went out back and practiced using Jonah's new dowsing instrument while the late-day sun began its descent. The monkshoods, not in blossom yet but seven feet high beside the shed, wagged in the baking air. A moth drifted along, blind as it was lost, its flight helplessly clumsy, as if it were a dead leaf blown on capricious breezes. I sat at the kitchen table and folded my hands into a tight ball, feeling every bit as lost as that poor moth outside and nervous about what the night would bring.

"Cassandra?"

I jumped in my seat. "You've got to stop materializing out of thin air like that, Laura."

"Sorry. Didn't hear you come back."

I let her know that my boys were aware she was here, knew nothing more about her circumstances, and it was best it stayed that way. Did she like stuffed eggplant? Because I made enough last night to feed the whole county. I hoped she didn't mind leftovers for dinner. She said leftovers were heaven compared to the junk she ate from bus stop vending machines and gas station deli-marts on the way here.

The meeting of Morgan, Laura, and Jonah, which was as unmanaged and weirdly upbeat as I might ever have thought possible, happened all in a jumble with Morgan crashing, as he often did, through the back screened door which slapped into its jamb like dropped planks, Jonah right on his heels, shouting, "Cass, it worked, we—"

"What worked?"

"We—" said Morgan, reddening.

"The divining rod worked," Jonah answered, catching his breath and staring at Laura. "Hello again."

She stared back, said, "Hello there," and for a singular instant it seemed like she was a long-lost daughter, that all three of these children were mine.

"Laura, this is Jonah's brother, Morgan."

"Hey," they said to one another.

Jonah said, "If you were talking about something important we can head back out."

"That's all right," Laura said. "I don't mean to push you out of your own house."

For the first time since moving into Mendes Road we ate with the shades drawn. It was warm out and the air inside was close as a crypt, but I was afraid enough on Laura's behalf that I'd trained the two fans we owned on the table and pulled down the window sashes in case someone outside got it in his head to prowl. None of us bothered to remark on these precautions, probably because Laura was as nervous as I, and the twins sensed it was better not to ask. Still, we managed to talk all over the map, in dribs and drabs, about baseball, poetry, math, soldering, the Cocteau Twins, whether I should continue to wear makeup, and the art of divination—my abandonment of it, Jonah's and now Morgan's fascination with it—all at one sitting. It didn't take a diviner to see that in another life, on another Earth, if the world were different, these three could be the closest of friends. We might well have carried on for many more hours, so familial was the mood, had the phone not rung. My phone that rarely rang on any given day.

Charley's voice on my outmoded answering machine. I heard his first few words and picked up in part because I didn't want the others to eavesdrop whatever message he might leave, in part because it dawned on me that Charley, of anyone, might be my sounding board. Even my possible pillar. He had been in times past. For privacy I took the call in my study, which was nothing more than a small room choked with books, drawings by the twins, a file cabinet filled with teaching notes and client invoices, a huge map of ancient Greece, some empty shelves where I used to store rolled geodetic surveys—now exiled to the attic—and assorted other stuff.

He called to say he was finished with packing his mother's belong-

ings and that he was about to wrap everything up. The house closing was scheduled for the beginning of the next week, after which she'd be headed to warmer climes and he would return to Wiscasset. "Before," as he put it, "the summer people spend all their money elsewhere and I wind up in some boatyard scraping barnacles off the bottom of hulls for a living."

"I doubt that's your fate, Charley."

Hesitant, voice lowered, he asked, "Are you all right?"

Masking my anxiety seemed impossible anymore. Besides, I didn't harbor any desire to hide myself from Charley. I said, "No, not really."

"Do you want to talk?"

"I can't."

"Can't or won't or shouldn't?"

"All the above," understanding that Charley knew me far too well to bother with any sort of obfuscation, that he carried strong memories of how Cassie Brooks thought and acted as a girl and, in some ways, as a woman. It occurred to me that Charley was the one person who might, long ago, have acted as my trusted confidant, the one with whom I could have shared the secrets about Emily's death and Roy's violation. How I wanted to share with him now what was happening, lean into him a little for strength. But I had made my promise to Laura. I was the confidante now. I was the one who needed to be the rock.

So here was the great hurdle, I understood, while I sat talking with Charley and watching the window-framed stars begin to appear. As simple as the first equation Jonah ever learned or when Morgan discovered that the best way to catch a ball was to watch it straight into his glove. Laura was silenced and so was I because we never learned to speak about these most important things. We weren't illiterates, weren't mad, or fools. We each loved the idea of our lives enough. Just we didn't know how to say we were afraid or why. We didn't know how to say ourselves. It was high time that I, for one, learned.

"Charley," I said, "I do want to talk with you."

"Any time, right now if you like."

"I can't right now. There's someone here," hoping not to sound too

mysterious. "But tomorrow should work. I need to talk with somebody first."

"Something is up, isn't it."

"Yes and no."

"'Yes and no' means yes. But look, I'm here for you whenever you like. Just give a call when it's good for you."

"Thanks, Charley."

We said our good nights and I sat quiet in the study for a few minutes before rejoining the others, whom I could hear talking away, even laughing, in the kitchen. My eye ran from island to island on the map of Greece. Naxos, Rhodes, Samothrace. Icaria, where Daedalus's son was buried after flying too close to the sun and plunging into the sea—no more fortunate a child than Martine de Berthereau's in Vincennes. All that the map finally stood for were stories upon stories upon stories. Paris and his golden apple, Helen of Troy. The oracle at Delphi whose shrine was inscribed with the most simple yet impossible advice ever offered, *Know thyself*. And yes, my story, too. All we had ever been were stories, and saying ourselves, unveiling our stories, was the best, the only, chance at divining ourselves.

29

Laura slept in my room that night and I made up a bed on the sofa. Once the lights were out, I opened the living room windows, and the plentiful music of crickets and tree frogs that lived in the nearby wetland filled the air. The ticking clock and its loud chiming made it hard to sleep, so I got up and stopped the pendulum. The warmth of the room was stifling, despite the nighttime air that wafted languorously through the windows. I lay there dressed only in an oversized white shirt that Nep had passed down to me years ago. Didn't draw the sheet over me. In my tired mind floated the image of my father there on the porch that afternoon, tranquil in his failing body. Next morning, as I knew he would have advised me if he could, I had to convince Laura to call her mother and Niles.

It wasn't cigarette smoke filtering through the window that awakened me with a jolt this night but the rank, wet breath of the smoking man murmuring in my ear. Nor could I speak or shriek or move, though I tried. My mouth was stuffed with the sheet, and my hands were caught together in the garrote of his strong hand, pinned behind my head. It wouldn't have taken much to asphyxiate me, so I breathed deeply through my nostrils and ceased kicking my legs when he tightened his grip even harder and got his free arm around my neck. I

have the boys, he said—Roy said. His voice was that of the boy I had known, not a grown man, yet it was unmistakably his. But it's the girl I want—

Then heard a scream outside in the dark and woke again, this time for real, on the sofa and drenched in sweat, all alone.

Taking the stairs two at a time, I ran first to Morgan's bedroom and snapped on the light. He was gone. Maybe he was with Jonah. I rushed down the hall, grabbed in the dark for his doorknob but soon realized the door was wide open and when I switched on the light saw that Jonah's bed, too, was empty. Shouting their names, I scrambled back along the hallway and burst into my room to find Laura sitting up in bed, blinking, yawning, a haze of sleepy confusion on her face.

"Do you know where the boys are?"

"No, what's—?"

"Laura, I want you to stay right here"—slipping on jeans and shoes—"and not breathe a word or answer anybody if they call your name, unless it's me. You hear me?"

"Yes," she said. Her face was drained of all color.

"I'll be right back."

"Don't go," she pleaded, feebly, shaking her head.

"I'll be right back. Just don't move."

As I lurched downstairs, skidding on the last steps, grasping the newel post to keep from falling, I continued to shout their names, and though I sensed the effort was pointless I went through the house turning on every light in the place, including the quartz porch lamps. The flashlight we kept under the sink was missing, so I bounded out into the night without it. Standing in the middle of Mendes, I squinted both ways in the black. Warm wind gentled the treetops. A ways up the road, a car I didn't recognize, a van rather, was parked on the shoulder half-hidden by bushes. I jogged toward it and looked in the windows as best I could in the sloe murk. Trying a door, unlocked, I opened it, called Morgan's name, even climbed in and blindly patted around. Maybe somebody had simply broken down and left it here until morning for the wrecker to tow it into the shop. Wishful thinking.

Back behind the house I could now see, in the strong light thrown from the blazing windows, that the shed door hung open. There was no sign of the boys anywhere, though. For a moment, I simply stood and felt the drumming of my heart in my chest, heard my labored breath, and scanned the surrounding gloom. I soon caught sight of a subtle pinprick of white, floating up and down, rhythmical out there in the obscure chaos of woods beyond the shed. As if ensnared by it, or implicated, I was drawn away from the yard and into the confusion of bushes and prickly brambles toward the eye of light. I held up my hands and arms as I walked to shield me a little from the invisible branches and rough-leaved shoots and barbed multiflora that whipped about my face. "Jonah? Morgan?" I asked, the light much closer now.

"Cass?" I heard. Jonah's voice.

He held the lamp of the flashlight to his chin, the beam directed upward. It cast grotesque shadows that bore an awful resemblance to the death mask he had playfully held over his face in the Bryants' library.

"Give me that," I said, taking the flashlight and pulling him to me in a tight embrace. "Where's Morgan?"

"He went up the road looking."

"For what?"

"For one of the Skoler kids, is what we thought. He was in the backyard. Threw some rocks at our windows to wake us up."

Jonah and I started immediately back toward the house. "For godsakes, why didn't you come downstairs and tell me?"

"Morgan wanted to show him what's what, that's why. But when we got outside we saw it wasn't a kid. We chased after him up the road, but I couldn't keep up. I saw them cut over into the marsh, and I—I was looking for them out back. That's where I heard him scream."

The very idea of Morgan screaming left me in a state of blank despair. We reemerged from the woods into the yard. The house, which I had never seen in the middle of the night with every last one of its lights on, looked like a squat, square, brilliantly illuminated ship, a steamer all lit up in its midnight mooring, readied for a predawn voyage somewhere. The shadows thrown by tree trunks and the shed

stretched all the way to the edge of the grayed lawn, and out into the darkness beyond.

"I've got to call Niles," I told Jonah as I unlocked the back door and we went inside. The kitchen was warm and close and unforgivingly bright. "Then I'll go look for him while you stay here with Laura."

"That's whose name we heard him say when he woke us up, you know."

The dispatcher told me he would send a patrol car over. I asked was it possible for him to contact Niles Hubert and, hearing him demur, assuring me the officer would be able to determine if that was necessary, I hung up, took a deep breath, and telephoned Niles at home. We weren't on for more than a few fast words. He was going to be angrier with me than I imagined he already was when I didn't follow his instruction to remain indoors with Jonah and Laura, not to venture outside. But no way was I going to leave Morgan out there by himself.

Next came a flurry of compressed moments the most prescient diviner might never have visioned. A series of actions that seemed to occur simultaneously — paradoxically — in both slow motion and at breakneck speed. Just as I was about to head back outside and call my son's name until he answered me, he pounded on the front door, shouting my name instead. Although his face was cut from running through brambles and his bare feet were muddy up past the ankles from wading through brackish swampland, he wasn't as injured as that scream had compelled me to believe. I threw my arms around him, pulled him inside, and relocked the door. Then, as Jonah and Morgan talked wildly about what they had seen and done, I turned, unthinking, and ran tripping up the stairs, only to find that Laura was gone. Another search of the house, all three of us crying out her name. But she had vanished.

Of course. The whole exercise had been a trap, a setup. He needed to lure all three of us away from her and did so flawlessly. Even that scream had been a sham, part of his program to draw me out in search of my boys so he might get to Laura undeterred. It wasn't as if he didn't know the inside of our house. He would have had plenty of time

while we were on Covey to learn its rooms. I hardly needed to walk up the road to confirm that the van was gone, but I did, and it was.

The diviner in me, the sometime forevisioner, had been betrayed by herself. I had betrayed the mother in me, and the daughter. I had betrayed not just Laura but the friend I had tried to be to her, the supposed friend to whom she had come to for help.

Niles arrived even before Bledsoe and Shaver and, quite abruptly, several converging others, the spinning cherry and silver lights on their cars filling the branches of the trees and clapboard siding with a surreal, gaudy stream of color. It was like Henderson's all over again, but rather than a pristine blue-skied afternoon, it was a waning crow-black night. Niles and I went inside while the others set off, some on foot, some in their vehicles, in search of the missing girl and her abductor. Niles sat at the kitchen table, looking haggard there and strange in his civvies with the holstered gun, the badge, the noisy two-way. The twins hovered at the periphery. He needn't have said a word for me to know what was running through his mind, nor did he much bother. He said, simply, "So?"

"Yes, I admit she was here."

"And?"

"And she disappeared again—she was taken—within the last half-hour."

"You saw her leave with somebody?"

"No."

"So how do you know she didn't leave by herself?"

"Because I just know that isn't what happened."

He asked me to explain and I told Niles everything. He sat listening, writing notes in his pad, neither prompting me with questions nor expressing any opinion about what he heard. "You didn't call me" were his flat first words in response to my account, spoken without looking up after closing his notepad.

"Niles, I made a promise I wouldn't tell anybody she was with me. She would have walked right out the door if I refused."

"I wish you had let me know."

"She came looking to buy time. I owed that much to her and myself, too."

Niles turned that over in his mind. He looked at the boys, each of them one at a time, then back at me. "I know you feel a deep connection to Laura Bryant. Do you have any idea where she might be?"

"You're asking me to divine her?"

"You divined her once."

Although I wasn't going to argue that point again—indeed couldn't, since Niles was no more wrong about this than Laura had been when I denied it to her—I did know where Roy had taken her. I saw them quite clearly on the overgrown, unmarked path to the caves, Laura stumbling behind him as they traipsed through the dense darkness, her hands knotted with rope—no, it was wire—an even crueler version of the garrote I myself experienced in my nightmare vision.

"I know where they are," I said.

Niles rose to his feet, conferred briefly with Shaver, who would stay at Mendes Road with Morgan and Jonah on the off chance Roy Skoler had it in mind to return here, then asked me if I needed to bring a jacket where we were going. Warm as it was, I put on a light Windbreaker if only to be able to offer it to Laura when we found her. I gave each of my sons a kiss, telling Morgan to wash his face and feet, asking Shaver to call a medic if any of his scratches were more than superficial, and left with Niles. Bledsoe and another patrolman followed us, lights flashing but no blaring siren, as we sped along straightaways and a series of switchbacks that led up toward the place where I had parked only the day before. When we got close, Niles doused the overhead lights and two-wayed Bledsoe to follow suit. Now we crept forward as both cars directed their searchlights on the woodland curtain that edged the road. Soon enough we sighted the van—of course, Laura's "long car"—parked with a kind of forlorn overconfidence just off the road, not quite hidden by swaths of rhododendron. Its shiny bumper and back windows winked under the glare of searchlights.

"Stay here, Cass," Niles said, climbing out of the car. He leveled his flashlight in the direction of the van, holding it aloft with one hand, its

butt end resting on his shoulder. In his other hand, his drawn gun. The three men fanned out and approached the van from several directions. I knew it was abandoned, so got out and walked around to the front of Niles's car, where I leaned against the hood to wait. Four-thirty. The sky already paling faintly along the eastern horizon of gently rolling mountaintops. The rosy-colored fingers of dawn would be spreading over the ridge in an hour. *Rosy-colored fingers* — was that how Homer phrased it in *The Iliad* or *The Odyssey*? The epic of war, or the epic of homecoming?

Niles returned. "Nobody inside. Where was it from here you thought they went?"

We threaded our way, marching single file through woods I had maneuvered both blindfolded and with eyes wide open, such that the predawn darkness meant nothing to me. The first birds, restless thrushes, had begun fluting away, unseen as always in the highest branches. Underfoot, the grasses and ferns were sopping wet with dew, making the trek slippery wherever the path bent steeply up or down. Niles and the others had apparently silenced their radios and none of the men conversed along the way. "We near yet?" were the only words Niles said to me.

And for myself, what was in my mind? My boys, naturally, along with my lost Laura. As for this overarching instinct that had settled within me, this inward observance, I had to hope it wasn't mere wishful thinking, but rather a true perception. A divining. Nor was it long before I would discover whether what I had pictured turned out to be just some empty, dashed hope, or a vivid forevision.

I was pretty sure I could hear the distant trickle of the creek splashing its way along the crooked, rocky bed. With that, I raised my arm and stepped to the side so Niles could stand next to me. I pointed ahead, indicating we were very near now. Whispered once more what I had outlined to him during the ride over, about the little conclave of recesses in the rocks, the Indian caves.

This was where Roy would have brought Laura, I assured him, and, following his directives, stood away while the three men closed in,

their flashlights darting about crazily in the penumbral light. Other than the cracking of broken branches echoing across the forested hogback, the softly shushing creek well below, the calm birdcall, the nearby world had gone mute.

Then, the birds lost their voices and I knew what it meant.

"Roy," I shouted, running ahead of the officers headlong toward a flat apron of granite just past the cave where I had hidden so long ago after Christopher's death. "Roy Skoler," my voice as sharp and furious as I had ever heard it, seeing him standing there, a shadow among shadows. Other voices rang out at the same time, on every side of me it seemed, a surround of wild utterances. As I passed the mouth of my cave, I tripped, fell hard on the hard stone, turned and saw the tenebrous outline of Laura there, reaching out toward me with her hands joined together as if in supplicating prayer. I tore the gag out of her mouth but didn't untie her, in part because there was no time, and also because she was safer, for one more long minute, where she lay.

This final act was not remotely what I had envisioned. Maybe my gift, if such a word obtained after so much dread and discord, had led me here to this place and moment. But it was some other instinct that brought me to my feet and sent me straight toward Roy Skoler, who hovered, then dashed sideways, then backed away nimbly, in a perplexing effort to both thwart and bewilder me. I didn't know what I was doing. This was all accomplished without rational thought intervening or directing my feet. I called his name once more with almost ethereal, unreal calm now. *Roy Skoler,* those two words, like disembodied curses.

Now so close to the man that I could see his encumbered eyes and hear his thin fast breathing, he rasped at me, "I should have saved you the trouble of turning into such a fool," and dodged to the left with miraculous celerity.

I mirrored his every movement, my eyes locked on the man in the glowering light, still speechless but needing to speak, to say myself.

"Roy Skoler" was all that came out of my mouth, his name for the third time but only in a whisper now. If names were doors to ideas,

then Roy Skoler's harbored for me all the ugliness that animated this man.

"But I didn't kill you. I loved you. You owe me your life," he said, trying for the last time to snare me.

"Loved me? Owe you? I owe you nothing, you monster."

"Nothing—" he echoed, and simply stared, almost contemplative in the growing light, while behind me Niles and the others came crashing through the underbrush and right out onto the rocky shelf, shouting at me to move away, firing out his name as if the syllables were bullets, ordering him to get on his knees with hands up, telling him it was all over.

It was not over like that, though. Instead, I witnessed Roy Skoler slowly blink like some antique doll whose mechanism was exhausted, turn on his heel, and begin to flee in a kind of slow motion, only to disappear altogether, hovering for an impossible moment before falling into the shafts of stone below. Before I was quite able to understand what had just happened, I heard a thrush call out, then a chickadee, and then a bird I could not identify, until the air was filled with birdsong, nothing unusual really, the kind that resounded in this remote place every morning, even during the coldest winter.

30

GABRIEL NEPTUNE BROOKS, Nep as he was known, passed away a handful of days after my doppelgänger Laura Bryant had been found alive, shaken but unharmed, in that cave above Henderson's valley. He had gone to the kitchen for a glass of milk. Maybe he thought it would quell the heartburn he was feeling. My mother found him lying on the floor, the carton of milk beside him having drained its contents in a large pool, the refrigerator door still open. A massive coronary chose a more final independence for my father. Independence from losing more of his self to the disease of fading memory. Despite my earlier sense of what was impending, I found myself upended by Rosalie's news. Yet, in a curious way, I understood that he had been a breathing ghost these past, often exquisite weeks. He had already lifted away from the earth just a little. Or, that is, begun melding with it.

My father was cremated, as he had requested in a sealed letter written to Rosalie and me back when he was first informed about his condition. His ashes were broadcast—thrown like seed from our hands—into the pond, again according to his instructions. *Dust to dust, water to water,* he wrote.

A slab of bluestone from the land was chiseled with his name, his

dates, and *Husband, Father, Grandfather, Diviner* on its face and placed flat on the ground down by the pond dock, where we planted a large bed of magenta campions around the memorial.

Just as I had done when I was pregnant, I moved back in with my mother for a while, along with the boys this time, so she would not be forced to suffer through a difficult season all by herself. Truth be told, I needed to recover along with her. She had taken me in while I awaited a birth—I would now take care of her while she adjusted to this death. Morgan was stunned by Nep's sudden absence and threw himself into his ballplaying as a means of getting through his grief. Jonah all but moved into his grandfather's barn, if not his life, spending productive hours out there fixing things from Mendes Road he deemed broken, that lawn mower for one. Rosalie gave Jonah full run of the workshop with the sole admonition he not hurt himself. If I didn't go fetch him to eat lunch and dinner, and to extinguish the overhead fluorescents at night, we might not have seen the boy at all. As for Rosalie, she relied on her prayers, her pastor, and her iron-strong belief in God and an afterlife to ease her through her mourning.

"He's in heaven now," she said, in an unexpected, gratifying judgment of his final reward. The godless man she had always insisted was headed into infernal flames now rested his weary head on a silken pillow in heaven?

"You think he's surprised to be up there?" I asked.

We were alone, hanging his washed clothes on the line, readying them to be donated to the church thrift shop at his request, also in that letter, an olive branch extended to his wife, I imagined, as affirmation he respected her faith.

"He's surprised, all right, surprised it's there at all. I can picture him looking around right now saying, This isn't so bad. Why didn't I believe sooner?"

"If there's a heaven, Nep is in it."

"There is and he is," she said, and this was the last time we ever discussed my father's fate beyond life. I admired her hardheadedness and softheartedness. I admired her, period.

My own response to Nep's death was slow and sure as an orchid's blooming. I may have had a year to prepare myself for this eventuality, but the hard, pitiless fact of death was nothing that discipline or anticipation could curb. Preparation was as futile as hoping to avoid death itself. And yet, what I had learned from the man was permanent enough that, other than our not being able to add fresh experiences together, he was as alive as ever. It was like he simply happened to be in another room, out of sight and hearing. That said, I wasn't quite as consoled by my own life's activities or faith as my mother and children were. Many were the days when I found myself wishing he'd come out of that other room and speak with me about any little mundane thing. My aching for him to walk through the door and say something would abate in time, I knew, but never finally go away.

Astronomers have a word for the uncommon occurrence of planets aligning in the sky. Syzygy, they call it. I've never seen one, though Rosalie and Nep did once when they were young. Newlyweds, they had come up to Covey to visit Henry Metcalf for the first time. Henry never traveled much farther afield than Ellsworth but wanted to meet his niece's man. One night during their stay, three planets lined up in the expansive starry sky. They saw it together from the balsam grove at the highest point on Covey not far from the family cemetery, the very grove where I now sit, a peaceful place which on a clear night is like a planetarium without walls.

What Rosalie witnessed was an astronomical event she would tell entranced science students about for years. For his part, Nep said that in their audacious symmetry, where the rest of the universe of stars and worlds was reveling in pure disarray (— Like joy incarnate, as he put it, according to Rosalie), the row of silver planets seemed courageous to him, if a bit unnatural. A line, he said, like a person's life, only finds its value when plunged into the great whirl and movement of things.

My mother told me about this syzygy sighting of theirs when we first arrived on the island last week, while we made our traditional mother-daughter hike around the island. She confided she was pretty sure that was the night Christopher was conceived.

"Why didn't you ever tell me before?"

"You never asked," she said. "Besides, maybe it's just another one of my myths."

"A lovely one, if it is," I said, thinking about how Laura and Nep had formed two parts of a syzygy with me.

Nep stood at the farthest end of our fragile lifeline, our throughline. Fading off the grid now. Laura was nearer its beginning. And I—who wept on Charley's shoulder while he whispered how sorry he was, how he had hoped good pilgrim Nep had a marathon of years left—was the link between them. I, the diviner who learned from her father and began to find herself by divining a stolen girl. The ancient Greeks, as ever, had it right all along. We understand our character by measuring it against and within the character of others.

The news that emerged from Henderson's in the days after Roy Skoler's body was removed from the ravine below the cave cliffs was ultimately understandable but only if measured against some demonic ideal. Bones, some quite old and long defleshed, were unearthed by Klat's dozer, the one assigned the task of carving out a man-made lake in those lowest flats of Henderson's valley. A graveyard skillfully sequestered there for what would prove to have been years, a couple of decades. It was an unceremonious excavation, but the consequences were salutary in the long run. At least the remaining truth about Roy Skoler was brought into the difficult light. All the girls, and there were several of them who had called out to me that day when I sat waiting for Laura to be discovered, had died similar deaths. Broken necks indicated that hanging had been his preferred method, his fantasy of implementing death in the air going all the way back to Emily's fatal fall, it appeared.

Building history backward, as investigative and forensics experts of such tragedies can do, defying time and its most coveted secrets, it came out that Roy had collected girls from far and wide in counties a day's drive from Corinth. Missing persons no longer missing but uncovered by the dozer's blade had been held, it was determined based on date of disappearance versus presumed date of demise, for a

considerable period of time. No reason to think he hadn't kept them, his unfortunates, in captivity in that same hunter's cabin, although it would appear he knew very well what he was about, given how bare of any evidence that shanty was. No reason also not to conclude, as time would tell, that his modus operandi had all along been to prey, scavengerlike, upon the female siblings of lost boys, having researched the disappearance of brothers and then approaching them with the promise of reuniting them. One theory suggested he would go into periods of remission after successfully carrying through one of his adventures from abduction to death, given how many years apart these girls' deaths had occurred, or so their remains proposed in the scientific theater of odontology, DNA, and decomposition analysis and extrapolation. In other words, I had saved Laura's life.

This moment of finally knowing what the hanged girl meant marked the end of my quest to conform. My foray into the ordinary hadn't lasted long, but I knew it would not bring me to a better life. Besides, there was no ordinary in this world. I had tried my best to stop divining but understood that it was in my blood. No, it was my blood. I missed myself and wanted her back. Laura, too, would emerge from all this, I knew, and that was a triumph. She, with all her poets and journals, would, as I had, find her voice. Say herself. And I am here voicing what I know now. Saying myself. A different sun rises each day for every set of eyes that watches it. Mine, scanning the horizon to the west where it breaks through the fog banks, are now searching out the bow of Mr. McEachern's ferry.

The balsam fir grove gives off a mild green scent. A welcome smell that never fails to remind me of Christmastime, even in August. A gift-giving scent, a celebratory perfume that transcends any season or religion. This promontory of tenacious, hardy shrubs and pines is scarcely a couple of hundred feet above sea level, but the views are commanding both toward the open ocean out east and Mount Desert south and west. Baker Island and the Cranberries are still shrouded in morning mist but I can distinguish their outlines, conifer-capped pink granite plates in the green calm water, and see Baker's lighthouse beacon flash-

ing. It won't be long before the fog banks roll out to sea, into oblivion, and the gentle curve of the Earth is plainly visible once more to the naked eye. When I was young I used to bring a book here and while away hours by myself, sometimes watching for bald eagles and ospreys overhead, or a pod of whales running along in heavy swells, other times tracing that horizon-curve way beyond what my eyes could see and imagining how very big the planet is. And how small.

I hiked up here this morning so I could be the first to see Mr. McEachern's mailboat rounding the edge of Islesford on its passage out to us. Last night, I asked Rosalie if she didn't mind getting the boys fed and off on their blueberry-harvesting excursion, as I wanted to take a walk before dawn, head up to the balsams, spend an hour or two by myself before Charley arrived for his first sojourn here with us, with me. She loved taking care of Jonah and Morgan, especially when we were on Covey, so my request was granted without a moment's hesitation. The twins had always filled the great absence of her Christopher, the loss that would haunt my mother all the way to her heaven. Now, with Nep gone as well, she was more than welcome to indulge herself as my fellow loving custodian of the twins. Besides, the boys missed their grandfather. What better proxy could they have than this woman who knew him better than any of us?

Nep did manage to escape a funeral in church, but he couldn't escape the inevitability of a large memorial service at home. All the same faces he had seen on Independence Day, and many others besides, gathered once more on the rampart, again in the early evening, on a Saturday later that July. Charley—shattered by the revelations about Roy Skoler—drove back down to be present, and it was then our childhood friendship matured. The night before the service, he came over to the house to help us set up the folding chairs that were loaned to us by Rosalie's pastor and arrange tables for the reception after the memorial. Once Rosalie declared everything ready enough and thanked us all, hoping we would excuse her as she was exhausted and wanted to go to bed early, Charley and I dropped the boys off on Mendes Road and went for a drive to the river to take a walk in the

glowing twilight. I myself was anything but tired. Wired, sad, fearful, yes, but also at peace with what a rich life I had experienced with my father. If Jonah and Morgan felt a tenth of the love and loyalty he had shown me—and which I did my best to match—they were fortunate sons. Charley took my hand and we roamed along. Some furry brown bats, the birds of the moon, coursed out over the slow-moving water, snatching up mosquitoes and other hatchers.

"I need to tell you about something, Charley," I began.

"Whatever you want," he said.

"You know about my divining."

"I'd be interested to know more."

"Well, it's usually a mundane exercise—"

"More mystery than mundanity, it'd seem to me."

"Well. Normally what I find is water, because that's what I was taught to look for and that's what people in these parts call on me to locate. But this spring when I was dowsing in the middle of no-where . . ." and told him everything I had never before shared with any one soul. He needed to know whose hand he was holding, whom he was about to embrace.

Several friends spoke at Nep's memorial service. Niles recounted the ways in which he had been a father to many of us gathered here, himself included. Charley recalled with warmth how Nep's ability to see what others failed to see had inspired him over the years. Sam Briscoll, representing the three wise men, praised his old friend's un-earthly skill at fixing the broken things people brought him. If he'd been given enough time, Sam said, and if people had wisdom enough to let him, Nep could have gotten this whole world of ours running quite nicely, thank you very much. Partridge spoke about how he had always thought the Earth was round until Nep proved it had other dimensions.

Speaking last, I thought it best the man be allowed to express him-self to those who loved him. I repeated some of the many truths Nep had told me over the years, reprised my favorite Nepisms. What you divine is a reflection of yourself, he always said. Divining is one of the

great chances a mere mortal has to reach out and touch the sacred. Divining is a human rather than a divine experience since it only works when a man or woman stretches so far into their humanness they allow themselves to be exposed to the deep simplicity of everything. When you're divining you're talking to a part of yourself that knows what you knew all along.

He believed, and I agreed in the closing words of my eulogy, "Divining is finally just another form of prayer."

Afterward there was a reception that Nep himself would have loved to attend. I couldn't help but remember the conversation we had, speculating about whether the good was erased along with the bad when one's memory was gone and how Nep promised he would get back to me with the answer if he could.

Nep, I thought, I'll always be listening. While we mourners, we sad celebrants, conversed on the lawn beside elegant tables laid out with food and drink, and while Jonah and Morgan played Nep's beloved jazz albums on his record player, which they'd brought out to the back porch, a woman I had never met walked toward me, where I had wandered down by the pond. She had a hard face, kindly but creased as a piece of paper crumpled by mistake and then smoothed flat again. One of the few at the gathering who wasn't wearing black, she had a solemn air like a dark veil about her anyway. Hers were quick searching eyes, the eyes of one in need, but who was nervous to ask for help.

She introduced herself. Her name was Grace Sutton, she said. She was deeply sorry about my father's death and wasn't sure whether this was the right moment to discuss such matters. I invited her to tell me what was on her mind. She said Nep had hoped to drive over to her place when he got to feeling better, see if he could help her. They had spoken about a year ago, perhaps a little longer, about his coming by again. She lived up north past Cooks Falls. A ways up the side of the hill above the town and river that ran through it. My father had divined her place once, she told me, kneading her hands and looking down at her feet. He really helped her family out of a bad situation.

I assume this had to do with a dead well and so asked her if she and her family had running water, or stagnant, just now.

"No, nothing like that," was her response. Without getting into details, there was more that needed doing.

"If you think you could see your way clear to coming up," she faltered.

Before she even fully finished asking her question, I told her yes. I couldn't promise her I would find what she sought. But I would be honored to try.

ACKNOWLEDGMENTS

I owe a great debt of gratitude to Marty Cain, David Royer, and Jim Linn of the American Society of Dowsers, wonderful and patient instructors from whom I learned basic dowsing techniques in Danville, Vermont. Anyone interested in the multifaceted art of divination might do well to join ASD, which has chapters across the country. It should be noted that most practitioners refer to their work as *dowsing* more often than *divining,* but I found the myriad implications of the term *divining* irresistible, even necessary to my own art.

I would also like to thank the sociologist Robert Jackall, who has done extensive fieldwork with police and detectives and generously offered me thoughtful insights and ideas about crime and investigation. Peter Straub and Mike Kelly gave close readings to early drafts and made a number of crucial suggestions, for which I thank them with fraternal affection. Books I found especially helpful while writing *The Diviner's Tale* are V. S. Ramachandran's *A Brief Tour of Human Consciousness,* Andrew Lang's *Custom and Myth,* George Serban's *The Tyranny of Magical Thinking,* and Christopher Bird's *The Divining Hand.* Tomáš Joanidis helped me believe in the path anew when I got lost. Others who encouraged me along the way are Henry Dunow, Lynn Nesbit, Howard Norman, Robert Olen Butler, Micaela Morrissette, Douglas

Moore, and Glenn Erts. I thank them all. Thanks also to Andrea Schulz, Tom Bouman, Rachael Hoy, Summer Smith, Michelle Bonanno, Laurie Brown, and the whole intrepid Houghton Mifflin Harcourt team, as well as my eagle-eyed copyeditor, Barbara Wood, for their kind support. My editor, Otto Penzler, is a natural-born diviner whose wise guidance through the many valleys and fields of this project has been true-compass every step of the way. Finally, without Cara Schlesinger the first word here wouldn't have found its pendulum arc to the last.